T0350026

Swords from the Desert

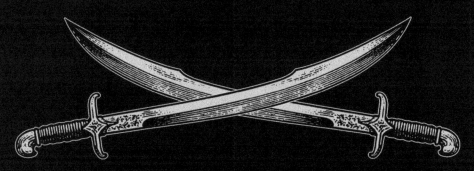

Harold Lamb

Edited by Howard Andrew Jones
Introduction by Scott Oden

UNIVERSITY OF NEBRASKA PRESS
LINCOLN AND LONDON

Library of Congress Cataloging-in-Publication Data

Lamb, Harold, 1892—1962.
Swords from the desert / Harold Lamb ;
edited by Howard Andrew Jones ;
introduction by Scott Oden.
p. cm.
Includes bibliographical references.
ISBN 978-0-8032-2516-9 (pbk. : alk. paper)
1. Crusades—Fiction. I. Jones, Howard A. II. Title.
PS3523.A4235S94 2009
813'.52—dc22
2009010878

Set in Trump Medieval by Kim Essman.
Designed by R. W. Boeche.

Contents

Foreword

While researching material for his histories of the Crusades, Harold Lamb began to read Arab accounts of the time and became fascinated with their culture. In a letter printed in the appendix of this volume he wrote that "the Arab, and the *saracin*-folk, were more intelligent than our Croises, more courteous, and usually more daring. They had a sense of humor. . . . Read side by side, the Moslem chronicles of Ibn Athir, Raschid, or Ibn Battuta are much more human, expressive, and likable than the monkish annals of the crusaders." Lamb found inspiration in these old chronicles, and before long was writing stories from the Arab point of view. First came "The Shield," a novella narrated by Khalil el Khadr,* who figures prominently in two of the Durandal stories.†

A few years later Lamb returned to an Arabian narrator, Daril ibn Athir, a former swordsman turned physician. His three adventures form the jeweled center of this collection. The first two were published almost back to back; the third was published some seven months after and is apt to leave those who read the adventures in sequence scratching their heads. In "The Road to Kandahar," Daril allies himself with the stalwart Mahabat Khan, scion of Jahangir the Mogul, and the story's conclusion leaves Daril with Mahabat Khan and his Rajput allies to journey to Jahangir's stronghold. When "The Light of the Palace" opens, Daril is introduced to another Mahabat Khan, likewise a leader of Rajputs and scion of Jahangir. Daril neither knows him nor makes mention of having known someone very similar. Indeed, it seems clear that it is the same fellow and that Lamb has

---

*Khalil is Lamb's first Arabian narrator, which should not be confused with Lamb's first Moslem narrator, Abdul Dost. Dost narrates four short stories collected in *Warriors of the Steppes* (Bison Books, 2006).

†Reprinted by Donald M. Grant.

ignored the existence of the preceding story. As Mahabat Khan is a prominent character in both novellas, it is no mistake but a deliberate choice. No correspondence on the subject or notes on the story seem to have survived, so Lamb's reasoning remains a minor mystery.

Whatever the explanation, in "The Light of the Palace" Lamb returns to the court of Jahangir the Mogul and the brilliant and lovely Nur-Mahal, mother of she for whom the Taj Mahal was erected. Nur-Mahal's astonishing ability to not only survive and rule in a male-dominated society but to rule wisely, fascinated Lamb; she appeared three times in the stories of Khlit the Cossack and Abdul Dost, and four years later, in 1932, she was the protagonist in one of Lamb's best novels, *Nur-Mahal*. In some ways, "The Light of the Palace" is a dry run for the later novel, or at least it was a chance for Lamb to experiment with the characters who would form its core. When Nur-Mahal and Mahabat Khan's goals bring them to loggerheads, they are so fully realized that great fiction results.

One of this book's companion volumes, *Swords From the West*, would probably have been a more appropriate home for "The Rogue's Girl," one of Lamb's better stories from the post-*Adventure* phase of his writing career, but because it has an Arab physician as a minor viewpoint character, I placed it here to relieve a collection already groaning at the bindings. Two stories with mettlesome female protagonists round out this volume. Nadra, from "The Way of the Girl," is so capable one wonders why she desires the attention of the rock-skulled Yarouk, but apparently love can be both blind and politically incorrect.

Lamb was treated well in the Middle East, for his writing had gained a reputation for being well researched and impartial.* The U.S. State Department valued his opinion highly enough to consult with him about the region after World War II, just as the Office of Strategic Services (oss) had employed him undercover overseas during the war. Lamb had been posted to Iran, his cover being that of a writer doing research for his books—an easy enough cover, as that's exactly what Lamb was doing. An oss superior, Gordon Loud, wrote of him in 1944 saying that "he has marvelous contacts but fails to make the best of them, having something of the feeling that reporting information gained socially is an abuse of friend-

---

*Hasan Ozbekkan, a Turk writing for the *New York Times Book Review* (in reference to Lamb's book *Suleiman the Magnificent*) called him "completely objective and meticulously just."

ship and hospitality. This I tried to dispel, how successfully only results will show." Loud made several other points about Lamb in the briefing, among them these two:

- *Apparently [Lamb] thoroughly appreciates the reasons why he cannot write for publication on certain controversial subjects and is reconciled to this limitation, even though it hurts his idealistic conscience.*
- *Is extremely sensitive to Washington [not* oss*] "boners" regarding Middle East policy—is repeatedly kept awake over them, and continually says "What can we do to prevent them." My only answer was to keep reporting their reactions upon the Middle East, constantly building up evidence of their detrimental effect.*

A letter written by Lamb to a superior in December 1944 reveals Loud's analysis to be an accurate assessment. Lamb mentions the drafting of articles for the *Saturday Evening Post* to help bolster support for Middle Eastern concerns. Here is an excerpt:

The attitude of our pgs *Command in Iran is they have one job to do, to move freight to the waiting Russians, and that in so doing they need have no tangible relationship with Iranians. Some officers, who, like Wright, had set up contacts like language study groups, etc. were discouraged in so doing. Not that Connolly and his staff do not appear at certain functions in Iran and shake hands, or entertain twosomes and threesomes of Iranians. But the general impression produced is that our officers consider Iranians an inferior lot, and have as little contact with them as possible, while building camps like Amirabad and running the railroad. You know how this impression has been strengthened by wisecracking write-ups in* Time *and elsewhere.*

At the same time Russian officers are in close contact with our Command in the performance of their duties. Also our Command has been throwing weekly parties for Russians with back-slapping thrown in. General impression: we want the Soviet heroes for buddies, but not the Iranians.

Now when the Shah and his party made a tour of Khorassan the Iranian group was greeted ceremoniously by the Russkys, who turned out the guard at their inadequate posts, and arranged motion pictures of the journey. General effect: cordiality and proper appreciation shown by the Russians.

It seemed more than obvious that unless our Command made some reciprocating gesture, its relationship with the Iranians would go from bad to worse. I suggested to Cairo (Nov 18) what should have been done long since—to invite the Shah to make an inspection trip down the railroad (our section, Tehran to the Gulf) to view our new installations, camps, hospitals, etc. The Iranian party to be received

with due ceremony—perhaps we could throw in a parade or band
concert, and certainly we could muster camera crews to take some
footage for the Tehran and probably U.S.A. news-files.

  The trip would appeal to the youngster, Muhammad Reza, and
would fit in exactly with his (and the general official Iranian) anx-
iety to participate in the war endeavor. Whether the trip was made
or not, the gesture would send up our stock.

The letter goes on to describe Lamb getting approval to set the plan in
motion through the Iranians, which he proceeds to do through his friend
and contact Muhammad Sa'id, Minister of Foreign Affairs. Later in the
same letter Lamb relays that Sa'id told him he "had been the only person of late to take the pains to go to all parts of the country and to understand it from the Iranian point of view. His aide pressed me afterward as
to the probable date of my return."

I do not know whether Lamb managed in the end to arrange a tour for
the shah; that would take some extensive digging through oss archives.
This snapshot of his oss service, though, shows that Lamb's own sense of
honor, fair play, and simple common sense was being troubled by American policies of the time.

After the war, Lamb's home was filled with lovely gifts from leaders
throughout the Middle East, including some gorgeous illuminated Koran
pages, pottery, sculpture, and so forth. The shah of Iran became a close
personal friend and visited the Lambs at their home, and Harold and his
wife, Ruth, spent much of the year (except the summers, which they usually spent in Switzerland) in parts of the Middle East. Other luminaries
and movers and shakers from other fields visited them at their house, including Cecil B. DeMille, who lunched there often.

At the time of his death, Lamb was a director of the Friends of the Middle East, Inc. It's hard to know what he would have thought of America's
Middle Eastern policies in the last decades, but it seems safe to say that
we could have benefited from his guidance.

This book, though, far removed from such concerns, transports us to
distant times as seen through the eyes of wanderers and heroes who rode
the caravan paths. They are splendid tales and worthy additions to the li-
braries of those who love adventure.

Enjoy!

Acknowledgments

I would like to thank Bill Prather of the Thacher School for his continued support. This volume would not have been possible without the aid of Bruce Nordstrom, who long ago provided Lamb's *Collier's* texts and other research notes. I also would like to express my appreciation for research assistance from Roland Popp and the advice of Victor Dreger, Jan van Heinegen, Alfred Lybeck, and James Pfundstein, gentlemen and scholars. Lastly I wish again to thank my father, the late Victor Jones, who helped me locate various *Adventure* magazines, and Dr. John Drury Clark, whose lovingly preserved collection of Lamb stories is the chief source of seventy-five percent of my *Adventure* manuscripts.

Introduction

SCOTT ODEN

In 1959 explorer Wilfred Thesiger wrote that once a man left the deserts of the Middle East he would "have within him the yearning to return . . . for this cruel land can cast a spell which no temperate clime can match."[*] Such a sentiment finds resonance in the life and work of Harold Lamb.

We most often remember Lamb as the premiere adventure writer of the Pulp Era, as the creator of such memorable characters as Khlit the Cossack, Kirdy and Ayub, Daril ibn Athir and Khalil el Khadr. Indeed, he was all of this and more. Born in 1892, Harold Albert Lamb was a contemporary of T. E. Lawrence, the famed Lawrence of Arabia; while no evidence exists that the two men ever met or corresponded, their lives nevertheless followed a similar arc. Apart from their more glaring differences—that Lamb was a native New Yorker and Lawrence the illegitimate son of Irish gentry—at a young age both men poured prodigious energy into the study of the old Orient, what today we call the Middle East, and especially into the era of the Crusades. But, while Lawrence's initial interests were archaeological, Lamb fashioned the rewards of his Eastern passion into stories. In Lamb's own words:

> I wrote all the time—set up my stories in the attic at school [Columbia University] and printed them on a hand press and then carried on with the Columbian literary magazine.
>
> In 1914 my father broke down and I found a job as a make-up man on a motor trade weekly, then tried to do financial statistics for the New York Times and write stories at the same time. The stories were gleaned from the oriental digging, and Adventure printed them. An understanding editor, Arthur Sullivant Hoffman, allowed me to write anything I wanted.[†]

---

[*]Wilfred Thesiger, *Arabian Sands* (New York: E. P. Dutton, 1959).
[†]From the dust jacket of Lamb's *Kirdy: The Road Out of the World* (New York: Doubleday, 1933).

While the Great War (1914–18) formed a watershed moment in the life of Lawrence, the moment where his name became legend, it was no less significant to Lamb. When America entered World War I in 1917, Lamb joined the 107th Infantry (formerly the Seventh New York) as a private but did not see any fighting; a month after his enlistment he married Ruth Barbour—she who would be his constant companion till the end of his days.

Lamb continued writing and selling, with the prestigious *Adventure* being his primary market. By 1927 he had also branched out into nonfiction with the publication of a critically acclaimed biography of Genghis Khan; more would follow. Still, Lamb wrote a staggering array of fiction for *Adventure*: tales of Cossacks and Mongols, crusaders and Moslems—from intricately plotted epics cast on a grand scale to romantic interludes worthy of Scheherazade. Adding to the verisimilitude of his work was Lamb's skill with languages. He was fluent in Latin and French, the language of Near Eastern exploration since the days of Napoleon, as well as ancient Persian, some Arabic, and a bit of Turkish . . . not to mention Manchu-Tatar and medieval Ukrainian. He assembled his own personal library of research material, with special emphasis on "the medieval travelers, Persian and Russian chronicles, [and the] histories of elder China."*

Lamb bolstered his scholarship with a propensity for travel. Not content to study the Orient from afar, he and his wife journeyed extensively through the lands he wrote about. Thus, when Daril ibn Athir, narrator of "The Road to Kandahar," sees "a wide and lofty plain, set with fruit gardens and water ditches and the yellow walls of villages. Lines of vineyards rose against the nearest hills, and pomegranate bushes with their dark, shining leaves nearly hid the water ditches," one can be certain it was a vista Lamb himself beheld while traveling in southern Afghanistan.

The roar of the '20s gave way to the dour '30s. Lamb weathered the Great Depression better than most, balancing the needs of writing, travel, and study with the demands of a growing family; he sought new outlets for his work as the pulps withered on the vine. More and more he focused on his histories and biographies, books whose even-handedness and popularity elevated him out of the pulp ghetto and into the role of serious historian—a role that earned him an excellent reputation in the Middle East.

---

*Lamb, *Kirdy*, dust jacket.

Much of the fair-mindedness in Lamb's work extended from a genuine affection for the peoples and cultures of the Orient: he respected their history, found their chronicles to be much more accessible—more human—than those of the Europeans, and found much to admire in their courtesy and their humor. This esteem manifested itself in his well-rounded portrayals of fictional characters and in the objective treatment of biographical subjects. This is not to say Lamb turned a blind eye to the faults and foibles of the Moslems. Far from it. But neither did he play to the stereotype. Lamb purposefully eschewed the Western caricature of Arabs as childish zealots and instead presented them as possessing in equal measures nobility and pettiness, piety and profanity, charity and greed, mercy and cruelty. In short, he allowed them their humanity.

Though one can only speculate, it is easy to imagine how the men and women Lamb met on the road must have provided him with a deep pool of inspiration: from jests and maledictions to gestures and expressions; from the cut and texture of a rich merchant's *khalat* to the fork of a camel driver's hennaed beard. Such miniscule details, when woven amid the threads of history, served to resurrect the dead in the eyes of his readers. But Harold Lamb's greatest gift, and surely this is beyond speculation, was his ability to restore to the past its epic sense of blood and thunder, its grandeur and its drama.

Apart from his work, Lamb does not seem to be the sort of man who courted drama; he appeared reserved by nature, quiet and devoid of that sense of personal flamboyance that has become the hallmark of the modern author. He said of himself, "When study oppresses I go straight to the Northern lumber camps or the decks of a schooner. My relaxations are chess, tennis, and gardening. I am six feet one inch in height, weigh 160 pounds, and have prematurely gray hair."*

But the outbreak of World War II brought a new wrinkle to Lamb's life as this learned, lean, and active family man was tapped by the oss to advise and gather intelligence—incidentally, the same task the British Foreign Office recruited Lawrence for in 1914—against Axis interests in Iran. In his foreword to this volume, series editor Howard Andrew Jones has much to say regarding this phase of Lamb's life, and there is obviously much more that remains to be discovered. Suffice it to say, Lamb's lifelong interest in the region's history, culture, and politics—coupled with

---

*Lamb, *Kirdy*, dust jacket.

his reputation as an author and historian—afforded him rare insight into how the Allies could best benefit from Persian involvement . . . and how the Persians could best benefit from Western interests. It is not known how seriously the Allied Command took Lamb's recommendations (though if history is any indicator, not very seriously at all), but he emerged from the war with both his honor and his reputation intact.

Lamb spent the remainder of his life on familiar ground, engaged in travel and study. He maintained a close friendship with Muhammad Reza, the shah of Iran, and continued writing histories and biographies, as well as articles and stories for the likes of *Collier's*, the *Saturday Evening Post*, and *National Geographic*. He also turned his hand to writing screenplays for a burgeoning Hollywood.

As all things must, the end came in 1962 when, at the age of seventy, Harold Albert Lamb passed away. He left behind a legacy of impeccable scholarship, stories, and books that would excite and inform his readers for generations to come.

I fell under Harold Lamb's spell in the early 1980s, after reading *Alexander of Macedon* for a school project. While my teachers were competent, they lacked Lamb's flair for bringing history to life; I remember checking the book out from my school's library time and time again, noticing after each reading some small facet I had missed before. Later, I came across an original edition of *The Crusades: The Flame of Islam*, and my esteem for Lamb increased a thousandfold.

Like that book, the stories collected here represent the perfect blending of storytelling and history. You'll meet men and women who must have surely existed, like Daril ibn Athir, a swordsman-turned-physician whose voice, to my ear at least, sounds curiously like Lamb's own; the far-wandering Bedouin Khalil el Khadr, lover of horses; wily Alai, who dwells in the house of Genghis Khan; and many more besides. Listen and you'll hear sounds from a time long past: tent poles creaking in a desert breeze, the silver chime of bells woven into a camel's halter, steel rasping on steel, and the splintering of lances . . .

Welcome to the old Orient as Harold Lamb knew it.

Swords from the Desert

The Rogue's Girl

The sun was going down behind the roofs of Paris. A chill wind came up from the river, whispering over the bridge of Notre Dame. One after the other, far-off bells clanged and chimed for vespers, and Jeanne put away her fiddle. That is, she tied a cloth 'round it and started homeward—a slight, ragged girl with slim legs thrust into muddy slippers.

The wind tossed the tangle of red hair upon her shoulders as she bent to count the day's earnings in her hand. Six copper coins she had, a clipped piece of silver, an old ring with a broken moonstone in it and a link from a gold chain. A great lord had thrown her this link as he rode past, but Jeanne doubted it was gold.

At a money-changer's stall she held it out, and a claw-like hand reached for it—felt of it and rang it down upon the counter. And thrust it back to her contemptuously.

"Brass!" The money-changer sneered. "Not the value of a sol."

"But," cried Jeanne, her gray eyes innocent, "a seigneur with six spears and a trumpeter to follow him gave it me."

"*Eschec*! Will the like of him cast gold to a rogue's girl? Now that ring you have is worth a chip—"

"Don't burn your fingers." Jeanne had been looking at the pale moonstone all afternoon and she liked it.

"Half a crown."

"My faith," she grimaced, "do you think to buy a crown jewel for silver? I'll be wearing it myself."

With a toss of her head she was off across the bridge, pausing only to bargain for cheese and bread. She nibbled at her supper as she edged around a veiled leper who sounded his clacker mournfully. It was late— almost dark between the leaning houses—and she circled wide where men-at-arms loitered over a watch fire. Jeanne was sixteen years old and she knew well where harm and where safety lay for a fair fiddling girl in the alleys of Paris. Humming to herself, she tossed a copper into the basket of a begging woman, mimicking as she did so the air of the seigneur who had thrown her brass for gold. Then she shrank against the wall, hiding her face in her hood.

The horsemen splashed through the mud of the alley, heedless of the women. The leader, a bearded man in red Burgundian colors, carried two shields, and Jeanne saw that one had been broken. Down toward the river galloped the riders, swinging away from the watch fire.

"My faith," Jeanne muttered, "they go apace!"

She wondered, as she turned from the alley into another, why a led horse with empty saddle had been with the men, and why they chose a way to darkness and water instead of a lighted square. But she had seen much of the feuds and the fighting of the lords of Paris.

Abruptly she stopped, peering into the dimness before her. A man lay there, outstretched and motionless. A tall youth with yellow hair darkened by running blood. Jeanne knelt down and touched his chest, her fingers feeling the iron rings of mail. But he was breathing.

Quickly the girl glanced about her. No one else was in the alley and the walls were blank and silent. Jeanne bent over the white face of the wounded man, and it seemed to her he must be dying. She drew a long, helpless breath, and hurried to the end of the alley through an archway to the black void of a stair.

"Giron!" she called, and whistled melodiously.

After a moment a figure broad as a bear appeared before her, and another followed, bearing a candle. They had shaggy heads and they smelled of the wine cellar from which they had come.

"There's a poor dupe," she cried, "turning up his toes yonder."

The two rogues grunted and followed her to the wounded man, where they blew out the candle and searched the ground by him.

"Thunder of God," whispered the broad fellow, "he's been stripped by them that laid him down. Aye, pouch and rings, all gone."

"And belt and cloak," added the other. "Sword and knife gone—like a peeled turnip he is."

But before the candle had been put out, Jeanne had caught a glimpse of a lean, proud head and gentle lips twisted by pain. "Nay, Giron," she exclaimed, "carry him down to the cellar and look to his hurts."

"Let him lie," muttered the big man with an oath. "See you not, Jeanne, he is a high Mark? He'll be cold in another hour, belike, and if he be found in our hands, they will e'en hie us off to the Big Jump."

He meant that this was a seigneur, whose death in their cellar would mean hanging for all of them. Giron was one of the most skilled dice coggers and picklocks in the city, while his companion, Pied-à-Botte, was a veteran mockmonk and mumper. They felt aggrieved that the fallen man had not even a belt worth taking on him, and they had no mind to set their necks in a noose to help him in his dying.

"Nay, he will live," cried Jeanne. "See ye not how strong he is, and a stranger, by his dress? And if he is a lord's son, ye will not lack pay for this hour's work. Be quick, before he bleeds his life away."

She kept at the rogues until they bore the man down to their fire in the abandoned wine cellar and laid him on the straw. But they had neither clean clothes to bind up his hurts nor water. Jeanne tried to wash away the blood with wine, in vain.

"Wait!" she cried. "I will bring one to tend him."

Ten minutes later she was climbing to the top of a dark stair, with her pulse throbbing. At the landing she found a lantern that cast specks of light upon a black curtain, disclosing curious writing embroidered in gold upon the cloth. Jeanne could not read, but she knew this writing was not honest French—since she had come to stare at it once before. And at the curtain she hesitated.

Behind it lived Ibn Athir, the Arab. Some said he was an alchemist who knew the art of drawing the essence of gold out of quicksilver. Others said he was a sorcerer who could summon to him the demiurges of Satan in the fire of his furnace. Surely the great ladies visited him to buy spells for their beauty, or secret potions. Yet Jeanne had seen him give medicine to a wine crier who had a fit in the street below.

"*Maitre* Athir!" she called, crossing her fingers before her eyes. A strip of light showed beneath the curtain, and she heard slippers moving over stone.

Then the light vanished, and Jeanne almost turned and fled as the curtain was drawn aside and a tall figure confronted her within the gloom of the doorway. "Who seeks?" a deep voice asked.

"'Tis Jeanne, the fiddling girl," she explained. "Oh, Master Athir, will you come now, at once, and bring a medicine to save a young lord who has been cracked on the scrag—on the head?"

"Who is this seigneur?"

"I know not. I found him in the alley, and he can say no word."

Athir disappeared from the doorway and after a moment came out on the landing wrapped in a long, gray kaftan, the hood drawn over his head. In one of his wide sleeves he carried a bundle, and he nodded to her—she thought that his dark eyes were not evil, but only amused. "Lead," he said briefly.

The two rogues and the girl watched while the Arab drew the mail shirt from the wounded lad and ran a lean finger over the wounds—for the silvered mail had been hacked through across the chest. He felt the faint pulse beat in the wrists, and drew the slashed flesh together, applying an aromatic gum that stopped the bleeding. Then he bound up the wounds, and skillfully poured a little fluid down the throat of the unconscious man.

"Will he live," Jeanne asked, "now that you have worked this magic upon him?"

Athir shook his head. "Verily, little demoiselle, I have worked no sorcery. The drink will bring sleep to him presently. Such a blow on the head may do great harm, but this youth is strong as a colt, and—*inshallah*—if God wills it, he may yet live with a clear mind."

"Yonder whack on the scrag," observed Giron from the fire, "was a foul blow. Aye, 'twas dealt him when the poor lordling lay outstretched on the ground."

"And how so?" demanded Pied-à-Botte.

"Did I not see the cut o' the blade in the mud? Aye, right against this young cock's comb. Now bend thy peepers on this."

Giron pointed out the line of a red bruise running across the forehead of the wounded man. "'Tis the mark," he said, "of the steel cap that kept him from being cracked open like a melon."

"And where," Pied-à-Botte inquired, "is this helmet? It lieth not i' the alley. Nay, who would carry off a split cap?"

"Why, them that stripped his gear from him. See ye not, addlehead, that they took every mark of his name and rank, and left him for dead."

Suddenly Jeanne bethought her of the three riders with the riderless horse and the broken shield galloping toward the river. "Then," she exclaimed, "I saw them, and they were followers of my lord of Burgundy, with a red-bearded lord leading them."

"A red beard close-clipped upon his chin?" demanded Giron. "A hawk's beak and a roving eye?"

Jeanne nodded.

"God's thunder! That will be Renault. Aye, the duke's lieutenant he is."

The name of Renault was well known to the rogues of Paris. They called him the Gardener, saying that he kept the gallows-tree loaded down with fruit, and the grave diggers ever busied at turning up the soil. This red Renault was the confidential agent of John the Fearless, Duke of Burgundy. So if Renault had struck down this stranger secretly, the duke had desired his death. And it was not safe to cross the path of John the Fearless.

"Here we be," muttered Pied-à-Botte, "a-nursing of this wight."

A shadow of dread fell upon the two rogues. That day they had seen the archers of Burgundy mustering at the street corners, while the butchers came forth from the markets with poleax and knife to join them. Rumors ran through the alleys that the duke had become master of the city. Certainly he held the gates, while the retinue at his house—the Hôtel St. Pol—was more like an army. Both Giron and stout Pied-à-Botte could not help wondering how much Renault would pay to hear that the man he had thought slain was lying alive in a certain cellar. And Jeanne read their thoughts.

"Asses, with long ears!" she cried. "You would flit off to the duke's men and gab for a silver pound. And then what would befall you? Why, Renault, who hath taken pains to hide this deed, would swing you up to dance in the air, to still your tongues."

The straw beside her stirred, and a deep voice muttered drowsily, "What is this talk? Where is—my horse?"

Aroused by their voices, the wounded man had raised himself on his elbow, to stare wearily at the fire. His brown hand quivered as he raised it to his head, then fumbled at his side for the missing sword.

"Messire," said Athir quietly, "you were struck down before nightfall and left to die. Your horse is lost, with all you carried on you, and these people—"

"Get me a mount. I must go on!" He rose to his knee, thrusting aside the Arab's restraining arm as if it had been an empty sleeve.

"Nay, this night you cannot sit a horse, messire. Wait, and sleep."

The sleeping draught had begun to take effect, and the boy's head swayed on his shoulders. Only by an effort did he keep his eyes open. "I tell you," he said hoarsely, "I carry word to the king, and it may not wait."

"The king!" Giron and Pied-à-Botte, stared, round-eyed, but the alchemist glanced shrewdly at the half-conscious messenger.

"Then, messire," he suggested quickly, "write it down, or tell it me."

"Am I a clerk, to write a missive?" The wounded man shook his head and swore under his breath: "*Sieur Dieu!* No one but I may bear it." He tried to stand up, but sank back on the straw instead. "Aye, Sir Rohan and De Trault, they lie dead by the road—"

As his eyes closed and his limbs relaxed, Athir touched his shoulder. "Your name," he whispered urgently, "what is it?"

The two rogues edged closer, their ears cocked, and the wounded man smiled a little. "You may well ask that, but you'll not know it." And in another moment he was asleep.

Athir, however, could guess at a good deal. By his profession he was brought close to the court, and for some time he had heard whispers that the rising star of John of Burgundy would soon eclipse that of the sickly and irresolute monarch of France. Did not John the Fearless virtually hold Paris in his grasp—so that he might at any hour close the gates? He had gained the support of the guilds by promises, and had rid himself of some nobles of the king's party by a reign of terror in the streets.

And now John of Burgundy had the monarch of France a guest in the Hôtel St. Pol. Few men gained admittance to Louis without the duke's consent, and rumor had it that the Lord of France could not leave the gardens of St. Pol until the duke chose for him to do so.

The king, no doubt, had officers and servitors to attend him, and even John of Burgundy would not risk harming his person. But Louis was a prey to moods, and the Burgundian persuaded him that only in his house would His Majesty be safe from the mobs of Paris. Athir suspected that John of Burgundy had not wished this stranger to reach the presence of the king with his message, and if so it was no matter to meddle in.

"Keep him here," he advised Jeanne, "if you wish him to live."

Then he went thoughtfully up the narrow stair. As he did so he heard above him a sound as of a rat scampering on the stones. Hastening his step, he gained the top and glanced quickly to right and left along the alley. The only light came from the stars and a distant lantern, but Athir had eyes accustomed to dark nights, and he made out the figure of a man slipping away under the wall—a man clad in a beggar's cloak and hood, yet moving away with a stride that was no beggar's discouraged shuffle.

Whereupon the Arab waited until the alley was deserted. Then, muffling himself in his kaftan, he vanished silently in the other direction. John of Burgundy had eyes and ears that served him well for hire of nights, even, perhaps, in the rogues' alleys.

Jeanne did not go to her room, in a neighboring attic. While Giron and Pied-à-Botte snored in their cloaks, she sat in the straw to tend the fire, and ceaselessly her eyes strayed to the face of the sleeping stranger. At times she reached out to touch his bandaged head and run her fingers timidly through the yellow hair dark with dried blood.

Hugging her knees and wide awake, she played a game of pretending—that this unknown man belonged to her, and looked at her with eyes of love.

Early the next morning Ibn Athir answered a tap at his door to find Jeanne standing by the curtain. The girl had made a hasty visit to her quarters and had washed carefully, adding a touch of rouge to her cheeks and a flimsy bit of lace to the throat of her dress. She said nothing as she wandered about the alchemist's room, glancing idly at the brick furnace, the crucibles and glass vials and the piled-up folios.

"Is it true, Master Athir," she asked at last, "that you make draughts of magic for the great Marks—the noble dames?"

"Sometimes."

Jeanne's tongue seemed to fail her, and she flushed. "I mean the things they call—love potions. You know well the draughts that make—other people—love these ladies?"

"Verily, I know them." Athir sold talismans and potions to his patrons, while he smiled inwardly at their superstition.

"And such a draught will work no harm to him—to the one that drinks of it?"

"Little Jeanne, such potions are for the seigneurs' ladies, who pay for their whims."

"My father was a seigneur even as they, but a minstrel of the southland with an empty purse and a great thirst in him, which brought him down to singing ballades to the crowds while I fiddled among them, thanking them for the silver. A year ago he died, and I have made good shift for myself. I can pay only a small price, but, please, Master Athir, mix me the draught with magic in it for I need it sorely."

The Arab looked at her curiously, seeing anew the soft hair, the clear, troubled eyes. And he wondered, as he went to his table, what minstrel had caught the fancy of so fair a girl. He measured out a little red fluid. "Juice of the root of manna," he explained, and added a pinch of dark powder that vanished from sight. "'Tis star dust brought from the Egyptian desert where the heart of a flying star fell. It hath power to arouse great love in a human, but be sure that you keep near to him who drinks it."

"I will do that." She nodded gratefully and hastened away with the red elixir in a vial.

In the cellar the wounded man, alone, was pacing restlessly by the embers of the fire—he had been asleep in Giron's charge when Jeanne had left him to seek the alchemist.

"What hole is this?" he cried. "Who brought me hither?"

Jeanne lowered her eyes and clutched the vial tighter. "Messire—I did. Truly, you are sore hurt and have not strength to venture forth."

"Thy name is Jeanne—I heard it spoken last night—and meseems I owe thee much." The boy smiled impulsively. "Wil't help me more?"

"Aye, but first," she added warily, "you must eat, and drink."

She hurried to place bread and cheese on a clean cloth, and to pour wine into a cup. After a second's hesitation she emptied the vial of red fluid into the wine and brought it to him. He gulped it down and chewed at a fistful of the bread, while Jeanne sat in the straw pretending to eat, but watching him breathlessly.

The drink had an effect upon him, for his eyes brightened and he seemed to throw off his weariness. "Thou art no rogue's girl," he said. "Nay, an elf-maid, thou, escaped from Merlin's tower."

Jeanne lowered her eyes swiftly, and choked on a bit of bread.

"And thou wilt see my need," he added eagerly. "Hearken, little Jeanne—"

With an effort she swallowed the bread, feeling herself flush from throat to forehead, and wishing of a sudden that she had not dabbled in magic. She wanted to fly from the cellar but she could not.

"—I know naught of Paris, nor have I a friend here, save thee. I am Hugh of Bearn, once armor-bearer to Sir Rohan of Navarre. We were sent from the south to bear a message to thy lord, the king. At Limoges tavern were we beset treacherously by a dozen riders, who slew Sir Rohan and De Trault. I fought clear of them and got me to a horse, and rode hither without sleep or rest, for now I must carry the message to Louis, who, they say, is captive to Duke John in this town."

The girl drew a breath of relief and glanced at him curiously.

"This is the message: The armed host of Navarre hath joined with my lord of Armagnac. It is now on the march toward Burgundy. Nor will it cease that march until Louis is released out of the hands of the Burgundians and set free among loyal men in Tours." He caught her hand impatiently in his. "How can I write such tidings in a letter? Nay, I must find me a way into the presence of the king and bespeak him openly. Sir Rohan said that when Louis knows that armed power hath risen to his aid, Duke John's web of scheming will be broken."

Thoughtfully Jeanne nodded. "But how would you find a way into the Hôtel St. Pol, Messire Hugh?" she asked. "Have you a plan?"

"Get me a good horse, and I will make shift to do it."

"Then wait!" Suddenly the girl rose and caught up her fiddle. "Don't pull a snoop—don't go out to look for aught, until I come back. For, truly, Messire Hugh, I can aid you in this." At the stairway she turned to glance back at him shyly. "Will you promise to await me?"

"If you make haste!"

In her own way, Jeanne did hasten, skipping through narrow alleys and under archways, toward the great street of St. Jacques.

When she came abreast a gray wall with gate towers and tree tops showing over it, she walked slowly, her eyes alert. This, she knew, was the entrance to the Hôtel St. Pol, with its gardens. She had visited its courtyard before, to play for the seigneurs, and she meant to try now to slip through into the building itself, and gain the presence of the king. She had seen his face in the streets, and she thought that no one would heed a fiddling girl. Then, if fortune served her, she might cry aloud the message that Hugh of Bearn was bringing from Navarre. These great lords, no doubt, would pay little heed to a girl's word, but still the message would be spoken, and the king himself might send for the real messenger—

The archers lounging before the half-closed grille gates turned to stare at her, and one of them thrust a pike shaft before her, grinning.

"*Pardie*," another grunted, "'tis the fiddling wench who hath half the rogues' brigade at her summons. Let her go, Mulph."

Safely in the courtyard, Jeanne plucked idly on the strings of her fiddle while she surveyed the prospect. On the left was a blank wall, on the right the stables and quarters of the men-at-arms. At the end of this, a roadway led into the gardens. In front of her rose the bulk of the hôtel it-self, with barred embrasures for windows, and a single arched gate, where stood men of the inner guard and an officer talking to a priest.

She went up to them boldly, and touched the officer's arm. "Messire, I have word for Renault."

He shrugged indifferently, "So have a-many."

"'Tis a word about the crack he did last night," Jeanne whispered.

The Burgundian frowned swiftly, and she smiled up at him, trusting that he would not know all the lieutenant's spies by sight, and would have to admit her.

"Eh, well." He turned to the pikemen of the guard. "One of you bear her in and look to her. Renault is away for the nonce."

Jeanne had expected that the lieutenant might be out of the hôtel, but she had got herself within the doors. Listening intently to the scraps of talk she caught in the halls, she went with the pikeman obediently as far as the door of a tower room that seemed to be a private reception cham-ber. "Now verily," she said wistfully, "I have never seen my lord of Bur-gundy. Is it his wont to pass this way?"

"Nay—he walks i' the garden, and thou'lt not see him."

But Jeanne thought otherwise. Humming to herself, she rested her head against a bar, listening patiently. Her guardian tired of watching her and yawned heartily, then strolled out into the corridor. When she heard him in talk with another soldier she slipped to the door.

Without a sound she edged behind the two and into the corridor away from them.

Almost running—for the guard in the tower room might miss her any moment—Jeanne reached a narrow door and opened it swiftly, giving in-ward thanks that no sentry stood there. Closing the door behind her, she glanced up, and down the stretch of lawn and tulip beds, at the Burgun-dian nobles who sat in talk by a fountain—at the distant group of squires and servants, and at the two figures who walked apart, opposite her, in the shade of a high myrtle hedge.

One, in a plain gray mantle, thin and stooped, she knew to be the sick Louis. The taller man in a green hunting jerkin, with a horn at his belt and a whip in his hand, must be John of Burgundy.

Without hesitating, as if she had been summoned to do that, the girl raised the fiddle on her arm and drew the bow across the strings. It was a dance she played—"Gentilz galans de France"—as she moved out over the grass, the sunlight striking on her red-gold head.

The two figures by the hedge were nearer, but they paid no heed to her. Instead, a man in a long velvet tabard who carried an ivory staff strode toward her, overtaking her.

"What mummery is this?" he demanded.

"'Tis the doing of my lord the Duke," she retorted, without ceasing her playing. But, as she did so, she caught a glimpse of the pikeman who had her in charge emerging from the door. And the staff bearer caught her arm.

She lowered the fiddle and cried out in a clear voice:

"Sire—"

The pale face of Louis turned toward her irresolutely, when the pikeman came up, swearing under his breath, and at a word from him she was pulled back and bustled toward the door. Behind her she heard the voice of John of Burgundy:

"A fiddling wench, Sire, seeking a coin." And then, louder, "Give her silver, from my hand."

"Hearest thou?" grunted the pikeman in her ear. "His Grace will have a word with thee, anon, when Renault is here. Nay, thou red vixen, we'll bide his coming here, within sight of His Grace. I'll have no more of thy trickery!"

Renault, however, was delayed. With two mounted men and a spy in beggar's garb he was searching the alley by the market to finish the work that he had begun the night before—having heard from the pseudo-beggar that Hugh of Bearn still breathed in a rogue's cellar, after a sorcerer had brought him back to life by black enchantment. Renault swore that a good knife-thrust would put an end to any spell.

At that hour Giron and Pied-à-Botte were warming themselves in the sun at the alley's mouth, waiting for Hugh to come out. One glimpse of the Burgundian helmets, and the two rogues were flying to hiding. Down the cellar stair they tumbled, hissing to the wounded man to hold his tongue, for the Gardener was riding by with two armed churls.

"Eschec!" Giron whispered. "'Tis the big Mark wi' two blades, come to the spot of his night's work."

In a moment Giron began to feel the skin crawl upon his back and skull. For the horses did not trot by. They halted, stamping, and iron clanked as men dropped from the stirrups. Then slow steps came upon the stair, and the gloom of the cellar was lightened by the gleam of a lantern. Giron shrank back into a corner.

A man in a mail shirt appeared, the lantern lifted high in one hand, a drawn sword in the other. At his shoulder walked the silent lieutenant, the point of his red beard jutting forward and his eyes narrowed. Renault paused to make certain of what the cellar hid—the two rogues shivering against the wall, and Hugh of Bearn standing motionless, unarmed, with bandaged head and tight-clenched hands.

"So," quoth Renault, his beard bristling in a grin, "the dead hath come to life. I regret, messire, that necessity compels me to send you back into the grave you have just now quitted."

He waited to hear the southerner beg for mercy, but he waited in vain. Hugh shrugged his shoulders and smiled.

"A pity," he said, "that you must strike such a foul blow twice. Give me a sword, and I pledge you there will be no bungling."

"Nay," Renault grunted, "I swear by the *tete-Diou* there will be no mistake this time."

He had left a man to watch the horses, and now—being ever careful in such matters—he called to the other Burgundian: "Slay me those rats by the wall."

To Giron, who had been watching for a chance to slip up the stair, this was the voice of doom. He roared in fear, and in desperation flung himself at the swordsman with the lantern. Midway in his rush he lowered his head and crashed against the other's chest. Unprepared for this butting, the Burgundian fell heavily, throwing out his arms. The lantern clanked on the floor and went out, while the sword slid over the stones. Before the light vanished, Hugh leaped for the blade and caught it up.

Then he stepped swiftly aside, hearing as he did so the familiar whistle of steel through the air. Renault had cut at him savagely, and missed. Hugh let himself down quietly on one knee, holding his sword upright, beside his head.

The cellar was almost in darkness—only a faint light coming down the stair. Giron and the soldier were struggling and cursing on the floor, drowning all other sounds.

"*A moi, Picard!*" Renault shouted, and changed his position as he did so. Mailed feet clattered down the stairs as the third soldier hastened to obey. Then there was a crash, a yell of pain, and renewed scuffling.

Pied-à-Botte had followed the example of his chum, and Hugh judged by the sounds that the two rogues could hold their own at this hand-fighting on the floor. But Renault was slashing about him methodically—knowing that a man without armor would have no chance at matching cuts in the dark with him. And he glanced ever at the gray square of the stairway.

But Hugh had no mind to try a run for it. "Nay, Renault," he called, "this way!"

At once the other's sword struck against his uplifted blade, the sparks flying. Hugh's blade yielded and then twisted suddenly around the Burgundian's as he rose to his feet. The two swords were in touch now, grinding together.

And Renault sought to lock hilts—to bear back the slighter man with his greater strength. But the southerner's blade yielded again, and parried deftly when the Burgundian tried to thrust, for at this game of touch in the darkness the skill of the wounded man was a match for the brawn of the lieutenant. Sweat dripped into Renault's eyes and he panted, maddened by the void before him and the elusive, clinging length of steel that quivered against his own.

He forgot that the southerner's strength must soon give out, and he bethought him of his dagger. His left hand plucked it from his belt and he stepped forward to strike. In that instant the other blade left his own and thrust through the links of his mail. Fire scorched Renault's side, and red flames filled the black void before his eyes. He fell forward into the flames.

Five minutes later, when Hugh had struck a light and kindled the lantern again, Renault lay unconscious on the stones. At sight of the blood-stained sword above them in the southerner's hand, the two soldiers gave up wrestling with Giron and Pied-à-Botte.

"Watch over these fellows," Hugh said, "for I have horses waiting above to take me to the St. Pol, and something—" he pointed to the wounded Renault—"that will open the gate to me. Now help me lift him to his saddle."

They did that, and the gabs and rummies of the alley came out to stare. The rogues and the dogs of the town whispered and sniffed as the horses paced under arch and balcony toward the house of John of Burgundy.

The archers at the gate gave back before the stranger with the bandaged head who cried to them that Renault had been sore wounded.

"And where is your seigneur?" he demanded.

They said that His Grace the Duke was walking in the garden.

"Nay," Hugh retorted, "is not your king here?" And when they pointed to the garden road, he turned that way, holding the unconscious Renault. He guided the two horses between the myrtle hedges, across the wide lawn, with a score of guardsmen walking by him, whispering. He saw the two figures apart, beyond the fountain, and turned that way.

While the Burgundians and the nobles of the court looked on curiously, he let Renault down into the hands of the soldiers, and, before anyone could speak, he cried to Louis, "Sire, a message from Navarre!"

The words reached the ear of the king, and before the onlookers recovered from sheer astonishment at hearing a reigning prince addressed by a strange lad from the saddle, Hugh had dismounted and come forward to kneel within a stone's toss of the two lords. And John of Burgundy broke the silence in an amused voice:

"His Majesty hath not come to the garden to hear messages of state. Go thou, and wait upon the chamberlain in the evening." Carelessly he ran the whip he held through tense fingers—taking swift note how Louis glanced irresolutely about—and he added thoughtfully, "But let us see the letter thou hast, or a token of thy mission."

And the southerner, who had nothing of the kind to show, laughed. He pointed to the wounded Renault, now outstretched upon the grass.

"There lieth the token, my lord—your follower who tried twice to slay me upon my way hither."

The silence that followed was again broken by the Burgundian: "This is mad talk, and out of place. What proof hast thou? Speak!"

Duke John knew well that he could not now dismiss this man, for too many ears had heard Hugh's charge. But he saw that Hugh had come alone, without companions or witnesses.

"There is one," responded the southerner instantly, "who can give proof to my lord the King."

Again his arm went out, to point toward the door where Jeanne stood, spellbound with anxiety, beside her guard. And Jeanne hesitated not a second. Slipping under the arm of the soldier she was across the lawn, her fiddle clutched tightly. She gasped as she came within the ring of those about the pale man in the gray mantle, and she plumped herself down beside Hugh. Her clear voice cut through the rising murmurs:

"Sire, 'tis truth, every whit. The Gardener scragged him i' the alley and tripped his gear away, and I brought the Arabian sorcerer who fetched him back to life, and I tried to carry his message to you, so they should not waylay him again. Now the *Seigneur Dieu* must have brought him hither unharmed, and by that token you must hear him."

All in a breath she cried it out, and laughter echoed her. Some of the listeners shouted angrily, and John of Burgundy with one swift glance at her eager face understood that here was a witness he could not deal with.

"Away with the rogues," he ordered, "and end this mummery!"

But before his men could lay hand on the two, the stooped figure in the gray cloak stepped forward. Louis had found his voice at last.

"Silence!" he cried; and after a moment: "Speak, thou," he bade the southerner.

Twilight was falling over the gray river, and vespers chimed from the bell towers when Jeanne came back to the door of her lodging, sitting sidewise on the great horse behind Hugh of Bearn. And out of the shadows of the doorway sounded a warning hiss:

"*Eschec!*"

Two shaggy dogs seemed to be crouched there, but the girl recognized Giron and Pied-à-Botte, clutching packs upon their knees. "And what?" she asked.

The big picklock came to the stirrup. "Flash the drag, little Jeanne. We're for St. Denis before the Red Duke twists our gullet in a rope necklace. Come away!"

"Nay," she laughed, "there's no fair fiddling out of Paris."

Giron grumbled under his breath, jerked his thumb at Pied-à-Botte, and the two rogues vanished with their packs. Jeanne looked at the ground. "You'll be wanting, Messire Hugh, to ride from the city before the hour of closing the gates. The duke, they say, hath a long arm and a long memory for vengeance."

But he was looking at the bright head hovering near his arm. The sight of her caught at his heart as if she had laid some witchery upon him. "And what of thee, little Jeanne? Sure it is the duke will not forget thee."

"No harm ever comes to me."

"Then will I see to it." He put his arm about her, pressing his head against the tangle of red-gold tresses. "For I will be riding to the south, and I will be taking you with me. 'Tis fair in my hills."

"There's no good fiddling out of Paris, messire," she said slowly. "And I—I am of these streets, having no love for your hills and olive trees and cattle."

"That is even a lie. Giron hath told me how you have ever the love of the place of your nourishing. And I will not cease from wanting you. So if you abide in Paris, so do I. Faith, now you must hide me from the duke's anger and heal me these wounds of mine."

"Healed you are already, Hugh of Bearn! You fought a champion this day at hand strokes."

"Yet never will I be quit of the spell you have laid upon me, little Jeanne."

Full into his eyes she looked swiftly, seeing in them a strange hunger. Fear of what she had done filled the girl. "May the good God forgive me!" she cried, and turned to him suddenly. "Now get this horse of yours going, and I will show you the way."

Around strange corners she guided him, to a tall house. Dismounting here, they climbed to the top of the stairs and Jeanne went to the curtained door. At her summons the dark figure of the Arab appeared. He welcomed them gravely, for he had heard what had passed at the Hôtel St. Pol.

"'Tis a cure he must have," Jeanne pointed to the southerner, "for the—for that—oh, you know well the elixir I mean. He hath taken from it a kind of fever, and, *pardie*, it was a sinful thing I did."

Glancing at the flushed faces of the lad and the girl, Athir smiled. "Jeanne," he said, "I know no remedy save one for this ailment Messire Hugh hath now."

"Then give it him."

"That only can you do—I have naught will serve him."

Dismayed, the girl chewed her lip, until she flung up her head with quick resolve. "Tell him, then—I cannot. Tell him what elixir I had from you, and gave him secretly."

Turning to his table, the Arab took from it a long vial half full of a red fluid which Jeanne recognized instantly. "This? I keep it for patrons who are more credulous than wise. By Allah," he smiled, "it is no more than spirits of wine which we call *al-kahol*. And this—" he took from a bowl a pinch of gray powder—"is pepper. Nay, little Jeanne, there is no elixir of the kind you sought."

"What," demanded Hugh impatiently, "is all this talk of drinks?"

Jeanne drew a long breath and her eyes flashed warningly at the Arab. "It is no matter," she said with dignity. "Come away now, I pray thee, Messire Hugh—to thy hills, if it must be. But come quickly."

The Shield

Thus said Khalil el Khadr, my good lord, the far-wandering, the wise, the truth-telling, and the never-fearing lord my master, favored of God—Khalil the Badawán who came from no city but the sands of Yamen, who rode to the great city of the iron men, the Franks—and of this city was his tale, often told to me, the unworthy, the scribe. Upon teller and hearer be the peace of God! Thus said he:

Praise to the Giver, who hath bestowed upon men the earth, with its vast spaces to wander in!

It was the year 603.* It was near the setting of the sun, in the bazaar of the metalworkers, which is a narrow street looking out upon the water. The water of the port of Costatinah was dark.

Men say that the water of the seas is black, and that is a lie. It is both gray and green, but to one who stands looking out upon it, when the sun dips toward the sea, it hath the seeming of darkness—yet not beneath the sun. There is gold beneath the sun. And this shining gold of the port lighted the street of the metalworkers and the scheming face of Abou Asaid of Damascus, who sells daggers and sword blades.

"Hearken, my lord Khalil," said the weapon seller, "there is talk in the city."

"There is always talk," I made response.

But he stretched forth his hand and pulled together the leather curtains of his stall, so that he could look out and see who passed by, without being seen or heard.

"It hath reached my ears," he said again, "from the seamen of the harbor, that a fleet comes from Venice."

"Thine ears be overlong," I made answer then, "and thou art little the richer for it, O Abou Asaid. What is Venice?"

---

*Of the Christian era. Khalil's Costatinah is Constantinople. This and many other places named by the Arab scribe are altered hereafter to European names.

"If thine ears, O my lord Khalil," he reproached me, "were inclined more to politics and less to the step of strange women, thou wert the wiser. Nay, Venice is the city of the Greater Sea whence come the hosts of the iron men, the Franks who have invaded the lands of the Muslimin. They are the barbarians, the faith-breakers, the slayers.

"They are fearless men. Their swords have two edges and are straight and heavy. A blow from such a sword breaks the rings of mail and the bones beneath. I have met them in Palestine.

"May they eat shame! This is a new host, and the fleet is vast indeed. The galliots bearing the warriors are as many as the sands of Yamen; the fighting galleys are beyond counting, and the store ships stretch from sky to sky."

Twice, thrice, even four times had these hosts of the Franks descended upon the barren coast of Palestine by land and sea—so my father and his father had said. At this time there was peace between Muslimin and Naz-arene in Palestine. So I wondered why this host had set forth from Ven-ice, and why it was coming to Constantinople.

"There are great lords upon this fleet," Abou Asaid resumed. "Naz-arene lords from far Frankistan, and the king of the Venetians. He is an old man."

"It will be a fine sight," I said then, "these kings and their clans and their horses."

Abou Asaid looked out through the rift of his curtains and ran his fin-ger through his beard.

"The Emperor of Constantinople will not think it a fine sight," he ex-plained under his breath. "He is a Greek."

"Yet he is a Nazarene." So I said, to get at the kernel in the shell of the weapon seller's words. And, indeed, Abou Asaid disgorged the thing that had been troubling him.

"The fleet of the Franks is coming to take Constantinople."

Now I had seen the emperor of Constantinople. Because I had come to the city on a mission, I had been allowed within the palace. The mission had been to escort a princess, the daughter of the emperor out of Roum, to Scutari and into Constantinople. Other Nazarene lords had been in the escort, and though they called me a *saracin*, which is a robber, we had not quarreled on the way. And to hear my tales of other lands, the emperor, who was called Murtzuple, summoned me into his presence.

His palace had walls of beaten gold and azure, and its marble floors were carpeted. Upon the walls, done in mosaics, were pictures of the wars of his ancestors. There were many walls.

And this Murtzuple himself had a bold bearing. He is a dark man with a sallow skin and restless eyes. Generous he is, for he gave to me a silk robe of honor and a horse of his own stable—a white horse of a Frankish breed, too heavy in the leg for my choice. And brave he is—though according to the custom of his fathers I was searched for weapons by eunuchs, and held by the arms and the cloak when I stood before him.

Two Frankish warriors he had on his right hand and three on his left, who leaned on their shields, fully armed. Not a rat could have run upon this emperor without being cut down. Yet it was in my mind that Murtzuple had no liking of this shielding by the suspicion-rid eunuchs and the lords of his court.

Except the Seljuk Sultan of Egypt and the Great Khan of Cathay there is no prince in the world so dignified and so treasure-burdened as this emperor who sat in the throne of the caesars.

And in all my journeys I had not seen a city so wealthy, with such massive walls as this city upon the Golden Horn.

"Surely that is a lie," I said to the weapon seller, when I had thought over his words, "because there is peace between the Nazarenes. And this is one of their holy cities."

Abou Asaid smiled and all the lines came out on his face.

"Little know ye, O Khalil, son of Abd 'Ullah, the Badawán. Of well-sired horses and edged weapons and girls who walk with antelope grace—of such matters thou art conversant, beyond doubt. By the breath of Ali, have I not sold daggers to the Greeks fourfold in the last days? Eh, they labor at building stone casters on the walls. But I have heard what I have heard!"

And at last he made clear to me why he had called me into his stall.

There would be war, he said, between the Greeks of the city and the Franks from over the black water. We would both profit by it if I were to go again to the palace of the Blachernae, where the Emperor Murtzuple sat in council, and swear that I was ready to serve him with a hundred men. Already I had some slight favor with the Greek emperor, and Abou Asaid would drum up the hundred men from the scoundrels of Galata and arm them himself.

The emperor, Abou Asaid explained truthfully, was already served by men-at-arms from Genoa and the island of England that lies beyond the

Gates. These barbarians from England were named Saxons; and in his host were also warriors from the far north—tall men with watery-blue eyes and yellow hair, and Tatars from the steppes of the East. They were men of all faiths and many Muslimin.

I was a *saracin* in the eyes of the Greeks. But the lords who had come with me from Roum had told in the city how I was a chieftain's son who had fought in the battles of Granada and Palestine. And Abou Asaid had praised me as a swordsman unmatched and an Arab without fear. And that was a lie, but the praise was pleasing.

"The emperor can reward greatly," he ended. "Thou hast of him already a journey-gift. What then will be his service grant?"

"Aye, what?"

"Why, a score of fair-faced slaves—precious stones to fill thy cupped hands—perhaps a province or a ship."

It was Abou Asaid's thought that he would share this wealth with me.

Indeed, I had no mind to the venture. Among my people there is a saying that a sword once drawn is not to be sheathed without honor. What part had an Arab in the quarrels of the Franks? I held myself as something better than the barbarian Tatars and Saxons. As for Abou Asaid, he was a merchant, with a purse to be filled.

"Consider, O my lord Khalil," he cried when he read no agreement in my eyes. "This Greek hath a fair mind to thee. Nay, he hath honored thee with a horse of his stables, so that when thou goest forth, there is a canopy held over thee and a trumpeter to go before, in token thou art an honored guest of Murtzuple. In gratitude—"

"Make an end of words. I will not set foot upon this path."

The gifts of the emperor had been for service rendered, and as for hospitality—he had let me stand before him with my arms held.

"Then consider this, O son of Abd 'Ullah. If the barbarian Franks take the city, they will care not at all for horse or canopy—or trumpeter. They will cut thee down for a *saracin*, and thy days will be ended without honor."

A horse had passed the stall where we sat. Such a horse as would have brought joy to Omar the Mighty—a gray desert-bred, slender of limb, with arched neck and eyes of fire.

This gray beauty picked his way through the narrow street of the metalworkers, and daintily as a favorite slave of a great prince who goes where he wills. And the rider of the *kohlani* was a girl-child, who was surely no slave.

No man sat before her, and she herself sat not upon one side, after the fashion of the Frankish woman. One knee was crooked over the low saddle peak, and her face was toward the *kohlani*'s head.

Her face I did not see through the crack in the curtain, but her long hair was the hue of gold. About her brow was a narrow silver filet, and she looked not to one side or the other.

"Upon thee the salute, and long years of life!" I bade farewell to Abou Asaid, the father of plots, and sought my horse.

As usual, my Greek trumpeter and his mates who held the canopy were taking their ease in some nearby wine shop and I called them not. There is a time for ceremony and a time for solitude.

I mounted the white stallion with a highbacked Frankish saddle, covered with cloth of gold, and reined after the splendid gray horse. I had seen that the rider was not veiled, so she could not be a Muslimin. Only one servant—and he a craggy fellow on an ignoble nag—followed her; her blue cloak and vestment bore no precious stones. She could not be the daughter of a wealthy sire. And yet the *kohlani* racer would bring a chieftain's ransom.

I wished well to see the horse near at hand and the face of his rider.

Girl and servant paced up the street of the metalworkers and turned into a muddy alley where the wooden houses nearly came together overhead—a place of foul odors, with children naked in the mud and women that screamed like the harridans they were.

From the alley the gray horse climbed to an open place, paved with flagstones, and began to trot. As if the way were familiar, he threaded a path among scattered marble columns and made toward a great square structure of stone.

There was a gate in this half-ruined wall, and through the gate went the horse and the girl with a rush, as of a dart loosed from the hand. Within the gate it was dark, but in a moment we came out upon the grass of a long enclosure. Here the glow of sunset lighted the sky with its first bright stars.

It was Al-Maidan, the Place of Horses.* At this place the Greeks held races and watched combats between beasts. Tiers of stone balconies looked down on the grass plain, but at this hour the seats were empty.

---

*The Hippodrome.

I pushed past the servant, who turned with an oath when he heard the rush of my stallion. I loosed the rein and spoke to the white horse, who stretched his great limbs in a ponderous gallop. Eh, the Franks chose their horses for weight, not for pace.

Ahead of me the gray *kohlani* skimmed over the racecourse like a hawk unhooded. I gained not at all. And yet the girl heard the beat of the stallion's hoofs and reined in, turning the gray horse sharply to meet me. I drew in the ring-bit and pulled the stallion back on his heels a spear's length from her.

In her hand was neither whip nor dagger. The cloud of her light hair was about her glowing face, and her eyes were those of a child who knew no fear.

Nay, she flinched not when she saw my helmet with the pointed peak and long nasal and chain drop, my black cloak and high-girdled scimitar, and the round shield upon my shoulder. Armed was I, and had come upon her unawares. An arrow's flight away the servant was beating on his nag with his stick.

"Praise be to the Maker," I cried in my Arab speech, "of such a horse, and so fair a woman."

For a second she looked into my eyes, and the blood warmed in my veins.

"Who art thou?" she asked at once, and though she seemed to understand my speech her words were in the Greek tongue. At the same instant she motioned back the vagabond who was coming at me with a stick. He hung back, grumbling.

"I am Khalil the Badawán."

It was well for the pair of them that she held off the barbarian with his staff, for if he had touched me with the stick I must have slain him, and I had no mind to do that. She was a maiden of quick understanding and surely a Frank. Her eyes were gray—not the dark ox-eyes of Greek women. Even though she were the child of a noble-born sire, I could not dismount to speak to a barbarian Nazarene.

"I have heard of thee, Khalil." All at once she smiled, and it was pleasing. "Thou art a prince—of boasters. Men say thou dost ride in the quarters of the city behind a Greek trumpeter."

Eh, there was a sting in the sweetness of this barbarian girl.

"I ride in the fashion ordained by thine emperor," said I. "And at the court of this emperor I told the tales that were besought of me, but no man in this city of the Greeks hath heard my tongue boast of thy noble men and knights overthrown by this, my sword."

"Yet even now a woman hears and likes it not," she cried at once, tossing her head. "Nor do I owe ought of fealty to the Greek or his lineage."

It had not come into my mind to speak to this maiden. I had come to see the *kohlani* racer. Yet it stirred my interest when she maintained that she was no servant of Murtzuple. Why should a young barbarian girl dwell in Constantinople the Great, without kinsmen to guard her?

"This horse," said I, "is of royal descent. How came he to thy hand?"

Her eyes flashed and she smiled again.

"By the sword, my lord Khalil," she cried in her clear voice. "He was taken from the *paynims* of Palestine by a great and very bold man, who gave him to me."

"By whom?" I asked.

She made answer with pride.

"By Richard, Sieur de Brienne."

"Ricard," I said after her, and thought that I had heard the name spoken before.

But surely there were many knights of that name who had sewn the Nazarene cross upon their *khalats* and had sought death or honor in Palestine. It was clear that this paladin of the Franks had brought the gray racer to Constantinople as a gift to the maiden. And I did not think that he was father or brother to her. When I looked again into her eyes, I did not think he was her lover, because her pride was that of a child in a hero.

"Take care not to overfeed the gray horse," I said when I had feasted my eyes upon him. "And keep a guard at his stable. There are more thieves than rats in this city, and there are many rats."

"Try to take him!" she laughed up at me.

"From thy Ricard, I would take the horse," I said, "but not from a child."

It came to my mind that if there should be a battle between the Greeks and the Franks, the girl would be carried off by someone or other, and the gray horse might fall to me—

"Thou art a bold warrior, O Khalil," she made answer, after a moment, "yet I do not think thee the boaster men proclaim thee."

"*Y'Allah!*" I cried. "Thou art a bold barbarian. Upon thee be the peace. I have seen the horse, and I go!"

"Bethink thee, Lord Khalil," she said as I turned my rein, "the city will be a place of peril for paynimry within the week. Wilt thou not leave the walls before the Franks come with their power?"

Indeed, until now, that had been my thought. But in the siege and the tumult there would be an opportunity to win the *kohlani*, and I decided to await this opportunity.

"What is ordained may not be altered," I said to her. "Look well to the horse!"

My people have a saying: "When God's earth is so wide, why dwell within walls?"

Of this saying Abou Asaid reminded me when I came to his stall the following day to watch for the gray horse and the barbarian girl. He had sold most of his daggers and javelins to Greeks at high prices, and was bundling up his own belongings to fly from the city with the next *karwan*. He said that most of the Muslimin were leaving, for dread of the Franks, and he besought me earnestly to go with him.

From Abou Asaid I learned the name of the barbarian girl. It was Irene. Every day she had passed through the street of the metalworkers on the gray horse, and her face had become known, being beautiful. She lived alone in the city in a small stone house close to the church of the Greek patriarch.

The barbarian Irene was under the protection of the patriarch, so that the Nazarenes did not molest her. In the stone house with her were also an old woman and a man slave—the one I had seen accompanying her. Abou Asaid did not know where the gray horse was kept.

"On thy head be the folly!" he said in farewell. "At any hour the emperor may give order to close the gates. Come away while ye may!"

"The horse is to my liking."

"Oh Khalil, are there not maids enough in Yamen, that thou should'st cast eyes upon an infidel?"

Then a sudden thought struck him, and he demanded that I go with some of his lads and seize the maiden, and the horse, too, if I willed, and he would send his pack animals and servants by way of the stone house and halt there, under pretense of shifting the loads. Thereupon—so said he—I should bring forth the barbarian captive, veiled, and place her among his family. At once the *karwan* would move on with a great tumult and pass through the gate. At Tanais or Sarai such a beautiful Frank would fetch three to four hundred gold bezants.

So planned Abou Asaid, promising that a hundred gold pieces should be mine, in addition to the horse. There was great confusion and running about in the city, and all this might easily be done.

Abou Asaid was only a seller of goods, and desired greatly the aid of my sword on the journey.

"And if we be stopped at the gate?" I asked, to try him.

"Have I not eyes and ears, O son of Abd 'Ullah? Four days ago I went to the Domastikos of the imperial palace, after paying silver to his officers. To him I gave gold in a purse and when he had weighed the purse he gave me a *talsmin*. Look!"

Abou Asaid drew from his cloak a little staff, like a mace. Only there was a crown on the head of the staff, a gilded crown, and letters.

"With this token from the high lord I may pass with my goods and family and servants through any gate, save the palace itself. Who, then, would stop us?"

"Many," I made response, "if I rode the gray racer. Surely he is known from Galata to the Seven Towers!"

Abou Asaid combed his beard.

"I will give thee half the price of the girl Irene. Leave, then, the horse."

"Nay," I said, and again, "nay!"

When did a son of my clan soil his honor by taking the payment of a slave dealer? I could not drag the barbarian girl from her house like a pigeon from the toils. And Abou Asaid lacked heart to make the attempt himself.

He lifted his hands, shook his head and hurried forth to berate his boys at the packs. So he ceased to make plots for me, nor did I ever see him again. Yet I remembered the little mace with the writing upon it.

Instead of going with Abou Asaid, I went to look at the stone house where the gray horse was kept. It was on the side of the little river, facing Galata. And it was inside the brick wall of the place called a *monastir*.

The *monastir* had a garden of olive trees and poplars, and in a corner of this garden beside a dry canal was the house, a tiny house of veined marble with wooden pillars by the door. The space between the house and the corner of the brick wall was fenced in, and here the gray horse was penned.

When I spoke to him he came forward and permitted me to touch his neck and stroke him behind the ears. Then he pretended to bite at my hand and sprang away.

Eh, it would have been a simple matter to jump on his back—once a bridle was slipped over his head—and make him leap the canal, and rush through the outer gate.

But there was the garden. On this side of the canal it sheltered blind and aged men, Nazarenes who were cared for by the patriarch; and on the other side was the *monastir*, where monks walked to and fro in garments of brown hair.

They showed no anger at sight of me—I had slung my sword within my cloak. It was a place of peace. Pigeons stalked about in the sun, and by the edge of the canal sat a group of young girls with white cloths on their heads—as fair as lilies.

At the knee of a black-robed priest stood a boy of nine years who read aloud from a parchment roll in his hand. What he read I knew not, but his voice was clear as a flute, and the damosels listened attentively.

Beyond the trees, in the center of the garden, rose the cupola of the patriarch's church, as a shepherd's watchtower, rising from a knoll, guards against the approach of an enemy.

There was no enemy within the brick wall, though any manner of man might enter—for the patriarch and his flock, being servants of the Roumi's god, were above molestation. And there was a man sitting on the edge of the canal who preened himself like a peacock.

He was as bright as a peacock, a bearded Persian with plumes in his turban clasp, and a purple cloak, and a round shield slung on his shoulder, and an array of daggers in his girdle. His scimitar was too heavy to handle well—though he was a big man.

When I looked at him, he glanced at the pigeons and the Roumi maids and the sky, and at everything but me. Then it came to me that I had seen him leaning against one of the gates of the Place of Horses the evening before. I went and stood beside him.

"What seekest thou?" I asked.

He pretended surprise.

"I watch."

"Thou were sent?"

Out of the corner of an eye he looked at me shrewdly.

"I came. No one is forbidden this garden, O my lord."

"Or Al-Maidan. Yet a certain questing is forbidden."

And I opened my cloak to let him see the scimitar slung from my shoulders. And he rolled over on his haunches to stare and assert innocence.

"Nay, O Badawán, I know thee not. I swear by the breath of Ali I seek thee not. I was sent to watch—"

The words left his lips, and I heard a light step behind us. The barbarian girl named Irene was coming down the path from the church, an old woman trudging behind her. The footbridge across the canal was near my Persian, and so she approached us with only a glance of amusement for me. But she stopped and frowned at the warrior, who had turned his head and was making clumsy pretense of throwing crumbs to the fluttering pigeons.

Presently, when she did not move away, he rose up and swaggered toward the gate. She watched him with blazing eyes. When he was beyond hearing she turned to me.

"The city gates are closed, Khalil, and thou hast tarried too long."

"Look then to the charger."

I saluted her and went forth, yielding the path to the grave-faced men of the *monastir*. I have heard it said that the damosels who listened to the young boy reading were daughters of Nazarene lords, even of kings, and I wondered whether the barbarian were such. But she wore her hair gleaming upon her shoulders and they had their faces hidden behind white cloths. The closing of the gates seemed to bring her joy, as if it heralded the coming of one she loved.

I hastened to overtake the Persian, and saw him step from the flagstones of the court into the maw of an alley. And before I reached the turning there arose a din as of dogs and wolves.

There was mud in the alley and gloom between smoke-blackened walls, and in the gloom I beheld my Persian, roaring and laying about him savagely with his clumsy blade. A few thieves and scoundrels were circling him, plucking at his garments and trying to drive a knife into him.

It was no quarrel of mine. For all his slashing and outcry, the Persian was getting the worst of it. And it came into my mind that he would be of use to me.

With the flat of my scimitar I struck the faces of the low-born nearest me, and when they fell the others ran. They had not a bit of bravery in them, and the flash of steel was enough to send them off. But the Persian was beside himself, still dealing lusty blows into the air.

"Dogs! Dung-bred slaves! Oho—ye flee from Arbogastes. *Tamen shud!* It is finished."

He charged after the wretches, then galloped back to slash at the two who had fallen. But these had taken to their heels, and he came and peered at me, wiping the sweat from his eyes.

"Dogs of Satan—curs they be, a score of them. Oho, they tucked up their skirts and fled like hyenas when they heard my shout. Thou didst see it? Come then! My throat is dry with shouting the war shout. We shall taste Cyprian wine."

It had been my coming that routed the wretches, yet this bull-Persian saw fit to think otherwise. He scurried around looking for chance spoil, and finding none, wiped his bloodless sword in a fold of his cloak. Then he rearranged his daggers, adjusted his turban, and set off with his arm linked in mine.

Ever and anon he glanced over his shoulder, and he looked up and down the next street before diving into a Roumi wine shop filled with Bokharians and Genoese men of the sea. Here my graceless rogue took cup in hand and cried out for all to hear that he had done two thieves to death. Such affairs were common enough in the alleys of this quarter, near the docks, and little heed was paid Arbogastes.

"Take water, as thou wilt, O Badawán!" he grunted, seeing that I would have no wine. "Eh, what is the harm, among unbelievers? There is no harm! Of a truth, a single drop of wine is forbidden all believers, yet—behold, thou—I pour out the drop, and empty the cup myself. The law sayeth not, concerning cups. After all, the juice of the grape is trodden by the feet of fair maidens, and thou hast an eye for such."

He brushed out the two corners of his curled and oiled beard, and filled his cup again from the skin on the rack.

"From this day thou and I be brothers," he proclaimed. "How do men call thee, my lord?"

Long ago my people of Al-Yamen, the Ibna of Al-Yamen, had descent from the Persian warriors, in the dawn of happenings. In that day and time the Persian swordsmen were men of pride. Now they have become boasters without shame, and this Arbogastes was no doubt compounded of Greek and Turkish fathers. Nevertheless, because he saw by the braids of hair and eye and ear that I was of Al-Yamen, he claimed fellowship.

"Khalil, el Khadr,* am I."

---

*El Khadr—the Valiant.

"A chieftain's son. Wah—this day is fortunate. Ask of me what thou wilt, only ask! By ——, Arbogastes is a man of courage also."

He puffed out his round cheeks, and his dark eyes glimmered shrewdly. Arbogastes, in the dramshop, was a braver figure than Arbogastes beset in the alley. I think he knew that I had saved his skin, and wished to reward me in this way. The long purse at his girdle clinked heavily when he moved, and he moved his belly often. A captain of guards, I thought him, in the service of some lord from whom he had learned insolence. And another thought came to me.

"Surely I have heard of Arbogastes," I made answer, as if greatly pleased, "and of his master, who is not less renowned than the emperor."

Arbogastes was strangely affected by these words. He glanced about him swiftly, emptied his cup, choked, and leaned close to my ear to whisper with the sigh of a bull.

"The time is not yet for such speech. My master, the Maga Domastikos, the very high chamberlain, has his finger on events, and gathers men through his gates."

He blinked like an owl, to show that he knew more than he would say. His words had opened up the path I meant to follow.

"I will speak with the Domastikos. Take me to him."

"Thou? Well, why not? But why?"

"There will be a siege. The gates are closed. A panther maddens itself by striking often. After the Roumis* have stood an onset or two from the Franks, they may massacre the Muslimin within the gates."

Arbogastes nodded. He had thought of that, it seemed.

"So," I explained, "by taking my place in the suite of a lord who is the equal of Murtzuple, almost—" Arbogastes nodded again, with a smirk—"I may escape the massacre and perchance render some service to the lord. As for thee—"

"What?" The Persian jangled his purse and looked inquisitive.

"Thou wert sent to watch the barbarian maid, Irene." I judged this to be so, nor did his face belie it. "The Domastikos, then, has an interest in her—"

"By Ali, and all the Companions, he longs for the girl as though she were a jewel of great price! At the church of the Greek Patriarch, he saw

---

*The Arabs called the Greeks "Roumis." The French and English and Western Europeans were "Franks," and all Christians, "Nazarenes."

her and desired her at once. So, when he fared forth, he summoned me to follow her. It was no great task. I sought my lord and told him that she was nobly born, but her father, who was a Frankish *al-comes*,* was dead, and no men of her family were in the city. She was as a dove in a cage, without guardian—"

I thought of the warrior named Richard who had given her the gray courser, saying naught of this to Arbogastes, whose tongue wagged on.

"—may my days be ended, Lord Khalil, but this maid doth not fill mine eye. Too young, lacking wisdom, and too lean i' the shanks. Yet my lord Menas, the Domastikos, burns with fever at thought of her. For the present he desires not to be seen at her gate, or to risk the anger of the patriarch by snatching this dove from the garden. But there will come a time when he, my master, will be able to go to the cage and take from it this dove. Then he will give me many pieces of gold and I shall have another matter to attend to."

The whisper ceased and Arbogastes waited for me to promise him more gold. But that is an evil promise to make, with his breed. It is better to let them expect.

"*Wai*, Arbogastes," I said, "a reward awaits thee at my hand, if thou art faithful. By the weight of thy deeds shall this reward be weighed."

The palace of Count Menas, the Greek, was within sight of the church. As we passed the guards in red livery, we heard the bells of the church sounding below us. For the palace was on the summit of a hill, overlooking the hovels of Galata and the sea. I listened to the voice of the surf as we passed through the courtyard, where slaves loitered by empty litters and restless horses. By the time we made our way into an outer hall of columns—each the likeness of a woman in marble—Arbogastes had painted himself the victor over fifty lawless soldiers, and sworn by the Greek gods and the breath of Ali that he had slain six, and I two. Some of the nobles who waited in the hall smiled, but no one laughed at the Persian, and I thought that he was a favorite of the Domastikos.

From the hall we entered a corridor with an arched roof, where Arbogastes' leather boots rang heavily. Here he motioned me to silence, and we bowed the head to several noblemen who were talking together in low voices, glancing impatiently at bare cedar doors at the far end.

---

*Al-comes—count, or baron.

But the Persian bowed his way through the guests, knocked upon the portal four times and nudged me in the ribs when we passed through the cedar doors between two Tatars who stood with drawn sabers.

"That behind us is the whispering gallery," he breathed in my ear. "An opening runs from the ceiling to the wall near my lord's couch, and oft-times he amuses himself listening to the talk of those who think themselves alone in the gallery. Remember it."

It was not easy, the path to the Lord Menas. We climbed a winding stair, and at each turn there was a lamp in a recess, and in the darkness behind the lamp a curtain that moved and fell again when we had passed.

"Archers," Arbogastes whispered again. "Look at the carpet."

The carpet was leather, from which fresh blood might be wiped in a moment. At the head of the stair a Greek eunuch met us and stared insolently at me. From chin to toe he wore a plain red robe, and the square cap on his shaven head was cloth of gold.

With his staff he led us out upon a gallery where the floor was veined marble and a fountain cast rose scent into the air. Beyond the fountain was a dais, and here on a couch lay the Lord Menas.

"What word, O bladder of a mule?" he asked of Arbogastes softly.

He was a young man, beautiful indeed. The veins showed blue on his skin, his eyes were clear and bright. His yellow hair curled about his neck in oiled locks and there was henna-red upon his cheeks. His lips curved willfully, like a spoiled woman's. A single sapphire of great size gleamed on his bare throat and his crimson tunic was edged with ermine.

"The bird is in the cage, your Magnificence. And in the city—"

"I know the city. Why did you leave the garden before dark?"

"At the gate I was set upon by some rogues." Arbogastes had wit enough to dispense with needless lies when the Domastikos listened. "This Arab lord helped me put them to flight. He is a notable swordsman, though a Muslimin."

Menas spoke Arabic as well as Arbogastes, and now he looked at me suddenly.

"What seek ye of me, O son of the black tents?"

"*Wai*, my lord, it is no time for the Muslimin to go alone in the streets. I seek protection."

"How many men hast thou, O Khalil?"

"I have one sword, my lord."

"Wilt use it on my behalf?"

"At need."

"For what price?"

"For no price. Naught have I to sell or buy."

Hereupon he looked upon the fountain for a moment, pinching the skin of his cheek between two fingers.

"It needs no soothsayer, my Badawán, to tell that thou hast a need. All men have needs—some slack purses, some desires. What is thine?"

"A horse, my lord," I made answer truthfully. "Aye, a wonder of a horse."

And I told him of the gray courser, in the hands of the barbarian girl. The young exquisite deigned to smile.

"By the good saints Sergius and Bacchus, this Arab covets the colt, not the filly. Why not go with Arbogastes and take it?"

"Whither? The gates are closed."

"True." He still smiled, as though contemplating something that pleased him. "And, after all, a *saracin* might not easily presume to ride off with the horse in the patriarch's garden. What then?"

I made bold to tell him of my plan.

"When thy men make away with the barbarian girl, then I will bridle and lead out the gray courser, as if bearing him to thee."

"And so, must I lose a racer worth a few hundred denarii in the Hippodrome?"

Now when a youth has his heart set upon a woman, and at the same time dreams of making himself an emperor, he is not apt to haggle at a horse. I had seen that which I had seen—the bearded Maga Ducas, or Lord of Ships, stalking impatiently in the anteroom. Aye, and the captain of the yellow-haired barbarian mercenaries as well.

Truly this youth held a high place in the Greek court, if he dared to keep such men of war gnawing their beards in his hall. And he had ambition, or they would not have waited upon him.

So I weighed my words accordingly, knowing well that unless I bargained with him, his men-at-arms would take the gray horse for him or for themselves. Such Greeks and barbarians have no true love of a fine horse, yet they would have sold him for a price.

"I have a white charger from the stable of the emperor himself, my lord," I ventured, "and this royal beast I shall give to the hand of thy captain, when I take the gray racer."

He looked at me sharply, considering the advantages of Murtzuple's charger, and nodded.

"Agreed," he said in Greek.

Thus he spoke with the desire to test me, but the thought came to me not to reveal my knowledge of the Greek, that I had from the galley slaves of the Gates.

"This Arab," spoke up Arbogastes, "understandeth not the noble language of your Mightiness."

"Be it agreed, O Khalil," the Lord Menas said again in my speech, and I bent my head.

"Between us it is agreed, my lord," I reminded him, "yet forget not that I have agreed to stand at thy back and draw my sword in defense of thy person—that only, and not to be thy servant, at command, as is this Persian."

"Body of Bacchus, thou art a man of many conditions and few promises. A true rarity, I vow, in Constantinople—"

There was a sudden commotion of running feet near at hand, yet unseen, a long shout and a clamor of voices. Menas listened, but his soft voice went on:

"And so thy boldness is forgiven thee. Abide with Arbogastes and await my further word."

He had been toying with a silver ball, and now he let it drop into a bronze basin that hung beside the couch. At once a boy slave slipped from the shadows behind the couch, and another from beyond the fountain. They ran to the heavy velvet curtain that hid one side of the chamber and drew it back. There was no wall. We looked out upon a tiled balcony overhanging an arm of the sea.

It was the hour of sunset, and a red pathway lay upon the sea—a pathway that led from the city to the tiny sails of many ships coming out of the west.

"The Franks!" cried Arbogastes.

"It is the Venetian fleet," assented my lord Menas, picking up his silver ball. Suddenly he laughed. "A fleet of gallant fools."

Again the half smile curved his lips, and he touched the glowing sapphire, speaking in Greek to the red eunuch.

"They spent their wealth on followers and accoutrements; they reached Venice with empty purses and bold words. They had pledged eighty-five thousand marks of silver to the Doge for his fleet, and war galleys to clear the seas and provisions for a year—to take them to Palestine. Lacking the half of this sum, they pawned their lives for the remainder—or would have done so, had not the Doge persuaded them to capture Zara for the Venetians instead.

"So the paladins, the men of iron, stormed Zara and gave its spoil to the accursed Venetian merchants. Then came to them an upstart—Alexius—who claimed the throne of Constantinople, and these mummers turned aside again to play the part of rescuers, forsooth. They have come to conquer the Greek empire for Alexius, so to pay their passage to the Holy Land. They would be masters of the city of the caesars, and enlist here a mighty host to set free the city of Christ from Moslem bondage. Fools, to go against Constantinople the Great, that never has been taken by mortal man. Aye, their lives are in pawn!"

In high good humor was my lord Menas, and the eunuch vanished with his staff. Arbogastes plucked at my robe, signing that we should go from the presence of the Domastikos, So, with a salutation we went, unattended.

And at the first turning of the stair I heard a shuffling of feet and whispers in the recess behind the lamp. I feared an arrow and so turned to peer into the gloom, which was a passage and not an alcove as Arbogastes had said. Verily, this was a house of many surprises and of hidden things.

I saw the eunuch, two spears' lengths down the passage, and behind him another man. This was a warrior, wide of shoulder and dark of face, in mail from toe to helmet—his surcoat so stiff with dust and streaked with rain that the device was dim.

Yet I had seen that device before. The man was a Frank and a captain of warriors.

I had faced him once when the Franks pillaged a village near Edessa. They had taken horses and cattle from the village, and had slain else all living things, the women, and the sick, and sucking babes.

There had been no Arab warriors at that village nor any battle. The Franks who plundered it were filled with the lust to slay. Yet I have seen others who nursed wounded Arabs—

The Frankish baron who burned that village had been Richard de Brienne. And the captain of his men-at-arms was this same mailed swordsman who waited behind the eunuch until we should have passed.

So much I saw in a glance, before the eunuch stretched out his long sleeve and the Frank bent his head to hide his face.

"What is it?" asked Arbogastes impatiently.

"A slave in a red robe," I made answer.

But memory had stirred in me. It was this slayer, the Sieur de Brienne who had bestowed the gray horse on the girl Irene. But why had his captain come with hidden face to the house of the Lord Menas?

That night I slept in the barrack of the Tatar archers, and in the palace grounds the next day there was not sign or portent of the Frank. I asked Arbogastes if an embassy had come to the city from the barons of Frankistan, and he laughed.

"Oho, they will come with their ships to the sea wall, not before."

He told me also that the Greek prince, Alexius, with the fleet had truly a just claim to the throne, because the father of this prince lay blinded and in chains in the prisons of Murtzuple. The father had been emperor for two years, and before his time, poison and the knife had shrouded three Greek emperors. As to whether Murtzuple or Alexius had the best claim to the throne Arbogastes neither knew nor cared. Nor did the Tatars or the Northmen or the Genoese mercenaries care.

"My lord Menas hath bought the captain of the Northmen and the Lord of Ships," he added. "He hath rolled out casks of Chian wines, and whole sheep roast in the courtyards. We fare well, and by that same token there is work laid up for us."

So thought the warriors who crowded around the wine casks. Some, when their tongues were loosed, said my lord Menas wished to gather a great array so that when the Franks were driven off he could say that it was his doing. But others—and these were the Genoese who sipped their wine instead of gulping it—whispered that the Domastikos meant to overthrow the emperor suddenly and then seize the crown.

The barbarians from the north of Frankistan said nothing at all, though they drank more than any—dipping their horns into the kegs of mead. They grunted together and sang without mirth—tall men in rusted chain mail who walked with pride, and yet drowsily.

They had been paid to fight for Menas. They were faithful to the gold that bought them.

I wondered what had driven them from their country to serve a Greek. The Tatars yearned for spoil, and the Genoese hated the Venetians. Like dog and wolf was the feud between these twain.

But no man knew the mind of my lord Menas.

The following night it was that I heard the voice of the Frank who was the follower of Richard de Brienne. It was late, and the singing of the Northmen had waked me from sleep. The feel of before-dawn was in the air, and I rose to walk through the corridors. I meant to go to the balcony from which we had seen the ships. I wished to see what the galleys of the Franks were about, because they had withdrawn from sight the night before now. And I went warily through the long corridors and up the marble stair where drowsy slaves stood beside the oil. The armed sentries of my lord Menas were not to be seen, yet. I had heard the corridors were guarded.

Before long I had lost the way and entered a dark chamber. Here I ceased to go forward and paused to listen. Close to my ear a man's voice spoke and another answered clearly.

One was the voice of my lord Menas, the other the strange Frank—hoarse and growling with much argument and wine. They seemed to be in agreement, though their words I understood not.

The chamber was empty, and the voices echoed in its stone walls. I heard another sound and leaped to one side.

Near at hand the air moved, and feet thumped on the hard mosaics. In the light from the passage behind me, I beheld the figure of a man and the gleam of a knife that struck at me, the blade ripping through my cloak. The man groaned loud, and fell. In the same instant that he stabbed, my sword cut him under the ribs and grated against the spine.

Like a slit waterskin he tumbled down and ceased to move. I drew back from the blood on the floor and looked at the wall. Aye, there was a niche, as if made for a statue, and beside it a square of fretwork, bronze by the feel of it. My fingers passed through it and felt the breath of cool air. This was surely a whispering chamber, and at the other end—what? The opening in the wall ran perhaps to the sleeping-place of the Domastikos. By chance, hearing the voices, I had stood before it, and the guardian of the chamber—he may well have been a deaf mute—had sprung out at me from the niche.

Then it was that I had assurance of the truth of this. A wide portal in the mosaic chamber flung open, light streamed in, and two Greek spearmen stood beside me. Two black savages entered, bearing torches, and behind them came my lord Menas with mincing gait.

Verily, from the other end of the gallery, he had heard the leap and the groan of his slave, and now he glanced at me from under lowered lids.

"Thy blade is bloodied, O Khalil," he said softly. "Wipe it, and sheath it."

The spears of the Greek warriors were close to me, yet I delayed not to wipe clean the scimitar on the tunic edge of the dead slave, and sheath it, and uprise with folded arms.

"And now, Khalil—what is this?"

"Upon thee, my lord, greeting of the dawn! I sought my way to the balcony, for sight of the ships. At this spot the slave leaped and struck with his knife—here—" I lifted my cloak. "No word passed, nor could I see him. So I slew him, and will take therefore no blame."

The Domastikos glanced at the grating, and at my bare feet—for it is our custom to remove our slippers at the entrance of a dwelling. Holding a linen, musk-scented, to his nostrils, he bent over the dead man.

"A good blow, Khalil. I see thou art a man of the sword."

I had slain his guard by the whispering gallery, and it would have availed me not to plead that I had not overheard the words that passed at the other end. Nor could I read the eyes of the Greek, though I watched for him to make a sign to his spearmen.

"Eh, Khalil, the fault lies not with thee!" And he smiled.

Aye, he smiled, and his nostrils quivered just a little when he withdrew the cloth, and still he showed no anger.

The eyes of a leopard glow, and its muscles twitch—even to the tail—when it settles itself to leap. A mask was upon the face and eyes of the Greek lord, and I was assured that he had not pardoned me, and would exact my life—not for the death of the slave but because I had chanced into the listening gallery when he held speech with the Frank.

With his men or his treasure I might have made free, and have been pardoned. But not with his secret—not at this hour. I think he had wished to order the spearmen to advance upon me, and had decided otherwise. A sword well handled is a match for two long spears, and Menas was neither impatient nor a fool.

"My lord," I made response, when he waited, "may God requite thee for thy mercy. It is true that I have meant no harm to thy men, being ignorant of the customs of this, thy palace."

"Thou art, as Arbogastes maintained, a bold man," he said idly, gathering his cloak about him. "I have a mind to such. Go then, and await my command."

Who may alter what is ordained? Who may look upon the writing that is not to be altered? I had not plotted against the Domastikos, yet he sought my life as surely as a trodden snake strikes. And this was because his palace was a pit of traps and a breeding place of suspicion. Within it I might no longer dwell, and I walked forth before he could send an order to the guards at the outer gates concerning me.

In all Constantinople there was no sanctuary for me, save one.

And so it came to pass that when Arbogastes sought his post of duty that morning because he had been at his wine in the past night—he found me sitting on the bank of the canal, by the bridge that led to the house of the barbarian girl.

He glittered and shone, indeed, like a peacock. From somewhere he had got himself a bronze breastplate with eagles upon it, and he was busily counting different coins from his right hand to his left.

Then he counted them back again and shook his thick head.

"By all the devils, one hand tallies not with the other! And by the beard of Ali, this ducat hath been shaved of half its gold." He blinked and glared from reddened eyes. "The dog cheated me!" He said he had been throwing dice at the tavern nearby, and regretted leaving it, being muddled in his head about his gains and losses.

"Eh, Arbogastes," I said to him, "I had thought thee an *al-comes* in this new armor. Verily, thou hast the figure of a swordsman."

He ceased his counting to simper and swell his chest. Indeed he had the figure of a fighter if naught else.

"And the dog cheated thee?" I went on.

"*Y'Allah*, he did! My dice were clipped and loaded. I won two casts in three, and he robbed me of my gains, the son of a bath tender!"

"That is evil. Nay, then, I shall keep thy post, and thou shalt return to the Greek and gain back thy winnings. Only come at dusk to take my place."

Arbogastes felt of his lean purse and blinked. He had upon him the thirst that is bred of spirits, not wine alone, and saw no reason why I should not watch in his stead. No men of Menas's household would enter the garden of the patriarch.

"Be wary as to the wench," he grunted. "I go!"

"Then say naught in the tavern of my watch in this place, or ill may befall thee, Arbogastes."

He nodded—he could see that.

So throughout the morning and until the sun began to sink past the dome of the church, I sat, sleeping a little, but rousing when the monks

or the slaves of Irene came near the bridge. The girl I did not see, but the
gray horse was led out and fed, and I knew that she was within.

Then came Arbogastes, with lurching step and darkened face.

"Ho, brother," he cried, "the gates of plunder are open! Hearken to the
bells! Come, and let us take what we may."

His purple cloak was gone, and his wallet likewise. In truth Arbogastes
looked more like a wight plundered than a plunderer.

"Eh, what has happened?" I asked.

"The Franks have happened—may they taste of Eblis! So the tale runs
in the bazaar. They drifted across from the Scutari shore this morning,
with their horses in the palanders and the men-at-arms in the barges, all
of them lashed to the oared galleys. They sounded trumpet and horn and
made a landing near Galata, leaping into shallow water with their spears
on their wrists, and leading forth their chargers from the great ships. The
fools have taken Galata and set up a camp on the mainland."

"And what of the Greeks?"

Arbogastes curled his beard, which reeked more of musk than ever.
The wine in his veins was singing a song, and he looked on the bare garden as if it were paradise.

"Murtzuple is a wolf, and a wolf, O my brother, is not easily penned.
He hath drawn back his hosts, behind the city wall. The Franks will break
their spears on the wall, and when that has happened they will taste grief
because they are separated from their ships and their brothers, the Venetians. Come, Khalil, this will be a night of nights!"

The wine in him did not bind his tongue; it was not fitting to leave
him thus in a place of prayer. And it did not suit me to forsake the garden then.

"Where be the men of the Domastikos?"

"Allah, am I an oracle that I should know?" The Persian scowled and
yawned. "I think they will muster in the *registan* of Tiodore* at dawn."

"Then go thou and sleep. I shall keep thy ward."

"Nay, I must fare to the palace of the Domashitish—" he hiccoughed
and blinked owlishly—"of the Domtishok, our master. 'Tis the hour for
my waiting upon him with word of the Frank wench."

"If that thou doest," I said, "thou wilt be slain and the skin taken from
thy body and stuffed with straw and hung out upon the sea-wall." I had

---

*The Forum of Theodosius.

seen such bodies, blown hither and yon by the wind, and torn by crows'
beaks.

"Nay, why should my lord do that to me?"

Now I had no wish to tell the stupid Persian what had befallen me in
the palace.

"Why did he choose thee in the beginning, instead of one of his servants?
Why did he show favor to a bullock like thee? Because when thy task is
done, and the girl is taken to him, he can then slit thy throat—lest any of
the Nazarene priests remember having seen thee sitting at her gate."

There was much truth in this, but Arbogastes saw it not.

"No buffalo am I!" he growled. "I am a swordsman, a *bahator*."

"Do you wish to be skinned?"

"Nay—"

"Then go and sleep. But first tell me the password."

Arbogastes seemed not to hear, and he began to snore on his feet. I
shook his shoulder.

"The word—what is the password of the Greeks?"

The wine and the drowsiness were heavy upon him and he only grunted
until suddenly he found words.

"Another cup!"

Eh, there was little good in seeking the word of him. He staggered away
up the path, and I sat down to think. The ache of hunger was in me, but I
could not go to the Nazarene church and beg for food like a slave.

It was then, a little after dusk, when all the monks had gone into the
church, whither they were summoned by a great bell, that the barbarian
girl Irene came and sat down by me.

Between her hands she had brought dates and a pomegranate and barley
cakes, and when I had twice refused them, she leaned closer to look into
my eyes.

"I have given Khutb, the gray courser, to eat, and why not thee, O
Badawán?"

So I began to eat slowly, and she leaned chin on hands to watch the
gleam of the new moon behind the barrier of cypresses, and listen to the
clong-clang of the bell.

"The Greeks yonder," she said after awhile, "pray for the overthrow
of the Franks. But the Franks will take the city, and then there will be a
new emperor."

I thought of Menas, who had talked with a captain of the iron men.

"There be fifteen thousand Franks and some few Venetians without—there be two hundred thousand Greeks and mercenaries within these walls."

"Are they one at heart? What happened today?"

I told her and she became thoughtful. Twice a hundred thousand men behind such walls are not easily overcome, and it was ever the fault of the iron men to venture onward foolishly.

"My father was castellan of Edessa," she said. "More than one onset and onfray have I seen. I do not think these treacherous Greeks will stand before the lances of the Crosses on open ground. I would well to be upon the walls—"

Perhaps she was lonely, perhaps excited by hope of the morrow, because she told me how she longed for the coming of the Crosses. The Lord Richard de Brienne had joined the iron men, she had heard, and she was to become his wife.

This paladin of the Franks had tarried once at Edessa—for her father kept open hall and was well content with company and song of minstrels. At that time Irene had been no more than a stripling; eager to follow the hawk, and to ride forth with her father, who was one of the wisest of the Franks.

The Lord Richard had looked twice upon her and had asked her for his wife, and the father of Irene had said that a year must pass before she was of age for marriage.

So the warrior of the Cross had fared forth after plighting his word to the damosel, and straightaway Irene forgot dogs and hawks and the loves of childhood for love of him—and she had waited more than the year, for her father was slain, and his followers and servants and his feudal hall were lost to her. For that is the law of Frankistan.

Aye, four years passed, and she heard of the deeds of her lord in Syria and Jerusalem yet saw him not. Edessa had fallen to my people and the Nazarene priests had sent her to the protection of the patriarch of Constantinople. She had brought with her the gray horse, Khutb, the betrothal gift of the Lord Richard.

All this was clear, not by her words alone, but by her voice and the eagerness in her. In this barbarian girl there was no deceit.

"How is he to be known, this Ricard," I asked.

"He is prouder than other men and his eyes shine when he speaks. His hair is black and his skin is dark, and he is taller even than thee, O Khalil."

How was I to learn aught from this? It seemed to her that Richard of Brienne was verily a saint in chain mail, guileless as a boy, grave and courteous to all who met with him. His blue eyes were without fear—

"What device bears he on his shield?"

"No device, save a red cross. If ye seek him, O Badawán—" she tossed her head valiantly—"look for him in the heart of the onset. Wilt thou draw sword against him, for the gray horse?"

"It may have been written," I said, and upon the words I heard a scraping near at hand, as of a scabbard tip or spear butt.

In another moment I felt assured that a man was breathing heavily within an arrow's flight.

Darkness had fallen, and the gleam of moon and stars revealed little under the trees. I touched the girl Irene upon the shoulder and whispered to her.

"Go thou into the house. There is danger."

She made no sound of fright, but rose swiftly and ran lightly over the bridge, into the stone dwelling. By then I felt that there were more than three who crept up on me. Eh, they were heavy men and the wood was dark. But they could see me at the edge of the canal.

I rose and ran to the narrow bridge, and turned upon it, scimitar in hand, as five figures burst from the path and ran toward me. The leader wore a Greek helmet, and held an officer's short sword. The others carried spears—I could see no bows.

"Ha, Khalil!" cried the swordsman. "Whither went the maid?"

Now, I had turned upon them because it is better to stand than to flee. I knew the speaker for a captain of my lord Menas, and whether he came for me or for the barbarian girl there was no knowing. Perhaps they had come in this fashion, like panthers, to escape the eyes of the patriarch's folk in the church.

So I thought twice, and thrice. The girl Irene was not of my seeking, and yet—she was brave, and alone. Her fate was ordained—it were folly to take her part, and yet in standing by there was shame.

Then the captain spoke.

"No harm will befall thee, O Khalil!"

He spoke too readily. Why should he have pledged this thing un-asked?

"What do ye here?" I asked in his speech.

"We have come for the barbarian."

Again, he was too eager. What reward had my lord Menas placed upon my life?

"The maid is in my keeping," I answered, thinking of many things.

Upon these words a spear flashed from the hand of a Greek, and gleamed before my eyes. I leaped back, falling heavily, and the weapon struck into earth behind me. To the eyes and ears of the Greeks it seemed that I had been pierced, and they came forward with the low shout of men who have made their kill.

Eh, it is well said among my people, "When ye set fire to the thicket, be wise and watch out for the tiger." The Greek captain had swung up his short sword when I rose to one knee. My scimitar was in hand and I slashed him deep over the thighs.

It was a good blow, touching no bones, and his sword fell upon my shoulder, his helmet to one side of the bridge, his body to the other. His men cried out in rage and astonishment. From the shadows of the house wall I spoke to them sternly:

"Pick up thy leader and bear him hence! Would thy lord Menas wish to leave his officer in the garden of the patriarch—thus?"

It was as a bone cast to dogs, and they snarled and muttered, half fear-ing. Through the open gate in the wall I ran, and into the stone house, where no light shone.

And the girl Irene cried out my name—"Khalil!" Something, no doubt, she had seen upon the bridge. "Whose followers be these?"

"Death's servants. Aye, bringing slavery for thee, and for me the shroud that is never to be cast off."

Swiftly I told her of the desire of my lord Menas and the watch that had been kept upon her.

"I know!" she cried impatiently. "There were spies—a Persian who watched. Yet the Domastikos would never dare carry a maid from the patriarch's garden—"

"Ha—these Greeks dare not go back to their lord without thee."

For this must have been the party sent to bear her to Menas. They had looked for Arbogastes and, finding him not, had ventured within the garden. Then, hearing my voice and knowing me, they had sought to slay me first.

Only one path was open to us. The house was in a corner of the high wall. To climb such a wall with armed men baying at heel were folly—if there were not others without. To abide in the house were witless. Plainly it was written that I should be as a shield to this maid. Had she not been thrust into my keeping? Surely we had shared the salt, though she thought little of that.

My safety lay in mounting at once the gray horse Khutb and springing out upon them. And if I did this, leaving the maid to the mercies of the angered Greeks, I must taste everlasting shame.

I closed the house door and barred it. Taking the girl's hand in mine, I ran into the rear enclosure where Khutb was stabled. At once the slender courser trotted toward us, snuffling and making great play of biting and springing away.

"*Taghún-taghún!*" I cried at him. "Be at peace; there will be work enough for thee!"

Bridling him, I forced the ring-bit between his teeth, listening the while to the Greeks pounding on the house door. The hag and the peasant had roused, and I bade them pull down the bars of the stable yard and then seek safety over the wall—little it availed them, I fear. There was not time for the saddle.

A Greek ran into the yard as I lifted the maiden to the back of Khutb.

"Hold to my girdle and lower thy head!" So I sprang up, speaking to the gray horse and drawing tight the rein.

Eh, he was a horse among many. Like an arrow from its string he darted through the gate in the fence, the Greek leaping aside. My erstwhile charger, the pot-bellied, cow-hoofed white stallion, would have taken an arrow's flight to plunge to full career. There was still a harder feat in store for Khutb.

The spearmen were standing about the bridge and door, so I reined aside and put Khutb at the canal. Ha, that was a sight and a delight! He pricked his ears, shortened his stride, without swerve or check, and rose into the air—I gripping with knees and hand in his mane, for the girl, off-balance, clung heavily.

Khutb landed daintily, with not a hand's breadth to spare. And then, once more, I urged him to trot and gallop, sweeping along the deserted path that led to the garden gate.

A shout went up behind us, but the gate was far, and we had passed through before the Greeks stationed there could see our faces in that dim light.

And so we rode forth into the alleys of Constantinople.

To the khan of the Bokharians, where lay my rug and horse—the big white charger—I took my way, finding the inn deserted, or nearly so. The Muslimin had fled the city, and the Armenian linen workers, and the Syrian bath-men who frequented the khan, were out thieving and defending their thefts. It was also dark. I placed Irene in my compartment over the stable court and bade her sleep.

To the dog of a Bokharian who had leered at our incoming I gave a piece of gold and a warning to hold his tongue, and then I groomed Khutb and fed him a little barley. Then I rubbed down the white charger without haste, and bridled him and waited for the coming of a man to serve me in the thing I planned to do.

"Y'Allah! O madman—O miscreant!"

So cried Arbogastes when he ran into the courtyard seeking me, no longer drowsy but red with fear and haste.

"What has come upon thee, my brother?" I saluted him.

"Misfortune—calamity. Such calamity. And thou—breeder of woe—hatcher of evil—thou hast heaped all this upon my head!"

In truth he lacked his plumed helmet, and his hair was disordered. In a breath he told me what had befallen him. The Greek who kept the tavern where he had lain in sleep, this dog of a Greek doubtless fearing the anger of the Domastikos, had wakened him and sent him forth, when Menas's men came seeking through the bazaar quarters. Arbogastes fled, not knowing what had happened—only hearing the curses heaped upon his name and mine by the searchers.

"It was thy doing, Khalil," he howled. "Thou didst beguile me and send me from the garden, and steal away the girl from my lord, and the horse as well. It was all thy doing!"

"By the eyes of ——, I did not plan it. It was to keep life in me I fled, on this horse."

What need to swear to truth? Arbogastes merely raged the more and mustered courage to threaten.

"No more tricks, Khalil! Did I not befriend thee and earn thee honor with Menas? A fox is not more deceitful than thee. Now am I dead and by torture, unless—give me the girl!"

I rubbed down the stallion's flank with clean straw and thought for a moment, Arbogastes waxing bolder and fingering the sword he never meant to draw.

"How many are searching for us?" I asked.

"All! Every warrior and slave of the palace. Ten thousand. My lord Menas rides from street to street casting about for the wench, and all the blood hath left his face—nay there is enough spilled under his sword this night. His torches are in every corner. They will be in this quarter of the merchants in an hour."

Verily, the Greek is a man of strange moods. That Menas should forget the siege and the throne to cast about for a masterless maid! Yet he had not altogether forgotten.

"And in an hour thou shalt taste of his tortures, Arbogastes. Had I not been in the garden at twilight instead of thee, ere now they had shrouded thee."

The Persian wiped his thick lips and ceased to threaten.

"What road is open to us?"

"O brother," I made response, "the way is dark for me, but thou art a swordsman, a man of courage and a favorite to boot. There is a way for thee to life and reward."

"How?" he asked, suspicious and fearful at once.

"Canst find Menas?"

He shivered, saying that of all things that were the easiest done, the hardest to avoid. Upon this I summoned the Bokharian who had been trying to hear what we said, and bade him bring reed pen and ink and the cleanest parchment he had.

And upon this parchment, while that precious twain stared and wondered, I wrote as follows:

> To the high and merciful Lord Menas, the Chamberlain, greetings—I Khalil, the Badawán, have fulfilled my pledge to thee, and in token I send thee the horse that was promised. I have the gray racer, and may God be the judge of thy promise to me!

"What says the writing?" Arbogastes scowled at the Arabic characters. I told him, and bade him take the charger to his master and earn reward.

"He will demand tidings of the Frankish maid—and thee."

"Tell him, then, the truth. Thou hast seen me here, and the girl is in my cubby above. This khan-samah hath seen her."

Taking the scroll, Arbogastes rolled it up and thrust it into his belt; then he grasped the rein of the imperial charger and stood first on one foot, then on the other. His beard bristled in a grin.

"Look here, Khalil—surely thou wilt not tarry here, to be cut open like a cornered hare! Tell me where thou hast a mind to hide, and I swear to thee by my honor and the graves of the Companions that I will lead Menas away, to seek thee in another quarter. Arbogastes can be like a fox in wiles."

He tried to look shrewd and honest at the same time, which is no easy matter. "Since thou hast asked," I made answer, "tell him to search for her, and he will, at the church of the Greek patriarch."

Arbogastes grimaced and looked twice at me. In such an hour as this my lord Menas might send his men into the garden of the Nazarenes, but to force his way into the church itself would be sacrilege and would arouse against him the flame of fanaticism.

No sooner had the Persian swaggered off than I beckoned toward the Bokharian, who had been slinking about the courtyard like a wolf around a sheepfold. Him I ordered to hide away the gray horse Khutb, even as he knew me to be a man of my word. If the horse were found by the Greeks, he would live to regret it at my hand—if the horse were well hidden, he should have from me a pound of gold.

We could no longer keep Khutb at our hand, and the departure of the splendid steed saddened me.

To Irene I explained that Menas's searchers were between us and the church—if not on guard at the church itself—and so that way was closed to us. From my garments I selected the cloth-of-silver robe of honor that the emperor had bestowed on me, also a loose cloak and a small cap of Greek cut. This I bade her put on. No maiden of such beauty would be safe in the streets of Constantinople on the morrow; nor could she hope to hide longer from Menas's spies in woman's dress.

Though loose, the garment did not look awry on her, for we were both of slender build. The flood of her yellow hair was hidden by cap and cloak, and so—the Bokharian being out of the way—no one saw me venture forth preceded by a handsome youth in nobleman's attire.

"Where can we go?" the maid asked me, as she tried to match her step to my stride.

"Whither God opens a way," I said, and there was indeed no other course but that.

So it came to pass that we beheld something that was near a miracle. After dawn we found ourselves near the line of the great city wall, whither companies of men-at-arms were hurrying. No heed was given us, and we passed up one of the tower stairs with a throng of Tatar archers.

The assault of the city had begun.

Before us lay the blue circle of the sublime port, and the galleys and palanders and small craft of the Venetians. Far off to the left we could see the camp of the Franks, and the line of their mangonels and batterers. And we looked for a long time.

See, the city of Constantinople runs down into a point, far into the sea. It is like a triangle of three equal sides—the base upon the hills, and the apex the gilded roofs of the imperial palace.

Against this tip of the triangle the waters of the two seas beat sonorously. On the side of the triangle where we stood was the port, with its canals and landing stairs and long wall that was higher than the deck of a ship. At intervals great towers rose from the wall, and on these towers were stone casters and smaller machines that shot forth balls of naphtha fire and sheafs of flaming arrows.

They were firing upon the small ships of the Venetians, which were answering with arrows that did little harm. I saw a heavy stone crash through the deck of a barge laden with men and break it in twain like a single stick.

It was as Arbogastes had said—the Franks were beating in vain against the wall of the city. A brisk wind off the sea was driving the mists away, and we saw masses of Greek soldiery moving up the steep streets, going away toward the land gates. Other companies mustered in reserve in the *registans*. And all the housetops and palace balconies overlooking the sea wall were crowded with watchers, slave and noble—harlot and Greek princess, laughing and pointing.

Above all the city towered the single statue that can be seen from far out toward Asia, the gigantic white woman with the countenance of the dead.*

Aye, Constantinople was like that stone woman, mighty and unchanging, looking out upon the world with the dead eyes of an ancient thing—

"They give way!" Irene cried. "They wear the Cross, and they give way!"

---

*This must have been the colossal statue of Juno.

In truth, the smaller vessels of the Venetians were drawing off, disheartened. Nay, there was reason for it!

Was ever such a siege as this? The Franks were so few that they beset only a little part of the great walls, and for every warrior of the Franks, ten men leaned on their weapons within the wall and laughed.

The girl, her hands clasped and her eyes moody, had no thought of hunger or peril, or the passing of the hours. Her gaze was fixed on the ships with a great yearning. Somewhere before her was the warrior Richard, on land or sea, perhaps wounded, perhaps slain.

When the sun was high, she clapped her hands and touched my shoulder. There was movement among the war galleys of the Venetians. The oar banks rose and fell, and the long vessels pointed their noses toward the sea wall of the city.

The wind had died down, and the swell lapped gently against the stone jetties and foundations. The broad banners and long pennons of the galleys swelled and flapped, and soon we heard the roar of their drums add the shrill cry of their *nacárs*.

"See," she cried, "this is the real onset!"

It was a goodly sight—the shining vessels crowded with men in armor. The largest galley came with a rush toward the wall near our tower, and turned, weighing oars. It drifted up against the wall, the oars on that side being pushed far back toward the stern. Soon they began to splinter, and the side of the galley rose and sank within a javelin's length of the battlement—too near for the mangonels to cast stones upon it.

But the Greeks became very active, thrusting out beams to topple upon the crowded deck and loosing flights of arrows. The shields lashed upon the rail of the ship gave some protection and every rower had a small shield bound on his arm. And the fore and after-castles and the great raised deck amidship were on a level with the battlement.

And the little platforms on the tall masts overtopped the wall, so that the Venetian crossbowmen were able to send their shafts into the men on the wall.

For a time there was tumult, of breaking timbers and war shouts, and thunder of drums. A score of galleys had drawn up in line with their leader, and from the masts of others came arrow flights that clattered against our tower.

But to these shafts Irene gave no thought. She was leaning forward to watch the platforms that were thrust out from the high bow of the ship.

Venetians surged across these platforms and leaped at the parapet, and we heard the clatter of sword and shield fighting.

Thus for a moment the issue of the assault was in the balance. And in that moment I heard a voice that grated upon my ears. A shout swelled up from the well of the tower stairs, and it was an officer of my lord Menas who had cried the order, a Greek who had seen me more than once in the palace of the Domastikos.

I rose and put hand to scabbard. I looked toward the palace of Menas, and as God ordained it, I beheld him afar in the open gallery, at ease upon his couch, his officers about him. Aye, even the red eunuch with his bloodless lips, his arms crossed upon his breast.

But they were looking at the ships, and the struggle on the wall. Again the officer shouted from below, and the Tatars who had been plying their bows, stepped back and exchanged glances.

They were savage folk, clad in the hides of beasts, yet they were rare archers and had slain many with their shafts. Their leader spoke to them, and they loosed their bowstrings and thrust their bows into the leather cases at their girdles.

"God gives!" they said, one to another.

And they thronged down the stair where a trumpet sounded and other armed companies of the Domastikos began to run down from the wall, marching off into the alleys somewhither.

"What is this?" I asked the Genoese officer who had been trying to train the naphtha thrower upon the great ship.

He was staring, wide-eyed, with snarling lips. All at once he laughed down in his throat and shook clenched fists up at the palace where Menas was no longer to be seen.

"May he be eaten by dogs! May his soul shrivel in purgatory! *Auraur!* —it is treachery!"

And he, too ran down the stair, shouting that they had been betrayed by the Greeks.

"Look!" whispered Irene.

With half the men running from this stretch of wall, the Venetians were gaining the upper hand. An old *shaikh* led them now, beckoning with a long straight sword, bareheaded. His hair was white, and his long black cloak whipped about his lean body. I have heard it said that this *shaikh* was the chieftain of all the Venetian warriors, by name Dandalo, the Doge.

Once they gave way, the Greeks broke and fled, and a new banner was hoisted on the nearest tower—a gold banner with the semblance of a lion. As far as we could see along the wall the Venetians were swarming and shouting.

Eh, it was indeed a miracle, that ships could have carried a city wall. Except Menas had drawn off his men, the matter might have ended otherwise. But it happened as I have said.

And more than this happened. We could see the array of the Franks drawn up along the distant shore, and the glittering host of the Greeks that emerged from the gates to give battle to them. At first I thought that Menas had taken off his men to join this host. Yet the time did not suffice, and it were folly to yield the wall of a city, to sally from the gate.

No man knew what Menas was doing, or why. But the standards of the emperor, Murtzuple, were in the center of the Greek host on the shore.

The mist had cleared away, and the sky was a clear blue. The host of the Greeks was shaped like a horn, with the ends projecting far beyond the line of the Franks. My eyes are good. I saw the archers of the Franks advance—they moved, it seemed, like midgets crawling across a giant stage.

This was the moment when the wings of the Greek host should have closed on the flanks of the iron men, and buried them under numbers. But the horsemen of the Greeks were all in the center, and the far-stretched wings waited to watch.

Slowly the knights of the Cross, the iron men, formed in line, mounted, with spears upraised. They meant to charge the Greek center.

Then a trumpet blast sounded from beneath the glittering standards of Murtzuple.

Aye, we heard the blast—we upon the wall. There were many trumpets and all the Venetians were standing in silence at gaze. So were the Greeks on the housetops. Then the Greek host began to move, slowly at first.

It moved back toward the gates, instead of onward toward the Franks. The trumpet call had been a signal to retreat.

What had happened? The All-Wise knows! Perhaps the Greeks, despite their numbers, had lost heart—perhaps Murtzuple and the grandees had seen the Venetians carry the sea wall and feared for the city. Yet I, Khalil el Khadr, beheld fifty thousand flee before ten thousand, with not an arrow sped, not a sword bared from sheath.

And now the vulture of misgiving ate at my heart. I had taken under my protection this maiden, clad in the garments of a young grandee. What was to be her fate? I could not leave her, and how could one sword protect her?

For the vials of wrath and fear had broken upon the city. Greek companies—and they of my lord Menas's command—were hastening tardily to attack the Venetians, who diverted them by setting fire to wooden buildings in the nearest alleys, using the same casting machine and naphtha jars that we had watched. Smoke spread under the sun like a veil of ill omen.

We were climbing the narrow streets to escape from the wall. And on every hand was heard the wailing of women. From their dark holes the vagabonds of the city rushed out, to tear at rich garments with their claws.

"Treachery!" A Greek captain lashed his horse through the beggars, and shouted, striving to make his way toward the gates on the far side, where was neither fire nor mob. "The emperor hath betrayed us!"

His charger stumbled and staggered, and a ragged man slashed a knife across its tendons. The horse screamed and fell, the officer falling among the beggars, who closed over him silently. As rats swarm over a bit of meat, jerking and tearing, so these foul creatures rent the Greek among them, until his voice was no longer to be heard.

I threw my cloak over Irene and hastened up wooden stairs that led out of the darkness of the alleys. Smoke was thick in the air and others were pushing and thrusting to run past us. So were we borne by the mob, through a throng of Greeks, into a great open space.

And here was half-silence and the heavy breathing of a multitude, and grating of iron mail and stamping of horses. Armed men were standing in some formation throughout the *registan*. There were restless Tatars and red-robed spearmen and—in advance of a group of mounted nobles—my lord Menas.

He bestrode the white charger from the imperial stables, and the horse was caparisoned in purple, like an emperor's mount. The baton held in his left hand and resting on his knee was tipped with a gold crown, and he was speaking to the multitude. The warriors in this place were his. And then I remembered Arbogastes' words, that they were to muster in the Forum of Theodosius.

"—It is an hour of danger, good people"—so the voice of Menas proclaimed from afar off—"yet it will pass. Behold, my companies go to drive the Venetians from the wall! Behold, my power is mustered here!"

He stretched out his right hand as if offering a gift.

"The imperial city is unconquerable. The Franks are few and fool-hardy. Except for the cowardly flight of your former emperor, Murtzuple, we should have driven the barbarians from the coast. We can still hold the hills—aye, even while I speak, Greek hands are tearing the Lion of Saint Mark from yonder tower."

The listeners who had climbed upon the pedestals of the statues and the balconies of the houses craned their heads and shouted, some one thing, some another. The truth was that no one could see through the smoke.

"My Northmen hold the Galata gate!" Menas raised himself in his stirrups, as if his eyes could see all this. "O my people, these barbarians shall never enter the grounds of the thrice-to-be revered patriarch or set hand upon the holy altar of Saint Sophia. The prince, Alexius, whom they would set over you as lord, is no more than a dupe—your churches, your souls they seek to enslave under the Latin yoke. I have foreseen this."

Shouts arose anew from the grandees clustered behind him. The Lord of Ships had the biggest voice.

"Take arms—follow the Domastikos, who remained to save you when the emperor fled!"

Others began to make outcry:

"Blessing be upon Menas, the savior! Who is mightier than Menas?"

Those who stood behind me began to push and strain to get nearer, and someone cried that Menas should be made emperor. When men are fright-ened they will follow anyone that stands firm, girdled in courage.

"Menas reigns! God and the Emperor Menas!"

The nobles about him began to scatter silver and gold coins into the mob, and the shouting became so great that he could no longer be heard. His warriors tossed their spears and the people in the balconies wept and threw down flowers.

And yet his words were false, and he alone had betrayed the city, hop-ing in this hour of calamity to win the throne.

He had withdrawn his men by order from the wall. Surely he had known the fruit of that, because he had been looking forth. Aye, instead of has-tening to the side of the emperor, he was buying the mob by coins and words.

The crush about us was so great that I stooped and lifted the girl Irene by the knees, bidding her climb to the pedestal of the statue against which we had been forced. Others were sitting on the marble block, and she stepped up to the figure itself, sitting upon its knee and swinging her feet, smiling down on the Greeks, who cried out applause—believing her some noble's son trying to gain a clear view of the new emperor. Menas himself glanced toward her, but knew her not.

The statue was of gilded stone—a powerful man, unclad, sitting with tense muscles, and frowning. It was a pagan god called Hercules, and it seemed as if he were angry at the fickle Greeks.

And then, as if the ancient gods of the pagans had spoken aloud, the shouting and rejoicing in the *registan* ceased. From one of the streets uprose the roar that has one meaning, and no other. It was a thunder of hoarse voices, a steady clanging of steel and crashing of hoofs upon flagstones.

It was still a long way off, yet it came nearer. Out of the maw of this street ran a tall man, with the mail hacked from his bleeding shoulder, helmetless and unarmed. He was a Northman, and the throng made way for him until he could catch the eye of Menas and make his voice heard.

What he shouted I know not, but no messenger of good tidings came ever thus.

He pointed behind him, and Irene stood up, her cheeks flushing red.

"The Franks!" she cried. "Give way, ye Greeks, before the Crosses!"

In that moment my lord Menas showed himself no leader of warriors. There was need of an instant order, and a clear voice. Yet he turned his head to speak with this noble and that.

When he should have spurred forward his horse, he let fall his rein. And when that moment had passed, the multitude began to make itself heard again.

"The Franks! The city burns!"

Some began to slip away, and blows and cries of pain were heard. By now I could see the iron men.

They were pressing steadily down the street, driving remnants of the northern warriors before them. Their steeds were accoutered in mail, with glistening headpieces. Their long swords flashed up and down, and their faces were hidden behind nasal and vizors.

With shields—battered and stained—before their bodies, and with deep shouts of triumph, they emerged from the street into the square. Some of the Greek spearmen faced about and dressed weapons, looking first one way, then the other.

"*Ekh*, brother," grunted a Tatar at my side, "this hay will be cut by those reapers. There is loot on the other side of the city."

He made off, and others followed, sparing not the mob in their way. In another moment thousands of men were trying to run out of the square and the flame of fear took hold on their souls.

"Wo!" cried a soldier, beating about with his sword. "We are surrounded."

The worst of all fears is that of peril, unseen, at a man's back. The multitude of slaves and common men became a tide, rushing and swirling, seeking its way from the forum. And to escape the clutch of this tide, I leaped to the pedestal of the statue.

Eh, the scum of the city ebbed away from the man they had acclaimed emperor, disappearing down every alley and stair until only the red-cloaked spearmen and the mounted Greeks stood between Menas and the fury of the Franks. The mailed riders plunged into the confused ranks of Menas's followers as strong men leap through surf, and though they were few, their weight and the terror of their swords opened a way for them. I touched the girl Irene on the knee.

"We can abide no longer. Come!"

But, standing on the thigh of Hercules, she was staring eagerly at the combat, and when I urged again she shook her head angrily. Go she would not.

Nor did I go from the place. Verily it is written that a man's grave is dug in one spot, and in that grave shall he lie at the appointed time. It had come into my mind that I had sworn to my lord Menas to stand at his back and defend him if his life was assailed.

Though his followers had set upon me, he himself was not proven forsworn. Though a man flee from peril, he may not rid himself of the stain of a broken oath. I climbed down from the stone and made toward him.

A little while ago there had been two thousand Greeks about Menas. Between them and twice a hundred Franks, the struggle had been doubtful. Now the French and Flemish archers were coming out on the balconies—from the houses they had entered to loot—and had put aside plundering to send their shafts into the close-packed spearmen.

Nay, they picked out the knights on horses, and emptied saddles swiftly. The Lord of Ships rose high in his stirrups with two arrows through his throat, and the Greeks gave back toward the statue of Hercules. More of the Franks trotted into the forum and charged with their battle shout. I reached the Domastikos and took his rein.

"My lord," I cried, "there is a way to safety down those stairs. Dismount and take with thee the servants of thy household. Give me fifty chosen men, and I will hold the steps."

His cheeks were bloodless, and his fingers fumbled with the chain at his throat. He was as if stunned by a blow on the head, without voice or will. Then his eyes lifted and gleamed with purpose.

My lord Menas had recognized the barbarian girl. And in that moment of calamity he caught at two of his riders, crying out to them to take the Frankish maid and carry her down the steps.

They went with misgiving and backward glances.

"My lord," I cried again, "thy men give way. Is this a time to think of women?"

Yet his eyes were fixed on her, and he was voiceless, a shackled slave. He nodded at me and smiled.

"Nay, Khalil, thou hast led her to me."

Then he groaned as if feeling the sting of a wound. His two nobles were near the statue, but before them now was a Frank. And surely the horse this warrior bestrode was Khutb.

I cursed the Bokharian who had without doubt offered the gray horse to the first knight of the invaders, for protection. This knight rode as one accustomed, with mailed knees gripping tight and a loose rein. Eh, the horse responded to his touch.

He reined between the two Greek nobles, and took the sword stroke of one upon his long shield, slaying the other with a sweep of his straight blade. Wheeling Khutb in a whirl of dust, he parried the heavy blow of the surviving Greek and swung up his sword. The Greek flinched aside and fled.

The men who had pressed around me were gone. There was heavy dust and smoke in the air, and a great outcry. I could no longer see Menas.

Anger gripped me, at loss of the horse, and I ran forward, catching the rein of the Frank as he lowered his sword.

"Dog of a Nazarene," I cried, "the horse is mine, and if there is aught of honor in thy soul, thou wilt dismount and let the sword be judge between us."

Now in my haste, I had spoken in my own tongue. Half his face was hidden by his vizor, but I saw his lips smile.

"The steed is mine," he made reply in Arabic, "and I will prove it upon thy body, O son of Yamen."

And he cast himself from the saddle. Striding toward me, he let slip his shield, seeing that I had none. So I knew him for a brave man—aye, and soon I knew him for a swordsman.

His blade was lighter than most Frankish weapons, and his long arm lashed out so swiftly, I gave ground. Once I parried, and he beat down my arm.

For a space we struck without ceasing, I striving to slash within the other's arm, yet there was no evading his sweeping stroke. The mail links on my shoulder were hewn through and I could feel the blood running against my ribs.

Again I gave ground and as he strode forward I leaped, striking at his neck. My blade met steel that was not yielding. And I, Khalil, stood weaponless, my scimitar clattering on the stones. The Frank had struck it from my hand with his sword.

"Yield thee, youth!" he said, and again his lips smiled.

I had been too sure of my swiftness, too certain of my strength. Eh, I made the head bow of submission, saying—

"This also was to come upon my head."

And then Khutb, who had been standing near, walked up to me and thrust his nose against my hand. The Frank threw up his steel vizor and loosed the coif at his throat.

I looked into his eyes and behold, he was of my height, and his skin was dark as a desert man's. His eyes were blue, and clear, and surely his age was no greater than mine. Moreover the damp hair at his brow was black. On his sun-stained surcoat there was no device, but upon the shield he had thrown down was a red cross, greatly scarred and stained.

Still I looked at him. He had been riding Khutb, and a thought came to me.

"Art thou the Lord Ricard, from Palestine?" I asked.

"Aye so," he assented, "I am Richard from Palestine. Who art thou, to cry my name?"

"Thy prisoner, Khalil el Khadr, chief of a thousand blades. Nor will I cry *aman* to thee, so slay if thou wilt."

He glanced around and sheathed his long sword, then folded his arms, planting his feet wide, to consider me, smiling.

"Was the horse thine, O Khalil?"

"He was. I stole him from the mock-emperor, and that jackal of a Bokharian gave him up to thee."

"Aye so."

"And now have I a word for thee. The Frankish maid who waits thy coming is yet unharmed and unscathed. But it is a task of tasks to shield her, and—go thou and speak to her."

He followed my eyes to the statue, where the barbarian girl was standing, half hidden by the smoke.

"That is the daughter of the castellan of Edessa to whom thou didst give the gray *kohlani* as a betrothal gift." I judged that he was surprised beholding her in youth's garments, for he looked again at me, narrowly, and again at Khutb.

"Come!" he said. The Lord Richard was a man sparing of words. Striding toward the statue, he came to stand beneath it and that elfin Irene smiled down at him. Though she wore cloak and vest, tunic and pantaloons, her beauty was none the less for that.

The cold blue eyes of my lord Richard glowed, and he caught his breath. His two hands he held up to her, and she leaped down. Gently he placed her upon her feet, nor did he take his hands swiftly from her waist.

It seemed that she, who had been glib of tongue with me, was stricken with his silence, for she lowered her eyes and answered hardly at all, though he questioned her. What passed between them was in the Frankish speech, and to this day I know naught of it.

My lord Richard paid no heed to what went on, to right or left. His lean, dark cheeks were flushed, and when he turned upon me there was a mask of anger or sorrow on his face. He beckoned up an archer who had been loitering near, and spoke with him.

"O Khalil," he said, "who is that *al-comes*?"

I looked where he pointed, and beheld Menas, no longer Domastikos, no longer emperor, but captive on his white horse, with a hundred other Greeks—all surrounded by staring and jesting Frank men-at-arms. And all of them bore a red cross on their shields. For this reason I judged them to be the followers of my lord Richard, and verily this was the case.

"He," I made response, "was emperor for an hour—between the flight of the Greek host and thy coming. Before that he was Menas the Domastikos."

"Nay, Khalil, like a hawk swooping low, thou hast seen many things, but not this. The Emperor Murtzuple fled from the other side of the city when we entered the Galata gate."

"Aye, my lord. And then Menas harangued the mob and had himself acclaimed master of the Greeks, here, in this forum. Thy swords and the faint hearts of his followers, and—" I thought of the few moments delay when Menas had looked upon Irene and had lingered until the path of safety was closed—"his own lust defeated his scheme."

"Wise Khalil!" The young barbarian smiled, leaning on his sheathed sword. "This is a rare day, and thou art a rare paynim. For thy shielding of this damosel ask of me any gift that I may in honor grant."

It was boldly and clearly spoken. Yet I could not without shame ask of him my liberty for the small service I had done this Nazarene maid. My soul warmed when I thought of Khutb, but how could a captive claim such a steed? I dared not look at the gray horse.

So I bent my head and he spoke again.

"One thing more thou mayest do in service to this maid. But wait—"

He pondered a moment and swung away, to walk between his men who called upon him loudly and with laughter after the barbarian fashion. Irene followed him with her gaze, as if a little bewildered.

Verily, four years may alter a man, and it may have been that she found my lord Richard somewhat different than she had supposed. At their betrothal she had spent with him no more than seven days. Yet beyond any doubt, she loved this youthful paladin of the Franks.

Of a sudden a thought seared my brain like an arrow. Richard of Brienne had sent his captain secretly to Menas before the siege. The twain had talked together for long hours, and then the captain had been sent forth again secretly.

"O one without wit!" I cried upon myself. I beheld at last the full of Menas's treachery. He had agreed to betray the city, for a price no doubt. He had agreed with the Franks how they should set about the siege.

And then, mistaking both the strength of the city and the hardihood of his own men, he had sought to seize the throne and drive out the invaders, after Murtzuple had fled. In truth, he had not known which way to turn when the iron men rode into the square. He had played the part of a snake with two heads and had been well scotched.

For a space the young peer of the Franks talked with the defeated usurper, apart from the ranks, and then the Lord Richard came back and gave some orders to the archer. How should I know what was in his mind? My shoulder ached and my soul was sick.

"Eh, Khalil," he said, "knowest thou the statue of the giant woman?"

"It is in the Forum of Constantine."

"Aye, go thither with this, my follower," he nodded at the archer. "Show him the way. He will lead thee to the *sheriff** of the Montserrat Franks. Tell to this *sheriff* thy story, all of it, and come back with them to this place."

"I am thy captive." And then a demon of anger plagued me, for the pain in my shoulder. "Nay, send thy *kapitan*, the man who plotted with the Domastikos!"

If the Lord Richard had few words, he had a clear mind, and quick.

"Point out this *kapitan*!"

I looked through his followers and again; but the powerful Frank who had come secretly to the house of Menas was not among them.

"He is not here. Yet I knew him beyond a doubt, having seen him at the sack of the village where thou wert pleased to carry off the gray horse."

"So thou didst hear this man of mine talk with Menas—when?"

The word was like a lash, and I told the barbarian lord what I had seen in the palace of the Greek, thinking that he was playing with me idly. In truth, before this I had thought to be slain. This Richard was not a man of mercy.

And verily his brow became dark and he stirred not for a space, except to knot his fingers on his belt.

"What a coil!" he said under his breath. "May God have mercy on his soul!" And he bade me sternly speak not again of such matters. "What now?" he cried when I still tarried.

"My sword," I explained.

The city burned, and the plunderers were like hungering wolves. If I went unarmed through the bazaar and the alleys, I should be set upon by vagabonds. I had seen the Greek captain of cavalry die, and if my fate was near me, it were better to die here under the Frank's sword than to be torn into pieces.

Aye, if Richard were playing with me, as he had with Menas, there was no good in a few hours more of life. He motioned to the archer, who picked up my scimitar and thrust it out toward me. Then the young barbarian did a courteous thing. He spoke quickly to the warrior, who shifted the

---

*A nobleman holding rank in an army.

sword so that it lay with its point in one hand, its hilt across the other arm, toward me.

"May it be remembered, on thy behalf!" I cried, taking it, and bowing. And then I dared his anger again. "This maiden—wilt thou have her in thy care henceforth?"

Whereupon the barbarian Irene looked from under her lashes at the youth, as a maid will when she judges matters for herself in veiled fashion. As for Richard, his eyes glowed upon me strangely.

"Never harm shall come to her, while I live."

With the archer stalking beside me, staring at every tumult, I made my way through the throngs. Doubt was heavy upon me, because I was being sent to a strange chieftain of the Franks, and because I was very weary.

By the smell in the alleys I knew we were passing through the Jews' quarter. It was the custom of the Greek tanners to carry the filthy water from the tanneries in carts and dump it under the noses of the Jews. Here the houses leaned close together overhead, and it was a place of gloom under the smoke-veiled sky. I turned aside and sought the square as my lord Richard had directed.

We had passed a few Franks, riding through the streets in groups, and some had halted us, until the archer talked with them and we were permitted to go on.

This archer had a green hood close drawn over his head, and a fat face red as fire and eyes that seemed to be asleep, but for all that he did not cease watching me. When we came to a throng in the square he pushed through, making way with both elbows, and pulling me with him.

The crowd had gathered around an old man and a girl. The old man was a Greek merchant of the poorer sort, and by the tears on his cheeks it was clear that the girl was his daughter. She had flung herself on the ground, and her face was smudged and stained as if she had been rubbing dirt upon it. Her garments were soiled and disordered, as if she had thrown them on in haste.

Two horsemen and a dozen warriors were about her, and these were Franks. The taller of the two riders was richly clad in a fur-edged mantle, with a gold chain at his throat. His shoulders were heavy, and his lips, and his eyes were a faded blue.

I knew that he was an officer of some kind because he had a small baton tipped with a gold crown in his belt—but I did not think he had been in the fighting that day.

He was looking at the Greek girl, and at two of his men who were pulling her up by the arms, trying to make her stand on her feet. To him the archer went, and they talked, glancing at me.

Then this *sheriff* spoke impatiently to the two warriors, and the old Greek wailed. Someone laughed, because the *sheriff* had given order to strip the garments from the young girl.

She struggled without weeping, and it was clear that the dirt had been put upon her face to hide her beauty, for she was lithe of limb and erect of stature, and her terrified eyes were like dark pearls. When even her sandals had been wrenched from her, the tall Frank leaned down and took her chin between thumb and forefinger, to scrutinize her face.

Again he gave an order, and this time the Frankish warriors hung back and muttered. It speaks ill of a leader when he asks of his men a deed that shames them. At length one of them sought on the ground and picked up a long cord. With this he bound the wrists of the silent girl, and tied the free end of the cord to the tail of the *sheriff*'s horse. As he did so, my guard, the archer, spat.

"That will teach the wanton to come to her feet at call," so said the Frank. And he spoke in Arabic, to me. "What seekest thou, dog?"

Before this never a man had named a chieftain of the Ibna al Yamen so, and lived. I drew the edge of the *khalat* over my forehead and looked upon the ground.

"Thy tongue shall feel the dagger, an thou answer not," he went on, his lips drawing back upon his teeth. "I have dealt with thy *saracin* folk before now—"

"Lord," I cried, lest he add worse to my shame, "I was sent to lead this archer to thee, and to tell thee a tale—"

"Who sent thee?"

"The Sieur de Brienne."

At this he fell silent, and I told him of the maiden Irene, and of the fight in the square.

"Is that all the tale?" He rubbed his long chin and eyed me as if I were the bait of a trap. Verily it was a strange thing that I should have been sent to this man. The gray-haired Greek, thinking this a favorable instant, flung himself on his knees and embraced the *sheriff*'s stirrup, and moaned when he was kicked back upon the ground.

Nay, before then I had seen men of the breed of this Frank—*wazirs* and *khayias*—who had been given the staff of authority and had become swollen with the pride of their office.

"Thou liest, Khalil—the damosel Irene abides at Edessa. She is poor enough in goods and gear by now—is she fair to look upon? Has she beauty?"

"Aye, Lord."

His eyes searched me, and he felt of chin and lips.

"Well, we shall see this morsel for ourselves. I mind, she was betrothed to me four years ago—to me, Richard, Sieur de Brienne, now constable to Montserrat."

Eh, before then I had ached, but now my soul burned. I led the way back to the Forum of Theodosius with laggard step, followed by the archer, and by the constable, who was Richard of Brienne. And he was followed perforce by the Greek girl, who shook her hair about her cheeks to hide her sorrow.

Presently he bethought him of her, and bade the archer cut her loose. She fled into the shadows and the very vagabonds of the refuse piles gave her their cloaks.

But my lord of Brienne told me that I was dull of ear and wit—that the Frank who had fought with me was the knight Richard d'Alencon, who was such another young fool. So said the constable, and I thought that surely there had been a feud between the twain.

Four years had wrought a change in this Frank. He was handsome still, but his blue eyes were seamed, and his pride had altered into arrogance. He still held his heavy shoulders well, yet he talked with me, a *saracin*, of the beauties of the young Irene and how he had ceased to think of her since the death of her father, who had been a power in Edessa.

"And the gray colt—Khutb—has she it still?"

"Aye, Lord."

Then it was that utter misery came upon me. This boar of a Frank who wore raking spurs would ride Khutb. This also was to come upon my head.

Fool! Thrice fool, to listen to the talk of a dreaming maid and to think to find her youthful paladin in the flesh as she had pictured him. Surely Richard d'Alencon had seemed to me to be her betrothed, and as for the constable—only sorrow and the death of her dreams would come to her at his hand.

A thought came to me, and I knew at once it was good. It is always good to end suspense, and a man may not journey past the spot where his grave is dug.

Coming close to the mailed knee of the constable, I spoke softly:

"Lord, there is another tale to be told. Nay, this is our way—"

Taking the rein of the charger, I turned aside into the Jews' alley where the smoke was now ruddy-hued afar where flames glowed. The archer kept abreast me, but the squire and the men-at-arms strung out behind, picking their way through the heaps of garbage.

"Lord, I dwelt in the palace of *al-comes* Menas, the Domastikos. There I saw thy man, thy *kapitan*."

What had passed between the man of the constable and Menas I did not know, nor do I know now. Nevertheless, beyond all doubt the bargain held treachery in it.

I heard the Sieur de Brienne catch his breath, and felt his hand move on his belt as he leaned lower to peer at me. The sun had set and the glow of fire was like a smoking torch afar.

"It was agreed between thy *kapitan* and the Lord Menas, for a sum in gold—" I laughed up in his face. "Menas is a captive and he has a woman's tongue for secrets!"

The hand of the constable gripped the short iron mace at his belt and swung it high, high above my head. He cursed and wrenched himself around in the saddle for the blow.

And my hand that had been upon the hilt of my scimitar rose, and my curved blade passed upward and outward beneath his beard. He gave neither cry nor moan, but fell forward against the charger's neck as I drew my sword clear and turned to face the archer.

Eh, that archer must have been heavy with sleep. His back was toward me and he was breathing like a bullock. It was no time for wondering. I thrust the dying constable from the saddle, and leaped into his seat, drawing tight the rein.

The charger reared, and from behind came the shout of the constable's men, who had not seen in that dim light the blow that slew him, but who had heard the clang of his fall, and had seen me mount to the saddle.

But the horse sprang forward, and I guided him aside into another alley. A bolt from a crossbow whipped over me, and the shouting grew until it dwindled and died behind me. The squire and the men-at-arms had stopped, perforce, to attend their lord.

With a sword at my hip and a horse between my thighs I considered what next to do.

Time pressed. I sought the *registan*, where I had left the young Richard. Looking back over my shoulder I beheld the giant statue of the white woman, with its face rose-hued from the reflection of flames. Aye, and a veil of smoke about its head.

Constantinople was burning. And the voice of the city was as a woman's voice, shrill with the ululation of fear. Vagabonds and grandees, slaves and masters fled from they knew not what. Cursing the fleeing, groups of Venetian sailors with axes struggled to get nearer to the flames, to cut away some of the wooden buildings in its path. I saw a slave stab his master to death, and a soldier of Menas, who had cast aside helmet and red cloak, grapple with the slave for the purse of the dead man.

I saw a Jew with a pack mounted on an ass, beating the ass in vain to make it go somewhither, and a throng of Frankish men-at-arms mocked him as they cooked supper and tended their hurts.

At the Forum of Theodosius were many men, but neither the knight Richard nor the barbarian girl. A tanner, with a club upon one shoulder and a sack on the other, bade me look for them at the palace of Menas.

"Ho, paynim! There is blood on thy horse. Hail to the new emperor—Death!"

He staggered and laughed and wandered away. There was a howling as of wolves that pull down living meat. Eh, these were two-legged wolves that held the streets this night. No man knew who had gained the upper hand in the city; some said that the Franks had fled and there were two emperors.

But in the courtyard of the Domastikos I saw hundreds of horses feeding quietly, tended by men-at-arms, and other Franks grouped around the pots and the fires that were barely cold from the morning meal of the dead Northmen.

I dismounted and let loose the charger in the courtyard. My mind was made up. True is it written, "Not an arrow is sped but its destination is marked upon it." The constable of the Franks had found his grave in the dark alley, and I—it seemed to me the hour of my fate was at hand. What availed a jackal's flight?

The inner court of the palace was deserted, except by the marble women whose hands upheld the roof; only two archers stood at the door beyond the whispering gallery. The niches upon the stairs were empty, the curtains pulled down.

But in the gallery of the fountain the young Richard stood, his hands thrust through his belt, his helm unlaced and put aside. A boy squire held his shield in readiness to his hand.

I looked for Irene and beheld her not. It was written that I should not set eyes on her again. In a chair by the ebony table sat my lord Menas, the henna-red standing forth on his pallid skin, his fingers groping at his throat. And apart from him swaggered a great figure in muddied surcoat and rusted mail.

And this was the captain of the dead Richard of Brienne.

"Where is the constable?" the young Richard cried. "Came he with thee?"

I made the salaam of greeting and answered thus:

"He came not, nor will he ever come. He lies dead in the alleys behind the tanneries."

Menas and the other looked upon me as if a djinn had risen from the fountain and confronted them, and the Montserrat captain cried out angrily. The youth listened to him and turned to me.

"The Sieur de Brienne was not in the assault. He had command of the Montserrat and Bavarian companies that held our camp. No one among them has been wounded."

"*Wai*," I said, "I saw him fall with a sword through his throat. His fate was at hand and no man may increase the number of his days."

Suspicion flamed in the bearded face of the Montserrat captain, and he shook his head savagely. He glowered at Menas, and his hand jerked to his sword. The young knight laughed and stepped between them.

"Nay, Barthelemi—I summoned thee to meet thy master. Go, now, and bury him. And—mark me, Barthelemi—I know you came hither to plot with this Greek prince. That was a traitor's mission. For the fair name and honor of thy master, seal thy lips. And go!"

The man called Barthelemi looked long upon the youth, then turned on his heel and left as if indeed his lips had been sealed. At once the knight spoke to Menas, and the Greek started up from his seat.

"Domastikos, my men have come to me with tidings. The Montserrat companies and the Bavarians hold the center of the city. They should have kept to their post, our camp in the plain. Thy men also were drawn up and waiting, yet not for my onset. I know the man Barthelemi came to thee and there was an agreement made—and now I say to thee this." He stepped to the side of the gallery and drew back with his own hand the curtain that had shut out the red glare of flames, the tumult of the streets and the gleaming lights of the Venetian galleys along the sea wall. "It is the hour, Menas, when the dregs of treachery are bitter. What passed between thee and our allies, I know not. But the hour is past when your Greeks and the Italians of Montserrat could have seized the city."

Menas half smiled, as if the words of the young Frank had no meaning in his ears.

"Bethink thee, my lord," went on the knight, "whether it is not better to play the part of an honest foe, who has yielded to greater power, than to make public thy compact with the constable of Montserrat who is dead?"

Still Menas kept silence, outwardly amiable.

"If I had not withdrawn my men from the wall, the Venetians would never have carried a tower," he said at last.

Richard looked at him steadily.

"As to that, I know not. The Sieur de Brienne often spoke to the commanders of our host, describing the great treasures in this city. He had a thirst for gold, and authority, and more than that I will not say, save this—" he paused in his long stride in front of the Greek, and waited until Menas met his eyes. "The Sieur de Brienne lived as he lived, and no man may call despite upon his name, now that his spirit has passed."

For an instant his fingers touched the mail gauntlet in his belt, and Menas bowed assent. At a sign from the knight, the shield bearer escorted the Greek from the chamber.

Verily, Menas had spoken truly. These men of the Cross were gallant fools. A handful of them had stormed Constantinople and hoped to launch a new crusade in this city of old intrigues and age-old treachery.

"Khalil!" cried young Richard. "How did the Lord of Brienne die?"

"He was slain by a captive that he abused."

He brushed his hand across his forehead.

"It was like him. There was no faith in him. But I shall say to the damosel Irene that he fell in the street fighting."

"Aye, be it so."

Foolish youth, who loved the barbarian maid from the instant he had first seen her—who knew that she awaited the coming of the Sieur de Brienne. And who would suffer no evil word to be said of the man who was his enemy.

How can two youths seek the same maiden to wife and not draw the sword of hatred?

"Why hast thou come back, Khalil? Alone!"

"I am thy captive, Ricard."

He held out his hand to me, laughing.

"Nay, and again nay. I have heard from the damosel Irene how thou hast shielded her. No prisoner, thou! Go, or abide as my guest, as thou wilt."

Now, I had seen what I had seen. The eyes of a maiden hold few secrets from the glance of wisdom. The thought had come to me that the barbarian girl would love this youth. He, too, was a barbarian, yet there was in him the bright steel of honor.

And he had overcome me with the sword. I longed to stand against him again and strive with the steel blades, for he was worthy, even of the girl who had warmed my heart—aye, she had stirred the heart of Khalil.

"May thy way be open to thee!" I made the salaam of leave-taking, and he took my hand in his. "Thou art a bold youth—even a brother to Khalil. I go."

And in the second watch of that night, with the flames at our heels, we rode through the portal of Constantinople the Great—Khutb and I. Nay, I lifted the gray horse out of the line under the eyes of all the Franks.

The Guest of Karadak

Once—no more than once—have I seen a man dig his own grave. Though his eyes were keen, in that hour he was blind. Though he was favored and fortunate and a conqueror, it availed him not at all in that hour.

Concerning this man, some say—

"It was written, and what is written may not be altered."

Others—and they are the mountain Kurds—say he was led to his fate by the hand of Sidri Singh. What my eyes have seen, I have seen, and I say that he dug his own grave, unknowing.

W'allahi, how many men have I seen in the hour of their death? I am Daril of the land of Athir. My clan is the Nejd and we are desert Arabs. In my youth I rode with the raiding bands—yea, and the banners of the clans. In those times the sword of Daril ibn Athir was not without honor.

When my years numbered fifty and eight I sheathed the sword, being weary of the war of clan against clan. It was the moment when the soul within cries, "Peace! Make thy peace." I lingered at the sitting-place of the expounders of the Law, and the burden of their words was not otherwise.

"Make thy peace, that thy years be not troubled."

But how—in what way?

I cannot read the written word of the Law. And where are the two who will agree as to the meaning of the words written? I listened, hearing much dispute, and learning little, for we of the *sahra* understand only a few words. It was said to me, "Give alms." I gave then my tents and carpets, the silver jars and the silk of Cathay, the red leather and blue, clear glass—all that my hand had plundered.

They then said to me:

"Go thou upon the pilgrimage."

And this also I did, taking leave of my followers and the keepers of my herds. For my sheep were numbered by the hundred, my saddle-horses by the score.

When I returned from Mecca and Bait al-Mukkudas to my district, I found there only a few of my men, who said that the herds had been carried off by raiders. They besought me to summon clansmen and companions-in-arms and ride and recover the herds. But I made answer that I had no wish to lift the standard of strife.

Nay, the blood was thin in my veins; the mail-shirt irked my stiff bones. I could no longer run beside a galloping horse and leap to the saddle; nor could I lean down from the saddle and slit in halves with my sword's edge a carpet laid in the sand.

"In poverty," I said, remembering some words of the expounders of the Law, "there is rest."

But who can sit in one place and eat out of another's bowl? Many men of the Nejd, remembering other days, came to me to have their wounds dressed and other ills healed, for they called me physician, praising my skill at letting blood from a vein, in judging the heat of fever. Thus the thought came to me to rise up and go upon a journey, naming myself a physician.

I would sheathe the sword forever, bearing only the unadorned blade of Damascus forging that I had carried as a youth. Daril, chieftain of Athir, would be Daril al Hakim—the physician. I meant to see new lands and visit the throne rooms of far kings—yea, the conquerors.

With this thought I set forth in the Year of the Flight, one thousand and twenty and nine.* I crossed the gulf to the coast of Iran. It is only a little way from the shore of the Nejd to the great island that lies in the throat of the gulf and to the land of the Iranis. Nevertheless, the *rais* of the vessel was afraid of pirates and more afraid of landing on this coast, though we had come to a walled town. He made me go down into a fisherman's craft, and the vessel turned its sail and went away.

I thought that I would buy a camel from these Iranis and go overland to the empire of Ind.

---

*By the Christian calendar, 1619. At that time the four great empires of Asia, stretching from the gates of Vienna to the Malay peninsula, were—as we moderns call them—Turkey, Persia, India, and China. In the narrative of Daril, Persia is called Iran, and the empire of the vastly powerful Moguls is Ind.

O, ye who listen, there is one thing true beyond doubt. He who sets forth upon a road may not know what the end of the road will be.

It was the season of the first rains, though no grass showed in the sand, and the cattle had not been led out into the valleys. I sat within the sea-gate of Bandar Abbasi, the walled town where the *rais* of the vessel had left me.

It is a good sitting place, the shadow of a brick arch of a gate. Here may be seen those who enter with their followers and animals. I listened to the talk of the shepherds and sellers of water who entered Bandar Abbasi.

I learned that this was a new port of the great Shah Abbas, the lord of Iran. Verily, it reeked of foulness and unclean dirt—the water was bad, and the horses, for lack of grain, fed on dried fish and camel flesh. Even the goat's milk that I drank tasted of fish. Many officers of the shah came and went through the gate, the lesser men hastening from their path and greeting them with low salaams, crying: "May God increase your honor!"

A hadji in a white turban spread his carpet opposite me and prayed in a loud voice at the hour of late morning prayer, and gathered listeners about him when he began to expound the Law. These disciples blocked the gate, and presently I heard curses.

Standing in the sun without, a Turkoman blind in one eye bade them clear his path. He puffed at a clay pipe that he held in his left hand, and he smelled of mutton grease and leather and dung. Indeed, the disciples of the hadji made way for him when they saw the long *tulwar* and the five or six knives in his girdle. The fingers of his right hand went from hilt to hilt and his one eye glared.

Seeing me, he took the pipe from his stained lips, and spat.

"By the beard and the teeth of Ali—what is this?"

He blinked at my striped headcloth and heavy, brown mantel, stared at my sandals and spat again.

"A dark, thin face. Ho, here is an Arab from Arabistan. Who art thou?"

"One who seeks the road to Ind," I made response.

"I know it well." The Turkoman came and squatted by me, on the side of his good eye. "It runs north along the river, then through the dry lands where the wells are a ride apart. Now it is a hard road; but after the first rains there will be water in the mountain gullies."

He pulled at his thin beard, eyeing me shrewdly.

"Ho, thou wilt need a companion to show the way, or horses—good mountain-bred beasts that will not give out—or weapons."

"Nay."

"Never say that." He wagged his head, his breath reeking of sour wine. "My brother, I know the track to Ind. I know the Kurds who will raid and rob thee, and the seven-times-accursed road guards of the Iranis who will lift thy wallet from thee as a price of their protection."

"Of thy wisdom," I made response, "canst tell me the hour of buying and selling in the *souk*—the marketplace?"

"In Bandar Abbasi there is no *souk*." He laughed. "The best of the animals were taken by the shah's *sipahis* in the marketplace—aye, and the girl-slaves. Now, the owners hide them. By the head of Ali, I can fetch thee a camel that is beyond price. A Bikanir racer worth a hundred silver sequins—aye, saddled as if for a prince and fit now for the road. Come and see!"

"Nay." I had seventy silver pieces in my girdle, and no mind for an affray.

"A white camel, swift-paced as the south wind."

"And are thy words as wind?"

This Turkoman was a fellow of resource.

"Abide here, O, *shaikh*," he cried, "and by the teeth of Ali, I wager thou'lt loose thy purse strings within the hour."

Rising, he departed, thrusting aside the beggars who thronged the gateway with their cries. Thrusting his pipe in his girdle-sack, he made off as one with a purpose formed.

True to his word, within the hour he came striding back, followed by a Baluchi with greasy ringlets who tugged at the nose-cord of a camel. And this, indeed, was a Bikanir fit to mount the courier of a king. Small in the head, smooth in gait, with belled trappings and a carpet saddle in place. Truly, a good beast, worth fifty silver pieces in the Nejd. The Baluchi made the white camel kneel near the brick arch of the gate and, when I had considered him, I offered thirty sequins.

"Now by all the companions and the ninety and nine names," swore the Turkoman, "this Arab would pluck the gall out of thee, little brother. I will attend to the matter, on thy behalf."

The Baluchi only smiled, twisting the cord in his fingers. He said the camel would bear a man forty leagues between sun and sun.

"At eighty pieces, this man makes no profit," put in the warrior.

I thought that the Baluchi might make little profit, indeed, for the tribesman meant to extort something from him.

"For the saddle also," I said, "I will give thirty and eight."

"Even an Armenian would pay more. With such a beast thou canst fly from all pursuit."

No doubt he thought me one of the Arabs who escape across the water from their foes. He knew much of the world, this Turkoman.

"From thy brother thieves?" I asked.

"Ho—from the ghosts of the dry lands, or the *ghils* that ride the winds. Nay, thou art bold of speech, O *shaikh*, and like unto a piece of my liver." He whispered hoarsely in my ear. "I will cheat the Baluchi who hath no more wit than a blind dog. I will persuade him to yield thee the racing camel for sixty and five sequins of full weight."

Thus we disputed the price, the Turkoman haggling loudly, now calling me his foster-brother, now cursing me for more than a grandfather of all usurers. In the end his haggling brought him no good. About midday came kettledrums down the street, and a thudding of hoofs in the dirt.

Crowding against the stalls on either hand, through rising dust, came a cavalcade of horses toward the gate. The leading riders cantered past, and I knew them for Kizil-bashis—Red Hats—the cavalry of Iran. They carried leather shields and tufted lances. They wore good mail shirts and the wide, red, cloth turbans that gave them their name.

The men around me pushed to get out of their way, and the white Bikanir rose to his feet, lurching hither and yon, so that the horsemen cursed, and one drove his stirrup into the belly of the Turkoman, who was unsteady on his feet and not inclined to move.

Before the warrior could get his breath, the Kizil-bashis were gone and a cavalcade of officers trotted through the dust. I saw the cloth-of-gold turban of a Sipahi Agha, a captain of cavalry. The best of the horses was a dun-colored mare.

This mare swerved and halted beside me. Its rider held a tight rein and sat in short stirrups. Upon him he had no mark of honor save a heron feather for turban crest. But the long, curved dagger in his girdle was gold-sheathed, with an emerald of great size upon the tip of the sheath.

"I will buy thy beast," he said to the Baluchi.

Those around me knelt and beat their foreheads in the dust—all but the Turkoman, who had drunk too much wine, and was angered, besides.

"Forty and five sequins were bid," he grumbled. "By the breath of Ali, my lord, thy price should be not less than that."

"Who bid the sequins?"

"He!" The thick-headed tribesman beckoned at me.

"And who art thou, O Arab?"

"Daril ibn Athir, of the Nejd."

"A warlike clan. Thy mission?"

"A *hakim*, journeying to Ind by the northern track."

The rider of the mare turned slowly and looked down at me. His full brown eyes were clear and alert. His body was thick and strong, his broad face sallow, his beard dark and close-clipped upon a wide chin. A man, I thought, sure of his strength—quick to anger, and accustomed to obedience.

This bearded Irani was leader of the Red Hats and, beyond doubt, an officer of the shah. From me he turned his attention to the camel, impatiently, and spoke to the servant who rode behind him. At once this follower counted out some silver pieces from a purse and cast them on the ground before the Baluchi.

"I bear witness," shouted the Turkoman, bending over to count the pieces, "that the sum sufficeth not. Here are no more than twenty sequins."

The rider of the dun mare seemed to smile, and spoke again. A foot follower hastened forward and caught the nosecord of the camel from the silent Baluchi. I looked for a tumult and outcry, since the bearded Irani had acted against the custom of open sale. Indeed, the Turkoman began to bellow like a wounded buffalo.

"*Hai-hai!* I bear witness, O hadji, the payment sufficeth not. Give heed, O hadji, and judgment—for this man hath been wronged and his property taken from him. Hearken to the complaint, O thou of the pilgrimage performed."

Then the throng turned to look at the expounder of the Law who sat across the street with his pupils. Indeed, he wore the white turban of wisdom and authority. His fingers trembled upon his beard, and his eyes went this way and that. But he spoke no word of blame to the rider of the dun mare.

In my land, across the gulf, the chieftains obey the customs of the clan, but here in Iran it was otherwise. In a moment I saw the proof of it.

Three of the Red Hats dismounted, at a sign from their leader; they ran suddenly at the Turkoman, who was too bewildered with wine to take heed. One caught his arms behind his back, another seized his girdle and beard, while the third drew a small and thin knife.

The Turkoman fought like a buffalo, twisting and bellowing and butting. Eh, the moment had gone by when he could have drawn his weapons—and what avail to struggle without steel in the hand?

He went down, and the dust rose as they rolled about. Before long the three soldiers held him beneath them, and one of them lay across his chest, gripping his head. The thin knife was given the one who lay thus, and while the Turkoman screamed, the wielder of the knife thrust suddenly, once and again. Then the soldiers rose off the man and went to their horses, the one with the dagger wiping it clean on my cloak as he passed.

"Say, O physician," cried the rider of the dun mare to me, "was it well done? Did the knife do its work?"

Wallahi—I saw then the face of the shaggy Turkoman, with blood running freely from under his brow. His lips drew back from his teeth—long, yellow teeth. No longer did he scream, but he panted with long gasps. His pallid blind eye rolled hither and yon, seeing naught. Indeed, he would never see again, for the knife had been thrust twice through his good eye.

"Truly, O my lord," I made response. "He is blind, but I bear witness that the deed was not well done."

And when the men of the Irani had withdrawn from the tormented one, taking his weapons with them, I stooped and began to staunch the flow of blood with a cloth from my girdle. The bearded rider reined his mare over against me, and I feared that punishment would be my lot, for I had spoken in anger.

"By the Ka'aba," he laughed, "physicians are like to the readers of the Law, being jealous of another's work and clamorous for reward. So, take this, and mend if thou canst what my man hath clumsily done."

A heavy gold coin fell beside me in the blood-spattered dust. The Irani noble wheeled away; his men mounted and fell in behind him, thudding through the gate. The Baluchi hastened to gather up his coins and come and squat by me. But the Turkoman, when I would have bound his head, thrust out his arms and rose up, staggering. He cursed the rider of the mare, and I knew then that the name of the Irani who had blinded him was Mirakhon Pasha.

"This was to come upon my head," said the Baluchi as we went from the gate. He spoke sadly, thinking of the little price that had been paid him for the camel, and I also thought with regret of the white Bikanir, because my desire to leave Bandar Abbasi increased within me.

"Still," muttered the Baluchi, "it was worse for him. He spoke in the teeth of Mirakhon Pasha. And he tasted his reward."

"Justly?" I asked, thinking of the hadji and his saying that men should taste of their deeds.

"*Vai!*" The Baluchi shook his ringlets and smiled. "Mirakhon Pasha is the master of the horse. If he did not use torment at times, men would not fear him."

"But he wronged thee in the matter of the price."

The man from the desert looked quite troubled, but presently his eyes brightened.

"Perhaps he had need of a camel. He goes upon a journey, it is said." And he looked at me eagerly. "Come, my lord, I can show thee other beasts that will please thee."

And before the evening prayer I bought a camel of him, with cloth and ropes for the saddle and a water skin, paying thirty and two silver pieces for all. Then I weighed the gold coin in my hand, the *tuman* that Mirakhon Pasha had tossed me.

"Canst find the Turkoman again?" I asked the man from the desert.

He nodded, saying that a wounded buffalo is easily tracked.

"Then bear him this," I said, "as a gift to the afflicted. Watch, then, that others do not see and take it from him."

This the Baluchi promised to do, but he explained that the Turkoman would not live long because the warrior had many enemies in Bandar Abbasi who would take his life in requital of old wrongs, now that he was helpless.

"O *hakim*," he said at parting, "thou art an old man, treading the way of justice. Take care upon the road. It would be well to wait for the great caravan of Mirakhon Pasha, who also takes the northern road tomorrow, through the mountains to the salt lake on the way to Ind."

But I thought of the Red Hat riders and the scarred face of the drunken warrior and of the trembling fingers of the hadji who had been afraid to speak. And when the Baluchi had gone upon his mission, I listened to the talk in the alleys and coffee stalls. Men spoke often of this caravan, and I learned the reason of its setting forth.

Mirakhon Pasha was the favorite of Shah Abbas, lord of Iran. Having the ear of the shah, he could gratify any whim without harm. No one dared complain of his deeds, and many stories were told of his strange entertainments. He himself did not drink wine, but it pleased him to make others drunk when they were sitting at supper or coffee. He would give his guests first the wine of Shiraz, and then the full white wine of the mountain vineyards, then spirits, both hot and cold. It angered him if a visitor refused the cup. More than one worthy person who angered Mirakhon Pasha was beaten from his threshold by the cudgels of his slaves—yea, beaten through the streets with great outcry.

The favorite of the shah was best pleased when his guests became maudlin. When they quarreled or rolled upon the carpet among the dishes, he clapped his hands. And perhaps his ears caught many inklings of secrets at these drinking bouts. Once in the fort of Bandar Abbasi, he sent for the daughters of the chief men and made them drink wine in his presence.

Indeed, then some of the hadjis murmured publicly, and—hearing of this through his spies—Mirakhon Pasha summoned them and said, smiling:

"Is it true that the people of Bandar Abbasi did not enjoy my entertainment? That is hard to believe, because I summoned jugglers and wrestlers and the best of my boy dancers and gypsies to perform before the hanims."*

He had brought in a throng of ignoble creatures that he carried about with him for amusement to perform their antics before these women, thus adding mockery to shame. And he had enjoyed himself very much.

"Eh," he said again, "if the entertainment was not sufficient I will call in the officers of the Red Hats the next time."

Thereupon the people of Bandar Abbasi grumbled in secret and praised Mirakhon Pasha loudly when he rode forth. Was he not the milk-brother of the shah? They had been nursed by the same woman, and the great shah always remembered this tie between them. Besides, Mirakhon Pasha pleased him.

For the favorite of the shah liked to wrestle with the heaviest of the wrestlers; he was a daring rider, and so great was his love of hunting that he seldom was without a leopard on his crupper to loose at antelope, or a falcon on his wrist.

He could put a swift horse to utmost speed and throw three javelins, one after the other, into a mark as he passed. Because of his great strength and sureness of eye he was dangerous with the sword in either hand. And

---

*Ladies—wives and daughters of distinguished men.

when he drew a weapon, he seldom sheathed it without slaying a man or a woman.

Perhaps because he trusted Mirakhon Pasha more than others, perhaps because he feared him a little, the shah had given command for him to go as ambassador to the court of the Emperor of Ind, to carry some valuable presents. And because pirates infested the Gulf at this season, Mirakhon Pasha had given up the idea of going from Bandar Abbasi on a ship, and was preparing to go over the desert road to the north and west.

Thus said the people in the marketplace of Bandar Abbasi, concerning Mirakhon Pasha, the lord or master of the horse. And when I had heard all the tale, I meditated and decided to set out alone upon the road. In setting forth, no man knows whether good fortune or calamity awaits him, but if he rides alone, at least, he will not suffer from evil companions.

And I had little in my bags. No more than sufficient millet and salt and rice and dates. What more is needed? I had, too, the copper pot and a slender knife and bow with forked arrows for striking down quail and sand grouse.

Except for my sword, with the damask work upon its blade and the ivory-and-horn hilt, and the silver in my girdle, no thief would covet aught of mine. Indeed, I have found that thieves come oftener to seek the goods of merchants and to hold them to ransom than they come to trouble an old physician who would fetch a small price as a slave.

So, as I had done in the Nejd, I placed my saddle-felt in a sandy hollow that first night. Here the road ran by a river of salt water, but I made my fire near a stream where the water was sweet and good. And, as in my land, I gathered roots and brush and tamarisk boughs sufficient to keep the embers of the fire aglow until dawn. This we do, so that a stranger may not miss our camp and our hospitality.

It is an old custom. Sometimes it brings strange guests. God knows best. That night the camel was already grunting in its sleep, and I had thrown more brush on the fire. I wrapped my mantle closer to my shoulders and loosened my girdle. The first quarter of the night had passed, but already the ground was chill. I was ready for sleep, because old blood courses slowly through the veins, and the blazing brush gave out a good warmth. My head was pressed against the sand when I heard the waterfowl flap up from the rushes, suddenly.

Eh, it was a sign. I listened, and in time heard horses moving along the hard earth of the trail. They moved slowly, often stumbling, and their rid-

ers did not speak. Drawing tight my girdle and taking my sword sheathe
in hand, I sat up. There were two horses and they came forward as if their
masters were fearful or wary.

And they halted in the outer blackness while one called—

"What man art thou?"

I rose and beckoned toward them. The voice had spoken in the Iranian
tongue, yet not as one accustomed.

"Come," I bade them. "The night is cold, and here is warmth. A *hakim*, I, from over the Gulf."

Then cried out a woman's voice, young and ringing with excitement:

"God hath led us aright. Here in the *thur* we have found a physician.
Come!"

Through the brush that had screened them came two men and a woman.
The leader was mounted on a foam-streaked Kabuli stallion, ungroomed
and lean. Lean, and haggard, too, the rider, who wore a cloak that had
once been part of a dress of honor. His turban was small, of a kind strange
to me, and rings gleamed in his ears. His cheeks were fallen in, his eyes
sunken, and he swayed in the saddle, supported by a wild-looking servant, armed with sword and shield. I thought at first the man on the stallion had been wounded.

"Are these the lands of Awa Khan?" he called to me hoarsely. "Can his
tower be seen from here?"

I took his rein and greeted him, bidding him dismount and sit. The
servant half lifted him down, though he looked like a man well accustomed to stirrup and saddle seat. When he stood on his feet he staggered,
and again the follower steadied him. I saw then that the armed servant
bore upon his shoulder a heavy bundle, cloth-wrapped.

"My lord," I made response, "I have seen no tower, nor have I heard
the name of Awa Khan."

"That is a lie," he muttered, glaring. "All these mountains know my
cousin's name, and he hath in his herds over a hundred sheep and a score
of horses. His tower overlooks the dry lake, and he—and his sire before
him—have had a hand in the making of wars."

"O *hakim*," the woman's voice whispered at my side. "Heed him not.
He has talked thus since the sun was overhead. His strength fails. Attend
him, and thou wilt not fail of reward."

She touched her arm, upon which was no more than a single silver
armlet. And her long, loose hair was bound at the brow by no more than

a coral circlet of little worth. Though she was veiled, one shoulder was bare—yea, and shapely, and her slight body under its thin brown mantle stood straight and unbending. Verily, I thought these travelers had in their company a fourth, invisible, whose name was Poverty. And they lacked not pride. For the servant had carried the bundle, lest it appear that his master and mistress bestrode pack animals.

While the servant spread cloths by the fire, I supported the master, and felt within his veins the heat of devouring fever. In spite of this he wore upon his body a shirt of heavy mail. Without cessation he muttered to himself, calling out the name of this man and that, as if he were attended by many followers. Later it became clear to me that he was naming warriors who had once been his companions. Indeed, he was himself a leader of warriors, but now when his wits wandered under the scourge of fever, he imagined himself still in the midst of an armed host.

"Ho," he grimaced. "Align the spears! Is thy shield to be carried thus, Rai Singh? Where went the standard? I see it not. Nay, was it in my keeping?" He peered around him, his blood-streaked eyes moving slowly under knitted brows. "The tower of my cousin should be here. We rode far this day—far."

Thus did his mind wander from an imaginary host to his quest for the tower of Awa Khan.

"After dawn," I said to the sick man, "thou wilt look for the abode of thy cousin. But now it is dark, and nothing can be seen."

Indeed, in this bare plain the starlight was dim, and the chill of the ground made a little mist—very different from the clear nights of my *sahra*. I helped the servant to lay him upon the bed. I loosened the turban cloth, but he would not suffer me to draw off the mail shirt. The long hair around his forehead was damp, and he breathed with swift gasps. I counted his heartbeats, and signed to the woman to come near.

"How long has he been thus?"

"Since three days. We wandered from the road, and now I think we are near a city of the Irani. Is it far to Bandar Abbasi, upon the sea? I will take my father there and he shall rest until he is well!"

"If God wills." I thought of the wearied horses and wondered if the sick man would live to reach Bandar Abbasi. "First he must be bled—a very little."

The woman then came close to me, looking into my eyes. She clasped her hands upon her breast and I thought that she was still a child in years.

"To draw much blood—twelve ounces—from thy father," I said, "would exhaust his strength. But to take a little from him will lessen the fever."

Her brown eyes clung to my face, and when the servant had thrown more brush upon the fire, I saw the beauty in the high forehead and the small lips and slender throat under the thin veil.

"Hast thou, O *hakim*, the skill to lay hand upon Sidri Singh, Rawul of Kukri?"

To this I assented, knowing not at all who Sidri Singh might be, but suspecting that his servant would set upon me with the sword, if harm came to the sick man from the bleeding. Indeed, the wild fellow hung about my elbow when I bared the arm of his master and drew the lancet from my girdle.

The flesh of the sick man had shrunk almost upon the bone, and the veins were clearly to be seen. I did not need to press and rub the skin, but pushed the lancet point into a vein. I had neither cup nor scales to measure or weigh the blood, but when it seemed to me that four ounces had been drawn I closed the vein with my finger and bound it. Then I bade the servant give him boiled millet, and to keep the fire high. When this was done Sidri Singh seemed to rest more easily, and ceased his muttering.

Though it was then an hour of the early morning, the maiden and the follower would not sleep. They sat beside Sidri Singh, talking in a tongue I knew not.

Indeed I had never seen such men upon the road. They had the pride of Arabs—yea, and more. Poverty-ridden, they did not hold out an empty hand, but spoke of payment to be given me.

Sidri Singh, bewildered by fever, might have lost his way, still I thought that the maiden and the follower knew the road.

In the morning the daughter of Sidri Singh came to me and spoke of her own will, saying joyfully that her father slept still. I rose and began to build a shelter for him, against the rising of the sun, cutting tamarisk branches and weaving their tips together, when the bearded servant came up from the stream and thrust me aside.

"He will suffer no other to tend the Rawul," she said. "When thou drewest the blood from the arm of my father, he swore an oath that he would cut thee down if the Rawul died."

A strange servant, whose pride was the pride of his master. He covered the tamarisk boughs with ragged and torn saddlecloths and stood at the entrance of the rude tent as if he were inner sentry to the lord of a host.

I looked here and there, but could not see that the wanderers had any food to ease the early morning hunger. So I soaked and heated rice enough for three, and bade the girl take her portion.

"O *hakim*!" she stormed at once. "Have I asked for alms? Have I held out a beggar's bowl?"

"And am I, Daril of the Nejd, so poor a being that guests should scorn me?"

Her brown eyes flashed and she pressed her hands to her cheeks. In the clear level light of sunrise she looked more lovely than by firelight, for her skin was delicate, and her dark hair tumbling from the circlet gleamed freshly.

"It is my misfortune," I said again, "that guests should come when I have no more to offer them than rice and dates."

At this she tossed back the long hair from her shoulders and smiled at me. Nay, though I could see white teeth under the silk veil, and her eyes half closed, smiling.

"Ai-a, my lord, thou art a man of birth and knowledge of what to do rightly." At once, having decided, she sat by me and ate eagerly. "I saw thy fire from far off. Hast thou no fear of thieves?"

"It is our custom to keep up the fire." And I told her how we made camp nightly in the Nejd.

"Aye," she nodded. "So did we once keep open the gate at Kukri." Then she was silent until I had wiped clean the bowl and taken it to the servant, the man she called Subbul.

The deep sleep of Sidri Singh rejoiced her who had borne the dread of sickness and the ache of hunger until now. She made merry in her way, smiling often, and asking many questions. I did not think she was older than fifteen years. Her name was Radha, and her father was a chieftain of the Rajputs. They lived on the border of Rajputana, nine days' ride to the east.

They had lost their dwellings and goods in a war, and Sidri Singh had planned to take her to the stronghold of a cousin, here in the barren plain of Iran, where she would be safe while he rode back and took his part again in this war of Ind. But when the fever had come upon Sidri Singh, she and the servant decided to turn aside to Bandar Abbasi, where the sick man could be put under a roof.

"The gods led us to thy fire, Uncle Daril," she cried again.

And she sent Subbul to see whether the horses had found grazing near the stream. Then she caught up a water jar and went herself to fill it at the stream and offer it to me. Truly, I thought that this was not wonted in Radha, for she carried the jar clumsily, yet offered it with grace, saying:

"Thou hast seen many years, Uncle Daril. Is there none to attend thee?"

"*W'allahi*, for many seasons have I wandered, companied by the *rafik*, the brothers of the road—yea, and the enemies."

"And war?"

Eh, when she smiled again, I did not refrain from boasting, telling her of forays against the Turkomans of the mountains and the Turks who were masters of Bail al-Makkudas.* To these idle tales of an old man she listened courteously, and it seemed to me that she herself had seen greater battles.

"And thy home?" she asked.

"Man's home is where his camel's saddle is," I made response, and she shook her head, saying that for her there was no abode but the battlements of Kukri.

Thus we talked, the man Subbul asleep at last—having eaten—under the tamarisk, and the cool morning wind stirring the white salt under our fingers. Perhaps it was the change from suffering and uncertainty to hope, or perhaps it was no more than the food, but Radha's spirits soared, and the wine of her laughter warmed even the thin veins of an old man.

"What men are these?" she asked suddenly, springing up to stare into the sun that was no more than spear-high over the plain. I turned and looked, shading my eyes.

Some twenty horsemen were cantering over the low ridges, and several of the leaders bore hawks on their wrists. One, in the center of the troop, carried a hooded leopard on the crupper of his saddle.

Even as we watched, a falcon was loosed at a heron that winged slowly over our heads, and Radha clapped her hands. The man Subbul awoke and joined us, and the twain stared at the circling bird of prey and the gaunt, clumsy heron. Farther and farther flew the heron, over the river, seeking refuge in the brush. But the rider with the leopard reined in and shouted suddenly. He had seen us. And in that moment I knew him to be Mirakhon Pasha.

---

*Jerusalem.

With his men he galloped over to us, leaving a single rider to follow and fetch the hawk. Sidri Singh still slept, and how could Radha hide from the eyes of the pasha and his men? She faced them, without alarm, and the milk-brother of the shah did not rein in until he was beside her, when he pulled the dun mare back on her haunches, and looked about the camp.

"What man is that?" he exclaimed, bending to peer into the ragged shelter where the Rajput still slept heavily.

And Subbul, who had posted himself beside Radha, strode forward without salutation.

"Silence!" he cried softly. "This is Sidri Singh, Rawul of Kukri, brother of the lord of Bikanir, defender of Anavalli, whose right is the right of beating drums to the gateway of Bikanir."* Thus he cried out the titles of his master, with the utmost boldness, as if Sidri Singh were the equal of the pasha. "My lord is stricken with fever," he said again. "Bid thy men withdraw, lest they wake him." But the dark eyes of Mirakhon Pasha lingered upon the veiled face of Radha.

"And thou, *hanim*?" he asked.

She bent her head, without coming forward.

"I pray thee, my lord of Iran, accept thy welcome from me, and ask not that Sidri Singh come to thee, for indeed he is ill."

So she spoke in her clear young voice, as if she stood among a thousand retainers, while the man Subbul dressed his shield and held high his head. But Mirakhon Pasha had eyes for no one but Radha. Indeed, as he sat the saddle of the restive mare—a horse among a thousand—he made a fine figure, in soft, green leather riding boots, and flowing *khalat*, bound by a cloth-of-gold girdle. The sword hilt at his hip gleamed with the fires of many precious stones. The leopard at his back shifted uneasily upon its pad, thrusting its head against him and rattling its chain.

It was clear to me then that Mirakhon Pasha, who had left Bandar Abbasi only an hour behind me, had come forth from his camp to hunt in the cool of the morning. He was attended by the captain of the *sipahis*, by young nobles and falconers.

"Eh, *hanim*," he smiled. "Thy welcome pleases me, and, by the breath of Ali, I would not disturb the slumbers of yonder Rajput."

To the nearest officer, he added:

---

*Bikanir, the city of the desert portion of Rajasthan held by a clan often at war with Chitore, the citadel of the reigning prince of Rajputs.

"What is thine opinion, Farash Agha? Is not this better quarry than the heron?"

Farash Agha, the leader of the *sipahis*, reined forward and touched henna-stained fingers to the glittering gold embroidery of his turban.

"Indeed, my pasha! I marvel that thou didst see the beauty of the quarry from such a distance."

"Then dismount and offer her a stirrup."

At once the young officer swung down and led his charger toward Radha. Subbul stepped between them with a muttered question. The men of the pasha's following were smiling and sitting idly in their saddles as if they had watched such happenings before.

"Mirakhon Pasha," explained the *sipahi*, "begs the *hanim* to accept the hospitality of his tents and the protection of his power. Indeed, she hath pleased him rarely."

"*Aye*," exclaimed another. "The journey begins well. A happy omen, this."

"My lord," said Radha gravely, "I go to Bandar Abbasi."

"But not now," responded the pasha. "Such a voice and such eyes would be wasted in Bandar Abbasi."

"Come," Farash Agha urged the Rajput maiden. "My lord is impatient of delay. He hath summoned thee to his tents."

Verily, when first Mirakhon Pasha had seen Radha he had been struck with her beauty. His eyes could judge a face behind the veil, and the slender form of the girl, only half hidden by the wind-whipped linen garments. He had claimed her, as swiftly as a hawk stoops from high in the air and clutches its quarry. Why not? This daughter of Sidri Singh had no following. And the milk-brother of the shah could go far. Mirakhon Pasha was no man to waste words or change his whim. If Radha had been the wife of an emir, with a hundred swords to serve her, he would have carried her off.

"Let not the price to be paid trouble thee," smiled Farash Agha. "My lord is generous. Is Sidri Singh thy father or husband? The price will be greater in that case."

Radha looked from him to the silent pasha, understanding now the meaning of their words. Though the blood did not rise into her forehead, shadows appeared under her eyes, and the hands, held so stiffly at her side, closed and unclosed. What she would have said then, or what Farash Agha would have done, I know not. Because Subbul's gaunt face darkened, and he drew his sword, rushing forward as if he would have struck the pasha.

He did not take three strides before a horse, swerving under knee and rein, shouldered him aside and, before he could gain his balance, Farash Agha was upon him with the scimitar. In one stroke the *sipahi* slashed open the Rajput servant's light leather shield.

Then Farash Agha parried a cut, and beat down the Rajput's guard, and passed his blade through the servant's body, under the ribs. He could use his weapon, the *sipahi*.

"*Shabash!*" cried the pasha. "Well done. By the breath of Ali, we have roused the sleeping lion."

Indeed, the clash of steel had brought Sidri Singh out of his slumber and out of his shelter. He came on hands and knees, because of his weakness, and only by grasping a boulder did he draw himself erect.

"Radha!" he called. "What is this?"

I think the fever had left him, and his brain was clear. But the strong sunlight dazed him and he turned his head slowly like a blind man, trying to understand. When he could see a little, he drew his sword and stepped forward, his beard jutting out, his eyes flaming.

"Do not slay him!" The Rajput girl cried out suddenly, and grasped the sword arm of Farash Agha. "Do not slay!"

But Sidri Singh still advanced, and I saw Mirakhon Pasha reach behind him. A servant thrust a javelin into his hand and he bent forward swiftly in the saddle; his right arm whipped down, and the javelin flashed in the air. Sidri Singh was not five paces distant, and the weapon struck beneath his brow, passing through his eye, the point coming out through his skull.

The force of the blow knocked the old man to the ground, and when I went to his side he was dead. Two others reached him before me—Mirakhon Pasha, who kneed his mare forward to see the result of his cast, and Radha, who knelt beside the body of Sidri Singh. No sound came from the Rajput, but the girl moaned, swaying upon her knees.

The other riders came up to praise the pasha's skill and swiftness. But he glanced at the sun and ordered the hunt to start again, saying that the first of the caravan would be up presently, and would spoil the sport.

Radha, rising to her feet, spoke to him. Her limbs did not tremble and her voice rang out clearly.

"Mirakhon Pasha, hast thou reckoned the price to be paid for this?"

"In gold coin or in jewels or perfumes?" he asked.

"The price will be beyond thy reckoning and it will be paid into the hand of a Rajput, though thy life be long and the day distant."

"Nay," laughed the pasha. "Is the Dark Angel then a Rajput? Sidri Singh was an unbeliever and he will look for me in vain through all the seven hells."

Then Radha covered her face with a fold of her mantle so that these men should not see her grieve. Farash Agha lifted her to the saddle of his charger and took himself the mount of a servant.

As for the pasha, he watched a slave pull the javelin clear from the head of the dead man, and then he spoke to me.

"O Arab, is it thy fate to appear before me in the company of such dogs?"

He was thinking of the other time in Bandar Abbasi, and seemed of two minds what to do with me. In that moment, indeed, my fate was in his hands. And so I answered him boldly.

"My lord, say rather it was my fate thus to encounter thee. For I had bled Sidri Singh, and now thou hast undone my work."

He looked down at me and smiled, brushing his red fingertips across his beard. But he did not give me leave to go.

"A bold tongue hast thou, Arab. We follow the same road. Put thyself under my protection, and ride in my caravan. By the head of Hussein, I swear thou wilt not lack patients!"

In this manner I joined the following of the Master of the Horse, for his request was indeed a command. Perhaps he really had need of a physician to attend his men, or perhaps he had a whim. He had slain Sidri Singh wantonly and had made Radha a captive, and it pleased him to make sport of me.

For many days I did not see Radha. Mirakhon Pasha gave orders that she should travel in a pannier on the same white camel he had bought at the gate of Bandar Abbasi, and that two black slaves should attend her. And word went through the caravan that she was *kourrouk*—forbidden to eye or ear. No one went near the white camel, and, when a halt was made, the black slaves put up a cloth barrier about her tent. So Mirakhon Pasha made it clear that she was his slave woman.

The pasha himself did not go near her at first. It pleased him to act as if he had forgotten her, and besides, many things happened.

The caravan came to the edge of the dry lands—a sunken plain without road or village. Here the south wind sweeps the plain daily with its fiery breath. The wells are deep, the water poor, and the wells lie a long march apart.

Though it was the season of the first rains, the sky remained clear and the watercourses empty of all save rocks and thorns. This meant that we must go from one well to the next before halting. A few men on fast camels could have done this without hurrying, but the pasha's caravan was like a moving village.

He had forty camels bearing the gifts to the court of Ind, and as many more to carry barley and chopped hay for the animals; he had his retinue, and its slaves, and the escort of sevenscore Red Hats, and the Baluchi camelmen. Besides, he had brought along nearly a hundred wild Kurds, lest the shah's cavalry turn upon him. Or perhaps the shah had sent the cavalry so that Mirakhon Pasha would not take the emperor's gifts for himself. I do not know.

The Kurds had their own chieftain, but Mirakhon Pasha paid them, and gave them many opportunities to plunder. Though the Kurds have no love for the Red Hats, and always make camp by themselves in their black goatskin tents, there was no fighting in the caravan. The Kurds feared Mirakhon Pasha more than their own chieftain or the ghost of the Desht-i-Lut—the dry lands.

Truly, he was a man without fear or remorse of any kind. He said we would set out near the hour of sunset and travel through the night, halting at dawn to rest and eat, and pushing on until we came to the next well. And when we set out from the last village, descending into the barren plain, he gave permission to his Kurds to circle back and plunder the village.

W'allahi, with a red sunset behind us and wailing in our ears, we moved down into the dark plain. Before long, even the Kurds ceased quarreling about the horses they had driven off, and the Baluchis muttered and took hold of the charms they wore on their necks.

A new moon shed light over the black wall of the hills beside us, enough light to make men and beasts appear as shadows. Here, in the gateway of the dry lands, there was silence. No wind sifted the sand, no brush crackled as the animals plodded by.

This silence of the dry plain was something I knew well; but the Iranis missed the sounds of the night in fertile land, where water runs, and birds stir in forest growth, or the wheat whispers under wind breath. Because the Kurds were mountain folk they also felt ill at ease.

"It is well known," said one who came to my side, "that this place is barren because a curse was laid upon it."

"It is worse in the day," responded another who had heard. "Then the wind slays, and the doomed have only time to cry, 'I burn,' before they fall lifeless. I have seen."

Nay, there was no end to the tales they told of ghosts that lingered in this accursed region. Finally all the talk ceased and the Baluchis halted their camels. The men crowded closer together, and all listened.

It was only a little sound they had heard, from far off. No more than a high-pitched chant, so faint that we could not hear the words or the voices of the singers. We could see nothing at all.

"It is the *illahi*," called out Mirakhon Pasha from the head of our column.

Truly, it might have been the chanted prayers of pilgrims returning from Meshed or Imam Reza. The pasha raised his voice in a shout—

"O ye of the pilgrimage performed, grant us a blessing!"

Though we all listened intently, the chant did not cease, nor did any man answer. I noticed that none of our riders galloped toward the sound to greet the other caravan.

"God alone knows," muttered the Kurd who had first spoken, "whether they be living or dead."

Mirakhon Pasha ordered the camels into motion and mocked at the fears of the Iranis, asking who had heard a dead man sing in the Desht-i-Lut?

"I will bear witness to one thing," he laughed. "They who lag behind will not live to see the other side of the plain."

He did not cease to make a jest of this fear of the caravan, and before dawn I saw how he dealt with another happening.

It was in the hour of dusk before sunrise when we had halted. The Baluchis had started fires, fed by thornbushes and the sticks they had gathered on the way. Into the pots over these fires the Kurds had thrown slices of mutton—there had been sheep as well as horses in the plundered village—and the warriors were warming themselves at the flames.

At this hour the men are sleepy and the beasts weary. The packs are not taken off, because the well is still distant an hour's ride, or two. The slaves stumbled about in the darkness, and the leaders of the caravan cursed first one and then another.

We heard a shout from one of our sentries, then the roar of a firelock. A horseman galloped through the kneeling camels, shouting for Mirakhon Pasha.

I heard a familiar sound—the drumming of hoofs, coming nearer.

"To horse!" cried the pasha, already in the saddle of the dun mare. A servant passed him his round shield with the silver boss, and he rode over to the Red Hats, calling out orders. Beyond doubt, it was a raid.

Farash Agha did not mount his horse. He summoned a score of his men and ran over to the line of kneeling camels, beyond the firelight. The Kurds acted after their manner, dashing away from the raiders into the shelter of darkness and then halting to see what would happen. Already arrows whipped by me.

All at once there was a great shouting. The raiders cried out loudly, loosing many arrows and circling the camp swiftly, trying to drive off our horses. They were long-limbed men wearing high sheepskin hats—Turkomans who had come down from the hills near at hand, perhaps to attack the pilgrims we had heard, or drawn by our fires.

They did not know the strength of the caravan until Mirakhon Pasha led his riders at a gallop through them, and turned to meet them with spear and sword. In the darkness the spear is better than the bow, and the sword better than all else. Soon I could hear the clash of steel blades.

In this moment of disorder I thought of Radha, and went to seek the white camel. A dozen of the raiders swept into the camp near me and flung themselves from the saddles to begin plundering. They ran toward the laden camels, and Farash Agha ran to head them off with his twenty warriors.

So the Turkomans—who are no great fighters afoot—were soon fleeing here and there, between the fires, among the yelling slaves and the grunting camels. I soon saw the white camel and the carpet shelter that screened Radha, and the two swordsmen who stood guard over her.

The thought came to me that I could steal up behind the watchers and free the Rajput girl, and go with her into the darkness. After that we could certainly manage to find horses running loose.

I crept toward the white camel, with one eye on the fires, lest I be ridden down. Mirakhon Pasha was back in the camp, his horse galloping on the flank of a warrior who was turning desperately this way and that to escape. But the pasha came up swiftly on his left side and struck savagely with his scimitar. The Turkoman flung himself from the saddle to the earth, but his right foot caught in the stirrup, and he was dragged by the galloping pony.

Mirakhon Pasha did not leave him thus. He swerved and came up behind the pony, shifting his sword to his left hand. When he was abreast the raider he bent low and his curved steel blade whistled in the air. It struck heavily, and Mirakhon Pasha jerked it free, recovered, and reined aside, laughing.

The Turkoman lay still, but the pony galloped off into the darkness with his right foot and half the leg still fast in the stirrup. Thus the pasha with one blow severed the limb of his foeman, while both horses were at speed.

This done, he rose in his stirrups to look at the white camel. I lay upon the ground without moving. There was no way of approaching nearer to Radha because the sky was growing light overhead, and the Kurds, who had seen how matters went, were hastening up to take a hand in plundering the bodies of the slain. Only two or three Turkomans were afoot in the camp, snarling like wounded wolves, hemmed in by the disciplined Red Hats. Their comrades had fled and the Iranis were pursuing.

So I crawled back to the fire, where the nobles were gathering around Mirakhon Pasha, praising him greatly. Riders came up with the heads they had cut from the dead raiders, and of these heads—eight or ten or a dozen—the pasha commanded a pyramid to be built.

When he saw me, the pasha shouted for me to bind up the wounds of the Red Hats, of whom nearly a score had slashes and arrow gashes. He watched me for awhile, as if to see truly whether I knew my trade. Then, restless as the chained leopard, he wandered off to look at the prisoners. Only a few had been taken—three or four, and all wounded.

"They will not ride again against a caravan of the shah," said the pasha.

Evidently his men knew what was coming, for they left the steaming pots of mutton to crowd around him, and the Kurds hastened up, grinning. I heard the pounding of mallets driving stakes into the ground, and saw that the tribesmen were being bound to the stakes. I did not watch the torture, but when we rode away I looked back and saw vultures dropping from the sky and sitting in rings around the bodies of the Turkomans who were still moaning.

So we went deeper into the dry lands, and the hills, the lair of the Turkomans, dropped behind us. And Mirakhon Pasha seemed to be in the best of humors. The raid had roused him to display his strength and, like the panther, he was no longer restless when he had struck down his quarry.

"Ho," snarled the bearded Kurd who had first spoken to me. "The kites feed well in the tracks of this Master of the Horse."

This tribesman himself looked much like a carrion bird, with his beak of a nose and his gaunt bare neck, and his little gleaming eyes set beneath thick brows. Verily, his plumage was black, for his one visible garment of black wool stretched down to his bare feet, thrust into up-curving slippers. He had girdled himself over the hips with many girdles of silk and worked leather. On his bare chest he wore a silver *talsmin*, taken from the body of some holy man.

"Is the pasha thy master, Sharm Beg?"

"*Vai*—we follow him."

The eyes of the Kurd dwelt on the striped cloth that covered my head, and it was clear that he wished to roll it and add it to his store of plundered girdles.

"And I, Sharm Beg?" I asked. "What will thy master do with me?"

"*Y'Allah*! Am I a sorcerer, that I should know? Thou art too old to bring any price as a slave."

Doubtless the Kurd thought that I had lived too long. Among his people there were sorcerers and perhaps a few priests, but no physicians. He came closer to look up at my sword, which was better than his own, and to pull moodily at his loose underlip.

"Knowest thou the way across the dry lands?" I asked.

"Aye."

"How many days?"

Sharm Beg withdrew his thoughts reluctantly from the matter of swords, and began to count on his greasy fingers, muttering to himself.

"Seven—eight days to the higher ground and the path that runs east to Ind."

"And if the water be bad in the wells—"

"*Inshallah*—it may rain."

"And if not?"

The Kurd frowned and cursed me.

"Thou art a fool and the son of a dishonored one! Mirakhon Pasha will find his way through—aye, the very ghosts of this place will aid him. Did he not shout to them and demand a blessing?"

Even the Kurds feared Mirakhon Pasha. That night we found the well to be deep—ten lance lengths—and the pasha gave orders to tie the leather water sack to a long rope, and the other end of the rope to the saddle horn of a strong horse. Then he showed his men how to drive two wooden stakes into the ground, so that the rope could travel over the crossed stakes when the horse was led away from the well. The dripping sack was drawn up to the stakes.

This the pasha did to keep his men from lowering too many water skins and wasting the water and quarreling among themselves—because the well was small and filled slowly once it had been emptied. Farash Agha stood over the well, giving water first to the nobles of the pasha's following, then to the officers of the Red Hats, and then to the men, in turn. But not all the skins were filled when we mounted and set out again.

Some of the slaves on poor horses began to lag, but the pasha would not delay the march for them. Indeed, he could not nor would he suffer them to ride the pack camels. At the sixth camp several of the slaves did not appear at all, but Mirakhon Pasha heeded them not.

Eh, we were deep in the bed of the dry lands. And still the sky remained clear and cloudless. On either hand, red ridges of rock lined the way, rising from the gray earth. Beyond the rocks, haze lay like a veil. Above the haze on the left hand stretched the dark purple line of hills.

Under the bright sun the caravan gleamed in many colors, through drifting dust—the crimson turban and silver-adorned harness of the cavalry, the cloth-of-gold and silver of the Irani nobles, the jewel-studded weapons, the pearl-sewn saddles.

But at night, under the half-moon, all were shadows. The men moved in silence, the feet of the camels thumping in a dull cadence like the pulsing of blood through the veins. It was in the seventh night that I heard Radha's song.

God knows why she sang thus. Hidden behind the carpets on the white camel, she could not be seen. Her voice, low and clear, rose and fell. No one knew the words.

At first the rhythm of the song bespoke grieving—but it was not the high ululation of women who mourn. It had in it both sadness and reproach. Then the song changed, and rose more swiftly.

And this, beyond any doubt, was a chant of battle. Aye, it shrilled with the whine of steel and clash of cymbals, and through it ran the mutterings of drums. Every man in the caravan listened, wondering.

"It is not good," grumbled Sharm Beg, who had come up to hear the better. "It hath the sound of sorcery."

But it amused Mirakhon Pasha, who vowed aloud that when he reached the dwellings of men, he would have her sing again. And the Irani nobles made jests concerning caged nightingales.

And that night the Kurds who were leading us lost the trail. We were passing over a part of the plain where the soil was streaked with white salt and strewn with rocks. Mirakhon Pasha halted the caravan while the tribesmen scattered to search for the track. They were gone for the time it takes to cook and eat meat, and they came back by ones and twos, some saying one thing, some another. In truth, the trail was lost.

By now the moon was down in the mist—a red ball hanging over the edge of the plain. For two hours, until the rising of the sun, there would be darkness. And the men, weary of stumbling over the boulders that lay on every hand, gathered in groups and talked angrily.

I made my camel kneel and sat against him to sleep, because there was no good in moving about, and no hope of finding the trail until day. Listening to the hubbub, I heard Farash Agha reproaching Sharm Beg:

"Thou dog! To blunder on the threshold of the hills."

The answer was a snarl and a curse. Farash Agha had all the insolence of the Iranis, and indeed Sharm Beg had not been with the advance.

"The light is bad," muttered the tribesman. "We will do well to wait here."

"The caravan of the shah is not a thief's cavalcade. Find the way."

"Allah! Have I the eyes of a gravebird, to see what is not to be seen?"

Others began to quarrel, and there was a sudden movement of feet and grating of steel.

"I tell thee, only the offspring of three dogs—"

The quarreling ceased as suddenly as it had arisen. A horse trotted up, and I heard the voice of Mirakhon Pasha, in a rage.

"O ye of small wit! O swine of the dungheap! I will stake out the one who strikes with a weapon."

The men drew away in little groups and in a moment I heard Mirakhon Pasha ordering the camelmen to see that their beasts were bound together. I had thought he would order them to wait in their places until dawn. The delay would mean a hard march in the heat of the morrow and, if we were far off the route, hardship and suffering. But to search farther in this darkness was no less than madness.

Still, the pasha ordered the caravan forward, saying that he would lead them. All around me the soldiers mounted and closed in, and the camels roared and squealed in protest. Mirakhon Pasha went off to the left hand, in utter darkness.

For an hour we stumbled over boulders. I could tell by looking at the polar star that Mirakhon Pasha was keeping a fairly straight course, and it seemed to me that the rocks were becoming fewer. The earth looked whiter, though the light was no stronger. I dismounted from the camel and led it, being weary of its lurching and sliding. Most of the *sipahis* were leading their horses, but the Kurds, on their shaggy ponies, seemed to be able to keep the saddle.

I felt dry rushes about my knees, and at the same time the air became chill. Mist, rising around us, hid the stars. It came into my mind to slip to one side and wait until the last of the caravan had passed, and thus ride free of the pasha and his men. Indeed, I could have done so, yet it was written otherwise.

The ground beneath me no longer had the feeling of clay or sand. At times it shook and sank strangely and the camels renewed their complaining. I reached down and brushed my fingers against the ground, putting them to my tongue. The taste was bitter salt.

"*Yah Allah!*" cried a voice in advance of me.

Then a horse screamed and plunged, with a sound as of mud quaking.

"The salt marshes!" Men repeated the words in terror, and the fright of the horses was no less. I remembered then that the merchants in Bandar Abbasi had said that at this end of the Desht-i-Lut there were swamps filled with rushes, where salt water, lying stagnant underground, had moistened the clay until it became as deadly as a quicksand. I sat down where I was, to wait and listen.

Yet Mirakhon Pasha would not halt. Again he gave command to go forward, and Farash Agha with his *sipahis* drove the camelmen along. I was pushed and thrust into the line, and I no longer wished to turn aside, because of the stagnant swamps. It was strange to feel the riders edging in and pressing close to the leaders. Where others had gone, they would be safe.

The air grew damper and more than once I saw white fire glow from the ground. The light seemed at times to be in balls that rested on the ground, and at times to ripple and glide about like snakes. There were

Kurds in back of me—judging by the smell of wet wool and leather—and they groaned aloud when these lights appeared.

They were afraid of devils, and most afraid that they would be separated from their fellows. But the camel train, led by Mirakhon Pasha, seemed to find good footing. The light no longer shone from the ground, and the sky behind us became paler. The mist turned gray, and I made out that we were climbing out of the rushes and the salt swamps, upon firm clay.

Did Mirakhon Pasha see his way in the darkness, or did his good fortune alone lead him in safety past the swamps? I do not know. The Kurds behind me said that the ghosts of the Desht-i-Lut guided him.

On the horizon a broad, red streak glowed and changed to orange and yellow, and soon we could see that we were walking among sandy hillocks. We were so thankful to be out of the swamps that we no longer thought of the road, or of the need of reaching water.

But when the sun struck upon our backs, we mounted into the saddle and looked on all sides. We were drawing nearer the mountains, and presently one of the Kurds cried out—

"Water!"

The horsemen trotted forward and the officers hastened to approach Mirakhon Pasha and praise him. For, below us, there lay a long pool of blue water in a sandy hollow. Before the sun was spear high we had reached the hollow, and the camels were kneeling while the slaves hastened to put up the pasha's tent and the shelters for the officers and Radha. I went down with Sharm Beg to fill my goatskin at the pool, and I saw him kneel suddenly and dip up water in his hand.

He drank a little and spat it out.

The water was bitter salt.

Sharm Beg vowed by God that he would not be the one to bear Mirakhon Pasha the word that the water was bad. He lifted his goatskin, shook it, and glared at me. Then, with one accord, we both walked to the highest knoll behind the camp, to look about us.

Eh, it was a strange place to which we had come. Here and there in the hollows were blue pools like the one we had left. To the east lay the long depression of the swamps, gray and green. All around us glittered and sparkled the white salt crust, save where red rocks reared up and cast black shadows.

The very air tasted of salt, and though the sun still hung low over the plain, heat rose from the earth and beat down from the sky. I remembered, then, that the merchants of Bandar Abbasi had warned me of this sea of salt, this dry sea.

By now the slaves had discovered the secret of the pool, and down below in the camp many figures moved about the striped silk pavilions. Only the white tent of Radha remained unopened, watched over by the blacks. The *sipahis* posted as guard over the forty camel loads that held the emperor's gifts gathered in little groups. Mirakhon Pasha did not appear at all. The heat down in the gully must have been great, and he remained with the nobles in the pavilions.

"They have wine," said one of the Kurds who came up to us.

All the tribesmen climbed the height to escape the thrice-heated air of the hollow. Sharm Beg and their chieftain sat in the shadow of a large rock, and the others curled up near them, to sleep. I drank up the last of the warm and ill-tasting water in my sack, because by evening thirst would grow upon these marauders and, though they would not ask water of me, they would then take whatever remained with me. Nevertheless, I chose to stay with the Kurds rather than join the Iranis, who knew no better than to drink up wine in such a place, and heat their blood to torment.

I could hear the Kurds talking among themselves, and at times, when one spoke in the Irani tongue, I understood that they were weighing the worth of the treasure in the forty camel loads. They knew that Mirakhon Pasha was lost in the dry lands.

"The camels will go well enough for two days," observed Sharm Beg, "but the horses are good for little more."

At such a time, when the road is lost and the men are restless and uncertain, each follower begins to think what he himself may have to do. And the thoughts of all the Kurds were upon the shah's treasure. Some said they knew beyond doubt that the camel loads held many pieces of gold-inlaid mail, and rolls of silk of Cathay, sewn with pearls and sapphires. Others vowed they had seen solid rock turquoise among the gifts, and weapons of Damascus work.

"The jackals looked up at the eagle's nest!"

Sharm Beg mocked the speakers, meaning that they hungered for what they could not seize. Loot is ever in the thoughts of the Kurds. They looked like vultures, sitting thus on their haunches, staring down at the weary men and the gaunt horses in the pasha's camp. But greater than their desire for loot was their fear of Mirakhon Pasha.

I wondered what I would do in the place of this lord of Iran. The horses could not be used before sunset. If water and grazing were not found the next day, they would be at the end of their strength.

To save all his men the pasha must leave his loads—all his loads—here by the pool, and mount his people on the camels. And which way would he go?

It seemed to me that the caravan route from which we had wandered lay back of us, beyond the salt marshes, to the east. So thought the Kurds. Could he lead the camels back, across that treacherous ground, in the darkness? The well might be far.

I slept, and did not rouse until the sun was near the hills in the west. The Kurds were muttering again, and below me resounded a tumult of flutes and kettledrums. It came from the pavilions of the Iranis, and I wondered if madness had come upon the followers of the pasha, until I remembered the buffoons and minstrels.

Eh, the wind made itself felt at last—the south wind that is like the breath of Jehannum, burning the skin and torturing the eyes. It swept among the tents, billowing the pavilions and raising a haze of dust. And the flutes and pipes made a mad kind of music for this dance of the wind.

"Look!" cried Sharm Beg, thrusting his foot into my ribs.

I rose, gripping my sword, but did not draw it. Among fifty foemen, what avails it to draw a weapon? Sharm Beg had reason in a later day to remember that he put his foot upon me. He was looking up at the sky, and I saw that heavy cloud banks had hidden the line of the western hills—clouds that moved up from the south, and soon hid the red ball of the sun.

The sky darkened and the Kurds hurried down to the camp to saddle their horses. They knew as I did that the heat and the scorching wind and the blackness meant the coming of rain.

The pavilions were being taken down, and the Baluchis struggled with the camels' loads, while the kettle drums whirred and the pipes shrieked. Surely the wine was in the blood of some of those Iranis.

Farash Agha stood at the stirrup of Mirakhon Pasha, who waited until the *sipahis* were in the saddle, and the camels roped up. He waited for no more, but gathered up his reins and trotted off. Nay, he did not turn back to seek the trail. He circled the pool and led the way toward the distant hills.

In a moment I understood why he had done this. The rain that was coming might not reach this part of the plain. But the storm would surely break down the slopes of the mountains, and there on firmer ground we would find the watercourses filled, or at least enough water in the hollows to keep us alive. It might be the next day before we reached it, and the wounded and the badly mounted slaves must needs taste what was in store for them, yet the caravan and the warriors would be out of the dry lands.

Thus did the pasha, being guided by no devils. Sharm Beg swore that he must have a *talsmin* on his breast, that such luck should follow him; the *sipahis* said in whispers that he had summoned up the storm by that mad music. But I have often thought that the invisible hand upon the pasha's rein led him toward those hills, and to that which he found there.

What need to tell of long hours of uncertainty? Upon the afternoon of the next day we found water. We had climbed into the foothills, where creepers grew over giant rocks and a scum of sage covered the earth. The storm never reached us, but the clouds covered the mountains ahead of us, and muddy water flowed down the gully that we ascended.

Now the wind whistled and roared over us and chilled our veins. The air grew colder. We gave the horses a little water and went on, having relieved our thirst. In a single day the aspect of the land had changed. The dry lands lay far below us, like a great gray sea. Before sunset we climbed out upon a high plateau, where the earth was damp and the brushwood and tamarisk thick.

Aye, more than that. We soon saw pomegranate and slender apricot trees ranged in rows and cattle grazing on the slope above us.

"By ——," cried Sharm Beg. "There is a village."

It was only a little village—twoscore wicker huts, a granary, and cattle sheds. It lay under the sheer wall of a cliff, by a stream that rushed and roared down a depression in the cliff, over a series of little falls. But it was a village of hill men, and as pleasant in our eyes as a green oasis. Nay, it had a citadel and a master, as we soon saw.

Above the huts and the tilled land rose a mass of rock and rubble from the cliff, and on the summit of this outcropping a wall had been built. Within the wall stood a white building and from it reared a tower, almost touching—so it seemed—the dark granite of the cliff.

"We have never seen this place before," said the Kurds. "And its name we know not."

The rain had washed the dust from the air. It was then the hour of sun-sinking, and the sky above the hills shone with a fierce and ruddy light, so that we could see everything clearly—the spray rising from the waterfall, the white walls of the castle and the dozen horsemen who picked their way down the ramp of rock and cantered toward us.

Mirakhon Pasha with his officers and twenty *sipahis* moved to the head of our column and there halted, while every eye fastened upon the leader of the oncoming riders. His black charger moved with the grace of a racing breed, clean and slender of limb, well-groomed of coat.

The master of the black horse did not rein in when his followers halted, but cantered within spear's length of Mirakhon Pasha, whom he singled out instantly. Nor did he dismount to address the lord of Iran.

"O ye wayfarers," he cried. "What caravan is this?"

Farash Agha reined forward a little. "This is the caravan bearing the shah's gifts to Ind, under command of Mirakhon Pasha of Isfahan."

"The lord ambassador shall be my guest!"

The stranger instantly saluted Mirakhon Pasha, but with no bending of the head. He touched the hilt of his sword that he wore girdled high, and raised his right arm. I saw then that he was no more than a youth, perhaps the son of the master of the castle, perhaps the leader of the men-at-arms.

He sat at ease, in the plain, worn saddle of the big black. Yea, he carried himself well—a rare horseman, slight of limb and erect. His dark eyes gleamed with insolence or laughter or high spirits. Unlike the Iranis he wore only a single close-wrapped tunic of white brocade and a small turban with a loose end falling upon his right shoulder. This head-cloth was bound in a strange way, by a slender fillet of crimson and gold.

"What place is this?" demanded Farash Agha, thrusting himself forward again.

Said I not the stranger could sit a horse? Evidently he did not choose to be addressed only by the officer, for his knees tightened and the black charger tossed his head and neighed, then reared suddenly with pawing hoofs. Farash Agha drew back swiftly from those hoofs, and when the youth of the castle had brought down his horse nothing was between him and the pasha.

"Karadak," he responded good-humoredly, "the tower is Awa Bahadur Khan's.

"And thou?" demanded the Pasha.

"Thy host."

At these words something stirred in my memory. I looked over my shoulder at the salt plain, now tinted by the sunset; I looked up into the shadow of the cliff at the single tower and the lofty summits of the range behind it, and I recalled the words of the dead Sidri Singh. Here was the tower above the dry sea.

Mirakhon Pasha had come out of the desert, following no road, to the tower of Awa Khan, the Rajput, the kinsman of Radha.

"And thou art my guest," laughed the youth in the saddle of the black charger.

There is a time for speech, and a time for silence and thought. That first evening in Karadak I kept close to the young lord of the castle, saying nothing at all. I never doubted that this was the place Sidri Singh and Radha had been seeking when the old warrior fell ill, and the girl turned aside to take refuge in Bandar Abbasi.

These were surely Rajputs. The young lord showed us the armory of the castle with its gleaming *tulwars* ranged on the walls, its shields of buffalo hide, its horn bows in their leather cases, and the stocks of reed and wooden arrows, with many old axes.

He himself carried a *khanda*, or curving blade, double-edged. He drew it at the pasha's request, and showed it, for the Master of the Horse had a keen eye for weapons. But in this hour Mirakhon Pasha thought only of satisfying his hunger.

The caravan animals and most of the *sipahis* and all the Kurds he had left to make camp beside the village, at the stream that descended from the waterfall. Into the castle he had brought his officers and intimates and servants with a few Red Hats. Twenty and four in all, as I counted.

Radha, likewise, he brought. She was led from the camel by the black slaves, who cast over her head a heavy shawl.

Hearing that this was the woman of the pasha, the men of the castle went apart when she passed through the courtyard, and the young khan turned away his eyes courteously. Was she not forbidden to the eyes of strangers?

Though I strained my ears as she entered the gate and ascended the stairs I heard neither spoken word nor outcry. Once in her chamber upon the upper floor, guards were placed at the door, and from that moment no man of the castle could approach the door.

More rigid than the law of hospitality is the sanctity of the women of a guest. Save for the servants of Karadak, I did not think that any man would go up to the floor above us. Unless—

How was I to judge what would happen? Radha did not yet know where she was. The Rajputs had not so much as glanced at her. And as for the pasha, he did not know that Awa Khan was the kinsman of his captive.

Indeed, he thought only of enjoyment after his long ride. He announced, through Farash Agha, that he would be pleased to have the evening meal within an hour. The Rajput lord gave command that this should be done, and the servants hastened to and from the kitchen house, preparing freshly slain fowls and stirring up the fires.

In a little more than the appointed time, the pasha was seated beside the master of Karadak in the hall of the castle with the Rajputs and guests ranged about the cloth on all sides—I sitting among the minstrels and the Red Hats and warriors of the garrison, in a place apart.

Truly, Awa Khan stinted not of his hospitality.

And the pasha plunged his fingers without ceasing into bowls of rice seasoned with saffron, plucked up whole roast pigeons, sweetened grapes and jellies. Then it entered his head to call for wine, and the young Rajput bade the servants bring honey-mead from the cellar. Farash Agha and his officers soon drank this and shouted for more.

"After the journey," grunted the pasha, "we should feast well. Come, we are not priests. What are these?"

He pointed at two great kettle-drums finished in black wood and finely worked brass. They stood on a shelf midway down the hall—a strange place for *nakaras*, and indeed, these seemed too large to be carried on the saddle.

"*Elchi-gi*," responded an elder Rajput, scarred from brow to lip, "My lord ambassador, those were the gift of the Raja of Bikanir to my master, who, with his descendants for all time, hath the right of beating his drums when he approaches the gates of Bikanir."

The pasha, his broad shoulders gleaming green satin, the candlelight winking among the jewels of his turban crest, glanced at his youthful host, who sat silent.

"Eh, thou hast honor, though thy years be few."

"I?" The slender warrior started, and smiled. "Nay, not I."

"He also, my lord," corrected the old Rajput called Byram by his companions. "He stood before Sidri Singh in the pass of Anavalli when the dead lay thick, and the clans of Bikanir advanced against the red banner of Chitore.

"That sword—"

"Peace, Byram Khan," cried the master of Karadak. "The talk was of the drums."

If the pasha remembered the name of Sidri Singh, he gave no sign. "Aye, the *nakara*. Let my minstrels sound them."

"They are the *nakaras* of Karadak," the old Rajput retainer uttered swift protest, "only to be beaten when Awa Khan musters his men, or approaches the throne."

"Nay," laughed the pasha. "I would hear them."

The Rajputs exchanged glances and the young lord did not speak for a long moment.

"If it pleases thee," he said gravely, "my guest."

How was the pasha to know that these warriors out of Ind counted such matters as dearer than food, or life itself? He did not know that their ancestors had earned honors of a strange kind—a privilege or name bestowed for fierce valor in a bloodied field. Nay, they weighed each word as if it held honor or disgrace. Tradition ruled them, who counted their forebears back to unknown gods, and gave the title of Raj only to the utmost bravery. I did not know, until a later year. The pasha was their guest, and if he had asked even their weapons, they would have yielded to his whim.

So the musicians of Mirakhon Pasha made a tumult of reverberations out of the drums, and the mountebanks beside me sang, while the flutes whined and the pasha began to be amused. One of the Iranis rose and danced, and Farash Agha began to argue with Byram Khan concerning weapons.

"For the mounted man," he maintained, "the lance is best. *Vai*—the arrow flies wide of its mark and leaves a horseman open to a blow."

"Against the lance," said Byram Khan stoutly, "the sword will prevail, for the sword can ward as well as strike."

"Parry a lance?" Farash Agha laughed loud. "That is idle talk."

Byram Khan lifted his head and pulled at his gray mustache.

"Spears serve well enough to strike down boars or scatter camp followers."

Now Farash Agha and his *sipahis* all carried the tufted lances, while the men of Karadak had come forth to meet us, armed with shield and sword and bow. And the pasha frowned, ill-pleased.

"By the breath of Ali," he asked impatiently, "where is the man who will venture against a lance—with a sword alone?"

"Here," growled the one called Byram Khan, nodding at his master. "Without a shield, he has guarded himself against a spear and a galloping horse—aye, until the rider tired. Well do I know, for I was the rider."

"I speak not of blunted spears, nor the pastime of boys."

"Nor do I"

Eh, the elder Rajput spoke like an Arab of my folk—openly, fearlessly. Little was the lord of the Iranis accustomed to such words, he searching for guile or a veiled threat. For that is the way of the Irani speech, to cover guile with praise, and insult with courtesy. His broad chin thrust out and his dark eyes swept the faces that turned to him.

Then did Fazl Ali, one of his courtiers, mistake the meaning of his glance, and rise, hand on sword hilt.

"O ye men of Karadak, could ye have seen the weapon play of that night a week ago, when our lord, favored of Allah and ever-victorious, rode forth into the ranks of his foemen, spreading about him a carpet of the slain, ye would know as we know that in all Iran and Ind no man can cope with him, with lance or sword or javelin."

Thus he boasted and Byram's head lifted suddenly as he scented a challenge; but the young khan spoke before him.

"The greater honor, then, to Karadak, in the arrival of such a guest as the lord ambassador."

Fazl Ali seemed disappointed in this mild response. He fingered his close-clipped beard and looked insolently about the hall.

"By the eyes of ——, are there no men in Karadak? I see only prating grandfathers and senseless boys."

He meant to amuse the pasha by baiting the Rajputs, dealing with them as he was accustomed to do with the tribesmen and merchants of Iran. Yet it was true that we had seen in this castle many elders and youths—men like Byram Khan scarred and stiff-jointed, and past the prime of life. Yea, and youths armed with the light and almost straight blade that is half dagger, half sword.

And here was a strange thing. They were no more than the eleven that had come down to greet us, with four or five cup-bearers and servants. The village below had been peopled with no more than a score of peasants, and many women.

Yet the castle of Karadak could shelter easily the half of a hundred, and the stables in the courtyard were ample for a hundred steeds. At the time of our entrance I wondered if other men were holding themselves beyond sight. But there were no other warriors this side the dry lands. And Mirakhon Pasha, always watchful against unseen enemies, had brought with him into the castle two for every Rajput.

Yea, and more. Two negro swordsmen guarded Radha in her chamber above us and a *sipahi* lancer loitered at the gate within hail of the camp, with its cavalry and Kurds.

At first, when I had heard the name of Awa Khan and seen the tower, I had hope of deliverance for the girl Radha and myself. Now I saw no hope—nay, I thought of stealing away when the pasha had finished making sport of the people of the castle. After the moon had set I could lift my camel from the line under the noses of the *sipahis*.

"True," laughed the young lord of Karadak. "Byram Khan is a grand-father many times, and I a fledgling."

He chose to ignore the taunt of Fazl Ali, but Farash Agha, sensing the mood of the pasha, hastened to add his word.

"Knowest not, little khan, that it is the custom to entertain Mirakhon Pasha with music. Where are thy minstrels?"

"Indeed, O my guest," growled Byram Khan. "We have no court minstrels. Yet Muhammad Dost and Kasim Khan are skilled after their fashion."

Two of the Rajput retainers came forward with strange instruments, slender horns of sandalwood and a thing of ebony and strings that sighed and whimpered under the touch of a bow. Eh, the note of the horns in the hands of Muhammad Dost bespoke sadness and grieving. This was no melody of feasting or the wooing of a maiden. It was the mourning of ex-iles, the sorrow of those oppressed by fate—yea, the slow cadence of rid-ers at a footpace.

Mirakhon Pasha threw himself back on his cushions, frowning. And I, also, remembered the song, the same that Radha the captive sang that night in the desert.

Perhaps it was the favorite melody of the Rajputs. I do not know. But presently a stir went through the listeners, and the musicians faltered on a note. Above our heads as it seemed, we heard the elfin echo of a distant voice. A woman's clear voice chiming in with the instruments.

Farash Agha had asked heedlessly for the musicians, and they had played of all things this song of the girl Radha. Had the *sipahi* held his peace, matters would have ended otherwise and that dawn of terror—but it was written thus.

The horns and the wailing strings began the second part of the song—yea, the onset of battle. And a shiver went through the Rajputs as I have seen Arabs quiver when they look to their swords at the shaking of the standard.* Clearer now the voice of Radha, singing in her chamber above, came to our ears. And the lord of Karadak sprang to his feet, silencing the musicians with a gesture.

Unseen, Radha carried on the song to its end, and the Rajput cried out suddenly.

"What voice is that?"

Reclining against his cushions, watching him with amused eyes, the pasha made answer.

"By Allah, that is the Rajputni, my bride." And he smiled at his host, stroking his chin with henna-stained fingers. "This is the night when she will be my bride, indeed."

The officers of the pasha whispered among themselves, taking pleasure in the amazement of the youth who had dared to act before them as the equal of their lord. They relished the jest, knowing that the khan of Karadak would not be suffered to question or approach the woman of the pasha. Was she not *kourrouk*—forbidden to the eye and the ear?

I wondered if the khan would ask her name, and whether the pasha would lie or not in answer. But he asked a different thing.

"Is she a hostage to the shah?"

The pasha smiled.

"Nay, she is mine given to my hands by her father."

A single glance went from man to man of the retainers of Karadak. They sat without moving, and their khan said no more. He signed for the musicians to play something else and stepped back into the shadows behind the stands of candles. I saw that his face had become white as the brocade tunic that covered his slender body. Farash Agha laughed and reached for his cup.

In the stir and noise that followed, I rose and slipped from my corner of the hall. For the moment the *sipahis* had forgotten me, and I meant to see whether I could go unseen from the courtyard before they thought of me again. Twice before this I had meant to leave their caravan, and other happenings had prevented. Now I vowed that I would escape from Mirakhon Pasha. As for Radha, God alone could aid her. If the other Rajputs fought for her, it would put them in their shrouds.

---

*The shaking of the standard—a signal once used by the Arab clans to go forward and begin to battle.

So I thought. But who can choose the path he will follow? I passed through the dark chamber leading to the courtyard, through the open gate of the building.

Clear moonlight filled the courtyard, beyond the shadow of the castle. I could see the *sipahi*, leaning on his spear by the outer gate, and—the pasha had ordered it left open—beyond it the flat roofs of the village, the dark water of the stream and the tents of the caravan.

Then steel fingers gripped my shoulder, and a voice whispered—

"O *hakim*, dost thou hear—and understand?"

The words were in the Irani tongue, but the speaker was the khan of Karadak.

"I hear."

"Thou art the prisoner of the pasha?"

"Yea."

Though I felt no touch of steel and saw nothing, I did not move or draw away, for the voice of the youth was like the whisper of a sword drawn from sheath.

"Who is the Rajputni maiden?"

"Radha, the daughter of Sidri Singh."

I had expected an exclamation or a curse, but the man behind me kept silence as if puzzled.

"Sidri Singh was at Kukri with all his followers—aye, he was in the field of war. How could his daughter be here without him?"

"They sought refuge in Karadak. *Inshallah*, they wandered to my camp across the dry lands."

"The swan does not mate with the vulture. The sun might alter its course, or the stars die out, but Sidri Singh would never give child of his to yonder swine. That pasha lied, but thou, O *hakim*, will tell me the true story and swiftly."

In that instant I began to respect the young Rajput. And I dared ask a question.

"Hast thou other men nearby?"

"Nay. I bade thee tell me of Radha."

"Then think twice—aye, and thrice, before giving way to anger, my lord," I warned him. "Nay, hearken to an old man, who has seen much slaying, and the death of the weak. These Iranis are wolves, and they will gut the castle and slash the blood hissing from thy people if thou oppose them."

"I will be judge of that. Speak."

So, having thought for a moment, I told him in brief words of the death of Sidri Singh and the man Subbul, and the carrying off of Radha. After all, this youth was her cousin, and it had been ordained that Mirakhon Pasha should come to this place.

My blood is old and thin. Yet in that moment it ran swift and warm, so that the scars of wounds in arm and breast and thigh—yea, I have known the tearing thrust of steel blade and the fiery smart of arrows—burned beneath the skin. I knew that swords would be bared in Karadak that night. How? How does the buffalo scent the water that lies in a gully beyond sight?

I did not hear the young Rajput leave my side. He did not go far, because I heard him whispering to a servant. Then, in a moment, my ears caught the heavier tread of an older man. Byram Khan growled words I did not understand. He departed, and once more the khan gave an order to the servant, who moved out into the moonlight of the courtyard.

"Art thou bound to serve the pasha?" So said the Rajput chieftain, standing close to me in the darkness.

"Nay."

"Good! Then go, old wanderer, from this gate and save thyself harm."

Now a moment before, I had desired nothing more than this. But in this moment curiosity and something more held me to my place. *Wallahi*—when did the men of the Nejd slink away like jackals from peril?

"I go in my own time," I said.

"Ho," he laughed under his breath. "The gray wolf smells out booty. An Arab will find loot."

"On my head be my deeds. Nay, I shared the bread and salt with Radha and Sidri Singh. I will watch the happenings of this night."

He seemed to muse awhile.

"By thy word, Arab, this pasha hath forfeited the immunity of a guest. Within the hour we shall know all the truth. And then—" He turned toward me swiftly. "Swear! Swear, thou, to seal thy lips with silence and to lift no weapon against man of mine this night."

"I swear, by the stone of Mecca!"

Indeed, I was ready to make this covenant. More and more my heart inclined toward the youth. He made decisions quickly, and I had not yet seen the man who dared oppose Mirakhon Pasha. This Rajput seemed utterly reckless. Could he plan wisely and hide his plans? I made test of him.

"Wilt accuse the pasha of an evil deed?"

"I?" Again he laughed, as if delight grew within him. "Another will do so."

"It would be better to fall upon him with thy followers."

"Is a hawk to be taken sleeping?"

While I pondered this, he turned from me suddenly and went toward the hall. I heard horses moving out from the stable, and saw they were two—the young Rajput's black charger and the dun mare of the pasha. A servant—the same who had spoken with my companion—led them, and the *sipahi* at the courtyard gate was full of angry questions, asking why in the name the pasha's horse had been saddled. Doubtless the khan had waited until he heard the horses before leaving my side.

Standing thus in the entrance hall between the feasters and the courtyard, I wondered what plan the Rajput had formed. The stair leading to Radha's chamber was behind me in the darkness, and it came into my mind that the young lord planned to go up with Byram Khan and strike suddenly upon the two negroes, slaying them and carrying off the maiden. So I would have done, in other years—had the girl been beautiful.

But the Iranis would be out of the hall at the first sound of struggle above them. Also, the khan would leave the greater part of his men to be slain. Still, he had saddled two horses—the best of the horses!

I thought that I, in his case, would fall sword in hand upon the feasters in the hall, trusting to surprise and swiftness to avail against numbers. Then I knew that this, also, was vain. How could the Rajputs, scattered among their guests, be warned of the plan? And what would prevent the warriors swarming up from the camp when they heard the tumult through the open gates of the castle? And, in the end, what of Radha, in the hands of the black slaves? I could think of no plan.

All this passed through my mind in the moment when the young khan walked to the heavy curtains of the banquet hall. With a sweep of his arms, he held them wide.

"Ho, where is the man who boasts of his lance?" he cried.

I could see the Iranis sit upright in astonishment. A gust of warm air, heavy with musk and mastic, swept past me. Mirakhon Pasha held a handful of grapes motionless under his lips.

"The sky is clear and the moon is high," said the young chieftain, smiling. "I have my horse saddled. Nay, we are weary of talk, and I would warm my blood before sleeping. Which is the best lancer among ye?"

By now the pasha's officers had found their voices.

"I!" cried Fazl Ali, springing up.

"By the ninety and nine holy names!" Farash Agha swore. "Dost name me boaster?"

"Art thou the one?" The young lord of Karadak spoke with disdain, scarcely veiled. "Come, my lord ambassador, wilt thou be judge of the joust?"

"What is this?" Mirakhon Pasha frowned.

"The play of Karadak, my lord. We have little skill at play of words or dancing, but it is our custom to mount and ride forth on such clear nights to exercise in arms. Yet thou art weary from the road. So this night we shall run a few courses in the courtyard."

The pasha noticed the change in the youth, the eagerness that he could not hide in his voice. It was clear to him, however, that the other Rajputs took such sport as a matter of course. They rose, making way for their guests. Then the broad face of the pasha grew dark, as I had seen it at Bandar Abbasi, and in the moment that Sidri Singh died. Like a wary boar, peering through the thicket, he scented the approach of something strange.

"O lord of my life," cried Farash Agha, thrusting Fazl Ali aside and salaaming low to his master. "Have I thy leave to clip the ears of this cub?"

"Look to thine own nose," cried one of the Rajputs.

Farash Agha glared about him, hand on sword-hilt. For the slicing of a nose there is only one reason, among the Iranis. Then, to mend his pride, he turned to the khan who had challenged him.

"I do not play with blunted lance points."

"Nor is there need, O Agha. Choose thou a lance, and I shall take the sword. If thou touch my garments, or draw blood, the victory is thine. If I parry the onset, taking no harm, I am winner of the joust."

The Iranis exchanged glances, being greatly amazed. They were in no mood to pass by a challenge, and even the pasha saw some rare sport before him. Warriors, minstrels, and nobles passed from the hall, jostling and talking, some bearing with them the great silver candelabra, and the Rajputs followed. Each man of Karadak paused where their young khan stood, and with each he spoke in his own speech. Then he hastened to the side of the pasha.

"Will it please thee to mount, my lord?"

Eh, he had thought to saddle the ambassador's mare, so that the pasha would not be constrained to remain afoot while others sat in the saddle. And he had also another reason that I suspected not at all.

The pasha mounted, Fazl Ali holding the stirrup. Once in the saddle, he took command of matters, placing the attendants with the candles close to him and summoning the warrior who held his javelins. The Iranis ranged themselves about him, some sitting, others walking about, near the wall of the castle, at one side of the door. There was laughter and crying of wagers—for, in a joust of lance against sword and shield, wounds are freely given.

The pasha began to be restless and eager as he watched the master of Karadak mount the black charger and rein up and down the enclosure, displaying the paces of his steed. Even the Iranis murmured approval, for the khan sat as one rarely skilled, and the clean-limbed charger sidled and trotted and wheeled at touch of knee and bridle.

Soon the leader of the *sipahis* appeared on a Turkoman horse, trotting in and out among the spectators, eyeing the youth of Karadak. For the khan had no shield. Nor did he wear a cloak. His tight-fitting white tunic made a good mark in the elusive light, mingled of the glow from the sky and the flickering gleam of the candles.

The pasha looked at his sentry in the open gate, and past him to the tents and dying fires of the caravan. The watchers fell silent, drawing closer to the wall, the Rajputs mingling with the Iranis.

"Begin!" he cried, leaning on the saddle horn.

The two riders cantered to the far ends of the courtyard, some sixty paces apart. Farash Agha raised his lance tip, and the Rajput drew his saber, saluting. Then the brown horse of the Irani trotted forward, and cantered, while the black charger, tight-reined, trotted, half rearing.

In an instant they were together, hoofs ringing on the hard clay of the enclosure. And those near me shouted loud. Farash Agha, gripping his lance in his right hand, pressing the shaft against his forearm, had thrust savagely at the young khan's girdle. Truly, he did not mean to play with blunt weapons!

The khan's sword flashed out, clinking against the wood of the lance, and the long shining point of the spear was turned aside, sweeping past him harmlessly.

"*Shabash!*" growled Fazl Ali. "Well done."

But the pasha and most of the Iranis looked disappointed. They hoped to see the Rajput cast, bleeding, from the saddle.

Again the riders turned and faced each other and Farash Agha spurred forward with a tight rein. This time his point wavered and thrust swiftly at the throat of the youth. Eh, the khan, leaning forward, parried upward. Again, the lance point slid off his blade without harm.

The Rajputs watched him with pride, breathing quickly. And when the riders turned for the third course, the pasha and his Iranis thought of nothing but the rearing horses, the gleaming weapons. This time Farash Agha tried another trick.

Leaning far forward, he gripped the spear shaft under his armpit and sat tight in the saddle, trusting by weight and strength to bear through the parrying stroke of the sword.

The young khan saw and acted upon the instant. The black charger darted forward, the rider slipped to the far side of the saddle. The blade of the heavy *khanda*, held high, smashed down upon the spear, driving the lance point sharply down into the earth.

Before Farash Agha could recover, the point had caught and held. Perforce he loosed his hold on the spear which remained, upright and quivering, in the center of the courtyard. *W'allahi*, it happened as I have said—the lancer was disarmed.

And before anyone could cry out, the master of Karadak wheeled his charger around to face the pasha.

"The play is ended," he cried.

He had seen from the corner of his eye what we now saw. From the door of the castle, out of the darkened entrance, stepped Radha.

Clearly was she to be seen, by the candles. Her hair, unbound, fell thick upon her shoulders, and her veil had vanished. Swaying, she stood in the half light, a dagger gripped tight against her slender breast.

For the time it takes to draw and loose a breath there was silence, while her eyes, shadowed by grieving, sought swiftly among the men. Her lips parted and she raised her head. Against the dark entrance she looked like a child out of *peristan*—an elf of spirit-land. But behind her loomed Byram Khan, his bared sword dripping blood from the channels, and his eyes afire.

"O my kinsmen!" she cried in a clear voice. "Avenge Sidri Singh. I shall live if ye live, or die with ye!"

Her eyes sought the pasha, and Byram Khan strode past her, shouting.

"The proof! To your swords, my children."

Hearing these words I thought that the Rajputs, all eleven of them, had dug their graves. True, the young khan might have ridden past the sentry at the gate. But, penned thus between the sheer cliff behind the castle and the high wall around the courtyard, how could the others flee? Penned in with the pasha and his wolves!

"God is one," I said to myself. "It will be over in a little time."

For the *sipahis* were no merchant-folk or peasantry to be charged and scattered. Full armed, alert and angered, they grasped at sword-hilt and ax-shaft, and Mirakhon Pasha reached back his right hand swiftly. The attendant behind him thrust a javelin into his fingers.

Without an instant's hesitation—without gathering up his reins or stiffening his seat in the saddle—the pasha launched his weapon, his heavy body swinging forward, grunting with the effort. He struck thus, as a panther leaps, with the release of mighty muscles, swift as instinct.

Clear in the candlelight I saw him cast at his mark, the young khan wheeling toward him ten paces distant.

No rider could dodge a javelin so thrown at such a little distance. Indeed, I did not see the shaft fly. But I saw it strike—against the far wall of the courtyard.

Mirakhon Pasha had missed his cast. Perhaps the flickering candles beside him had drawn his eye from the slim white figure wavering in the moonlight; perhaps anger had clouded his sight. I do not know.

But when the javelin shattered itself against the bricks of the wall, the pasha cried out as if in pain. The young Rajput, the two-edged sword swinging at his knee, spurred at him. The pasha also drove home his spurs, wrenching out his scimitar as the dun mare plunged.

The Rajput came in like flame out of darkness, laughing, leaning in toward his foe. The broad body of the pasha stiffened. The swords clashed once.

I saw it—the shining blade of the Rajput beat aside the lighter scimitar and seemed to stroke the pasha's breast in passing.

The pasha rose in his stirrups and cried out twice. Then the dun mare, rearing in frantic excitement, cast him from the saddle and he lay prone on his face, as a heavy sack, cast from a height, remains motionless.

"Guard thy lord!" shouted Farash Agha, who had seen from the center of the courtyard the fall of his master.

"Ho, my Agha!" cried the Rajput chieftain. "Where now is thy lance?"

He had recovered, reined back the black charger scattering dust and gravel, and wheeled toward the officer of the *sipahis*. I did not see their meeting. Steel clanged all about me, and the shouts of the Red Hats mingled with the battle cry of the men of Karadak. The dun mare, riderless, swerved within reach of my hand.

It was no place to remain afoot. Nay, an aged and feeble man would not long have survived in that place of death. I grasped the mare's rein, steadied her, and climbed into the saddle. In other years I would have leaped without touching horn or stirrup. I drew my sword, because in a mad fight such as this within walls, a gray beard is no shield, and every soul must guard himself.

I looked at the leaders. *Wallahi*, they were slashing like fiends—Farash Agha with his brow and cheek laid open, the Rajput scattering blood when he swung his right arm. The horses were turning swiftly on their haunches, and the grinding of the steel blades did not cease. A *sipahi*, his lance poised, stood beside them.

"*Allah!*" shrieked Farash Agha.

The Rajput's two-edged *khanda* passed into his body under the heart— yea, the half of the blade. And that moment, seeing his chance, the Irani warrior on foot thrust his spear into the Rajput's back.

How could I sit, mounted and idle, and watch a boy struck down in this manner? I kneed the mare forward and slashed at the *sipahi*'s neck above the mail. The edge of my scimitar ground against bone and I had to pull to clear it. The *sipahi* fell where he stood. It was not a bad blow.

Farash Agha slid from his saddle, but the young khan kept his seat and called out to me above the tumult.

"I have seen, O Arab. Ask thy reward in another day."

He was able to walk his horse toward the castle door where Radha stood by the candles, her faces bloodless in its cloud of dark hair. But he was too badly hurt to do more than cry encouragement to his men. I glanced about the courtyard. Never had I seen such play of weapons.

The Rajputs, without shield or mail, cast themselves upon their foes with nothing but the sword. Death struck them and laid them low in an instant, or the *sipahis* fell under their feet. The youths and old men of Karadak acted as if reckless of life. Indeed, they had but one thought—to spread swiftly the carpet of the slain before other enemies could come up from the camp.

And they bore themselves with the skill of warriors reared to weapons. By swift swordplay they slashed through the guard of saber and shield, and

leaped forward. And, lo, the fight was now an equal thing. The fury of the
Rajputs matched well the sullen anger of the *sipahis*. But I knew that if the
young hero of Karadak had not overthrown the pasha and Farash Agha in
as many minutes, the Rajputs would have been doomed before now.

Leaderless, the *sipahis* began to think of themselves, to gather in groups.
The sentry, who all this time had remained amazed and motionless, so
sudden had been the onset, instead of running in, began to beat on his
shield and shout in a high voice to the watchers in the camp below.

"*Hai-hai!* Aid, Kasim ad-Din! Ho, Sharm Beg! Aid—give aid!"

Who can tell the happenings of a hand-to-hand affray? Nay, the man
who tells much lies greatly! I saw one of the mountebanks still hugging
his guitar, dancing in fear from the swords; I heard a boy shriek for his father—and a man staggering along the wall, curse the name of God. The
candles had gone out, and a haze of dust rose against the moonlight.

I rode down one warrior, who tried to guard himself with his shield
as if the rush of a horse were the flight of an arrow; I followed another
horseman through the murk, rose in my stirrups to slash at his head, and
saw that it was Byram Khan who had got himself a horse in some fashion known only to God.

A face peered up at me out of darkness, and I thought it was one of the
Irani nobles. He was laughing—

"Ho—aho—ho!" Thus, on his knees, both hands clutched in his girdle, he was laughing, and it sounded strangely.

Two of the pasha's minstrels, with flying mantles, elbowed and jostled to be first out of the gate, though five horsemen abreast could have
passed through without touching stirrup. I thought then that the half-
dozen creatures of the pasha would not stand and fight like the *sipahis*.
Then I could see nothing at all for the dust, and drew rein.

A voice behind me called out—

"Close the gate!"

The two, who hurried forward and swung shut the wide portals of teakwood and iron, were men of Karadak, servants who had taken no part in
the affray. They turned the massive iron key in the lock and lugged the
lance-long bars into place. And the one who had given the order walked
up to see that all had been well done. It was Byram Khan.

The fighting had ended. When the dust settled down I looked about
the courtyard. Three other Rajputs were on their feet, and none beside
the three.

Truly the Rajput swordsmen had spread that night the carpet of the slain.

Nine *sipahis* and Irani nobles were already dead or soon to await their shrouds. Four, slashed and pierced in the bodies and heads, cursed and moaned for water. Four defenders of Karadak lay lifeless, and three little better. All the pasha's mountebanks and the remaining three of his men must have fled through the gate. Well for us that gate had been open! Cornered men will fight with fury.

Indeed, the desperation of the Rajputs, who had been resolved to prevail or perish together, had turned the tide of victory toward them.

Byram Khan peered at me, his eyes clouded and his breath coming in long gasps.

"Ho, Arab!" He gripped my arm. "How many swords will come against us from the camp below?"

I counted over in my mind the number of the caravan folk.

"Two hundred—nay, two hundred and twenty and eight, and perhaps they who escaped from here."

"What manner of men?"

"*Sipahis* and Kurdish cavalry."

Byram Khan looked at his three Rajputs, and at the long stretch of the courtyard wall. He looked at me and said, "God is one!" and walked away. His meaning was that what might happen hereafter would be in the hands of God, not in his.

I dismounted and went to the form of the pasha, thinking that if life remained in him we might hold him as a hostage against attack. Gripping his shoulder I turned him over, with an effort, for he was heavy. His pallid face was smirched with dirt; his lips, drawn back from his teeth, seemed bloodless, and his body below the ribs had been cut through to the backbone. His eyes stared unwinking into the moonlit sky.

Farash Agha I did not look at, knowing well his case; but Fazl Ali lay among the wounded and cursed me.

"The sword prevailed," he grinned. "But ye will never see the dawn."

From him I went to look at the wound of the Rajput chieftain. He sat upon a tiger skin, Radha kneeling and supporting his head. She held a turban cloth tight against his back under the shoulder blade where the lance point had bitten. They were talking low-voiced, for he could do little more than whisper. What they said, I know not, yet she seemed to be sorrowing and he heartening her.

"My lord," I broke in upon them. "Bid thy men carry thee to a couch and I will probe the wound."

"O *hakim*," he responded. "Until the issue is at an end I will not leave the courtyard, and thou art too precious a swordsman to be taken from the wall. Get thee to Byram Khan."

Nevertheless, he called me back and bade me do what I could for the other wounded while we waited, and this I made shift to do while the shadow of the castle crept across the courtyard as the moon sank behind the hills and a throng of warriors came up with torches from the camp.

This might have been the ninth hour of the night. Well for us that the wall was in shadow! Byram Khan ordered his three followers and four servants to move about and rattle shield and arrow case. The pasha's men halted beyond arrow shot and argued among themselves. Kasim ad-Din, the pock-marked chieftain of the Kurds, and Sharm Beg did most of the talking.

First they demanded the surrender of the castle, bidding us throw our arms over the wall.

"Come ye and make proof of our weapons!" responded the old Rajput.

When it was clear to them that the castle would not be yielded, there was more talk among them. Perhaps they suspected Radha of casting a spell upon their dead lord, for the wild Kurds are fearful of such things; or the few who escaped told them lies about our numbers, to justify themselves.

"Is Mirakhon Pasha truly dead?" they asked.

"As Farash Agha is," Byram Khan assured them.

Then they withdrew a little and sat down to consult among themselves. When the torches went out, they began to drift back to their camp. This seemed a trick and we watched until the dawn spread in our faces, revealing the tents and the groups of warriors among them. The villagers, fearful of the battle in the morning, had fled during the night, driving off most of their animals. The Kurds and *sipahis* had other things to think about.

Byram Khan said they would make the attack now when they could see what little was before them. But I began to meditate. The sun was spear high, and smoke rose from the fires of the camp. Nay, that day passed, without so much as an arrow shot against the wall. And I felt assured of what would happen.

The men of the caravan never attacked the castle.

Perhaps the *sipahis* would have done so, to avenge Farash Agha and gut the castle. But there was the treasure in the camel bales—the forty loads of gifts for the emperor of Ind, worth many times the looting of a small hill tower such as this. The *sipahis* did not attack because they were afraid to leave the Kurds in charge of this treasure and very likely afraid that if they were cut up by our weapons, the Kurds would fall upon them.

With such unexpected riches under their hands, and with Mirakhon Pasha gone from them, the Kurds thought of nothing but those bales.

Yea, in the end they all went away together, after supplying themselves with water and grain and meat. They went down to seek the road from which Mirakhon Pasha had led them. I have often wondered what befell thereafter in the desert, and what finally became of the treasure bales.

Those bales never reached the emperor. Yet a little of the treasure did go to Ind. In the next year, by the river road of Lahore, I saw some of it. A wealthy tribesman rode past, his saddlecloth silk of Cathay sewn with pearls, his scimitar blazing with sapphires and silverwork. Behind him came five camels bearing women, hidden from sight by rich carpets. Thus I saw Sharm Beg again.

On the third day I took my leave of the Rajputs, having seen that it was not ordained that the young lord should die. The spear had pierced upward under the shoulder blade and no arteries were severed. Indeed, he had upon his body the scars of five other wounds, each as bad as this. Though I had bidden him keep to his bed for the rest of that moon, I found him outstretched upon a mattress, clad in a fresh white tunic of brocade, his small turban wound with a string of pearls. And four men-servants of Karadak were bearing the mattress and the wounded youth toward the river garden where Radha sat.

"Nay," he smiled at my protest. "Thou hast said it was ordained that I should live. Who would deny his eyes the sight of such beauty in a maiden?"

Indeed, though veiled, Radha's face held the pride and gladness of one released from torment. She rose to greet the hero when his mattress was laid at her feet.

"From my lips, my lord," she said in the Irani speech. "Thou must accept the gratitude of Kukri."

"For a word from thee, I would have passed through the swords of Kukri," he responded.

In another man this would have sounded like boasting, but this youth was full of unexpected happenings. Surely, for cousins, they made much of ceremony. But I did not yet know the ways of the Rajputs. Radha, wrapped in her white garments of mourning, sat quiet in the ferns by the bank of the stream—aye, like a lily rising from the ferns, so straight was she, so slender and fair to behold. The eyes of the young lord took fire.

Thirty years ago, I would not have left Karadak thus—not without measuring my sword against his, and taking the maiden upon my saddle, if I lived. Thirty years!

"Grant me," I asked of him, "thy leave to depart."

"Not without a gift," cried Radha swiftly. "*He* will give thee, O *shaikh*, that which thou desirest in Karadak."

"Nay," I denied. "I have beheld the beauty of Radha of Kukri, and what gift is to be measured against that sight?"

"Well said!" cried the Rajput. "But thou hast lost a camel in this fighting, Daril." He turned and spoke to one of the servants who bowed and made off toward the castle. "Byram Khan will choose for thee a good horse, saddled and equipped." Suddenly he smiled merrily. "Thou art a strange physician, not to claim a reward. But I say thou art a better swordsman than physician, and wilt ever be!"

Thus he gave me leave to go. At the stables I met Byram Khan, mounted, with one follower also in the saddle. Presently a groom let out my mount, and lo—it was the dun mare of the dead pasha!

"Awa Khan hath a generous hand!" I cried.

Byram Khan gathered up his reins and rode forward, musing.

"That is true," he growled, "as I the captain of his swordsmen know well. But this mare is the gift of the guest of Karadak."

I thought of one person and then another.

"The Rajput maiden, then?"

"By her wish, aye, but she had naught to give."

"Then it was surely Awa Khan."

The old warrior shook his head, and let his charger trot through the village street, saying that he had orders to escort me forth upon a trail that led north to the caravan route to Ind.

"Awa Khan is not here," he said, "being in the army of his lord the Raja of Bikanir with seventy men from Karadak. He left me here to keep the castle with nine men."

Then I remembered that the young Rajput, the rider of the black charger—he who had overthrown Mirakhon Pasha—had never spoken his name. I had thought that he was the kinsman of Radha.

"Who is the swordsman?" I asked.

Byram Khan looked at me in surprise.

"Ask in Chitore—aye, or Ind. He is Kurran, a stripling of the royal house of Chitore, son of the ruler of Rajasthan. He is too young to be sagacious, but he can handle a sword."

"Then he is no kinsman of Radha of Kukri?"

The old retainer of Awa Khan passed his fingers through his beard and grunted. "Nay, Chitore and Bikanir have been at war for long years. They are still at war. Once, in the gorge of Anavalli, this youth Kurran and Sidri Singh fought hand to hand."

I thought then of the feuds of my clans in the Nejd. It was clear to me now that Awa Khan and Sidri Singh had been opposed to Kurran's clan in this feud of the Rajputs.

"Yet Kurran was the guest of Karadak," I said.

"Aye, he was riding from the mountains of Iran, with two followers, to join his father's army. He turned aside to rest at Karadak. Was the hospitality of Awa Khan to be denied the noblest blood of Ind? Being Kurran, we served him, and when this pasha came, though a dog-born dog, it was the duty of Kurran to offer hospitality."

W'allahi, they knew the duty of the salt, these Rajputs! Desert men, like the chieftains of my *sahra.* Within the tents, the feud is forgotten.

"Though no kinsman of Radha, this stripling prince drew the sword for her," I mused aloud.

"If he had not done so," Byram Khan said grimly, "the honor of Awa Khan would have been lost indeed. Being the guest of Karadak, Kurran took thought for the honor of Awa Khan." He meditated a moment, easing forward in the saddle. "And Awa Khan will be well satisfied when I tell him what was done, and how."

Thus we parted, he turning back to Karadak, I trotting forward along the mountain trail. I wondered whether Kurran would ride forth on this road with a bride. Byram Khan had not bothered his head about this. Indeed, it was hard to say what that young Kurran would not do. Thirty years—yea, and eight—I had carried such a maiden off in spite of the watching of her clan.

But one thing was certain. When I looked down at the smooth mane and the twitching ears of the fine mare, I thought of Mirakhon Pasha. Surely he had dug his own grave, being blinded by pride and lust.

The Road to Kandahar

It is written: Thy wealth will not save thee, if thy deeds destroy thee.

And I have seen a man who had a great store of gold under his hand, yet he was slain by his own deeds. It was in the year one thousand and twenty and nine,* when I was journeying to the land of Ind—I, Daril, the Arab of the *sahra*, the desert land.

I was then beyond the middle of life and I had sheathed the sword to follow the path of a physician, thirsting to see new lands. I had agreed to pay a camelman of Isfahan ten silver pieces to bring me safely to the frontier of Ind. He was called Sher Jan, and he was a rogue.

Yea, a man of loud oaths and many weapons—three knives of different shapes and a rusty *tulwar*. At times he would draw this sword and flourish it, but I never saw him clean it. In his girdle besides the knives he carried a beard comb and opium and flint and a pouch filled with powder, though he had never owned a musket. Sher Jan, with his forked beard and his deep voice, had the mien of a lion and the heart of a hare. He called me his lord and his friend, and one evening he spoke very boldly, asking if I carried much money.

This was the evening when we climbed out of the plain and entered the foothills where Iran ends and Ind begins. We followed a shallow valley that became narrower as we advanced, until the ridges of red rock loomed above us like walls. Yellow dust hung around the camels in clouds, until the air in this hour of sunset became a golden haze. The baked earth still gave off the heat of the sun, and the river of the gully was no more than brackish pools. By one of these Sher Jan halted, looking about on all sides and sniffing like a dog. Satisfied, he set his helper to work pulling tam-

---

*A.D.

arisk bushes and picking up dead roots, while he loosed the bales from the kneeling camels.

"What place is this?" I asked.

"The Kaizak-davan—the Valley of Thieves." He wiped his long nose with his sleeve and looked at me sidewise. "It is well named. If thou hast much money, O my lord, give it to my keeping for the night."

"Nay," I assured him, "our bargain was that thou shouldst protect my possessions from theft and tribute on the road."

"God knows," he muttered, "I deny it not. Yet consider, O favored one, if thy purse and gear be stolen from thee while I sleep, how am I responsible? While if I have them in charge, I must answer for them."

"Answer for thyself!" I cried at him.

Truly the camel driver had sworn to me by the triple oath that he was the master of a large caravan with many armed followers and that he made the journey from Iran* to Ind several times in the year and had bought immunity from the chieftains who might otherwise plunder caravans along the way. And it turned out that he had no more than eight camels, laden with red leather and honey and sweet oil, and no more than one sorry servant whose only weapon was a cudgel to beat off dogs.

"Upon thy head be it," he said calmly, meaning that if anything happened to me it would be of my doing, not his.

So I spoke no more, and went and sat, to meditate and enjoy the one good hour of these days when the sun was at the rim of the desert below us. In my belt I had no more than forty silver coins, of which I had agreed to pay Sher Jan ten. But I needed little.

I was alone. My horse, a swift-paced dun mare; my sword, a plain Damascus blade with a horn hilt. All other belongings I had given away when I set forth upon my wandering. Yea, wanderers are we, we Arabs of the *sahra*, the desert land.

It is better to be thus free than to be chained; better to ride with few possessions than with many, and far better to journey thus, toward a strange land than to abide in one place, bowed down by goods and debts and increasing cares. In my youth it would have been misery to be thus bare of gear and goods, and apart from the eyes of fair young women and the raids of the clans. Now, though I wore still the sword, I sought peace; men called me *shaikh* and *hakim*—elder and physician.

---

*Persia, then ruled by the great Shah Abbas. Daril and other Arabs called it Iran, but the modern name is substituted hereafter in the narrative. I have left the text as it was originally printed, even though we now refer to Persia as Iran. —HAJ

And yet I was not quite alone. The mare, coming close to my shoulder, stretched down her head, rattling the bit. In my argument with Sher Jan I had forgotten her. I rose, loosed the saddle and lifted it down. I rubbed the slender limbs with a handful of dry grass and freed her from bit and headband, slipping on halter and rope. Then I let her drink at the pool, and gave her a measure of barley and salt. As I was leaving her, she lifted her head and neighed.

In our small caravan we had no other horses. Sher Jan and his follower rode between the camel packs. I looked at Sher Jan and found him heaping more tamarisk upon the pile, already smoking and blazing.

"O one of little wit!" I cried. "If this be truly a place of thieves, why light such a beacon to guide them?"

"In this gully the fire will not be seen," he answered, throwing roots on the fire to show that he cared not for my reproach.

"Nay, look at the smoke."

Down by the pool, hemmed in by ridges of rock, the dusk had deepened, but the sky overhead still glowed, changing from shimmering blue to dull purple. From the heights before us the twisting smoke would be clearly seen against the last of the sunset. Sher Jan squinted up and wiped his eyes with his greasy sleeve.

"True, O *shaikh*," he made response, "but we must eat."

"On thy head be it then."

I went and sat by the fire, while he put water and salt and rice and strips of mutton into the pot. The air had become cold of a sudden, and the wind was chill from the snow far above us. It was then the beginning of winter, and Sher Jan said the snow lay in the passes ahead of us, in these mountains that he cursed, calling them the mountains of the Pathans. Yet he said that the city we would reach the next day was a veritable paradise, a garden spot within the barrens.

This city he swore to be the gateway of the empire of Ind—the end of his road, to which he had made covenant to guide me. And he called it Kandahar, rolling the word upon his tongue as if he loved well the sound of it.

"Verily," he often said, "that is a place good for wine and for profit."

But that evening, although he had set the stew boiling, we ate from a cold pot and at a late hour. Before the last light had left the sky the thieves came.

First my mare neighed again, then I heard hoofs striking upon loose stones. Sher Jan sprang to his feet, but when a dozen riders clattered down into the gully he made no move to draw weapon or to fly. He might have fled, because the horsemen all came along one path and at a hand pace, without attempting to rush us. I thought that one of them had been watching us for some time and that Sher Jan's fire would bring no good.

When the horsemen moved into the firelight I saw they were warriors of a kind strange to me, mounted on scrawny hill ponies. They were armed with light lances, with hair tufts under the points. Over their mail and leather shirts they wore immense gray-wool and sheepskin coats, while their reins were heavy with silver; and their leader sat upon a saddlecloth of embroidered damask.

To Sher Jan he spoke in a language I knew not, and my valiant camel driver with his helper made haste to open up his loads, the leader of the band riding from one bale to the next.

No more than one load of the eight did he order taken—bales of red leather—and divided up into four packs, which his men strapped upon led ponies. Then he of the damask cloth walked his horse over to me and asked a question. When I shook my head, he called out a name.

"Shamil!"

A rider who had kept far from the fire advanced at the summons—a drowsy man, finely clad in a green and white striped *khalat* edged with soft brown fur. He swayed in the saddle, and his eyes, touched up with dark powder, did not open at all. His lips and thin beard were stained bright red, and he acted as if he had been chewing too much opium.

"O brother of the Arabs," he greeted me in a droning voice, "pay down the road tax to this man."

"Who asks it?" I demanded.

His eyelids flickered as if this surprised him.

"I am Shamil, the treasurer of the Hazara band. Who art thou, and whence?"

"Daril of Athir, of the Nejd Arabs," I answered truthfully, "a physician upon the road to the empire of Ind."

"To serve whom?"

"If God wills it, the emperor, the Mogul of Ind." For I had been told that he was the most powerful of rulers, the most fortunate of living men, and I had journeyed from afar to visit his court. "Art thou a servant of the Mogul?"

Shamil laughed, gently.

"Nay, we are kites swooping down from the mountain. Pay us gold!"

I pointed at the shawl that held no more than a headkerchief, my lancet and such things.

"As thou seest"—for the man called Shamil seemed to watch me from under heavy lashes, and when I turned away I felt his eyes upon me—"I am no merchant, nor have I goods with me. What talk is this of gold?"

Then the leader of the band pushed forward, scowling at me and gesturing. He had noticed the dun mare picketed just beyond the firelight.

"We will take the mare," said Shamil, "and require no more of thee, O Arab."

Stepping between them, I laid my hand on my sword hilt. *W'allahi*, a man of peace am I, seeking no quarrel! But to take a man's horse in the barrens, without authority, to set him afoot in such a place was the deed of a dog-born dog. Sher Jan edged nearer, plucking at my sleeve and whispering to me to show no anger.

"Lay hand on the mare," I said to them, "and more than one man will die—thou, Redbeard, the first."

At this he opened one eye a little, and would have drawn back, but I held his rein. The leader of the Hazaras made as if to pull out the heavy battle mace in his belt, and I stepped to the far side of Shamil's horse. Sher Jan began to bellow imploringly, and it seemed to me that my road would end here. Against ten horsemen with lances I would not have lived more than a moment—long enough to dispatch the man called Shamil and perhaps, if God willed it, another. For I could strike swiftly and surely with the curved blade, and it was not my habit to draw a weapon without striking.

Shamil and the chieftain spoke together, and he of the damask saddle-cloth put back his weapon. Strange it was that he should heed the words of the unarmed Shamil. Long afterward I understood why they had no wish to shed blood in this place.

"By God!" cried he of the striped cloak and red beard. "If thou hast silver, O Daril, we will take it instead of the mare."

The horsemen crowded around, hearing our dispute, but not understanding what was said. There was nothing to do but to pull the coin bag from my girdle and toss it to Shamil, who caught it deftly enough, for all his sleepy eyes. The Hazara chieftain came over to watch him count the silver dirhams, grumbling because they were so few. But Shamil spoke in his ear, and he seemed satisfied, for he raised his arm, shouting to his men—

"Off!"

They trotted out of the firelight, shouting back mockingly at us until the cliffs overhead gave out the echoes—*Ya-hough! Ya-hou-ugh!* Sher Jan, bending shamefaced over the dying fire, pretended not to hear the taunts or my step when I strode over to him. Nor did he look up when I asked whether this were his promised immunity against raiders.

"Eh," he said, "I am not rich."

"What has that to do with thy covenant?"

"Listen to me, my lord! If I had wealth, then I could well pay the heavy tithes to the chieftains of the Hazaras and the Yuzufis. But God has not given to me wealth, so they take a little of my goods."

"Fool! How easily thou and I could have slipped through this gorge, if thou hadst not settled here for the night and lighted a grandfather of fires!"

He stirred the embers and shook his head.

"Nay, my lord. Above us are eyes that see in the night. Besides, the next time they would have taken all my goods, and I am a poor man with only eight camels to my hand, and five daughters and three small sons to feed."

Now I was very angry at him, because of the near loss of the dun mare and the vanishing of my silver.

"At least, Sher Jan," I reminded him, "thou wilt have no payment for thy guidance, since thy ten dirhams have gone off with these Hazaras, with my purse."

"God is great," the stubborn fellow answered readily, "because my lord is a *shaikh* and a man of his word. Also, he is a *hakim* of reputation; and soon in Kandahar he will have silver to repay his servant."

"Repay! What have I to repay? May dogs dig up thy father's grave!"

"Nevertheless," said Sher Jan calmly, "I asked my lord Daril to give his money to my keeping, and he chose not so to do. What happened, he brought upon his own head."

When he said this I kicked him into the ashes and sat down by the pot. Truly, it was not fitting for a chieftain of the Nejd, son of a chieftain, to quarrel with a carrier of goods. Convinced by my silence that he would eventually have his ten pieces, Sher Jan waited cheerfully until I had drawn the best morsels of mutton and balls of rice from the pot. He even growled out a song about the fragrant wine of Kandahar and the fine figures of the *lulis*, the dancing girls.

The next morning, while we climbed out of the gullies, past cliffs of veined limestone, I meditated upon the Valley of Thieves. The raiders had taken only part of the spoil they might have had. In my land, the riders of the clans would strip a stranger's caravan, but leave untouched the goods and animals of a friend. These Hazaras acted otherwise, and I thought that they were only one of many bands serving one leader. Verily, the mountains that rose, snowcapped, to the north of us might have sheltered many armies!

I was at the gate of the Mogul's empire, but what a cold and windy gate it was! Hugging his sheepskins about him, Sher Jan grinned at me.

"Only think, my lord, tonight we will walk in the alleys and look at the dancing girls, who have moon faces and sheep's eyes."

He hurried on the camels, muttering to them of grape leaves and grass that they would feed upon that evening; he shouted out blessings on the horsemen and merchants we met coming down the trail, and he swore that he had brought me safely out of the desert—I, who had been born in the *sahra*. All fear had left him, and when the valley became shallow and the red rock walls drew far apart, he ran up a ridge and beckoned me.

"Now, my lord, approaches the hour of ease and profit. Look!"

Eh, what my eyes beheld was pleasant as an oasis after the sand glare and dust of the track. We stood at the edge of a wide and lofty plain, set with fruit gardens and water ditches and the yellow walls of villages. Lines of vineyards rose against the nearest hills, and pomegranate bushes with their dark, shining leaves nearly hid the water ditches. We splashed through the ford of a gentle river, and I beheld at the northern edge of the plain the domes and minarets of a city above a gray scum of leafless poplars. And above the roofs of the city towered the foundations and lofty walls of the *kasr*—the citadel.

I saw distant camel and mule caravans going toward the gates of Kandahar, and I thought that indeed it was a good place, a strong place, one to bring power to its master.

Sher Jan made all haste, but his beasts were weak from lack of food, and the plain was wide. Not until after the hour of evening prayer did we arrive at the nearest gate and find it closed for the night. Sher Jan swore and then besought me to go with him to the Armenian village by the river, outside the walls. It was, he said, the order of the governor that the gates should not be opened after sunset. The governor was a cautious man, and Kandahar a frontier city, perched above the dominion of the Iranis, through which we had come.

W'allahi, our road was ended. No longer did I need the guidance of Sher Jan. I told him that I would go and seek for Arabs, who are to be found on every caravan road, and always outside the walls.

Asking first of one person, then of another, I learned that some Bedouins had their tents out on the road toward Ind, where they could graze their sheep and cattle. There I dismounted and gave the mare into the hands of the youths who came out of the black goatskin tents to greet me. Many times had I fought Bedouin raiders in the *sahra*; but here in a strange land we were as friends, and the blind chieftain of the band sent out and had a sheep killed in my honor, and his men thronged in to talk with me.

They heaped up the fire and filled the largest copper dish with the feast of mutton and rice, murmuring their pleasure when I ate heartily. We sipped many bowls of coffee. When the great bowl had been sent out to the women and the children and the dogs, we rested at ease on the rug.

The blind chieftain said that every year they journeyed from the hill country of Persia with horses, selling them in Kandahar.

"Dost thou pay road tribute to the tribes?" I asked, thinking of the Valley of Thieves.

"Yea, Daril of Athir. And when we are within Kandahar we again pay road tax to the guards of the Mogul."

"But the guards do not keep the road clear." I told him of my meeting with the Hazaras.

"Will dogs keep off a wolf pack?" He shook his head. "Nay, the Pathans of these hills rob where they will."

"Yet taking only a small part."

"That is their custom, and they obey the order given them."

"By the governor of Kandahar?"

The blind man bared his yellow teeth and drew nearer, until his head touched my shoulder.

"By God, the chieftain in Kandahar is no man for war. The Pathans obey a stronger."

"That must be the shah." I had heard tales of the might of Abbas, Lord of Persia.

"Nay, they obey a voice." The master of the tent mused awhile. "A loud and clear voice, calling to war and plunder. Some of my men have heard it, up yonder." He motioned with his head toward the hills. "That is why we linger here, to learn what the voice of al-Khimar will command."

Indeed, al-Khimar was a name to rouse the desert men—a name with memories of dark hours and great slaying. Al-Khimar, the Veiled One. Once a woman had been called that, and again a prophet in Khorassan—a false prophet.

"He has spoken to the tribes," said a youth, coming to sit by me, "promising many things and foretelling that which has already happened."

Yea, that is the manner of prophets, to promise and foretell, and to rouse a following. Verily, in elder ages there had been some who talked with God, and since then, many who lied and stirred up strife. But these Bedouins were full of mystery.

"Nay, Daril," they cried when I said naught. "This is no common man; he eats not at all, nor does he sleep. Only at times does he appear at his place. At other times nothing living is to be seen there."

"In one thing he hath shown his power," grunted the blind man, "for the tribes, the Hazaras and Baluchis and Yuzufis and all the Pathans, all obey him and do not harm each other."

"He told them to look for the coming of the great caravan bringing cotton and indigo and silver, and in the next moon it came," put in another.

"And many muleloads of silver did the tribes take from that caravan," added a third Bedouin, twisting his nose with his fingers, while the men of the tent sighed. It was clear to me that they envied the people of these mountains, who were guided to plunder by a truthful prophet.

"Why do they call this man al-Khimar?" I asked, not wishing to mock them.

"Because he is veiled. From eyes to shoulders he wears a veil of thin white silk."

"Then ye have seen him?"

The Bedouins exchanged glances. They knew me for a wayfarer and an Arab, still they hesitated to say what they had seen of al-Khimar. One at last admitted that he had been visiting the tribes in the hills above the town, when al-Khimar had appeared among them. It seemed that this prophet kept himself in a certain gorge or valley to which there was only one entrance. Hither went the people seeking him, sometimes finding him among his rocks, sometimes not. Yet no one had ever seen him leave the gorge. The Bedouins swore by the triple oath that no food was taken him, nor had he been known to eat. They who had beheld him said that he had a clear voice—far carrying as a muezzin's cry.

"His eyes!" cried one, "oh, his eyes! They burn with dark fire."

"What is hidden," assented the youth eagerly, "his eyes see. How else would he have known of the coming of that great caravan bearing silver?"

"All this is strange," grumbled the blind chieftain, who was old and irritable. "Is not a prophet a man? How can a man live up yonder with the eagles, without a fire, in such cold? Surely he eats."

"Nay," his followers cried at him, "it is a barren place, and he will accept no offerings of fruit or grain or any food. We have seen."

"What thinkest thou, Lord Daril?" growled the chieftain. "These boys of mine are foolish as foals not yet licked dry. They go from me and come back with tales."

Indeed the Bedouins are wild folk, inclined to run after whatever takes their fancy. Instead of going back with the money they had gained from the sale of the horses, they lingered here among a strange people, filling their ears with the talk of a veiled prophet.

"In what language does al-Khimar speak?" I asked, unwilling to show open doubt.

"In the speech of the Pathans."

"As one born to it, or as one who has accustomed himself to it?" I asked again.

"Verily, as one born."

Almost I laughed at them, for the harsh speech of the Pathans, bearded men shouting among their rocks, was little known to the Arabs, and how could they judge of it? Their zeal inflamed their minds, and to argue with them would only rouse them to anger.

"O men of the tent," I assured them, "I grant thy prophet is no common man. Still, a Pathan is as full of tricks as a dog of fleas."

"Al-Khimar hath no need of trickery," muttered the youth who wore the cloak and girdle of a warrior. His beadlike eyes peered at me from between twisted plaits of dark hair. "Fortunate indeed, Lord Daril, art thou, that thou drewest not the sword against the followers of al-Khimar. For those who pay not the tribute he slays swiftly."

In this manner we were gossiping, lying at ease, until the blind man should dismiss his followers and allow me to sleep. Being blind, he hun-

gered for more talk, and the night hours passed until a herd boy rode up,
calling out that riders were coming up the road toward Kandahar.

A Bedouin drew back the entrance curtain of the tent, and we saw lanterns moving among the trees and heard a man singing. The voice carried
far in the cold air, and I knew it to be a trained voice, a minstrel's. When
we saw mules laden with packs, and servants walking beside them, the
Bedouins who had grasped their spears and bows lay back at ease again.
Travelers with lights and luggage could not be raiders, looking for cattle
to lift or tents to ride down and plunder.

"By my head!" swore the youth of the raids. "These are men of the
Mogul."

When the first riders came abreast of our tent they halted, and the singer
ceased his chant. A black stallion, reined in by a strong hand, stalked up
to the embers of our fire, and a cloaked figure scanned us.

"Peace be upon ye," a deep voice greeted us.

"And upon thee be the peace," responded the blind man.

"How far to the gate of Kandahar?"

"An hour of slow riding." The old Bedouin began to be curious, because
the stranger, though not an Arab, had spoken in full-voiced Arabic. "O my
lord, there is no good in going forward, because all the gates are closed at
sunset and they would not open to the Mogul himself."

The stranger mused a moment.

"Is that done by order of the governor?"

"Yea, by his order."

"Thou hast water in this place?"

"Indeed, enough for all thy beasts."

Blind the Bedouin chieftain was, but he had learned to judge of what
happened near him by sound, and he guessed there were twenty to thirty
animals with the travelers. I, using my eyes, judged that there were three
nobles and six servants and twenty warriors in the escort, with two or three
mule drivers. By the number of soldiers and the few servitors, I thought
the strangers were officers. Indeed, that was the case, because the rider
of the black stallion turned his head, speaking a brief order, and the followers began to off-load the mules and set up small pavilion tents in the
meadow across the road, while the armed retainers dismounted and looked
to their horses. The boys of our tents ran to bring water.

"O my lord," cried the blind man, "thou who speakest our speech should take food and sleep within this tent. Verily, I am honored this night with two guests. By what name may I greet thee?"

Before anyone could answer, a slender noble came to the fire—a man whose crimson cloak was lined with down, whose girdle gleamed with gold thread, who swaggered with head high, his loosely knotted silk turban clasped with a single great emerald.

"Know ye not, O men of the tents," he cried in broken Arabic, "that I am Kushal, the songmaker? As to this lord, my companion, bring me wine and I shall tell you who he is."

Kushal's fine voice was that of the minstrel who had been singing up the road. The Bedouins stared, because his white tunic under the cloak was spotted with fresh blood. His young face seemed pallid, though his clear eyes sparkled with mischief. Someone brought him a jar of wine, muttering that it had been taken from a Persian *kafila* and not tasted until now. Kushal laughed and poured himself out a goblet, emptying it down his throat with a toss of his wrist.

"My companion—" he nodded toward the rider of the stallion who was talking in the road with the warriors—"is an officer of the *padishah*, the emperor, the Mogul."

"May God grant him fortune in his service," responded the old Bedouin courteously.

"Stay," cried the songmaker, "thou hast not heard his name. He is Mahabat, lord of ten thousand horse."

While Kushal poured himself another gobletful and drank, the blind chieftain frowned, responding briefly—

"May his honor be increased."

"There is more to hear," grinned Kushal. "He is Mahabat Khan, the most trusted general of the emperor." And he filled his third goblet.

"Mahabat Khan, the sword of the Mogul!" cried the Bedouin, suddenly angry. "Nay—" he caught my arm—"take the wine from this loud talker, or after another drink he will swear that his companion is the prophet of God!"

Verily, the Bedouin thought the minstrel mocked his blindness. Kushal laughed a ringing laugh, heedless of the restlessness of the men in the tent. I rose from my place, but the rider of the stallion strode out of the darkness among us. In dress he was somber beside the gleaming songmaker; his dark cloak and silver-inlaid mail bore no mark of distinction;

his gray *pugri* had neither heron feather nor jewel, yet his sword had a rare hilt of gold-worked ivory.

All this I saw in the first glance and knew that this man needed no ornament to mark him a chieftain. The thin, wide lips; the lean, dark head, with its hawk's beak, revealed at once passion and the iron will that controlled it; his straight back and supple limbs spoke of strength restrained. He came almost silently among us in his riding boots of soft leather. His dark eyes, brilliant under rugged brows, had the fire of untamed daring. *W'allahi*, this was a man to listen to and to follow!

Without impatience or annoyance he looked at Kushal, who stilled his laughter, and at the Bedouins who had grasped their weapons and risen from their places. For an instant his glance weighed me and passed on.

"Since when," he reproved the minstrel, "has it been thy wont to mock affliction?"

Now Kushal's mirth held no guile. He had been amused when the Bedouins took the goblet from him. Yet he had not understood that the *shaikh* was blind, that the old man had intended no jest. As for the anger of the others, he seemed more than ready to welcome a quarrel. Yet he bandied no words with his companion.

"Thy pardon, O *shaikh*," he said quickly to the old man. "Verily, by God, a stranger beholding thee and hearing thy speech doth not deem thee afflicted!"

A little mollified by the compliment, the blind man muttered—

"Eh, thou wert not born in the tents, songmaker." He turned his head toward the man in the gray turban. "And thou, who art thou in truth?"

"The son of Ghayur of the northern hills."

"Then thou art Mahabat Khan." Hastily the blind chieftain rose, calling at his followers impatiently. "O fools! O sons of dogs, ye have blackened my face with dishonor. Ye have eyes and saw not that this lord should be greeted as a guest. Go and kill a sheep and prepare the dish again. Leave the tent!"

Startled and protesting, the Bedouins laid aside their weapons and went forth to cook another feast. Most of them were children and grandchildren of the gray chieftain, and endured insults from him that would have been cause for a blood feud from the lips of another. The chieftain groped about until he caught the hand of Mahabat Khan, then led him to a seat on the carpet beside him, feeling to make sure that a saddle properly covered with a rug lay ready for the arm of his distinguished guest.

"I am Abu Ashtar the Blind," he said, "and verily this is a joyful night that brings to me the leader of a hundred thousand swords."

For Mahabat Khan to have declined his hospitality would have been a great disappointment to Abu Ashtar, who anticipated hours of pleasant talk with a distinguished guest who could speak Arabic fluently. Although he must have been road weary and, as we learned presently, had been involved in a skirmish that afternoon, Mahabat Khan sat by the old chieftain, drinking the tea and coffee brought by the Bedouin youths and sending away his own attendants who came after awhile to seek him.

Listening to their talk, I came to know that he was a Pathan born, who had sought service with the Mogul as a youth. Abu Ashtar had heard of his deeds, reciting battles unknown to me, and conquests of strange lands. Now in this winter Mahabat Khan desired to see his own people again. He had started off at once, taking only a small following and Kushal.

And when Abu Ashtar asked it, the minstrel sang to us, low voiced. He also was a Pathan, no more than a youth. The blood on his tunic had not yet turned dark, and his left arm seemed to be injured, for he would not touch the guitar slung upon his shoulder, yet the magic of his voice was such that we listened greedily while he sang of his deeds in one battle and another, and always of the glory of the Pathans.

He was a youth of fierce pride and heedlessness—a spirit that could no more keep out of trouble than an unleashed hawk out of the air. He boasted often of his skill with the bow and the sword, and yet was master of neither weapon. In battle his recklessness made him dangerous to his foes and himself, for he seldom escaped without a wound. It was a miracle that he still lived—a miracle, indeed, that he liked to sing about. A loyal friend, and an enemy greatly to be feared.

Hearing from Abu Ashtar that I was a physician, Mahabat Khan requested me to treat a sword cut on the minstrel's arm. Kushal drew back his cloak and showed me a slash running from his elbow joint through the muscles of his forearm—the wound that had soiled his garments.

After I had drawn off the hastily knotted bandage, I washed it and heated in the embers a broken spearhead that lay in the tent. With this I seared the cut, Kushal smiling at me and praising my skill to show that he heeded not the pain, even while his face blanched. Then I dressed it with oil and bound it up again. With his good hand Kushal slipped a silver chain from his wrist and offered it to me.

"Nay," I said at once, "we are guests of Abu Ashtar, and shall I take payment for easing thy hurt?"

"Why not?" he smiled, and added, "perhaps the gift should be gold instead of silver."

He meant that I might have been offended because he offered too little. When I assured him I would take no reward, he laughed.

"By my head, Daril, thou'lt never go far at the Mogul's court. There the greatest physicians ask the biggest prices."

He told me how he had the wound. That afternoon Mahabat Khan's cavalcade had been stopped by a band of Hazaras who demanded a road toll.

"I told him that the roads were God's," the minstrel cried, "and they responded that we should taste of woe if we paid not the toll. Then swords were drawn and many were slashed on our part and theirs, and the man who gave me this was carried off without his arm."

"Then ye have beaten off one of al-Khimar's bands," I cried, glad that men had been found bold enough to stand against these robbers.

Mahabat Khan glanced at me questioningly, and I told him what had befallen me in the Valley of Thieves, adding much that I had since heard in Abu Ashtar's tent. The Pathan lord listened intently and said gravely that he had heard of a veiled prophet in the hills.

"But not a tax-gathering prophet," laughed Kushal.

Mahabat Khan asked the old Bedouin if the governor of Kandahar had not armed strength enough to put an end to such exactions.

"His strength is like a camel's," responded Abu Ashtar with a grunt, "good for work in the alleys and the plain, but no good for climbing mountains. *Bism'allah*! When the governor sends horsemen after the raiders they catch no one; when he sends search parties into the upper gorges they find no one. When he patrols the roads, the men of al-Khimar wait until the merchants go forth or come a second time and then take thrice the toll, so that travelers take pains to pay the price to the Veiled One without delay."

"And if they pay not?"

Abu Ashtar shook his head.

"At first some merchants who did not pay were put to death in their houses in Kandahar. The men of the Veiled One come and go unseen. Since then no one has refused, until thy coming. As to thee, who knows? Thy great name may safeguard thee, and perhaps al-Khimar will content himself with slaying one of thy men."

"If he does that," swore Kushal, "he will have made a blood enemy of Mahabat Khan and ye will see the Veiled One torn out of his rocks. Mahabat Khan does not suffer a man of his to be slain, unavenged."

Eh, it was a little matter, the talk of that evening in the tent of the Bedouins—the compassion of the Pathan general upon the blind man who made two feasts in one night for unexpected guests. Yet I had reason to remember the talk.

In Kushal I gained a friend. When Mahabat Khan withdrew to sleep, the minstrel insisted I should come to his own tent, a comfortable place well strewn with carpets and robes. Thither the next day while Kushal still slept, after the midday meal had been brought us, came one who cried my name loudly.

"Lord Daril! Fortune awaits thee."

This was Sher Jan, my camel driver, and I cursed him for making a tumult in the camp of the strangers.

"Nay, thou'lt bless me when I have told thee the reason for my coming, O my lord. The most splendid of reasons. I swear to thee by all the holy names that I have not ceased to labor for thee in the last night. I proclaimed thy skill in the streets and taverns, and this morning a servant sought me with a message. There is no other physician worth his price in Kandahar."

This was not strange, because Persians skilled in medicine were more apt to attach themselves to some powerful noble or prince of a reigning family than to shut themselves up in a frontier town. And Arab physicians are much sought after.

"The message is written," continued Sher Jan with broad satisfaction, "and I have it in my girdle. The servant wore clean linen and gave me—" he swallowed hard and twisted his words—"directions how to reach the house where there is need of thee. And that is not all."

He grinned and stooped down to my head.

"By God, the summons is from a *hanim*!"

He meant either a wife of a noble or a daughter, and this pleased me little. For the hardest work of a physician is in visiting the women behind the curtain. In my land, where my name was known, the Arabs let me look upon the faces and, at need, the bodies of their sick daughters. But in Persia I had been forced to judge the health of an ailing woman by feeling the pulse in the arm she thrust through a curtain, and by a few questions.

I looked at the missive Sher Jan drew forth—a tiny square of scented paper bearing a few words written in a skilled hand.

> Greetings to the Arab hakim. An afflicted woman hath need of thee and reward for thee.

"Why was not the summons from the lord of the house?" I asked, wondering.

"By the Ka'aba!" observed Kushal, sitting up on his rug. "Thou art the first man, Daril, to ask that when a fair *hanim* summons thee."

Our talk had roused him, and he stretched his good arm out for the paper. When he had read it he laughed.

"Allah, what more canst thou wish?"

"Lord Daril," put in Sher Jan, gazing at the minstrel approvingly, "the servant said that his mistress was alone, without the men of her family."

Then, surely, she was a singing girl or public dancer, for otherwise she would be guarded. Still, the servant or Sher Jan or both might be lying.

"What is the matter with her?" I asked.

The camel driver lifted his hands and shook his head.

"O my lord, what does that matter? Anyway, she is very beautiful and it is certain thou wilt receive many times the ten pieces of silver. Remember—"

"Be still, brother of a dog!"

But it was not easy to silence Sher Jan's tongue. The witless man had determined to see me earn the silver that he thought I owed him and had cried my skill through all Kandahar. Probably he had been given some money to find me.

"Remember, my lord," he whispered loudly, "to reward thy follower. Take care to make the affliction seem to be a great one requiring many visits and bloodletting, and stiffen the price thereby."

"Wait, I will not delay thee long, Daril," cried Kushal, calling for his servant. "I must change these soiled things for better ones before approaching a *hanim*."

"Thou!"

"No help for it. Mahabat Khan is talking politics with the governor, and I must escort thee."

While he spoke he helped his man put clean linen on his slender figure, until he stood garbed in rose-pink brocade that heightened the color of the great emerald in his white headgear. Then he put on an embroidered coat with sleeves and collar edged with soft sable, and around his waist he wrapped a green and gold girdle, taking care to leave the coat open at his breast to show the fine brocade beneath. Then he washed his face and hands in water scented with attar of rose and slipped his feet into pearl-sewn riding slippers. *W'allahi,* never had I seen such a splendid youth! I could not help looking down at my dull black headcloth and heavy brown mantle and dust-stiffened sandals, while Sher Jan walked around the minstrel, grunting his amazement and satisfaction at this elegance.

I told Kushal that I had need of no escort and that he was clad for an audience at court rather than a visit to a sick woman, and that, in any case, he would not be admitted to the presence of the *hanim.*

"If she is really beautiful," he smiled, "I will admit myself; if she is ugly I will go off without troubling you."

Eh, there was no checking him. On a freshly groomed white charger he galloped all the way to Kandahar, putting my fleet-footed mare to her best paces. He offered to buy the mare of me and, when I refused, to cast dice for both horses. At the gate of the mud wall where some Mogul soldiery lounged, he reined in until they scrambled up to salaam to him, thinking him a grandee of Ind.

Perforce, we had to wait for Sher Jan and his follower, who had done their best to keep up with us, without avail. They were far down the road. This interval of quiet the minstrel spent in gazing at the bare ridges to the north, red bulwarks against the blue of the sky.

"Those mountains are like sleeping lions, Daril," he said under his breath.

The tawny masses did have the shape of crouching beasts, and Kandahar itself stretched up toward them along a ridge, as if one of the lions had thrust a paw down into the plain. Outside the gray mud wall were endless orchards and hamlets of many people, Tajiks, Jews, Baluchis—the followers of the caravan track.

Inside the wall the city rose, tier above tier, crowning the summit of the ridge, to the yellow-stone citadel where the banner of the Mogul rose and fell in the wind gusts.

Sher Jan came up, beating his nag that he had borrowed or stolen in the night—and led us through the crowds and dust and kneeling camels of the marketplace, crying out to clear a path for us. Then he turned up the street that led toward the citadel. It was so steep that stone steps had been built at places, a dirt path being left for the horses. But Kushal urged his white charger up the stairs, mocking me when I did not follow.

Not until we were within arrow shot of the gate of the governor's castle did Sher Jan halt and peer at the walls of houses and courtyards that lined the street solidly on either hand. He quested about, and knocked at the wooden gate of a court.

The portals opened at once, without question or the barking of dogs. Sher Jan drew back, suspicious at this silence, but Kushal swung his horse aside from the steps and paced in.

A dozen armed men, who might have been Gypsies or Baluchis, stared steadily at his magnificent figure. They were lying around a fire, shivering under leafless poplars, even in the sun, for the winds of Kandahar came out of snow-filled gorges. Kushal greeted them, and one stepped forward to hold his horse. The one door of the white house behind the poplars opened and a bearded Persian came and stared in his turn from the minstrel to me. Seeing Sher Jan, his face cleared and he hastened to my stirrup, bidding me dismount and enter. But he would not allow Kushal to accompany me, and the minstrel kept his saddle.

I followed the bearded keeper of the door through a corridor and up a winding stair that ended in a curtain. Here, as if she had been listening for our steps, a young slave appeared out of a niche.

"The *hakim*—the *hakim* of Arabistan," explained he of the beard, and the veiled girl giggled when she salaamed, slipping through the curtain and beckoning me to follow.

The Persian folded his arms and took his stand at the head of the stair, as if to show me that he would stay there until I left.

I parted the curtain and went forward, feeling beneath my toes the richness of a fine carpet. Into my nostrils crept the scent of rose leaves and of the incense that smoldered within a copper jar before me.

The only light came from a round, heavily latticed window by the far corner, and the sun's rays, coming through the lattice, pierced dimly the hanging wreaths of smoke. Near at hand I heard the fluttering of birds, the whirr of wings and tiny scrape of claws.

"The carpet will not harm thee, O *shaikh*! Sit, and fear not."

The voice was young and amused and so low that I barely heard the words above the stir of the hidden birds and splashing of a fountain.

"Nay, not there; here in the sun," it said.

So I seated myself under the window, drawing my mantle about me, and the speaker seemed to find more food for amusement in that.

"What is this? An old gray eagle! I thought thee a physician. Nay, thy manners smack of the tents, and thy sword is an omen of blood, and thy face is that of a father of battles."

"Can the eye of youth," I asked, "discern the wisdom of age? Judge thou whether I have a physician's skill or no."

By now I could see a couch under the round aperture, and upon the couch the outstretched form of a girl whose slender feet within touch of my hand were white as jasmine, whose ankles were bound with bracelets of flashing sapphires. Her head, unveiled, was no more than a shadow, beneath the smoke-clouded sunbeams. And yet the shadow seemed to be tipped with gold.

"But all physicians," she cried, "act in a manner that is not thine. Nay, they bow to earth and come forward with ready compliments and rare promises."

"No doubt they were Persians," I said and she laughed a little, for she spoke in the Persian manner, and boldly, as if she were a woman who knew how to command men.

"Wilt thou cure me by burning or by letting blood or by purging?" she asked.

"What troubles thee?"

She mused a space and said gravely that sleep would not come to her, and sometimes her eyes pained her.

"Stretch forth thy hand," I bade her.

I pressed my fingers upon the artery in her slender wrist. In leaning forward her head came more into the light, and I saw that her hair was yellow as sunburned wheat. And the touch of her skin was cool and moist, the beat of the pulse as true and mild as the drip of the fountain. I withdrew my hand.

"Thine eyes," I asked, "let me see them."

"The light pains them," she murmured, keeping in her shadow, and beginning all at once to chatter like a parrot aroused.

She questioned me as to my travels, and the road to Kandahar, and whether I had been robbed. To this I made answer that I had been captive to the Persians, and she clapped her hands, summoning the slave girl who brought sherbet, cold and sweet, and dates, full-flavored and good, like the dates of my land. I thought of Kushal, sitting impatient below, and smiled.

"*Hanim*," I said before tasting her offering. "I can do naught for thee. Thy health is good, and to my thinking all that ails thee is curiosity."

Once or twice before I had been summoned by women who had grown weary of confinement behind curtain and veil—who could go forth only to the mosque and the bath, and wished to hear talk of the world. In the shadow under the incense smoke her eyes dwelt upon me, whether amused or angry I could not know. I was ill pleased to be summoned thus at the whim of a girl, and the insistence of a camel driver; and yet, shameless though she must be, because unveiled, there was charm in the music of her voice.

"O father of battles," she said reprovingly, "thy hand is more accustomed to the sword hilt than the lancet. I am weary for my land and feverish with longing for my mountains, the snow mountains by the Sea of the Eagles."

Verily, such longing can be no less than fever, and I too longed at times for the bare *sahra* and its clear night skies. Because it seemed to me that she had spoken the truth, and because I was partaking of her salt and perhaps because I wished to keep Kushal out in the courtyard where he could not stir up any mischief, I talked with her, answering the murmur of her questions.

She told me her name was Nisa. She was a Circassian, born in the mountain land of Persia, a singer who wandered from city to city. For months she had been pent up in Kandahar, because she feared to take the road down into Ind, where the riders of al-Khimar might despoil her of possessions or carry her off.

She asked me about my capture by the pasha, and I told her the truth—that I had seen this pasha, the ambassador of the great shah of Persia, slain in a hill tower, and the gifts he was escorting into Ind scattered among thieving Kurds. Then she asked me if I had seen any nobles of the shah hunting near the frontier.

"I shall go back," she cried softly, "if I can find protection upon the road. Kandahar is full of merchants and hillmen and I am weary of it."

"Would the shah's nobles hunt in winter?" I made response.

"Yea, if the whim came to them."

I told her I had passed only one camp, at a distance, where I had seen Persian Red Hat soldiery and many horses, doubtless the frontier guards.

And then Kushal made himself heard. A guitar struck the first light notes of melody, and he sang—I knew not what. Nisa grew silent at once, and I thought that she must have watched us from the window, because she made no effort to look out to see who the minstrel might be.

But the song had the rush of galloping hoofs and the ripple of laughter and the harsh notes of anger, and when I rose and looked through the lattice, I beheld Kushal on his white horse among the warriors of the courtyard. They were sitting, agape, grinning and listening with all their ears.

It was a Pathan love song, this—a thing of fire and grief and passion, and the warriors enjoyed it. When Kushal ceased and bent his head over the guitar and adjusted its strings, Nisa whispered a question.

"Who is the young lord?"

I told her that he was a minstrel of Mahabat Khan's, and she rose to her knees to watch him, the sunlight coming full against her face for the first time. *W'allahi*, it was my turn to stare!

Unveiled, clouded with pale gold tresses penned beneath a silver fillet, her eyes dark as pools at night, her lips small and fine as the seal of a signet ring, what a face it was! Too young for richness of beauty, too impulsive for peace of mind—it was the face of a child of *peristan*, of elfland, willful and careless and still tender.

And that moment Kushal chose to ride up under the window. Perhaps he could see her through the lattice or perhaps he heard her whisper, for his ears were keen as his wits and his head was no more than a lance length from the opening.

Nay, she did not complain then of the sun glare or of aching eyes, for she pressed close to the wooden fretwork, and Kushal surely beheld her face. An instant he stared, his fingers fumbling the guitar, then he smiled and salaamed, crying—

"The praise to God who created fair women!" Musing a moment he put his thought into song, choosing a lilting Persian melody, thus:

> *Swords are sharpened for a blow,*
> *Tresses perfumed for a lover*
> *Everything is created so,*
> *Is it, or not?*

Nisa, resting on a slender arm, cuddled down to listen, and the slave girl clapped her hands soundlessly.

> *Eyes were given me to see*
> *Maiden's beauty. Thus, I fancy,*
> *Everything was made to be—*
> *Was it, or not?*

Not once did the songmaker seem to remember the armed henchmen at his back, nor did he once falter for a word.

Lips were given thee to kiss
And banish sorrow. Nay, thou sayest,
"Everything was made for this!"
Was it, or not?

The slave girl was sighing with admiration, but Nisa chose to laugh—a
soft trill that provoked and mocked, not less melodiously than Kushal's
song. Kushal's eyes lighted at the sound.

"Open the casement," Nisa ordered her woman, and when this was
done, she turned at once to look back at me. "Verily, Lord Daril, thy companion resembles a peacock in splendor and in self-conceit, and his voice
is as harsh as a peacock's."

Now Kushal's improvised song had been put in a Persian measure, and
was not to be compared to his native chants, but often I had seen a minstrel rewarded with a jeweled bracelet for less than that, by a pleased pa-
tron. Of course, Nisa being a woman, a reward was the last thing he expected.

"Throw him a coin," Nisa whispered quite distinctly to her maid.
"Nay, not gold—silver."

Naturally the slave girl giggled and, after a moment's search, a silver
dirham was tossed from the casement by the maid. Kushal's face darkened
and he sat rigid in the saddle, his eyes fastened upon Nisa's face.

"Close the casement," she whispered, glancing from beneath long lashes
at the motionless minstrel.

Although I was not ill pleased to behold Kushal's pride touched, I had
seen enough of the girl's pranks.

"Thou hast my leave to depart," she said idly, and slipped from the
couch to accompany me to the curtain, which was strange.

Here we met the bearded steward in argument with one of the warriors of the courtyard, and they both looked unhappy when they saw
their mistress.

"What is upon you?" she asked at once.

The armed retainer squirmed and held out a closed fist.

"*Ai, hanim*, a message from the lord who sang, he of the white
horse."

"What, then?"

"These words, 'The gift of Kushal Kattack, who has many times bestowed a diamond for a glimpse of a fair face.'"

The slender Circassian brushed back the tangle of her tresses and held out her hand. The man opened his fingers reluctantly and yielded up a single coin.

"This was his gift."

Nisa's left hand flew toward his girdle, as if to grasp the hilt of a dagger, and the messenger shrank back. Then, looking amused, she let the copper piece roll down the stair and waved the two servitors to follow it. They went gladly, and I thought that she had made them fear her anger before now.

Verily, by pretending that she had appeared at the casement for a price, Kushal had matched her treatment of him—and he had not stopped to think that we were shut up with a dozen of the Circassian's armed followers. When she dismissed the maid, after the two men, I began to watch for a storm.

"Art thou his friend?" she asked in a whisper.

I pondered, and nodded. For a night I had dwelt in his tent, sharing his salt. She looked at me searchingly, and twice seemed to check the words that rose to her lips. Seldom will a woman do thus.

"Then bear him this message—to him alone. Warn him thus, 'If Kushal abides in Kandahar a week he will meet the hour of his death.'"

She spoke impatiently and so softly that I barely caught the words. As to me, she said naught, and I went from her presence wondering. If he had offended her, why should she delay taking vengeance upon him? If she had reason to fear for him, why did she not summon him up and warn him herself? It seemed likely enough that Kushal had enemies in Kandahar—and everywhere.

When we had rid ourselves of Sher Jan, outside the courtyard gate, I gave him Nisa's message, and he smiled.

"No doubt she would like to see me run, as a jackal flees a lion's den."

"As to that I know not, and God alone knows what is behind a woman's words. After all, she is a singing girl, without shame."

To my surprise he turned upon me fiercely.

"*Allah karim*! Thou liest, Daril! Those eyes—" He meditated, with an inward struggle. "True, she is without shame, knowing not its meaning. She is a child, untaught."

"She said she was a singing girl, and she meets men unveiled."

"I thought thee wiser, Daril. I'll wager my horse and purse she knows no more evil than that pigeon."

He pointed up at a blue pigeon that had swept down out of the west, circling above the poplars. Fluttering, it dropped out of sight upon the roof of Nisa's dwelling. In the clear, level sunlight of late afternoon I caught the flash of silver upon one of its claws.

"A messenger pigeon," I laughed, but Kushal frowned.

"Why did she summon thee?" he asked moodily.

"To question me and amuse herself; nay, she has mocked us."

Kushal glanced again at the blank white wall of the house and reined forward savagely. While we had been idling in this fashion at the Circassian's, the followers of Mahabat Khan had moved forward into Kandahar, taking up quarters in a large house offered the khan by the governor, who had not known until this day of the coming of the foremost soldier of Ind. To this house Kushal now made his way, saying nothing at all.

And here I would have parted from him, to go back to the Arabs' camp, had not one of the troopers of Mahabat Khan galloped forth to meet us.

"*Hai!* For an hour the order of Mahabat Khan has awaited thee, to go at once to him at the governor's hall!"

Kushal shook off his meditation and gathered up his reins.

"The Arab physician likewise," added the man.

His voice had a ring to it, and his eyes looked ominous. Beyond him, in the pomegranate garden of the dwelling, other troopers walked about among their saddled horses, talking vehemently. I saw for the first time that these followers of Mahabat Khan were Rajput horsemen, warriors too proud of their own birth and worth to serve any lord of another race who was not a man of the utmost courage and as careful of honor as themselves. And at this moment they looked as if they wanted nothing more than to take to the sword and saddle.

"What has happened?" Kushal asked.

"Enough!" said the trooper, chewing his beard. "When the Sirdar—" in this fashion they named Mahabat Khan—"rode through the marketplace of this city, a man dressed as a pilgrim drew a *tulwar* and ran at him. Rai Singh, riding at the Sirdar's flank, saw him and spurred forward, taking the blow in his breast. Thus the man failed to do harm to our lord."

"Allah! And then?"

"The man of the *tulwar* fled through the bazaars, and we heard this cry, 'The stroke of al-Khimar!' Who cried out, we know not. The Sirdar drove his horse into the crowd, but the assassin escaped. Rai Singh died in these last moments, after the Sirdar had gone to the governor. Tell him so."

While we trotted toward the citadel the same thought came to both of us—that al-Khimar had dared take vengeance for the skirmish of yesterday.

At that time Baki the Wise was governor of Kandahar. Kwajah Baki, frugal and penny saving, a learned reader of books, a good man for accounts and management, who trusted no soothsayers but studied the stars himself, making calculations of fortunate and evil days. Wise indeed he was, but too fearful to be a good soldier, though he was the son of a Pathan chieftain and a Persian mother.

We found his palace to be evidence of his peculiarity. The walls were bare of tapestries, the carpets were mended, the servants meanly dressed. Even the merchants and officers who awaited audience with him had come garbed in common stuffs, and the worn slippers that they left at the threshold were no better than my sandals.

And Baki himself we found not in the fountain garden nor in the tiled reception hall, but perched in the high round tower at the rear of the citadel, at a table covered with rolls of paper. We were escorted to this chamber, where Mahabat Khan nodded to us and spoke our names to the governor.

Baki had the large clear eyes and pale skin of the man who goes forth seldom into the sun. His black cotton tunic and loose red *khalat* seemed to make up in color what they lacked in ornament. He looked fixedly at Kushal's elegance and turned his back upon us, with a curt greeting.

"As to the wound of thy follower," he said to Mahabat Khan, resuming his conversation without heeding us, "that is one of the least of the injuries inflicted by al-Khimar."

"Rai Singh is dead," remarked Kushal.

Mahabat Khan glanced at him and nodded again, clasping his lean hands between his knees. Baki and he sat upon the low carpet-covered platform that ran around the wall, while Kushal and I stood before them, there being no fit sitting place on the clay floor of the governor's workroom.

"O Kwajah," said the Pathan Sirdar quietly, "thou has heard. My men will expect me to find the murderer."

"How?" asked Baki crisply. He had a keen mind and the gift of plain words. "By now the man who did it is hidden in any one of a hundred cellars. By nightfall he will be lowered over the city wall, on his way to the hills. Once there, thou and I could search for a month and only see more men slain."

"Then he is from the tribes? He wore pilgrim's dress."

"So do a thousand others who journey from Ind to the shrines of Meshed and Mecca yearly. When al-Khimar is pleased to murder in Kandahar, it is his whim to dress his swordsmen so."

Mahabat Khan called Baki's attention to us.

"This companion of mine was wounded in fighting off raiders yesterday, and this physician was robbed of his silver in a place called the Valley of Thieves, all within thy territory."

The governor pressed his thin lips together and thrust out his chin.

"*B'illah*! Hadst thou advised me of thy coming, Mahabat Khan, I would have sent two hundred troopers to escort thee."

"The fault is not thine," Mahabat Khan said grimly, "but the responsibility is thine."

"Nay," retorted Baki, "it is God's, who made hillmen—Pathans and Hazaras. Were the Veiled One in Kandahar I could scent him out and make an end of him. But he does not leave his gorge. Only his men wander in and out—excellent spies by all tokens, because they inform him of the coming of the caravans."

"Were any caught?"

Baki spread out his hands.

"Two were caught and accused by twenty witnesses. I tortured them and put them to death thereafter, they swearing by the life of God that they knew naught of al-Khimar. And the next day a message was dropped from the wall at my feet, saying that they had died speaking the truth and al-Khimar knew them not."

Verily, he was a man of peace like myself, desiring quiet to finish his tablets of solar equations and movements of the moon.

"In the end," he said moodily, "it was clear to me that the twenty accusers were al-Khimar's men, and the twain that I slew were enemies of his. In this fashion he cast dirt upon my beard."

"A prophet who sheds blood!" Kushal cried.

"Yea," assented the governor, "who sheds blood to clear the path he means to follow."

"And that path?" Mahabat Khan looked up.

"Leads to war. Promising war and loot, he is rousing the tribes of the hills." Suddenly Baki rose, drawing his heavy coat about his thin shoulders. "Come!"

He unlocked the narrow door behind his table, and a gust of wind whirled into the chamber. We followed him upon a spiral stair that led upward past embrasures to the roof of the tower. Whoever built this tower of the citadel had meant it for a lookout. A solid parapet, breast high, ran around it.

Leaning against this wall, our robes tossed by the buffeting of the icy wind, we could see all Kandahar and the fertile plain below. It was then the hour of early afternoon, after the third prayers.

"Look," cried Baki the Wise, "and you will see why al-Khimar prevails against me."

Mahabat Khan was silent, his dark eyes running over every point of the citadel, as a chess player gazes at the men on the board, with thought for strength of attack and defense.

Indeed, this was a strong *kasr*, a fort to be held by few against many. On three sides a rocky ditch lay under the wall, which had been built of yellow stone, buttressed and sloping sharply upward four or five times the height of a man. The one large gate of black wood, ironbound and studded, was set in the maw of a squat tower. Instead of the usual litter of stables and stalls against the inner side of the wall, the space was clear to the inner citadel, also of solid stone, rising roof above roof toward this wind-blasted tower.

And the tower sat back squarely against the soaring ridge of the mountain behind us. I could have cast a javelin against the rocky face of the mountain, with its gaping fissures and jagged pinnacles.

To right and left, clear in the glow of the evening sky, other arms of the mountains stretched down toward the dark line of poplars that marked the highway from Ind to Persia. A dozen shadow-filled gorges led back to the upper slopes of the hills, and it was clear to me that raiders coming from the heights could choose their valley and strike and flee unharmed.

"Listen!" exclaimed Baki, shivering in his wraps.

Below the walls of the citadel all Kandahar was astir, perhaps aroused by the parties of Mogul guards who searched in vain for the murderer.

"*Ya hu—ya huk!*"

Beggars, scenting profit in the confusion, cried the louder, pulling at the horsemen and cursing those who beat them off. Dust rose about them like a veil, swirling up in the hot air that lurked in the alleys, smelling of camels and dirty cotton and burning dung. Women screamed down from the roofs, abuse mingled with praise and questions for all the world to hear.

"With three hundred men," said Baki, "I am given the duty of hold-ing Kandahar and collecting the tax of the Mogul. Half my men are Pa-thans, cousins of the hill dogs, fire-eaters, who would like nothing bet-ter than to loot on their own account. The landholders in the plain will not support me, because they say I tax them too heavily. The wandering folk who have come down to camp here for the winter are more afraid of al-Khimar than of me. Mahabat Khan, I watch, and I will hold the fort if I am attacked. I have posted guards at the trail that leads to the dev-il's aerie. Here!"

He led us to the west side of the tower and, shading my eyes, I looked down into the haze of a bare ravine under the city wall at the gray river winding through its depths. On my right hand the ravine wound up into the hills, and a thin column of smoke showed where Baki's outpost camped by the river, within sight of the tower.

"That is well done," said Mahabat Khan gravely.

Baki peered at him curiously, no doubt wondering if the Sirdar meant to complain of him to the Mogul. In truth this was not the place for Baki, a man whose years had been passed in the academies, who craved soli-tude and was fearful of the unseen. A strong hand and a ready sword were needed to keep this mountain gate for the Mogul.

"There is a way to take the slayer of Rai Singh," went on the Pathan, and Baki shook his head, thinking he would be asked for men or money.

"How?" he asked.

"Write thou a summons to al-Khimar, bidding him find the man and send him to thee, bound."

"For what price?"

"For no price; seal it with thy seal."

Baki and Kushal both looked at him to see if he jested, but Mahabat Khan led the way back to the cell-like chamber, and the governor wrote some words in Pushtu upon a paper.

"Who will take this, Mahabat Khan?" he asked, pausing.

"I will be responsible for that."

When he had signed his name, Baki rubbed some ink on a corner of the paper and pressed his signet ring into the ink, then rolled up the missive and thrust it into a plain wooden tube.

"O Sirdar," he said, as he handed the tube to Mahabat Khan, "thy com-ing hath cast the torch of strife into the framework of my administration. Should harm befall thee, my trouble will be grief indeed. So I beg of thee to go upon thy way, relating the plight of Kandahar at the court of our illustrious lord, the Emperor of Ind, so that aid may be sent me and my hand strengthened against these hill dogs."

"Aye," smiled the Pathan, "I will do that, after I have delivered the murderer of Rai Singh to my men."

Baki's eyes darkened and his lips closed in a straight line. Verily, he knew his own mind and did not lack conviction.

"Art thou the Sirdar, conqueror of Bengal, victor in twenty battles, lord of twenty thousand horse, or the son of Ghayur, meddler in feuds and thievery?"

"Both," responded Mahabat Khan, pulling at his mustache. "O Baki, when an obligation is laid upon thee, dost thou put thy hand to its fulfillment or mount thy horse and ride away?"

Baki smote thin fists together, his slender body rigid as a lance shaft, under its poor and ill-fitting clothes.

"By God, Mahabat Khan, it is my duty to hold Kandahar for the emperor! And thou, riding at pleasure, art bound to anger al-Khimar and give him the very pretense for war that he seeks!" He raised both fists over his head, struggling with anger. "At least, take care whom thou sendeth into the hills with this message, for al-Khimar will send thee back his head and then thou wilt have two blood feuds on thy hands instead of one."

"Then will thy troubles be at an end."

So said the Pathan, rising to go forth, and I pondered the riddle of his words until we had mounted and left the citadel. Then I saw a little of what was in his mind, for he signed to me to come to his side.

"Daril, hast thou a mind to serve the Mogul?"

"Yea, my lord—as a physician."

He smiled fleetingly, white teeth flashing under his clipped mustache.

"Thou art not a man of ready promises. Good! Ride to the tents of Abu Ashtar, and lead him to me before the first hour of this night, with three of his men."

"They are Bedouins, serving no lord. For what reason shall I bid them come?"

"Ask if they wish to increase their honor."

"How?" I questioned, knowing that they would demand to be told.

Mahabat Khan was little accustomed to quibbling over a command, but he seemed to know the men of the tents.

"Bid them come, and learn. Shall I be feasted by Abu Ashtar and not kill a sheep for him?"

Not with three Bedouins, but with eleven, did I come to Mahabat Khan's house in the second hour of that night. At first they had refused loudly, fearing both the walls and the guards of Kandahar, and doubtless with good reason, because of thefts committed by them in the past. But the Father of the Blind had the courage of his affliction, and it was a matter of honor to accept the Sirdar's invitation—of honor and good eating. When he had scolded his men for their fears and announced that he would go alone with me, they all began to think in another fashion and begged to come. Abu Ashtar rode a fine mare, with embroidered caparisoning and silk saddlecloth and fringed reins.

Kushal greeted him at the courtyard of the Sirdar's quarters and led him and his men to the fire, where a whole sheep was boiling. The song-maker explained that his master begged to be excused, as he was with the Rajputs in the chamber where the body of Rai Singh lay. Some of the Rajputs came forth presently and greeted us, taking no part in the feast, for they were Hindus. They seemed both restless and troubled, and Kushal was buried in his thoughts. But the servants brought forth many dishes, offering saffron and dates and sherbet with the mutton, and my companions stuffed themselves comfortably.

When we had licked clean our fingers, Kushal led us into the first room of the house. There, as we sat against the wall, I beheld in the dim light of a hanging lanthorn a tall Pathan striding back and forth. The step and the poise of the head were familiar, and presently I knew him by his beaked nose and lean chin to be Mahabat Khan.

W'allahi, but he had changed more than his garments! His loose, soiled *pugri* with its hanging end, his long wool shirt and rusty chain mail, his baggy breeches bound to the knee with odds and ends of cloth, and his once-splendid padded and embroidered coat—all these looked and smelled like those of a thieving hillman, and even the gold chain bearing some talisman at his throat, and the battered silver armlets were no more than evidence of plunder taken from a slain foeman. He walked like a man accustomed to stride over boulders and climb goat paths.

The keen eyes of the Bedouins recognized him; and they waited for him to speak.

"O Abu Ashtar," he said, "I asked only for three men—three who know the way to the den of al-Khimar."

The blind chieftain muttered uneasily:

"We are horse traders, strangers in these hills. How should we know the paths?"

"The talk was otherwise in thy tent. I ask for three men to go with Daril and with me."

Even then I could not believe that Mahabat Khan meant to enter the hills. I thought he was playing a trick, and the Bedouins answered in chorus that they knew nothing of the veiled prophet and his people.

"Are ye al-Khimar's men?" he said, smiling.

"Nay, lord. We are—"

"Choose ye the three who will go," he bade them. "Let Abu Ashtar choose. I ask for three to go up the river gorge, to point out the way to the *sangar*, and thereafter to watch our horses. No more than that; nor will any blame be upon them."

He went away then to talk with Kushal and the Bedouins turned upon me, accusing me of betraying them. I had a moment to reflect and decided how to answer them.

"What is upon ye?" I cried. "This Sirdar hath a feud with al-Khimar. Think ye he will go into the hills and betray ye? Fear ye the river gorge or Baki's guards?"

"Nay, we fear the anger of the Veiled One."

But Abu Ashtar had been meditating, and now he announced suddenly that his men should go. It was better, he said, to obey the Sirdar. If all went well there would be a reward. The truth was that Abu Ashtar had realized that he himself would be held as a hostage by the Rajputs, and he scoffed loudly at the misgivings of the youths who, he said, were eager enough to slink off and listen to the prophet, but reluctant to earn something for him. So the youth with the lovelocks bethought him and offered to go with me, and likewise two of his companions.

Why did I go with the Sirdar? I had brought the Bedouins to Kandahar and I was responsible for the three men to Abu Ashtar. And then it was not easy to refuse Mahabat Khan, who had power to cast us into chains, but who asked no more of us than suited our minds. Eh, before the end came I watched him take command in truth; but that was not yet.

Only once that night did he use his authority, when we four reached the eastern gate of the city. He drew aside the officer of the guard, and presently the gate was opened—against Baki's order. I have often wondered what the Sirdar said to that man!

For awhile we rode east, then circled through the outer camps, until we were heading west. So we reached the river far out from the wall and dropped into the path that wound toward the dark mouth of the gorge.

"*Sahib,*" I said, drawing abreast Mahabat Khan, "this venture is not wise. There is peril for thee; and as for me, if thou art harmed, Baki will crucify me, and thy troopers will light a fire under my toes. If harm comes to the Bedouins, Abu Ashtar will make an end of me."

"Thou shalt go with me," he laughed.

"Whither?" I wondered. "To deliver the message to that prophet?"

"Perhaps."

"That is madness, for al-Khimar cares naught for the power of the Mogul."

"Nay," he said, "it would be madness to hang about the streets of Kandahar after what has happened. Tell me, Daril, if thou wert riding upon an open road and an arrow sped against thee out of the brush, what would best be done? To ride on, or to turn thy horse swiftly into the brush?"

"To turn aside and hide, and then watch," I made answer.

"Aye," he said, "and that is what we shall do."

When we drew near the outpost in the ravine, the Bedouins thought that the Sirdar would ride in boldly and make himself known; and that would be folly, if eyes were watching from the hills.

Instead, he turned off the path and climbed a ridge, bidding us dismount and warning me to take care that the mare did not whinny. He led us among boulders and bunches of camelthorn without hesitating, and I thought that he had marked this course from the tower that afternoon. The Bedouins moved almost silently beside their unshod beasts. The mutter of the river filled the ears of the guards beside the fire. Perhaps they heard us once the pack pony stumbled heavily, and we waited, listening for a challenge, but I think they were content enough to stay by the road and keep their skins whole. A hundred men could have passed them as we did.

When the fire was too far behind to outline our figures, Mahabat Khan led us down again to the path and halted.

"Lead ye," he said to the Bedouins.

And when they would have pushed past, he checked them and whispered.

"I am called Mahabat Khan—aye, of the Lodi Pathans. I came to Kandahar to sell horses, and I have come hither with you to hear the prophet preach. Is that understood?"

"Yea," they answered.

They had been surprised when he led past the picket, and more surprised that he thought to warn them of a name and a tale to tell when questioned. And I too began to see that the Sirdar was not on strange footing in these hills. As for the name, there might have been a hundred Mahabat Khans within the borders of Ind. Who would think that he assumed his own name?

But now he was no longer the Sirdar. He had left his authority down below at the outpost. From now on he was to be Mahabat Khan, horse trader of the north, and if his disguise failed him he could expect to be held until al-Khimar was paid what ransom he might deem fitting. That, at the best—at the worst it meant a dead Sirdar and endless trouble for me.

Yet he seemed well content.

Within an hour the Bedouins drew rein and waited until we came up.

"There is the way," they said. "May God protect you!"

We had gone forward no more than an hour from the outpost, and the valley was still open, the gleam of the river clear to our eyes. On our right hand the slope fell away, divided sharply, and I stared into the utter darkness of a narrow gorge. Toward this they pointed.

"We will wait here with the horses. Keep close to the rock on your right hand."

The Sirdar dismounted; I said something about torches.

"Nay, Daril," the Bedouins said in chorus, "al-Khimar's men will shoot at any light. We will guard the horses and the packs."

"But the covenant was that you should show the way," I objected.

The air tasted of ice, and the wind cut through my robes, and my joints ached too much to relish climbing upon a mountain such as this that towered over us.

"Nay," they cried instantly, "Mahabat Khan asked only that we should keep the horses; the beasts cannot go upon that path. *Inshallum*, it is not very far to the *sangar!*"

Nevertheless, I saw that the graceless liars took the saddles from the animals and wrapped themselves in their blankets, lying down in a sheltered spot, as if they expected to spend the night in waiting. Mahabat Khan, seeing this, gave them leave to go back to Kandahar, if we did not return by the time the sun crossed its highest point the next day. I too would have liked the warmth of my blankets, and sleep. But how could I abandon Mahabat Khan and lurk with these horse tenders after my high words concerning responsibility? I could not!

Mahabat Khan strode off, and I followed. In a moment his figure was lost in utter gloom. I hastened forward and touched him before I saw him.

"What is upon thee, Daril?" he asked softly.

"The way is hidden," I said.

"Aye, this is a *tangi*—a water ravine. When we reach the heights we will be able to see the path."

It is not easy to dismount from the saddle and go forward on foot—not at all easy, after the third hour of the night, when the path winds up the rocky face of a cliff. For a man like myself in sandals, lean and stiff-limbed and shivering, it is like an ordeal of Tantalus.

Truly, this was a water ravine. Dropping farther below us, a stream rushed and gurgled its way to the river; even the stones that bruised my knee bones were wet, and the air smelled damp. After the first hour, the gorge narrowed and the stars were obscured; the wind beat at us in gusts, and presently the air began to be truly wet, because it rained.

By keeping close to Mahabat Khan, my feet did not stray from the path, which was well, because stones loosed under our tread rattled down through the darkness until they passed beyond hearing. I thought of the Bedouins and hoped that they too were wet.

My shoulders ached, and the calves of my legs. But Mahabat Khan, who had the harder part of feeling the way, did not lag. He must have had legs of iron.

At times we picked our course over a nest of boulders, and then Mahabat Khan was obliged to seek again for the narrow path that hung between the cliff and empty air. The wind no longer beat at our faces; it swirled up from below or swooped down upon our shoulders, and my thighs and ribs began to be wet.

At times we climbed upon our hands, over slippery stone and treacherous gravel. No longer could I hear the stream; instead, scores of tiny watercourses trickled and pattered in our ears, and, in that terrible gloom, it seemed as if we were wandering blindly, driven like sheep before wind. Nevertheless, I think we tended more and more to the right. Presently the wind ceased. Snow began to beat softly against my chin, under the hood of the robe, and to fall unheeded on my numb hands.

As if Satan had withdrawn a curtain, we beheld a strange dawn. The snow had ceased, and the cold increased; and our bruises ached where we had slipped and stumbled and clung. The stars stood in a clear sky, so deep a blue it seemed a shimmering black. Gray pinnacles came forth from behind the curtain of mist, where an old hidden moon shone. I could see Mahabat Khan's swinging coat and *pugi*'d head and the black knobs of boulders in his path.

We moved along a shallow ravine that twisted and turned among rock ledges, and, after the murk of the *tangi*, the half light overhead seemed like the true dawn. Presently Mahabat Khan stopped and looked steadily to one side. I saw a flicker of red light run up a chasm.

"Yea," I said to him, through chattering teeth, "Satan hath lighted a lantern to guide us."

He said that somewhere in these gullies a fire burned, and we had seen its reflection upon ice. But it was the cold and not fear that made my jaws quiver. Indeed, such chill as this I had never known.

We went forward more swiftly, looking for the fire. Once I beheld something that danced and beckoned in the shadows of rocks and went toward it. Eh, it was a grave, and an old grave, because, thrust upon dead branches and knotted to bushes, long rag streamers whipped about in the wind.

"Peace be upon ye," I whispered, hurrying after Mahabat Khan, until we both halted and stared about in the dimness.

"O ye wanderers," a voice shouted at us, "What seek ye here?"

I saw no man, but the voice had come from the gloom under a cliff beside us, and I wondered what manner of men kept watch over the graves in this lofty valley. Mahabat Khan made answer in the harsh Pathan tongue, speaking loudly and arrogantly, until the very rocks rang. The man who had challenged seemed satisfied, because he lifted a long wail like the howl of a wolf.

"Come," Mahabat Khan muttered, and we went on without haste, climbing toward a ridge that showed dark against the stars. Soon we beheld one advancing to meet us, who leaned on a staff, peering at our eyes in the starlight. He grinned and spat and went away without a word, motioning to us to go where we willed.

Thus we followed the path to the ridge and stopped to stare. *W'allahi*, we had come upon the encampment of the hills, not before, but beneath us!

A hundred cubits or more the ridge dropped away beneath our feet, to the bed of a short valley. And scattered through this valley a score of fires flamed bright. Around the fires squatted men in sheepskins and garments of every sort, and women and children behind them. Off in the brush several hundred horses were picketed.

It seemed to me that there were many different clans grouped at those fires, and Mahabat Khan took his time in studying them, saying nothing. On the other three sides the walls of ridged rock loomed sheer, rising out of the firelight. I thought that this pit of the hills was a good place of concealment—a thousand men might lie here for days unseen.

It seemed to me that another road must lead to the bed of the pit, because there were horses and mules and tents down below that could never have come up the *tangi*, or scrambled down the footpath that we were now forced to descend.

No one heeded us, because the men of the pit were all rising and moving toward the fires at the far end. Mahabat Khan swaggered among them without turning his head, yet using his eyes and ears to pick up scents, like a hound that has returned to his own abiding place after long years. There was a mutter of talk that I did not understand and a smell of wet mud and sweat and burned leather. The women hurried to fetch more wood for the fires, toward which the wave of hillmen moved, and I saw a white stake set in the earth here, on a level spot under the cliff.

It was the bole of a tree, the bark cut away from it, and around it the throng began to thicken, leaving clear about the stake the space of a stone's cast. An elbow was thrust into my ribs and a bearded face leered at me.

"In the name of God!" the man muttered. "The Arab doctor hath come to the hills!"

Eh, this man was one of the Hazaras who had visited me at Sher Jan's fire. Indeed, many of his companions stared at me, for my garments were not like the Pathans. They seemed both suspicious and arrogant.

"See, *hakim*," quoth another, in broken Persian, "the stake is ready for thee."

"He quakes," jeered a third, "and before long he will shrivel. We will build a fire around him."

I heard several of them draw swords out of sheaths, and the press around me grew greater. Mahabat Khan, standing near, made no sign. I thought that if there were danger, he would take my part.

"*Bism'allah!*" I cried. "Is this the hospitality of thy camp?"

"Nay," grunted the Hazara, "this is not our *sangar*. What led thy steps hither?"

"The other Arabs—they of the horse traders' tents—told me of a holy man in this spot."

A pockmarked Pathan, with a sword scar whitening his brow, pushed through the crowd to me and growled. "Who led thee hither?"

At last Mahabat Khan turned, stepping between us.

"I!" he said. "I did."

They all looked at him, finding nothing to say for the moment. I wondered if any would know the face of the Sirdar of Ind. But then horns began to quaver behind us, and drums rumbled. The Pathans forgot us and thronged about the cleared space, into which a score of the elder men were moving, swords in hands. Turning their left shoulder to the post, these old warriors made a circle about it.

"Hai! Ahai-hai!" one shouted, and the drums quickened into a fierce beat.

Mahabat Khan touched me on the shoulder and led me to a blanket by one of the fires. Here we sat, our faces toward the stake, the veiled women moving off a little from us.

"Silence is best," he whispered, "for a little, until this is ended."

The music grew louder; younger warriors ran from the crowd toward the elders, who were now moving slowly around the stake, swinging their swords over their heads. Eh, the youths had more supple joints. They hastened into rings, leaping and swinging their blades in time to the music.

Some had two swords, some a sword and musket. All the circles were now revolving about the posts in the same direction, and the swiftly darting blades made red light above the tossing heads. Faster leaped the warriors, the sword edges whistling in the air. Straining throats made deep-tongued clamor.

More swiftly the long-robed figures ran, long locks tossing about the turbaned heads. But never a blade clashed another, never a steel edge slashed a man. The cliffs roared back in echo:

"Hai-hai!"

Half smiling, yet his eyes agleam, the Sirdar watched the sword dance of his hills, seeming to expect some greater miracle of movement and madness. And it happened.

There was a rush of hoofs, a straining creak of saddles, and jangling of silver laden reins. Standing in their stirrups, nay, leaping upright upon the saddles, the men who had mounted horses joined the throng, rushing about the post. They tossed their swords into the air, caught them, and flashed the blades down at the dancers. Red firelight flickered on the bare steel.

The Pathans who sat about the spot were staring, loose lipped and shouting. Mud-stained children jumped about in their bare feet beside their mothers. More and more swiftly the drums resounded and the hoofs raced. Then some of the horses darted aside, figures swirled, and a man shouted in rage.

I had seen a horse stumble. Its rider must have slashed another Pathan—the same pockmarked giant who had confronted me. He gripped his ear, the blood running through his fingers; the greater part of the ear was cut clean away.

Shouting, he made toward the horseman who had wounded him. The drums fell silent, the horns ceased, and the dancers ran toward the two antagonists. Deep-toned clamor arose—men snarling at their companions of a moment before. Panting and mad with excitement, they would have thrown themselves at each other, for at such a time it takes little to turn play into slaughter, and many clans with many feuds had joined the dance. But the tumult was quieted before the first blow could be given.

Above the stake on a great flat boulder appeared a slight figure in a brown robe and green turban, and a high voice shrilled over the quarrelling—a single word.

I saw that this figure was veiled beneath the eyes. At its bidding the Pathans dropped their swords, the wounded man fell silent, and, in a moment, they turned to go back to their fires, as jackals turn at the coming of a wolf.

"What is this?" I whispered.

But Mahabat Khan frowned, his eyes intent.

"A time for silence," he repeated under his breath.

Still fingering their weapons, panting from the dance, the hillmen sought the fires. Some of them snarled at me; but they were too full of their half-stifled quarrel and too eager to hear what the man on the boulder might say, to bother about an old Arab.

"O ye of little wit!" he cried, in their speech.

Nay, at the time of his speaking, I understood not, but many have told me his words. For the words of al-Khimar were treasured in the memory of the hillmen.

"Know ye not that it is written, 'Nothing happens save by the will of Allah?' What have I seen? A horse stumbled, a man was cut by a sword, and ye thoughtless ones—ye less than children—would have taken life, here, before me!"

Slowly he spoke, pausing to give them time to hear and understand and mutter among themselves. Every word was clear as the clank of steel, and I thought that at one time al-Khimar had been a muezzin. The warrior of the slashed ear made as if to complain to him, but the veiled prophet waved him away angrily, and he went in among his fellows, unheeded.

I saw now why al-Khimar had appeared so suddenly. Behind the flat-topped boulder was a dark mouth of a cave. Within this he must have stood and watched. There were many clefts and ridges in the rock wall, but this seemed to be a cavern of some size.

"Why are ye here?" he asked, and looked from one to another.

The Pathans moved uneasily, and many thrust their swords back into their girdles.

"To obey," responded an old man, "to hear and obey."

"Take heed that ye do it!" Again he searched the crowd with his eyes, and the listeners held their breaths. "Have I come at this hour of the night to see ye wield swords? Are ye indeed children that ye may not wait for a space without a game?"

"Nay," cried a bearded warrior with one eye, "Shamil the Red Snout set up the stake and called upon us to show our skill. I am of the Yuzufi Khel—"*

Even their reverence for the holy man could not keep these children of the hills curbed entirely. They answered back like defiant sons and, like sons, received their chastening. I noticed likewise that when they spoke the echoes flung back the words. The louder they shouted, the louder roared the opposite cliffs. Foolishly, they tried to make themselves understood by shouting.

But al-Khimar, standing apart from them and facing the end of the valley down which we had come, managed to speak without stirring up the echoes. No doubt he had experimented until he had discovered how to do this, yet it filled the hillmen with awe—they knew that echoes were the voices of devils, mocking men.

"Thou art a pig's butcher!" gibed al-Khimar, and the valley rocked with laughter.

When the echoes rumbled—*Ho-oho-ho!*—they were frightened and fell silent again.

---

*The tribe of Joseph. Also, David and Solomon are favorite names in the Afghan hills, where tribes trace their descent from the rulers of Israel.

"Will ye take up the swords again and play at butchering—or listen to me?"

"Nay, al-Khimar," protested the Yuzufi, "we will listen."

And thus the veiled prophet quieted them by mocking them, and turned their thoughts to him.

"I dreamed last night of war," he said then. "Have ye forgotten that time I beheld in a dream the coming of the caravan with silver and precious stuffs? In this new dream a message came to me. These were the words of the message: 'Think ye your wealth will save you, if your deeds destroy you?'"

They murmured, saying that truly they had not forgotten.

"The gain was great at that time," quoth al-Khimar, "and now—very soon—it will be more. But you must win it by your deeds!"

"Ah!" cried the Yuzufi. "Lead us to Kandahar! We have waited and increased in strength, and now, surely, it is time."

"O thou shameless one!" shrieked al-Khimar. "If these men followed thee, many would be slain with little gain. Know ye not the citadel of Kandahar hath walls too high to climb? Behind walls the Moguls will be stronger than ye. Know ye not that the Sirdar of Ind hath come to Kandahar with a following? What talk is this? Nay, I dreamed of another matter. In the night this was revealed to me—a rich camp, with camels and mules. A camp of silk pavilions and ivory and red leather—of full wine skins and a thousand slaves."

The Pathans gazed up at him, plainly astonished, and Mahabat Khan chewed his mustache.

"Where?" shouted a man far back of us.

Al-Khimar pointed to the west.

"At the edge of the plain, among the foothills, I saw this camp."

Then a camel driver sprang up, his face distorted with amazement.

"By Allah, indeed!" he shouted. "There is a camp, down below, a day's ride. Yesterday I saw it, and it is filled with Persians, lords and servants who have come hither to hunt."

The shrill voice of al-Khimar soared.

"May their eyes be darkened! They will fall to our swords—save those who would better be held for ransom. Yea, we shall have slaves enough to glut the markets of Kandahar. For nothing happens save by the will of God! The fate of these Persians is not to be altered—the hour of their doom is written."

And for awhile he harangued the Pathans, promising to lead them to victory, rousing them again to eagerness and anger, though they needed little rousing. Thus he made them cease to think of Kandahar, and to long for the spoils of the camp below. Never before had the wealthy lords of Persia ventured so near the frontier.

He painted with words the attack upon the *lashgar* of the hunters by night, the overthrow of the guards, the swift charge among the tents, the slaughter and the pursuit of the fleeing, and the capture of young and fair women—until the mass of hillmen rose to their feet and shouted to be led down into the valleys.

"Not yet," said al-Khimar, when the roaring had died away between the cliffs, "not yet is the time. In two days—the night following the next." Then he lifted his slender arms. "Upon ye be the blessing of Allah!"

This done, he turned and stepped down from his rock, vanishing from the circle of firelight as swiftly as a shadow. He must have entered his cavern, because I could not see him anywhere behind the rock. A moment later, the red-bearded opium eater Shamil—whom I had defied in the Valley of Thieves—came and stood upon the rock, leering down at the fires as if all these men were no more than sheep to be led under the knife. As usual, his eyes were nearly closed, yet I thought from a sudden movement and a turn of the head that he had noticed me.

Mahabat Khan sat in talk with the Yuzufi, who was called Artaban and who wore about his neck a charm. It was a camel's tooth upon which a prayer had been carved by some holy man. Artaban carried it in a silver locket, hanging upon a plaited cord. He said to us, for he loved the sound of his own voice, that this charm made him safe from bullets or steel.

"Allah is my witness," he swore, "that bullets have gone through my sleeves and girdle and head cloth without harming my skin. I had it of a man I slew with my hands."

Truly this Artaban had a bear's strength in his arms. Grinning with yellow teeth, he showed me how he had slain the owner of the charm, seizing his beard in one hand and pulling to one side while with his other hand he thrust the man's shoulder in the opposite direction.

"Allah is merciful," he grinned again. "The night after the next I will flay one of the dog-born dogs of Persians alive. They had my brother for a slave and ripped him up with a knife."

Eh, the Persians love the Pathans as wolves love panthers; because the ones reverence Ali as the successor to Muhammad, and the others disown Ali. It is said that no feuds are as fiercely hot as the feuds of cousins, and no quarrels are as deadly as the strife of Alyites and Sunnites.

"And will al-Khimar lead ye to attack?" asked Mahabat Khan, looking about him idly, as if no more than courtesy had prompted the words.

"Nay," declared Artaban. "He gives us warning of what must be done; he chooses the fortunate hour of sallying forth; but I and the red Shamil and the Hazara chieftain lead."

"Truly, ye have many men."

Artaban grunted.

"Six hundred and more. There are guards upon the roads, and other men in Kandahar."

"It is a great miracle," said Mahabat Khan, sinking his voice, "that the Veiled One eats not and never ventures from his place."

"Allah is great!"

"What man could go without food for many days?"

Artaban pulled at his beard and blinked, flattered by the reputation of his prophet.

"Perhaps," went on Mahabat Khan gravely, "there be fools who believe such matters, but thou and I are men of intelligence, and we understand that even saints must have food—even though it pleases them to pretend otherwise."

"True, by Allah!" The one-eyed Yuzufi chieftain frowned and tried to look wise.

"Some say there is another way out of this cavern."

"Then let them look! I will not enter it."

"Does none go in?"

"Shamil—nay, I saw a man of the Waziri *khels* carried out with his toes turned up and a knife in his heart. Why not? Al-Khimar keeps all the offerings of his people—all the silver that we shall need someday—in there."

"True. Who does not know a day of need?"

"As for me, I take what I require."

Artaban struck his fist against his broad chest covered with chain mail to which some traces of gilt still clung. I wondered if the steel shirt were the reason why the Yuzufi had escaped wounds.

"So Shamil goes in," nodded Mahabat Khan, his head close to the tribesman's shaggy locks. "Surely he is the servant of the Veiled One."

"Nay, his watchman. Red Shamil keeps the silver and sees to it that none goes in. If one of us went in, how would we know that the silver and precious things were not stolen? The Hazaras and the Waziri are great thieves." Artaban spat.

I heard a man breathe at my shoulder and turned swiftly. The man called Shamil stood within touch of me, his eyes fixed on the ground, his thin lips sneering.

"So," he said harshly, "ye twain have come hither to hear the Veiled One? Will ye go to his place and speak with him?"

The Yuzufi dropped back a pace and stared, but Mahabat Khan considered a moment and nodded.

"Aye."

"Why?" demanded the watcher.

"I am of the Lodi Pathans and I have come far. I bear a message to al-Khimar."

"From whom?"

"That is for him to hear."

For a moment Shamil combed his beard, swaying his red head from side to side. I wondered what the Sirdar would find to say to the prophet. It would have been a mistake to refuse to go with Shamil—who among these men would refuse?

And suspicion was in the air.

"And thou, Daril," snarled the redbeard, "hast thou a message also?"

I shook my head, and he turned on his heel, motioning for us to follow. Mahabat Khan did not look at me, but he waited until I had reached his side before he advanced. His step and bearing told me that he foresaw no good thing awaiting us. Artaban and a dozen others trailed along to listen.

The fires had died to glowing embers, and, when we climbed up behind the boulder, we could see little except the dark mouth of the cavern. A cold gust of air touched our faces. Shamil bade us stand, while he went forward to speak to al-Khimar concerning us. I looked up at the stars, above the black wall of the cliff, and envied the Bedouins in their blankets by the river.

W'allahi! It is written that no man knoweth what the next moment will bring to him. I thought of many things, but not of what happened now. Shamil had vanished into the darkness, and I strained my ears in

vain, hearing only the coughing and shuffling of the tribesmen who had
lingered by the boulder.

Then I beheld a tiny spot of light that danced on the rock wall of the
cavern. It vanished, and a soft glow was cast upon the arched roof, slowly
moving toward us. I stared at it like a sheep. Mahabat Khan moved beside me. Steel slithered faintly through leather.

The flickering glow came nearly over us, when suddenly a glaring light
shone full into my eyes.

The light was from a copper lantern held in a man's hand. I could
see the hand and the long sleeve, but little else, for the frame of the lantern was so wrought that it threw its illumination only in front. In such
shadow and at such a moment the eyes seize upon a little thing, a familiar thing. I was sure that I noticed Shamil's curling beard. I think he had
brought the lantern from elsewhere and wrapped it in a soft blanket, because presently my toes caught in a loose cloth upon the rock floor. But
at that moment my ears were filled by a high-pitched shout—the voice
of al-Khimar.

"Spies! These twain be spies, sent by the men of Kandahar. Slay them,
ye men of the hills!"

The voice came from behind Shamil, and I thought that verily this
was a prophet of true words. One instant's sight of our faces, and he had
cried out at us. The hair prickled on my scalp, and I put my hand to my
sword hilt.

It was the part of Mahabat Khan to act now; he was the leader, his the
responsibility. I did not need to wait the space of quickly drawn breath
to see what he meant to do. Before the light shone upon us, he had drawn
his blade, and now he slashed at Shamil behind the lantern.

The watcher of the Veiled One caught the glimmer of steel descending
and sprang back. Mahabat Khan was after him like a panther, and Shamil
ran to the side of the cavern, the light swinging wildly. Eh, Shamil bleated
like a sheep, and I ran in to corner him. Nay, I should have remained at
the edge of the cavern!

Mahabat Khan whirled suddenly away, flinging over his shoulder a command to me to finish the redbeard. I heard his saber grate against steel,
and then the *clish-clash-clank* of many blades striking together.

Shamil was like a rat, slipping this way and that, evading me. He drew
and flung a knife that ripped through a fold of my headcloth, the guard

scratching my ear. Darting past me, he ran out of the mouth of the cavern, close to the rock.

I saw then that Mahabat Khan had taken his stand in the entrance of the cavern. His sweeping blade barely missed Shamil. But four Pathans were pressing in upon him, Artaban roaring his war shout, the foremost of them.

My eyes searched the cavern for a glimpse of al-Khimar, but in vain. He had vanished. And yet I saw one thing that was most precious. The beam of the lantern, which Shamil had dropped, struck against a cleft in the rock wall at the back of the cavern. I saw that the cleft was wide enough for a man to pass through and that the ground lay upward within it.

Mahabat Khan was engaged too closely with the four hillmen to withdraw. The mouth of the grotto was perhaps seven paces wide, and they were trying to slip past him to take him from the sides. Verily, the Sirdar seemed to be two men, bending from side to side, parrying and slashing with an arm of steel. With a quick thrust and snap of the blade he disarmed one of the Pathans. Nay, he did not cry out his name or make any plea for mercy.

It would have been easier to check a wolf pack by prayers. I made up my mind to join him and fall, if need be, with a weapon in hand, when Artaban began to shout at his companions to stand clear.

"Aside ye dogs! I will make trial of him, and the Veiled One shall see his blood run."

The Pathans to right and left of the one-eyed chieftain gave back, and Artaban sprang at Mahabat Khan alone. Between the faint glow of the outer fires and the radiance of the lantern their figures loomed half seen—tall forms that swayed forward and back while steel grated shrilly. Eh, it lasted no more than a moment.

Artaban slashed fiercely and the Sirdar caught the descending blade upon his hand guard. The steel snapped and flew against the rock. Artaban bent low and drew from his girdle a long pistol. Stepping back swiftly, he pulled at the trigger and the flint snapped down.

Many times have I seen such weapons snap without roaring, yet fortune favored the Yuzufi, for the pistol bellowed. I heard the bullet flatten itself somewhere upon the rock, and Mahabat Khan suffered no hurt at all, while black smoke swirled through all the cavern.

"Back!" I cried to him, seizing this instant of quiet, while the Pathans were peering into the smoke. "Here—"

He turned and ran toward me, and I snatched up the lantern. To light his way—there was no time for talk or hesitation—I ran into the cleft, finding it so narrow that the sides brushed my shoulders.

The ground was firm beneath me, and the lantern showed the marks of many footprints. For perhaps ten lance lengths I went up, the crevice growing wider, until I stood within a second rock chamber.

"Set the light down—there!" Mahabat Khan pointed with his sword tip, and took his stand at one side of the entrance.

Before doing as he commanded I turned the light in all directions. The walls were of the same red stone, ridged and crumbling, as the outer cliffs, yet darker. Space and darkness lay above us, and I saw no end to this place. Near my feet lay several blankets, a water jar and the stained leaves of a Koran. In truth we had come to the nest of al-Khimar—a place of cold and darkness.

"Good!" laughed Mahabat Khan, breathing a little quickly.

When I had listened to the muttering of the Pathans in the outer cavern, I whispered to him that it would be better to go away. Shamil was urging them to follow us, and Artaban and others were grumbling. Verily, their fear of al-Khimar served us well, because the hillmen were reluctant to enter the cleft where the dim light showed. We had vanished in the smoke; they had no love of this maw of the cliff. In a little while Shamil might persuade them to go forward, perhaps by leading them.

"We can hold this corridor," the Sirdar mused.

"And gain what?" I asked. "Nay, without water or food, it would avail us nothing."

He considered and nodded.

"Is there a way out?"

"God alone knows. Let us go and see."

After looking down the passage, he felt in his girdle and drew out a little wooden tube, the same in which Baki had sealed his message. He looked at it and tossed it down the cleft. "A bone for Shamil to gnaw on! Come!"

Picking up the lantern he shook it close to his ear to hear how much oil might be in it. Then he grinned and strode back into the depths of the cavern, I following. It was needful to go quickly or not at all.

It was a strange path, that in the belly of the mountain. Indeed, it seemed to be no path at all, but a goat's track that squeezed through rock walls and ascended from ledge to ledge, and once ran along a bridge of stone over a crevice that had no bottom at all. Here the air rushed up, and the flame of the lantern flickered and died down, so that I breathed not until Mahabat Khan sheltered it in a niche between two boulders.

He said that water had made this passage through the heart of the mountain, and showed me how the surface of the rock was worn, and how the very boulders were round and smooth.

At times we were forced to quest about and choose among many passages. The thought came to me that we might have chosen wrongly, and were lost in this cursed place; but Mahabat Khan was only concerned about the oil in the lantern, lest it fail and leave us in darkness. We were walking swiftly through a long corridor when a thought came to me.

"*Bism'allah*! The Veiled One must have gone before us."

Mahabat Khan looked at me. "Eh, Daril, I wonder if Shamil is not the prophet? Hast thou seen the two, at the same moment?"

I pondered this and shook my head. Verily the veil might have hidden that red beard. I suspected that al-Khimar really came forth and ate and slept among the Pathans, unknown to them. Other rogues had played that trick before. Among them, al-Khimar would be no more than a hillman, listening to their talk. Then, slipping into the cavern, he would put on his clean garments and the green headcloth and the veil, and come out upon his speaking place. Only at times did he appear thus.

"But the voice," I sad, "the voice was different."

"Even a common singer can do that," he reminded me.

"In the cave, when the light appeared, the voice seemed to come from behind Shamil."

"True," he nodded. "That is a more difficult trick, yet I have known conjurers to throw their voices elsewhere." He thought for a while. "By a gesture or little thing a man is known. What sawest thou of al-Khimar?"

"That he had a light skin and fine eyes—that he is slender in body, and his mind quick to read thoughts."

"And knows our faces," laughed Mahabat Khan. "Except for thee, he had put an end to us."

"If Shamil is not the man," I responded, "he must have gone ahead of us."

"Then God grant we catch him, for I need al-Khimar in my hands. Look!"

He held the light low and pointed. I saw that the ground was damp and that snow lay among the boulders. Surely it did not snow down here in the belly of the mountain. I turned my eyes upward. Stars winked down at me from between the dark sides of a gorge. We had come out into the open air, and Mahabat Khan spent some time in observing landmarks so that he could find the passage again.

A little farther on we stopped again. Here a sprinkle of snow lay upon the gravel and, clearly pressed into it, we saw the mark of slender and small feet, going in the way that we were going. But we did not see al-Khimar. The gorge opened out into a nest of blind ravines. We climbed a height to observe what lay around us.

Eh, thus we beheld many things—the snow-whitened peaks, tinged by the first glow of dawn, the dark mass of Kandahar far down ahead of us, the shadow-filled plain and the great crimson fire of sunrise. It was bitterly cold, and all my body ached; my knees quivered and creaked. When the sun flooded these lofty levels, I sought a sheltered spot and lay down.

"*Bism'allah!*" I said to the Sirdar. "I did not come with thee to join a Pathan sword dance, nor did I come to frolic in ice and snow. I am tired, and here will I sleep."

So I thrust my arms into my sleeves and slept, Mahabat Khan sitting beside me. When I waked, the shadows had turned, and he was still in the same spot, the lifeless lantern at his feet. He had waited to watch beside me, and I was ashamed of my weariness and ill temper.

"Nay, Daril," he laughed, "I have learned something. Now it is time we went down to Kandahar, or those Bedouins will be back and rouse Baki with their tales."

Those Bedouins were back indeed. They had been routed out of their sleep by a rush of Pathans down the *tangi* at dawn, and had had to flee without their saddles or blankets. Probably Shamil had remembered the guides who brought us to the hills and had sent a band down to bring them in. The tribesmen being afoot, my Arabs had escaped without hurt, but were gloomy over the loss of the saddles.

When Mahabat Khan and I walked into the courtyard of his house, they were saying that all the forces of the Veiled One had sought to take them, that they had held their ground as long as they could, in spite of the fact that we twain must be captive or slain.

Thus they were protesting. The Rajput followers of the Sirdar were in a cold rage, while Abu Ashtar cursed. When they saw us, all became silent except the blind man.

"By God!" said I to the Bedouins. "I marvel that you have your shirts—or that you did not leave your breeches in the hands of the hillmen."

I added that their flight had made us walk back; and to this they had nothing to say.

"Shall we beat them?" the captain of the Rajputs asked his lord, very willingly.

"Nay," said Mahabat Khan, "they are not to be blamed."

"But the saddles—and the packs?"

"I swear," put in old Abu Ashtar who had listened intently, "that these worthless and light-minded puppies of mine shall bring you other saddles."

"I ask a harder thing," responded Mahabat Khan gravely. "That they, and you, shall say no word concerning this past night."

"On my head," swore the blind chieftain.

"Aye," assented the Sirdar with a flash of grimness, "for thou shalt be surety for their silence."

Thus chastened, the Bedouins could only stare at me. They yearned to know how we had come back to Kandahar, because they were certain we had not come down the *tangi* again. I hinted that Mahabat Khan had stood off all the men of the Veiled One with his sword, and made great show of wiping the stains of dampness from my blade with a clean cloth.

Eh, it is written that the boaster digs a pitfall for his feet to tread. After I had mocked the Bedouins and looked to see whether the mare were safe in the Sirdar's stable, I began to be hungry. Mahabat Khan seemed to have forgotten food. I was not minded to beg of his men, so I went forth to find Kushal, who had gone into the bazaar.

Seeking him, I wandered into the shadows of narrow alleys, stooping beneath the woven roofs of stalls. In a dark place among sacks of rice and trays of tea bricks I heard a swift movement behind me.

I turned to look, but it was my kismet that I should see no more in Kandahar that day. A dusty sack was cast over my head and held about my shoulders. A hand reached forth and jerked the sword from my girdle, while a dagger's point pricked the tender skin under my ribs.

"O Daril," a voice whispered through the sack, "thou art a man of judgment. Walk between us quietly. We have no mind to slay thee—now, and in this place."

"Who art thou?" I said foolishly, for the voice seemed familiar.

"Thy fate!" I heard a laugh. "Come!"

W'allahi, in such a plight a man is less than an ass! With a sack held over my shoulders, all dignity was lost. Hands gripped my arms and led me back into the stall, stumbling over bales and rugs. For a moment sunlight shone on my head; then we entered the darkness of another covered place, smelling of hemp and spices and dirt.

Here I heard camels grunting and bubbling, as they do when the loads are put on. My arms were drawn behind my shoulders and bound together skillfully. Then my knees were bound, and my ankles.

I was lifted high by several men and dropped in what seemed to be a basket, but a basket that swayed and creaked under me. Then the ends of the cords from my arms and ankles were drawn taut and knotted—so that by bending my knees up under my chin I could ease the pain of the cords, but could not raise myself in any way.

The sack was lifted and replaced at once by a kerchief, tied loosely under my chin.

"To keep off flies, O Daril," whispered the voice.

"May God requite thee for it!" I answered.

"Hearken to this, O *hakim.* Thou art in a camel's howdah, and thou art bound upon a little journey. Men will walk beside thee who care not at all for thy life. They will carry spears. If thy voice is heard after this, for any reason, those long spearheads will be thrust through thy basket. Dost thou understand?"

"Indeed," I responded. "But let the journey be short, for I shall desire water."

"Water thou shalt have and wine."

I thought that the speaker mocked me, and I said no more. As if they had waited only for me, the men began to move about; the camel beneath me rocked and lurched to its feet, and the smell of it came more strongly through the wicker work of the pannier. Then we began to walk.

By the sounds around me, we passed out into narrow alleys, brushing through the stalls of merchants who cursed the ancestors of warriors who would lead he-camels through the market at such an hour. We turned hither and yon, and began to move more swiftly.

By the motion of the camel, I knew that we went downhill, and once I heard a clatter of hoofs and the voices of Rajputs riding past, but I thought of the spears and made no sound. My captors had laid branches in the open top of the basket, and through these and the kerchief I could see no more than tiny sparkles of sunlight and blue sky.

We halted for many moments in a place where horses were gathered. Men walked about on all sides. From the talk I suspected that we were among soldiers of the Mogul. When we went on again, a deep shadow passed over my head, and sounds echoed hollowly. We were moving under an arch, probably the outer wall of Kandahar.

After this had been left behind us, things were quieter. The camels settled to a swifter stride, when I heard faintly a voice close to my head. It whispered gain, a little louder.

"Ho, Daril—how is it with thee?"

Eh, it was the voice of Kushal, the songmaker, and I answered as softly.

"Where art thou?"

He laughed a little then.

"In the other basket."

A spear or sword blade slapped angrily the side of my pannier, and I said no more. I had wished to ask him whither we were bound, but what mattered it? We were going whither we were going. It seemed to me then—I had wondered at first if the Bedouins had not come after me to make me captive on some whim—as if we were bound for the hills.

Al-Khimar's men might have entered Kandahar in force, after the Bedouins, and seen me stalking like a witless gazelle through the bazaar. In truth, I did not dream of what lay before me!

After hearing Kushal, I knew that I had a companion of misfortune. It was warm in the pannier and, in spite of cords and the ache of hunger, I began to doze. Presently all sounds and smells drifted away and I slept.

The camel waked me by kneeling. It must have been late in the afternoon, for the sun was no longer overhead. I was lifted from my basket and carried under shelter, placed upon a carpet; all the cords were severed with a sword. Only a little at first did I stretch my limbs; they ached as if all the nerves had been pierced. At this moment Kushal cried out beside me.

"Thou!"

"Thy kismet," murmured the soft voice of a woman.

I pulled the cloth from my head and saw that I was under a tent, or rather, a pavilion of blue silk, set with a splendid carpet. The air had a scent of rose leaves. Kushal sat beside me, a kerchief in his hand, his bloodshot eyes flaming and his *pugri* and white damask garments clean and in order, in spite of his trussing. The severed ends of cords lay about him.

Beyond the tent pole, on a cushioned divan, knelt Nisa. She nodded at me.

"*Hai*—thou art not an eagle this evening but a frowsy old owl, Daril."

I knew now that her voice had warned and advised me after my capture. Verily, it seemed to change with her mood. But Kushal was gripped by the heedless anger of youth. His hands shook and his voice trembled.

"God be my witness!" he cried. "I shall never honor word of thine again. In the bazaar one came to me saying that Nisa had need of my aid. I followed, and was caught like—"

"A caged parrot," she giggled. "Oh, I watched thy struggles."

Suddenly and strangely Kushal mastered himself, became utterly calm; only, his cheeks paled and his eyes darkened.

"It pleases thee to mock me," he said.

Aware of this new mood, she glanced at him from the corners of her eyes.

"To repay thee for the copper coin," she murmured.

He shrugged his slender shoulders and turned to me.

"I heard thee say thou thirsted, Daril. Only a man without honor or a woman—" his eyes ran over Nisa, dwelling upon every part of her body, as a slave buyer might look at a new purchase—"without shame would deny water to a captive."

Nisa seemed to draw back before his glance. It was true that she went unveiled, and might not be trusted, as we had both learned, but the song-maker's new mood hurt her, and she too turned to me.

"Wilt thou have sherbet or red wine, Daril?"

"Water," I grumbled, for sherbet increases thirst, and wine was not for my tasting.

She clapped her hands, and that same maid tripped in, to return presently with a tray of fruit and china bows of clear water. I drank, and began to eat of the dates, but Kushal waved away the woman. This was foolish in him, for hunger and thirst are no allies in a moment of need, and it is more profitable to prod a panther than to anger a young woman.

"What seekest thou?" he asked Nisa. "Money?"

"Nay, the emerald in thy turban cloth."

Without a word Kushal reached up and undid the clasp that held the precious stone in place. He tossed it upon the divan at the knees of the singing girl.

"And what of Daril?" jeered the young Pathan.

But Nisa rose and went to the entrance, passing without answer. At once—they must have been standing on guard—two of her warriors came and took stand within the entrance, grinning at us. When I finished all the dates, I tried to get Kushal to talk, asking him in Arabic what all this meant and what might be in store for us.

"Ask her!" he muttered after a long silence. "She alone can explain her secrets. Last night, when I went to look again at her house, these same men told me she had gone away."

I remembered that she had warned Kushal to go from Kandahar; but it is profitless to try to reason why a woman does things. Each hour brings her different moods and different thoughts.

"Nor more than a day ago thou didst call her a child untaught," I reminded him. "What now?"

Kushal was not minded to smile at his misfortune. He lay down upon the divan with his arms beneath his head and pretended to care or think nothing at all about it. He had been taken captive and bundled into a camel pannier by a woman, and his honor suffered greatly.

"She could have had the emerald yesterday, for the asking," he cried once.

It occurred to me that she had said Kushal must leave the city within a week. The time, it seemed had grown less—something had happened since our first meeting with her. Sitting in silence I listened, and after a while became certain of two things.

We were in a strange encampment, and no small one. Horses were being watered—many of them. Men passed with a hurried tread, and such talk as I heard was in Persian or dialects I knew not. At sunset the caller-to-prayer made himself heard, and his words were not familiar.

There did not seem to be many women about, and indeed little was to be heard. The camp seemed to be muffled in quiet, yet in constant motion. After dark the maid brought us a good repast, and I ate Kushal's share when he would not touch it.

Once I made as if to go out of the entrance, but the guards stayed me, saying that it was not permitted.

"By whose orders?" I asked.

They pretended not to understand. So I went and sat and listened attentively. Eh, by its tracks a camel reveals itself—whether it be laden or not, whether it be old or young, weak or strong; and by the sounds of evening much may be learned of a camp.

These were no tents of merchants. Orders were given in the speech of the Persians, and arrogantly. When a group of men passed our tent, I did not see the glow of torches or lanterns—they moved about in darkness, often stumbling over pavilion ropes and picket lines. At such times, weapons clanged or clashed. I heard an officer curse some servants for allowing a fire to blaze up. By one thing and another I thought that this was an encampment of nobles, with strong guards, and that the leaders desired not to attract attention to themselves. All this was true.

About the second hour of the night Nisa slipped into the tent. She seemed to be grieving. Her bright hair fell in disorder about her cheeks; there were shadows under her dark eyes. Soundlessly she went toward the divan upon which Kushal lay. At his feet she seated herself, he paying no heed.

In a moment I heard feet approaching, striding free and heavily. A word of command was spoken. Our two guards sprang up swiftly, drawing back the entrance hanging.

Nisa crossed her arms on her breast and bent her splendid head until it nearly touched the divan upon which she knelt.

"*Shabash*! A man spoke harshly. "Well done!"

Peering into the outer darkness I made out several figures in long mantles, the gleam of tiaras and jeweled turban crests—for an instant only, because, at a second command, the guards let fall the hanging and the footsteps retreated. Beyond doubt these lords of the encampment did not wish to be seen.

For awhile Nisa sat in silence, brushing the flies from Kushal's head, her eyes dim with thought. Never have I seen a more beautiful pair than these two—the wild Pathan, cloaked in his pride, and the golden-maned singing girl at his feet.

Eh, many times have I seen the fire of love brighten and grow dim. Nisa was wrapped up in her love for this man, as strange and fierce a love as ever glowed in the eyes of a pantheress. As if fire had burned all other feeling out of her, she bent over his feet, sweeping away the flies with the end of her shawl, until suddenly she remembered me and sprang up, bidding me follow her. Only then did Kushal look at her, as a man might glance at a dog behaving in some new fashion.

Outside the tent, she led me swiftly toward a mass of horses and stopped under the clear starlight, where none could overhear.

"An order has been given to flay him alive," she whispered, and I began to understand a little why she grieved.

At Kushal, sitting the saddle of his horse and singing in her courtyard, she had hurled insolence and defiance. For Kushal, captive and defenseless, she grieved. And yet she had brought him hither herself!

"They will torture him," she went on, "unless—" she checked the words to glance fleetingly into distant shadows—"unless thou canst bring Mahabat Khan hither before sunrise—sunrise after this next."

I wondered what this encampment was and why they wanted Mahabat Khan and how she expected me to bring him; but I said nothing, since she was minded to speak freely at last.

"When the first rim of the sun is seen over the plain, they will bind him and begin tearing the skin from his throat and breast," she whispered. "By noon, they will have taken the skin from his back and at the end of the day he will be dead."

"No man may escape his fate," I said, to spur her on.

The white blur of her face drew near me and the scent of rose leaves came to my nostrils.

"Daril" she cried softly, "thou art a man of honor. Forget that I beguiled thee in Kandahar and made sport of him." She clasped her hands and laid them against my breast. "Wilt thou pledge me this?"

"What?" I asked. "And under what conditions?"

"To ride now, at once, to Kandahar, and tell Mahabat Khan all thou hast seen. Tell him that the life of his companion, the songmaker, is in his hands. He may come alone, or with his men." She leaned close to look up into my eyes. "Daril, a man such as thou wilt not believe a woman's oath. I cannot swear to this truth, but it is surely true that Mahabat Khan will suffer no harm by coming."

"To whom?" I asked. "Who sends for him?"

"I—I do. It will be better for him to come without escort."

"W'allahi! Will the Sirdar of Ind come forth unattended at a woman's whim? To visit a woman?"

"To save the life of Kushal—aye! He must!"

"What if he chooses to bring a squadron of Moguls and his Rajputs?"

"It is all one to me; but he will fare better alone. Nay, I swear—nay, Daril, a greater lord than thou or the Sirdar of Ind, swears on his honor that

Mahabat Khan will suffer no least harm. He will be entertained for a day, perhaps a little longer, and then he and the songmaker may ride free."

Reaching down, I took her wrist in my fingers, feeling the beat of the blood in her veins. Understanding that I was making test of her, she withdrew her wrist and pressed my hand under her breast against the heart. It fluttered and throbbed as if heavy fever were in her veins. Indeed, fever burned in her.

"Thou art beside thyself, Nisa," I said. "Mahabat Khan will not believe such a tale as this of mine."

At this she laughed softly.

"Nay, he will believe. I will give thee such proof as he will believe. Thus!"

She put into my fingers a hard object, about the size of a date, wrapped in thin silk.

"Kushal's emerald," she explained. "And here—" she gave me a tiny tube such as messenger pigeons carry—"is a letter saying that Kushal will be tortured, as I have said, unless he comes."

I let the things lie in my hand while I pondered. Indeed, the songmaker was captive in this camp. As to the matter of his death, I knew not. But I believed that Nisa hoped to save his life, if Mahabat Khan could be persuaded to visit this place. Clearly it would serve no one for me to remain sitting in this tent. I decided to go to the Sirdar and explain all that had happened. The responsibility, then, would be his.

"Give me a horse," I said, "and tell me where Kandahar lies."

She sighed, as if a burden had been taken from her back, and motioned toward the line of beasts near us.

"My men have a horse awaiting thee. Kandahar lies no more than two hours to the north."

"How can I enter at night?" I demanded, remembering that the gates would be closed.

"Show the silver tube to an officer." She waved me away, as if dreading any least delay. "God requite it thee!"

The tokens I thrust into my girdle and asked yet one more thing.

"Thy sword?" She clapped her hands impatiently, and presently a tall figure swaggered up leading a saddled horse. "Sher Jan took it. He has it now."

The figure halted suddenly, and I stretched forth my hand. Indeed it was Sher Jan, my companion of the road, and among his many weapons he had my scimitar in his sash. Reluctantly he drew it forth, and I girdled it on again, without a word.

"Lead him past the guards," Nisa commanded the camel driver, when I had mounted, and, in silence, Sher Jan holding my rein, we moved away. I heard the sound of sobbing behind me, where Nisa stood, the starlight gleaming faintly on her hair. After that I was more inclined to put faith in her words, because a fair woman often tries to bend a man to her will by tears; but if she weeps after his departure, it must be that she has cause for tears.

"So thou has taken service with a new mistress," I remarked to Sher Jan.

"Aye, indeed, my lord." He grinned up at me. "Oh the excellent food, and the wealth to be had!"

He had lingered at Nisa's house on the street of the steps and had wheedled himself into the attention of her majordomo. There was no good in reproaching him for turning against me; although it irked me that he should have handled my sword.

"And thy mistress," I hazarded, "hath found a new lord to serve."

But Sher Jan's tongue would not start wagging. He conducted me past the outer sentries and commended me to the mercy of God with great dignity.

As it happened I had no need of parley at the Kandahar gate. Torches were lighted over the gate tower, and I was challenged an arrow's flight distant. When I spoke my name, the small door beside the gate was opened, and I led in my horse—a shaggy mountain pony, worth very little.

"Mahabat Khan is above," said one of the Mogul soldiers, eyeing the pony and its saddle without approval. "He gave command to send thee up."

It seemed to me that the custom of the guard had changed in the last day and night; but I was grateful that Mahabat Khan should be at the gate. He was sitting on a couch in the chamber of the tower above the arch, by an embrasure that gave him sight of the road of approach. He looked graver than before, with deeper lines about his eyes.

"My men were searching for thee, Daril," he said at once. "How in the name of God didst thou get out of the city?"

"In a camel's howdah," I answered, but he did not laugh.

He was in no mood for trifling. I told my tale with few words, watching his brow darken the while. At the end he struck his hip impatiently.

"Am I to shepherd witless minstrels and doddering *hakims*? Where are the tokens?"

He glanced at the emerald and laid it aside, but the tiny message tube he turned over in his fingers before withdrawing the cap. He shook out a roll of paper no larger than the written prayers that some physicians give their patients to swallow by way of cure. It had only a line of writing on it, in a fine hand, without flourishes.

"A woman wrote this," he said. "It bears witness to thee, Daril, in this wise:

> "*The Arab* hakim *is a speaker of truth, and the hour of fate is the second sunrise.*"

Again he glanced at the tube, which had elaborate ornament inscribed upon it.

"How large is that encampment?" He used the word *lashgar*, which may mean the traveling camp of a lord, or the gathering place of a tribe.

I told him that they had led me out by the horse lines, and I had seen little. But I thought that several hundred men might be in those tents. At this he nodded.

"And the visitors who came to look into thy tent—what didst thou see of them?"

"They walked carelessly, spoke harshly, and wore costly attire."

"What is thy thought concerning them?"

"Mahabat Khan," I said, "at first I thought that some of al-Khimar's bands had made me captive. But the men of that *lashgar* were not Pathans. I do not think the girl Nisa serves this prophet."

Again he nodded.

"They, who hold Kushal, are Persians. While I sat beside thee on the height behind Kandahar, in the clear light of early morning, I saw at a great distance a long line of men and beasts moving up from the western defiles into the plain. They were soon lost to sight among the trees."

"Eh, then they must be the hunters the camp al-Khimar saw in his dream."

"Or otherwise. They are at least Persians who have crossed the frontier and kept very much to themselves." He mused a while, pulling at his mustache. "I sent two of my troopers out to look at them from a distance; my men reported that they number more than a thousand, and have baggage enough for a journey to Isfahan."

I wanted to ask why such men should have come up into the plain without seeking Kandahar, and why they should desire Mahabat Khan to come
to them. Then I remembered that al-Khimar had promised his hill people
that they should plunder this *lashgar*.

"It is well for al-Khimar that these Persians have come into the plain;
for, if his men had attacked such a strong force, the Pathans would have
been cut up and driven away empty-handed, and they might then have
made al-Khimar the victim of their disappointment."

Mahabat Khan looked at me with straightforward eyes.

"Daril, I think thou hast spent more time in the saddle of war than
upon the rug of the physician."

He told me to go and sleep, but not to leave the tower. So I unrolled a
rug and lay down by the charcoal brazier in the corner. The stone beneath
the rug was both hard and cold, and the smoke from the charcoal made
me cough, so I did not sleep at first. Mahabat Khan called at once to the
men below, and several of them came and saluted him. What orders he
gave I know not, but they went away with the manner of men who have
much to do in little time.

Horses were led out below, and I heard the little door open and shut.
The horses trotted away and began to gallop, before they were out of hearing. Mahabat Khan mused awhile, leaning in the embrasure, looking up
at the stars. Then, without calling anyone, he blew out the candles and
threw himself down on the divan.

When he heard me moving about, trying to ease my bones on the stones,
he laughed a little.

"These Persians have made Baki fearful," he remarked. "Also the plan-
ets foretell calamity to come—so he calculates. He is drinking wine and
making his calculations over again in his tower, after praying me to take
charge of the city gate."

"And thou?" I made bold to ask.

"Eh, the stars tell the hour of the night, but men make or break themselves."

He said nothing of Kushal or of what he meant to do; before long he
was breathing deep. I do not think he had had any sleep since two nights
before.

Just before I fell asleep the thought came to me, as such slight things
do when the mind is empty and drowsy, that Baki had warned Mahabat
Khan that, if he sent a messenger to al-Khimar, he would have not one

but two blood feuds on his hands. Indeed, matters had turned out as Baki had predicted.

I heard a stir below us before dawn, and Mahabat Khan rose and went out quietly. It was too cold to sleep anymore, so I sat up and fed more charcoal to the brazier and became aware of excitement that grew around me as the light increased.

Because Mahabat Khan had commanded it, I remained in the tower—that is, within call of the tower. The gate was still closed and held in strength by the garrison—threescore Moguls, short and stocky men, in good chain mail and leather, wearing burnished steel helmets. The Sirdar's escort of Rajputs sat by their saddled horses, with the air of men awaiting a summons. To them I went, seeking Dost Muhammad, the leader of the escort, who was striding back and forth, examining girths and stirrup leathers.

Dost Muhammad stood even taller than I, by reason of his white silk *pugri*; he was a man gaunt and restless as a racing horse and almost as sparing of words. His beard, brushed to either side his chin, was streaked with white. Verily, with his feathers and his stiff muslin skirt projecting out from his knees, and his white leather slippers and the tiny jeweled hilt of his light sword, he seemed to be robed for an audience at court rather than service of any kind. Yet Kushal had told me that he was terrible with the sword, when aroused. When I asked whether he was in command here, at the gate, he looked down at me, as if searching for insult, and said that Rajputs never mounted guard.

Then he remembered that I was the guest of his lord and he began to explain what all Kandahar was talking about. The men of the garrison sent out by Mahabat Khan last night—the party I had heard riding off—had scouted around the Persian *lashgar*. They had brought back three prisoners, sentries carried off from an outer post. These captives proved to be Red Hats, soldiers of the great shah of Persia. They had been persuaded—Dost Muhammad did not choose to explain in what manner—to talk and had admitted that twelve hundred or more soldiers of the shah were in that camp, commanded by royal officers.

The Red Hats swore that they did not know why they had been led beyond the frontier, although they believed that the hunting was only a pretense. They swore likewise, very earnestly, that their leaders had no designs on Kandahar, because no artillery or siege tools had been brought along.

"There are no greater liars anywhere," said Dost Muhammad, "than these dogs of Persians. Still, it must be true that their camp is a military camp, and it is well indeed for the Mogul governor that the Sirdar of Ind is here."

"Why?" I asked, for the captain of the Rajputs was too blunt to relish anything but plain words.

"When the eagle is perched on the edge of his nest, the hawk keeps its distance," he smiled.

He added that Kandahar, being the gateway in the mountains between Persia and Ind, was greatly desired by the shah.

For the present the shah and the Mogul were at peace, but it was the uneasy peace of powerful emperors, who complimented each other while they had their hands on their swords.

"Nay," said Dost Muhammad gravely, "those Persians have crept up to pluck Kandahar from Baki."

"What will the governor do?"

The tall Rajput had all the contempt of his race for the man of peace and trade.

"Baki the Wise! I went before him with the Sirdar after the dawn prayer, and he was like a man struck on the head. He begged the Sirdar to defend Kandahar, and hastened off to eat opium and pray."

Evidently Baki thought that calamity was descending upon him! Now it was clear why Kushal had been carried off. The leaders of the Persians had heard of the Sirdar's presence in Kandahar and wished to get him out of the walls, in their hands, away from the garrison. The Sirdar of Ind would be a splendid hostage, in their camp. But if he chose to defend Kandahar against them, their task would be no easy one.

"No doubt," I said, "they will pay the woman, Nisa, a fine price for bringing them the songmaker."

Although Dost Muhammad would admit no knowledge of this woman, it seemed to me that she had planned the trap for the Sirdar, knowing that Kushal was his friend—knowing that he would risk his own life to aid Kushal.

Mahabat Khan, by his prompt sortie of the night, had their plans. But what he would do now, I did not know. With three hundred Mogul men-at-arms and a handful of Rajput riders, he could not attempt to rescue Kushal; nor could he hope to defend the outer wall of the city against an attack of twelve hundred Persian Red Hats. Then, too, he had to watch al-Khimar, who was no doubt hovering like a vulture in his hills.

I saw only one thing for Mahabat Khan to do—to retire with the governor into the citadel and try to defend it as best he could. But Dost Muhammad chose to mock at this plan.

"When did an eagle fly into a cage?"

Indeed, Mahabat Khan did otherwise—and of all things this seemed to me the most mad and vain. He rode up to us alone, but clad in a cloth-of-silver robe of honor. He chose me and Dost Muhammad and two troopers from the Rajputs. He left the gate in charge of a Mogul officer and, when all the men of his cavalcade had mounted and reined behind him, trotted off toward the citadel.

In the garden by Baki's tower he dismounted, leaving our horses with the other Rajputs, who looked crestfallen when they were ordered to remain in the garden until his return. With only Dost Muhammad and me he walked under the trees to a narrow door like the one beside the main gate. This he unlocked and locked again after us, confiding the key to one of the troopers.

We had come out into a shadowy ravine and, before the Sirdar had gone a hundred paces, I knew the place. It was the same ravine by which we had come down from the heights the day before. Mahabat Khan, looking neither to right nor left, began to climb up among the boulders.

Before the shadows turned, we reached the spot where I had dozed during our flight from the Pathan's *sangar*. Here the Sirdar halted to gaze down at the city and the distant plain, which was motionless under a burning sun. No caravans moved along the road; no horsemen entered and left the villages. As birds quiet their noise and take shelter before a storm, the people of the valley had withdrawn from sight to await events. Mahabat Khan looked at everything and turned, striding into the rock-strewn gully that led to the caverns.

"May God prosper it!" I muttered, thinking of what we had left behind us in that place.

"Are there horses ahead?" Dost Muhammad wondered aloud.

Unlike the Sirdar he hated to walk; indeed, he limped already in his light slippers, and the other Rajputs eyed the rocky way with little favor. They would rather have galloped in the saddle down to Satan than have climbed afoot to Paradise! Mahabat Khan had given them a half-dozen split pine torches to carry, while he let me walk unburdened.

"Where is he going?" I asked.

"To preach to some hill tribes," Dost Muhammad muttered, "some men of that prophet."

W'allahi! It seemed to me then that Baki was wiser than we. I would have relished both wine and opium before entering that pit again.

"Yea," I said to the Rajput captain, "there are horses beyond us, but it is likely thou and I will descend into our graves before we mount a stirrup again."

This prospect of danger put an end to his grumbling. The hillmen he held in utter scorn. But it seemed to me that Mahabat Khan might stroke a wounded panther more easily than talk to those Pathans again. He must have counted on al-Khimar's absence from the valley this afternoon and on persuading the tribes to take his side in the coming struggle.

It is written that God deals lovingly with the bold of heart, and many times since have I thought of that saying. Mahabat Khan staked his own life and ours that day, and God put a weapon into his hand. Nay, he did not look for it!

It was Dost Muhammad who caught my arm and whispered—

"What is this?"

I looked up and saw, a bowshot ahead of us, al-Khimar sitting on a boulder in the gully. He wore the same brown mantle and wide green turban and veil, and his back was toward us. He sat like a man who rests beside the path he follows.

Mahabat Khan saw him in the same instant and sprang forward. He made no sound, but one of the troopers, shifting the torches on his shoulder, made some noise and al-Khimar looked over his arm at us. At once he sprang to his feet and ran. His mantle floating behind him, he skimmed among the boulders, holding something in his arms.

"Take him!" Mahabat Khan cried to his followers.

But before we had run ten bowshots, al-Khimar vanished. We saw him disappear into a narrow cleft of the rock that walled the end of the gully. This was the place where we had come out under the stars. At the cleft, Mahabat Khan checked us, bidding us light the torches.

It was no easy task. Mahabat Khan went on into the cleft, and Dost Muhammad knelt, cursing the damp wind of the place, while he struck flint against steel, dashing little sparks upon a wad of dry hemp that he placed in the end of the pine sticks. Many sparks died before the hemp began to smoke, and the flame caught slowly upon the wood. Then Dost Muhammad seized the torch and waved it until the fire sputtered and flared.

Still waving it, he ran into the rock passage, his men after him, and I following. We did not see anything ahead for awhile, but when we came down over the ledges, we made out two figures hastening below us.

Al-Khimar must have had eyes that could see in the dark, or he knew every step of the way. He might have had a torch or lantern of his own hidden somewhere, but he had not waited to light it, thinking that we could not follow in the darkness.

When Mahabat Khan and I had felt our way out of those accursed caverns, the path had seemed endless and terrifying. In reality it was not far to the chasm where the rock bridge led across.

Guided by our torch, Mahabat Khan was only a spear's thrust behind the veiled figure. Al-Khimar ran out upon the narrow bridge and slipped or stumbled. Suddenly he screamed, falling to his knees and clutching that which he held still in his arms. The shrill cry echoed and quivered in the chasm, and Dost Muhammad cursed aloud.

Sword in hand, the Sirdar bent over the kneeling figure. He reached down and jerked off the veil and stood thus without moving. When we came up, Dost Muhammad held the torch high, and we stared at the terrified face of the kneeling man.

Eh, we saw before us Baki the Wise. His eyes were fixed on the darkness beneath him, his whole body rigid with terror.

After a moment the Sirdar thrust back his sword and helped Baki to our side of the chasm.

"Light another torch," he bade us, "and retire beyond hearing until I summon you."

When this was done, we went and sat on a ridge of rock, breathing heavily, staring at the tall and gleaming figure of the Sirdar and the man who crouched at his feet.

What they said I know not. Mahabat Khan seemed to ask many questions, and Baki, after a space, began to complain shrilly. Swiftly Mahabat Khan cut him short and called to the Rajput captain.

The Sirdar looked and spoke like a man who sees his way clear before him, after searching through darkness and uncertainty. Although he was no longer on the brink of the chasm, Baki still labored with his fear. His eyes gleamed, when Mahabat Khan took from his arms the bundle that he had carried during his flight.

It was a gray sack of coarse cloth. The Sirdar thrust his hand into it, drawing out a little heap of silver coins. At these Baki stared anxiously, and I wondered what strange hope he might have in this money—sitting thus after that wild chase through the gut of the mountain. His face fell when Mahabat Khan handed the sack to me.

"Nay!" cried Baki. "Nay, that is mine!" He trembled and kept stretching out a thin hand toward the sack. Mahabat Khan looked down at him in silence for a moment, while the governor of Kandahar put forth his hand and drew it back like a child, desiring something greatly, yet fearing to be punished.

"Art thou," the Sirdar asked presently, "the servant of the emperor, to whom a trust was given?"

Baki nodded several times.

"Then let there be an end of al-Khimar," the Sirdar said. "And do thou, yield to me the command of the men and treasure of Kandahar, until such time as thou canst go before the emperor and justify thyself."

Again Baki assented, his eyes still fixed upon the sack in my hands. But the tall Pathan was not content with this.

"Wilt thou yield thy trust to me?" he asked again.

"Into thy hands," muttered Baki, "I give the government of Kandahar."

He glanced up at us with such malice that Dost Muhammad swore into his beard, and I felt misgiving. Truly, in that day of calamity few men would have wished to take the reins Baki let fall.

"And I accept the responsibility," answered Mahabat Khan.

At once he gave an order to his two troopers to take Baki back with them, going slowly along the heights and not descending to the garden gate of Kandahar until sunset. He bade them escort Baki to his tower, taking care to veil his face, and to keep him there, a captive, through the night.

Immediately Dost Muhammad voiced an objection.

"Mahabat Khan, the follower of this man slew Rai Singh. Let him come with us and make atonement."

The Sirdar did not reprove his officer for this speech.

"Within an hour," he said, "the murderer of Rai Singh shall face my sword, or thine."

Dost Muhammad uttered an exclamation and touched his sword hilt, stepping back. Then the troopers took one torch and Baki, and they hastened back, desiring to be out of the cavern. Mahabat Khan and the old Rajput and I went forward.

Nay, I would have chosen to go with the troopers. Surely Baki, who had taken the veil of al-Khimar, had laid many plots, and Shamil likewise. That Baki was a coward made matters no easier for us, because the intrigues of a weak and covetous man do more harm than the scheming of a bold rogue.

I thought that Mahabat Khan was taking a mad risk, to go among the Pathans. Baki had tricked him and nearly slain him twice. Indeed, Mahabat Khan was not the match of these men, much less the Persians, at scheming. By good fortune, when he ventured into the heights, he had made Baki captive. What more could he do?

But Mahabat Khan was a leader of cavalry, a man of his word, faithful alike to his lord and his men. He saw only one thing to do—to go forward until he was overcome. And God had given him one weapon—the knowledge that Baki had played the role of al-Khimar. This weapon he used in a very simple way.

It is ill to rouse sleeping dogs. The Pathans in the prophet's gorge were sleeping wolves!

Standing in the deep shadow of the outer cavern, we could see all of that great pit of the hills. It looked different by day than by night. The sun struck against the lofty cliff of dark red limestone, filling the bed of the pit with a ruddy half light. The gleam of dazzling snow on sentinel peaks far overhead filled our eyes.

Perhaps six hundred tribesmen sat and slept and gossiped and ate, scattered in clan groups among their horses. Some were testing sword edges, or binding feathers upon fresh arrows. Others overhauled the flints and priming holes of a few firelocks. The women and boys were making ready to bundle up their belongings on pack animals, to follow down behind the warriors, in the raid of the coming night.

Upon the opposite ridge, where we had first seen the *sangar*, stood a solitary sentry, wrapped in sheepskins. I saw the one-eyed Artaban chewing the last meat off a sheep's bone and then wiping his fingers on a passing dog. At his side squatted the red-bearded Shamil, casting anxious glances at times toward the cavern, as if he expected al-Khimar to appear.

Eh, they were like drowsy wolves, wary of the unknown, more than ready to quest, to prey when roused, a pack that awaited its leader. And in full sight of them Mahabat Khan stepped out upon the boulder with the Rajput officer at his side.

"O ye men of the hills!" he cried his greeting, in their speech.

At first the nearest children bobbed up to stare and run from him. Warriors turned on their elbows and grasped for their weapons when they saw the glittering garments of the two strangers. Men rose to their feet and gradually the murmur of the camp died into silence. In truth, they were too amazed to understand what was before them.

"I come from al-Khimar," Mahabat Khan cried in his deep voice.

This loosed the shackles of their amazement. Shamil sidled in, peering up at the boulder from his slits of eyes. Artaban grunted and pushed his way toward us, and presently a mass of them elbowed and swayed before the boulder.

"Who art thou?" demanded one.

"The son of Ghuyar, Chief of the Lodi people, Sirdar of Ind, under authority of the emperor!"

There was silence anew, while they pondered this, and then a great outcry of amazement. Mahabat Khan addressed them in their own Pushtu, and many were found to tell me later the words he spoke. Not a man or child of them but had heard of the battles won and the honors gained by the soldier of the hills. Only there were no Lodi clansmen in that throng, and these men who had gathered at al-Khimar's summons were resentful of authority and suspicious of new developments. They had the feeling of being tricked or trapped, and mutters of anger rose and swelled, until Mahabat Khan flung up his arm.

"Are ye wolves or men? Where are your leaders? Set forward the leaders, for I have come to speak at a *jirhgar* and not with wolves!"

A *jirhgar* is a council of elders and chieftains, with all the tribes listening. And because they were curious to hear what message Mahabat Khan might have for them, they began to call for their chief men to come forth. Artaban and half a dozen others ranged themselves under the boulder, and Shamil joined the group, peering up under his shaggy brows.

Mahabat Khan would not go down until they were seated, all six hundred of them, and then he went leisurely and sat upon a large rock, his hands clasped over his knee. As the hillmen were squatted on the ground, this set him a little over them, as if he spoke from a throne, and increased his dignity.

The straightforward manner of the man had calmed them. They saw that he had only one or two followers. I lingered in the shadow of the cavern. Their curiosity grew mighty indeed. Mahabat Khan had stepped out of the cave where al-Khimar was supposed to dwell; he had said that he came from the prophet. I think only Shamil recognized him as the Pathan who had ventured hither the night before last, and Shamil, with Baki absent, hesitated to cry out his knowledge. The others, seeing him clad in this new fashion, in daylight, thought not at all of the shaggy Mahabat Khan who had come among them by firelight.

"Al-Khimar," the Sirdar said at once, "hath given me his place among ye. I have come to lead ye to a battle this night, to the spoil that al-Khimar truly foresaw."

W'allahi! When a blunt man speaks thus, who does not believe? A schemer might have argued, and a prophet have exhorted in vain. But the Pathans, drawing a long breath, became attentive. Probably al-Khimar had kept them waiting overlong.

"I shall remain among ye," he said again, "I alone, until the end of things."

They did not believe this at first; but, as he spoke on, they began to consider and to believe.

Of all things he told them the truth—that twelve hundred Persians had been sent by the shah to take Kandahar by a trick; that this force was too great for the hillmen to attack alone; that, besides, the Persians were now camped in the plain out beyond Kandahar.

He described the camp, as his scouts had seen it. Then he talked about the great shah of Persia, revealing his trickery and cruelty, his way of venturing where he was not known and putting to death all who offended him. Yea, the Sirdar showed them that with the Persians quartered in Kandahar, the men of the hills would be hunted and driven from their *sangar*.

"My brother-in-arms, the songmaker, is captive in that camp," he said suddenly, "and at the next dawn the Persians will begin flaying him alive, unless I yield myself also to them. And I mean to be in that camp before sunrise."

They could understand now his need of making war upon the Persians. This was well, because otherwise they would have suspected a trick.

"If ye will," he cried very loud, "ye can take me and sell me to the men of the shah."

This was what they had been considering, but they denied it loudly at his challenge.

"Nay, Mahabat Khan," declared Artaban, "we are not traitors. But we are too few to go against twelve hundred."

Then the Sirdar revealed the plan he had made. He knew the Persians would not move out until dawn, because they would wait that long to see if he would give himself up. He meant to have the Moguls of the garrison sally out in the last hours of darkness and make an onset upon the *lashgar*.

Upon the heels of this charge he would lead the Pathans to attack the tents, thus taking the Persians by surprise at two points.

Eh, he knew these hillmen. The plan warmed their hearts. They would not have advanced alone against regular soldiery; but to dash in on the flank of the Moguls—to slash and loot among the tents!

"*Hai-a!*" they murmured, beginning to be eager.

Then it was that Shamil acted. He had waited until he saw the issue going against him, had waited vainly for al-Khimar to appear. Now he sprang up and pointed at the Sirdar.

"Fools! This is the governor's spy who tried to seize al-Khimar."

He had waited too long. Artaban was thinking now, not of the Veiled One, but of the coming raid.

"Nay," they cried, "this is the Sirdar of Ind."

Mahabat Khan took matters in his own hand.

"Choose, ye men of the hills, will ye go against the Persians, as Pathans should? Or lurk here like the thieves of al-Khimar?"

The chieftain of the Yuzufi was the first to spring up.

"By God, I will go with thee!"

"And I!" cried others, not willing to be thought lacking in courage. Many said nothing, but Mahabat Khan gave them no chance to quarrel about it.

"Will ye have me for leader, or him?" And he pointed at the enraged Shamil.

Now it is a strange thing but true that men are ever willing to pull down an old leader for a new one, and these Pathans loved both daring and dignity. A moment ago they might have slashed Mahabat Khan to pieces, but now they rallied to him.

"With thee will we go!"

"Then I shall be obeyed, from now—from this instant!"

His dark eyes swept over them confidently. And Shamil, struggling with his anger, learned the truth of the saying that a man who cannot master himself may not lead others.

"Wait!" He tried a new course, changing his words. "Wait for the coming of the Veiled One and hear his command!"

"Then would ye wait long," smiled the Sirdar, "for al-Khimar is sitting with Baki the governor in the tower of Kandahar. As for thee—" he turned swiftly upon Shamil—"may God judge thee, for thou hast slain a man of mine, taking him unaware. For thee there is but one choice. Wilt thou draw thy sword against me, or Dost Muhammad?"

The captain of the Rajputs stirred and came forward.

"Is this the one who struck down Rai Singh?"

"In the bazaar," assented the Sirdar. "I saw his face, and there are not two such beards in these mountains."

When Shamil appealed to the Pathans, they jeered at him. In truth, they had not known of the killing in Kandahar. They cared not at all about the life of Rai Singh, but they knew the law of the punishment of blood. Any relative or companion-in-arms of the dead man was privileged to draw his sword against Shamil, and the redbeard must look to his own life.

The law of the hills is inexorable—that no man may shrink from his quarrel. Even Shamil saw the uselessness of appeal, and his face grew hard. He looked once toward the cavern; his eyes no longer drooped, but glared hatred. No doubt he thought al-Khimar had betrayed him.

In the end he chose to fight Dost Muhammad. Mahabat Khan seated himself on his stone. True, the Rajput seemed both lank and old, and his small sword was lighter than Shamil's long *tulwar*. But Dost Muhammad grinned at the choice, motioning back the hillmen who thronged about him.

"Thou shalt taste what is stored up for thee," he said to the redbeard.

I wondered what Mahabat Khan would do if Shamil vanquished the Rajput, but he seemed not at all concerned. The hillmen thought the more of him because he had been willing to take Rai Singh's death as his own quarrel.

"Al-Khimar hath set thee upon me," Shamil muttered, and seemed willing to say more, but Artaban mocked him; and presently, the space before the rock being cleared, Shamil fell to watching the Rajput who had drawn his sword and stood in readiness.

The light blade of Dost Muhammad was a *khanda*, double edged and finely balanced, of blue steel. The *tulwar* of Shamil was longer and much heavier at the head—a weapon made for a wide slash. As to strength, I could not judge. Dost Muhammad stood almost rigid, balanced on his thin feet, while Shamil moved about restlessly as a chained bear, his jaw outthrust, his heavy shoulders moving under his tunic.

"*Inshallah!*" cried Artaban. "As God wills it, let the end come!"

The two swordsmen watched each other as keenly as hawks. Being afoot and with curved blades, the struggle would be decided swiftly. Shrewdly, each waited for the other to leap in, while the tribes breathed heavily and jostled, not to lose a single glimpse of the two men.

Suddenly Dost Muhammad paced forward, his curved blade held at his hip. This spurred on Shamil, who cried out and ran in, his mantle flying, his *tulwar* flashing out and down. The Rajput thrust out his long arm and parried, letting the long blade slide off his *khanda*.

"*Hai!*" cried Artaban. "The stork wards off the hawk!"

Shamil pretended then to rush in, twice, without being able to draw Dost Muhammad into a false guard. Then he slashed at the head and changed direction in midair, to strike the Rajput's slender hips. Again Dost Muhammad parried; and now the two blades sang and clashed so swiftly that I could not follow thrust and cut.

I saw that the tall Rajput walked forward slowly, and that by degrees he forced Shamil to guard himself. The *tulwar* man scowled, springing back again and again to escape those light cuts of the *khanda*. Then he saw the folly of falling upon the defense, and leaped forward, his long blade singing in the air.

Dost Muhammad sprang this time to meet him. The swords clashed and parted, and clashed anew. Shamil cried out, and swung up his *tulwar* to put all of his strength in one slash.

Instead of drawing back, the Rajput stepped in, his blade flicking sidewise across his enemy's breast. Shamil made his slash indeed, but the *tulwar* slowed in the air and fell from his hands. The front of his tunic under the ribs suddenly became red. The *khanda* had touched him and passed half through his body.

Dost Muhammad laughed and stood to one side, lowering his point. Shamil, dying upon his feet, gripped his breast, his knees sinking under him. His red beard stood out strangely, as his face became bloodless.

I looked at the Rajput. He was breathing evenly, wiping clean his blade with a cloth he had picked up from the ground.

"By God!" cried the one-eyed Artaban. "This man has held a sword before now!"

The slaying of Shamil silenced any who might have sided against Mahabat Khan. When the Sirdar told them that he sought for true men who would not turn away from weapons, and that men of another mind need not come with him, the Pathans all cried that they would follow him.

So he drew apart while they made ready, and Dost Muhammad refreshed himself with wine. He took me aside with him and told me the secret of Baki.

Baki the Wise was a man of a single craving. He coveted wealth—gold pieces and silver. He stinted himself to gather in money.

And when he had found that the revenues of Kandahar yielded little more than the emperor's tithe, he had bethought him of the hill tribes. Shamil, a merchant of Kandahar, had told the governor of this valley, of their favorite camping place and of the passage through the mountain that led to it. Shamil alone knew of this passage. They knew the superstition of the hills, and planned between them for Baki to appear in the valley, veiled, so that he would not be recognized. Baki had once been a reader of the Koran and knew its verses by heart.

He found that the tribes were afraid of him, and he gained real influence over them by foretelling the coming of certain caravans—a thing well known to him in Kandahar. He gathered tribute from the tribes, while he held them in leash by promising to lead them to war. Shamil, abiding with them, watched their moods.

Baki could come and go unseen from his tower, by the little door. So much he had confessed to Mahabat Khan when he was caught in the caverns. As to the bag of money, he had said he meant to give it to the Pathans, but more probably he had been taking it from the tower to a safer hiding place. It was not all his money.

The coming of the Persians had found him unprepared to make any defense. He had thought of loosing the tribes upon the camp, but had lacked courage to lead them. Truly, a man who gathers wealth is fearful of harm!

"He was taken like a hare, running from one hole to another," I said.

"But his scheming opened a way to strike at our enemy," said Mahabat Khan, and when Dost Muhammad came up he gave us careful orders.

He bade us return at once to Kandahar by the caverns. He wrote out an order for us to give the leader of the Mogul garrison. All the garrison was to be led out under Dost Muhammad and the Mogul captain, about the fourth hour of the night. All must be mounted. With the first trace of light over the plain, they were to attack the Persian camp from the Kandahar side.

He would lead the Pathans down the *tangi* and the river valley, and be in position to attack from the west at the same time. Dost Muhammad listened intently and nodded, saying briefly—"On my honor!" He asked how many men should be left to keep the citadel.

"One," said Mahabat Khan grimly, "to watch Baki."

Dost Muhammad looked at me instantly, saying nothing. I knew that he meant to put me in place of his men, who would not relish being left behind. The prospect filled him with quiet joy, and he was only disconsolate because we could not ride back to the city.

He saluted Mahabat Khan and turned away. At the cave mouth we both looked back, beholding only the tumultuous preparations of the tribes—and the cold body with the red beard, outstretched by the boulder. So elated were we that we did not reflect how unruly were these same Pathans, and how Mahabat Khan would be cut off from all word from us.

"*Hai*, Daril," cried Dost Muhammad, "the sniff of a battle gives life to thy aged bones."

"Nay," I said, "my old bones rejoice because life is in them after I had thought myself dead."

More time had passed than we thought, and it was after sunset before we reached the last height. The descent in growing darkness was both slow and painful, and more than once we went astray. By the time we beheld the wall loom up before us, Dost Muhammad was cursing by all the ninety and nine holy names and more names of Hindu gods. The gate was locked, and we had to shout before servants came with torches and went to fetch the Rajputs with the keys. Dost Muhammad was fuming voicelessly, asking how in the name of all the gods he was to rouse and muster and lead out three hundred men at the time appointed. He calmed a little when he found it was no more than the third hour of the night. He hastened to the tower where, as I had suspected, he bade me take the responsibility of Baki, so he would have all his men.

This was a mistake, and I was doubtful about standing guard over the governor of Kandahar in his own tower. True, Baki was still veiled, his arms bound, and the tower chamber darkened. I did not think he would wish to reveal himself in this garb.

"Send me the Bedouins and Abu Ashtar," I responded, "and I will remain here."

Full of his coming battle, Dost Muhammad hastened off. Presently the eleven Bedouins appeared, full of curiosity.

They all peered at Baki in the starlight of a window and satisfied themselves that this was indeed al-Khimar. To put an end to their questions, I invented a fearful story of how the Veiled One had been chased through caverns that led to the underworld, and how Mahabat Khan had fought with him on a bridge of rock over a bottomless pit.

This gave them something to think about, for each one was trying to memorize the story, to improve upon it at the next telling. Baki understood me, but had nothing to say.

After awhile, I too became thoughtful. After all, of what was Baki guilty? We did not know for certain that he had sent Shamil to slay Mahabat Khan. Indeed, why should he have desired the death of the Sirdar?

In the hurry of events at the gorge I had not spoken of this; now I dared not ask Baki about it, before the Bedouins. It seemed to me that the prisoner was restless and breathing heavily, and that he roused up whenever hastening footsteps passed under the tower. Dost Muhammad had told the Moguls that Baki was taking opium, which was a well-known failing of the governor. No one came to ask about him, and presently all was quiet around the tower.

Then this quiet was broken horribly by the voice of the captive. He cried out in a shrill whimper that made the Bedouins gasp.

"*Ai-a!* This is a night of fear. The wolves are sitting on their haunches and blood will fill the gullies before dawn. Oh, the terror!"

He continued to moan and exclaim, rocking back and forth.

"May God forgive me, I see the death of a thousand souls! I see shadows riding in a host through the plain!"

Then he sighed deeply and flung himself back on the couch.

"May God be merciful to me—it was not my doing. May their blood not be on my head."

"Allah!" whispered the blind Abu Ashtar. "He prophesies!"

At first it had startled me, until I reflected that Baki was no doubt playing a trick of some kind, to excite the Arabs or gain his freedom. But it
was otherwise. The man was gripped by a great terror, and so real was his
fear that we began to share it.

"By God, Daril," said Abu Ashtar again, "this is truth indeed. What is
happening in the plain?"

Baki kept on moaning weakly, at times starting to speak and then checking himself to break into new lament. The Bedouins were thrilled.

"The garrison is gone out," muttered Baki, and turned his head toward me. "Has not Mahabat Khan led down the Pathans to attack the
lashgar?"

Since Dost Muhammad had spoken before him, I saw no good in trying to conceal our plans, and told him what was passing.

"Then they are doomed," cried Baki and, as if breaking the chains that
held him silent, he cried out harshly—

"You do not know that Shah Abbas, king of kings, lord of Iran and Irak,
and master of Persia is in that *lashgar*!"

For a moment I did not understand the significance of his words and
then I doubted that this could be true.

"That is surely a lie!" I said.

"By the triple oath I swear it," he moaned, and then angry impatience
swept over him. "Daril, the shah is in that *lashgar*. The Persians Mahabat Khan captured told him many things, but not that."

I was too astounded to wonder then how Baki came to know this. For
awhile I pondered, the Bedouins, breathless with interest, pressing closer
not to miss a word. *W'allahi*, they thought that this was indeed a noble
prophecy!

A little at a time I pieced things together in my mind. Nisa, with her
passenger pigeons flying from the west—her eagerness to make Mahabat
Khan captive—her promise that a king would be surety for the life of Mahabat Khan, if he gave himself up. Nay, she was one of the women spies
of the Persian court; and she had been willing to trick Kushal to aid the
ambition of Shah Abbas.

So the whole matter became clear in mind, as a mirage drifting away
from the hot plain shows the bare rocks and gullies that are really there.
It was like the Persians to plan such a trick—to pretend that the shah had
been hunting in these mountains, that the shah was really entertaining
Mahabat Khan as a guest. But once in Kandahar with his troops, the gate-

way of the hills would be Persian indeed, and not soon would Mahabat
Khan win his freedom.

"Fool!" cried Baki, trembling. "Canst thou not see what is about to
happen? The Persians will beat off the Moguls and those hillmen; they
will follow up to Kandahar and enter it easily. They will come here and
take thee and set thee on a stake, on a greased stake, to die slowly, for the
length of a day."

"Allah!" breathed the Bedouins, agape. Verily, this was about to happen.
I knew well that Shah Abbas would not venture over the frontier without
a strong guard of his warlike nobles, the *atabegs*, and hundreds of his veteran mailed cavalry, the *kurshis* and his men-at-arms, the Red Hats, who
would rather slay than plunder, and rather torture than slay.

When I thought of the fury of the shah and his men, surprised and attacked in his camp, my bowels became weak and ached mightily.

"It is certain," cried Baki, "that he has other forces in support across
the frontier within a day's ride. There is only one thing to be done, Daril.
I have gold—some gold, hidden here in the tower. I will show thee where
it is, and thou and these Arabs can take it, and bear me across the hills
into Ind. We can take a boat on the Indus and be safe from all harm. But
we must hasten!"

Indeed, I was tempted. Who would not be tempted, knowing that this
miser must have gold enough hidden away to yield us luxury for years?
No doubt he would try to trick us again, but the Bedouins and I would
know how to deal with him.

"We can leave the city now without hindrance," whispered Baki, still
shaken by his fear. "But in two hours it may be too late."

I went to the embrasure and looked out. Clouds hid the stars and an icy
wind swept and swayed through the gardens of the almost deserted citadel. There was no telling the hour. I knew it must be long after midnight,
and that the air was full of a rising storm. So much the better, if we fled.

I had not sworn to guard Baki, yet I had promised Dost Muhammad to
remain here. Was Mahabat Khan my lord, that I should hazard torture to
hold his prisoner here? Yet I owed him the duty of companionship and of
salt. I thought of Mahabat Khan riding into the storm with his wild hillmen at his back, and it sickened my spirit to leave him thus.

"O Father of the Blind," I cried to Abu Ashtar, "what thing wilt thou
do in this situation?"

He answered promptly—

"Daril we cannot fly, leaving our tents and women out there."

When Baki would have spoken, I checked him. A thought had come to me, a memory of words that Baki himself had spoken to the Pathans when he exhorted them to war against the Persians.

"Saidst thou not, in the valley," I asked him, "'It is written: Thinkest thou that thy wealth will deliver thee, when thy deeds destroy thee?'"

"I said that, indeed, but the Pathans are fools to be swayed by such words. Thou and I, Daril, are otherwise. We are men of wisdom."

"God forbid!" I responded, "that my wisdom should be kin to thine. I am a man of peace, but I have never reined my horse from a place where my companions tasted death."

It was clear to me then that I must go at once and warn Mahabat Khan of what Baki had revealed. But how? I wished then for a Rajput trooper. It is easy to sit by and see others hold the reins of command, but it is far from easy to take up the reins they let fall! The Bedouins were waiting for me to decide. They longed for gold; greater than their longing was their fear of what was breeding in the storm.

"Find horses!" I bade them. "Find and saddle my mare, and tarry not."

Some of them departed at once, being more than willing to do this. In truth, they knew where to look for mounts, because within the time it takes to light a fire they were back at the tower with thirteen mounts saddled in every fashion.

"Nay," I cried, "what is this? We cannot take al-Khimar with us. Some few of you must remain here with him."

All speaking at once, they refused unconditionally to stay in the tower; even Abu Ashtar refused. They were like sheep that would not separate in a storm. So we had to bind Baki more securely and fill his mouth with a cloth, stripping off his turban and binding his jaw tight with its long cloth. At least he would not cry out, and we left him to what God had ordained.

Putting Abu Ashtar in the center of our cavalcade, I mounted my mare, and we galloped through the dust-swept streets, out of the open gate. Only slaves and women saw us go.

To find six hundred men in hiding somewhere upon a wide countryside in a starless and windswept night is a task for hunting dogs or a real prophet. We only knew that Mahabat Khan had come down the shallow valley of the river and would be somewhere west of the Persian *lashgar*.

We turned toward the river and heard it rushing past, making a deep roar. Up in the hills the storm had filled the watercourses, and the river raged. We had great trouble making our way down it, plunging through tilled land and skirting tossing willow groves. Dogs howled at us in a chorus that echoed the voice of the wind. We saw no lights, although we passed dark hamlets several times.

We trotted over the high road upon which I had come to Kandahar. Then the gardens became less and the open brush more plentiful. Our horses were restless, and we had to rein them in in order to listen; this availed us little, for the brush crackling under the wind and the mutter of the river filled our ears.

"On such a night," cried a young Bedouin, "we could steal into the Persian horse lines, unheard."

"On such a night," I responded, remembering other experiences in other years, "we could wander into a Persian guard post, unknowing."

By now it seemed to me that the *lashgar* must lie upon our left. But it was useless to try to feel our way toward it and hope to meet the body of Pathans before running into the camp. Whether we encountered friends or foes, we would probably be greeted with arrows.

I decided to follow the river, thinking that in this accursed blackness we would at least be keeping in one direction, and that some stragglers would surely have fallen behind Mahabat Khan's force.

Then the rain came down, driving suddenly upon the backs of our heads and shoulders.

We shivered and went on in silence. In the end it was not our searching that came upon the Pathans. My mare whinnied, and another horse answered, a spear's length away.

I bent low in the saddle and called out, saying that we were friends, seeking the Sirdar. Something stirred in the blackness and a voice answered—

"By God, so are we!"

Three or four Yuzufis had become lost and were wandering around, as witless as ourselves by the river. They told us that Mahabat Khan had passed an hour ago, turning east before the rain began. At least we knew that he was not by the river, and I ordered my men and the Yuzufis to spread out, keeping within call of each other, and to push on swiftly.

So we went ahead after a fashion, yelling and stumbling and trotting heavily in the mud. As to our line, it soon became a thing of madness, for

I heard Bedouins crashing through brush behind me, and once I ran into a Pathan who was going across my path. Only Abu Ashtar kept his temper, saying that all things had an end.

This, indeed, had a sudden end. A heavy voice cried out within touch of my rein hand—

"In the name of Allah the compassionate, the merciful—are ye women, nightmare ridden, or dogs become mad?"

The voice was Artaban's. The Yuzufi chieftain had heard our clamor over the beat of the rain and had hastened back to silence us. We had come upon the right wing of Mahabat Khan's force. A little more to the right, and we would have pushed into the *lashgar* of Shah Abbas.

I told the one-eyed chieftain that I must see Mahabat Khan at once. He was a man of deeds, and he took my rein in one hand and Abu Ashtar's in the other and strode off without another word.

It is a strange thing but true that all the other eleven Arabs heard us and gathered docilely behind me, like a disciplined escort, whereas a moment before they had been plunging about anywhere. Nay, the Yuzufis with us chose to slip away to their comrades, without revealing themselves, no doubt dreading their chieftain's tongue.

We splashed among groups of men squatting in the rain, and presently found horsemen about us, dismounted and standing by their beasts. Hillmen such as these do not love night marches or fighting in a storm, and it was a miracle that Mahabat Khan had brought them thus far and formed them after a fashion. He had taken command of the two hundred riders in the center.

By the time we found him the rain had ceased, although the wind still blew with force. The clouds raced overhead, yielding a little light—or rather, the utter darkness seemed less. Mahabat Khan was in the center of a group of Hazaras, telling them of a time when he had marched at night in Bengal during the rains and had missed half his command, at dawn, a hundred miles down the Ganges in boats. I took him apart, dismounting and standing in the mud, and he listened silently to what I had to tell—that Shah Abbas was before him in that *lashgar*.

He did not reprove me for leaving Baki without a guard. I had expected reproof and anger, and a hurried command to withdraw. But he kept his thoughts to himself and gave no command.

"It is too late to do otherwise," he said quietly. "I could not get word to Dost Muhammad."

After a moment he laughed a little.

"Eh, Daril, one thing is sure; Shah Abbas will be wet this dawn!"

The Pathans around us fell silent and began to gather up their reins. Abu Ashtar lifted his head, and Mahabat Khan left me, springing toward his horse.

Somewhere ahead of us, over the whine of the wind, a roar of hoofs resounded, and a deep shouting. A smashing of brush, shrill neighing of horses—a growing clatter of steel, a bellow of a firelock. Dost Muhammad was in the Persian camp.

With a shout Mahabat Khan swung upon his saddle.

"*Hai!* Come with me, ye men of the hills!"

And with a roar like the angry rush of the river, the tribesmen followed his voice.

Know now, many years after that battle, that if Mahabat Khan had not led us forward instantly as he did, we would have been worsted at once. Sentries shot arrows at us, and drums rolled in the blackness. We had gone only a little way, when men began to run out in front of the horses.

Here and there lights flared up from torches in the hands of frightened slaves. They only made the darkness thicker elsewhere. We plunged in among the tents, knocking many of them flat, the Pathans halting to slash at the Persians who struggled under the wet cloth.

But Mahabat Khan led his riders on.

"Forward ye men of the hills!"

So we left many Persians behind us, to be dealt with by the Pathans afoot. Arrows sang past my ears, doing little harm to anyone. It was no place for bows. Mahabat Khan had ordered his followers to wield their swords, and those long *tulwars* did fearful work in the confusion. As to firelocks, I heard only that first shot. The rain and the swift onset made the clumsy muskets of no use at all.

The Arabs and I had followed the mass of Pathan riders, who in turn followed the Sirdar. And presently we all saw lanterns and torches grouped in front of us. Here a hundred or more *kurshis*, mailed riders, were forming under officers, struggling into the saddles of rearing horses. Eh, few of them had had time to put on their armor.

Mahabat Khan tarried not at all. He spurred over the slippery clay at the Persians. A horseman swung out to meet him, and Mahabat Khan reined in, lifting his sword arm. His horse, checked in this fashion and made frantic by the flaring lights, slipped and slid, all four legs locked.

In this fashion they crashed into the foremost Persian, knocking his horse off balance, so that beast and rider went down beside the Sirdar, who leaned forward and slashed at a second soldier. The man tried to parry, cried out, and reeled with his head split open.

The sight inflamed the charging Pathans, who might have hung back and broken if they had not seen Mahabat Khan go through the Persian array like that.

"Allah, il-'lah!" they shouted from straining throats, and the clatter of steel and creaking saddles resounded around me.

After that all order was lost. My Bedouins scattered like dogs in a field of running hares, and many of the torches went down in the mud.

In truth I knew not what was happening. Men told me afterward that the main force of the Persians had rallied around the shah, to make stand against the Moguls who had not cut their way in as far as we.

I reined in under some trees and looked around. Artaban galloped past, waving a torch in one hand and a sword in the other, his dark face frenzied. He was alone.

I saw one of the Bedouins ride down and kill with his scimitar a fleeing Persian. Then he dismounted with a shout of triumph to rob the body, which was richly clad. It was folly to dismount at such a time. A bearded *kurshi* saw, and wheeled and galloped down upon the Bedouin, sticking him through the body with a lance.

I had drawn toward them, and the Persian saw me, dropped his lance and made at me with the sword. I gathered the mare under me and half turned, to take him on his left hand. He saw, rose in his stirrups and slashed down at me across his horse's head. I wished vainly then for a shield, knowing that such a stroke is hard to parry. At such a moment the mind races and the arm moves slowly.

The *kurshi* towered over me, blood dripping from a slash in his cheek, his teeth gleaming through his matted beard. He leaned forward and down as he struck.

I thrust up my sword, catching his blade against my hand guard. The force of the blow knocked the sword from his hand, and he drew back, reaching for a knife hilt. I slashed at his throat and felt the blade strike into flesh.

He staggered, and urged his horse on past me. Looking back, I saw him slip from the saddle.

"Daril!"

Mahabat Khan was calling me, and I made toward him, finding him escorted by no more than two Hazaras, one holding a torch gingerly—more than ready to drop it, if the Persians beset him. Mahabat Khan was breathing heavily, his fine tunic darkened with mud and blood. He bade me take the Hazaras and find the tent where Kushal had been held. Then he trotted off to seek Dost Muhammad.

As soon as the Sirdar had turned his back, the Hazara cast down the torch. I remembered that Kushal had been on the far side of the camp. When we galloped thither, we found little fighting going on. A light gleamed within the pavilion of blue silk.

The entrance was closed, and I dismounted, bidding the tribesmen hold my horse. I lifted the hanging and stepped inside. No living thing was here, but upon the couch, outstretched in death, lay a woman.

I went to her side, looking down at the familiar yellow tresses, the slender throat, and the blue-lidded eyes. It was Nisa.

Her lips curved a little, as if smiling, and her splendid head rested on one side against a cushion, as if she had settled herself to sleep. There was still a flush in her cheeks and warmth in her hand, when I touched it. She had been slain within the hour—slain by many stabs. Nay, the one who did it must have been angered indeed, thus to mutilate so fair a body.

The candle flames rose and sank as gusts of air came through the pavilion, and the changing light made Nisa's eyes and lips seem to move. I closed her eyelids and drew her shawl across her breast. At that moment I remembered only the time when she had pressed my hand against her heart.

I am an old man, and many times have I seen death, sudden and fearful, but for a girl to die thus alone and in the midst of maddened men was pitiful.

The entrance curtain was flung back, and I turned, sword in hand, seeing Kushal enter. His *pugri* was gone; his wet, dark hair hung about his bloodshot eyes. He staggered like a man badly wounded or utterly weary.

"Ha, Daril!" he cried at me, and flung his sword down upon the carpet.

"Hast thou done this?" I asked, pointing at the couch.

"I?" He planted his back against the tent pole and laughed with blood-less lips. "I loved her. Knowest thou what she has done?"

The tumbling words seemed to give his spirit relief, and he talked on:

"Daril, we twain were here in the hour before this dawn. She had waited for the coming of Mahabat Khan, and I taunted her, saying that he would never come at her summons. I hoped he would not come. I knew she had betrayed me to these dogs of the shah. In the hour before dawn she de-spaired of the Sirdar, and talked with the guards of the tent. Then she summoned that fellow of thine, the camelman, Sher Jan."

He sighed, holding himself more erect.

"She bade me go with Sher Jan, before the first light, saying that it had all been a trick. I went at once, and Sher Jan guided me past the outer guards unseen. Then I met Dost Muhammad's cavalry and heard of the attack to be made upon the *lashgar.*"

He looked wearily at the weapon he had thrown away.

"Daril, I begged a sword and a horse, and fought my way hither. There were Persian lords at the tent, and lights. They had come for me and had revenged themselves on her."

Upon this I meditated, understanding that Nisa, the singing girl, had made Kushal captive, to serve her lord the shah. Then, when the hour came for Kushal's torture she had freed him, and waited in his place.

Why had she not gone with him? Was her pride too great for this? Did she hope at the last to outwit the Persians? I knew not. The heart of such a singing girl, wayward and passionate and full of longing—who knows it?

Kushal had gone to the divan and thrown himself down, pressing his forehead against her feet, in the very place where she had sat a day and a night ago, fanning the flies from him. He would not let me look at his wounds; he bade me go and keep the entrance and let no others in. Nay, he thought no more of the battle.

My two tribesmen said that now the fighting was all in one place, and this meant that the shah must be surrounded by the Pathans and Moguls. The mist had turned gray and was drifting through the trees, and some-where the sun was rising. The wet pavilions and the dark boles of trees were clearly visible.

The sound of the fighting changed, and my Hazaras gathered up their reins. Horses galloped toward us. I mounted into my saddle. No sooner had I done so, than riders swept out of the trees and past the blue pavilion. Others followed in a dense mass, rushing like fiends out of the veil of mist. They were Persian cavalry, with nobles riding haphazard among troopers and mounted slaves.

In the midst of the throng rode a man of short stature and wide shoulders clad in cloth-of-gold. He was in the saddle of a tall black horse with gilded reins. I caught a glimpse of his broad face, dark with anger, as he lashed on his charger.

It was thus that I saw Abbas the Great flee from Kandahar, and he went as if Satan followed behind him.

But it was Mahabat Khan who pursued the Persians, bareheaded, with Dost Muhammad at his side and two hundred Moguls at his heels. They crashed through the camp and vanished into the mist. I stayed at the blue pavilion, where Nisa's candles burned fainter, and Kushal mourned.

After victory, after the last blow is struck, and men begin to feel the ache of wounds, the spirit flags and the body is heavy. Then a man cannot sleep and desires not food.

I watched the Pathans exulting as they looted the tents, dragging out carpets, piling up weapons and leading off the horses they had taken. My Bedouins rode by, clad after their custom in the gilded mail and the silk turbans of the shah's men. They carried new shields and had gleaned the best of the horses, and were singing about it all. I smiled when blind old Abu Ashtar rode past, singing with the rest, his arms full of plunder. By God's mercy he had suffered no harm in all that fighting.

But later in the day I came upon the body of Artaban. In spite of his charm, or perhaps because he trusted too much in his charm, he had been slain by a lance that passed clear through his throat. Too often had he boasted that steel could not pierce him.

Shah Abbas escaped by the speed of his horse, taking refuge across the border, where other Persians awaited him. I did not see this pursuit of an emperor, because I remembered Baki and galloped back to Kandahar to take charge of him again. Thus I was the first to enter the gates and shout the tidings of the battle.

I hastened to the tower chamber and found it empty. The cords with which we had bound Baki lay upon the stone floor beside the cloth that had served for a gag. The rug and the cushions were torn from the divan, revealing a wooden chest as empty as the room. Baki had been able to free himself from his bonds and to flee from the citadel, taking with him a great weight of gold.

Nay, I knew before the end of that day that he had taken the gold.

He had placed it in sacks upon a horse and had gone through the gate unseen. He had turned his horse toward the river. It was Mahabat Khan who summoned me and took me to Baki.

The Veiled One lay curled up like a bird that had dropped from the sky. He lay in the mud by the river, crushed and beaten down by weapons and the hoofs of horses. Only by his tattered garment and the shreds of his veil did we know him. And all around him Pathans searched eagerly, picking out of the mud the gold coins that had fallen from the burst sacks.

"Eh, Daril," said Mahabat Khan, leaning on his saddle horn, "that is Persian gold. The *atabegs* of the shah, who are my prisoners, have told me the tale. Baki offered to open one of the gates of Kandahar to the shah if Abbas would come secretly with a strong body of men, as if to capture the city. Baki asked a price of ten thousand pieces of gold for Kandahar, and the shah agreed."

He looked away from the body, frowning.

"Five thousand pieces were sent to Baki by the hand of a singing girl, Nisa. I think he meant at first to take refuge in the hills, when the rest of the gold was his."

I thought of another thing—the coming of Mahabat Khan had disturbed both the Persians and Baki, and each had tried to be rid of the Sirdar, in different ways.

In the end Baki had become afraid and had fled with his horse in the darkness along the river. He had been seeking the Persians, and thus, in the first light he had appeared before the maddened shah and a hundred riders. His death had been swift—what a death! Nay, Shah Abbas had believed himself betrayed, and in that dawn of fighting his mood must have been dark indeed.

Thus Baki disappeared, and no man saw him again. But to the Veiled One death brought honor of a strange kind. The Pathans recognized the body of their prophet, and mourned. My Arabs told their tale of his last vision in the tower, and to all of them it seemed that the Veiled One was indeed a holy man.

Who was to say otherwise? Not Dost Muhammad or Mahabat Khan, who took me with them in fellowship to Ind. Not I, who was glad to behold Baki at last safely in his grave. Many hillmen stopped to pray and to tie rags to his shrine, and the sick journeyed far to this holy spot.

But I, when I passed through those hills again, I thought of what is written—that a man cannot save himself by his gold if his deeds destroy him.

The Light of the Palace

Chapter I
A Horse and Servant for the Hakim

Thus said Daril the Arab, he who was known as Ibn Athir, the wisest of
physicians, the far seeing and long wandering. Thus said he, who in his
day and age beheld the Conqueror of the World, and the battle of the ele-
phant, and knelt before the Light of the Palace. Thus is his tale:

Why sit in one spot? The wise ride afield.

This thought of all thoughts came to me after Ramazan of the year one
thousand and thirty and two.* Until then I had been content—I, Daril ibn
Athir of the clan Nejd. I had been no more than the physician of my folk,
and I had grown weary of the folk and of the land of Athir.

Something had come into my heart. Men, journeying up from the sea
with the camphor and leather caravans, had lingered as guests in our
tents. They told us of the sea that lay beyond our desert and of a rich land
beyond the sea.

This land they called Hindustan, or the country of Ind, and the ruler
of this empire they called the Mogul, swearing by the triple oath that the
Mogul was the most fortunate of men. The wonders of his court their
own eyes had beheld—the tents of cloth of gold, the treasure great beyond
counting, the slaves more numerous than our sheep.

---

*By the Christian calendar 1620. The story of Daril ibn Athir was first written
down by a Persian scholar in the seventeenth century. The Arabs of that time were
too proud of the sword to take up the pen. It will be noticed in Ibn Athir's narrative that he passes over his undeniable skill as a physician but dwells fondly on
his success against a Rajput swordsman.

Aye, their words put the thought into my mind. And I resolved to journey to the land of Ind, to behold this chieftain, the most fortunate of men.

So, between the first stars and darkness, I left my folk. I gathered together a horseload of cloths and rice and fruit and some silver. Girding on the best of my swords, I set forth upon the road that leads to the sea.

Who knows, when he sets forth, what the end of the road will be? Upon the sea there are no paths, and the ships go hither and yon, when the winds rise, at the will of God. Also, men are visited by the sickness of the sea that makes food an abomination in the belly.

During this sickness my silver was stolen—all but eleven pieces wrapped in my girdle. The wind blew us to a land that was not Ind, and for several moons I journeyed with merchants, serving as a swordsman to protect their goods, they giving me food of sorts but no horse.

It was after the noon prayer one day that we came out upon a road bordered with trees and to the outskirts of a temple-ridden city. These temples were not like our *masjids*, being of stone worked into the semblance of figures of women, men, and beasts like men—aye, and serpents carved out of stone.

The merchants went off to the bazaar, and I sought the horse market. Here I found turbaned folk, and some Persians in striped cloaks, whose animals were ill nourished, besides having saddle sores.

I waited, sitting upon the carpet with other buyers, until I beheld an Arab who wore the green cloth permitted to one who has made the pilgrimage to the Ka'aba. Of him I asked a question.

"Indeed," he laughed, "this is a city upon the border of Ind."

"The praise to the All Compassionate!" I cried.

The name of this horse dealer was al-Mokhtar, and he was full of wisdom mingled with guile. He had in his string two or three splendid mares, and he said that the people of this land did not refuse to ride mares. He had also some swift-paced geldings and a riffraff of baggage bearers.

The first day I said naught to al-Mokhtar concerning the purchase of a horse, though I was determined to have one. I saw that the people of Ind went about on their own feet for the most part, or sat in carts, or—and they were the nobles—lay in litters upborne upon the shoulders of slaves, of whom there was no lack. Yet I would not take the road until I had a horse beneath me.

The second day al-Mokhtar showed his string to a wealthy emir who took two of the mares at high prices, paying for them with a pearl or two and many promises. Meanwhile I had marked one of the trader's poorer beasts, a small roan, a little lame.

But he held his head well, and when the other horses ran he showed good paces. This roan I determined to buy if he could be had at my price.

When al-Mokhtar had completed the sale of the mares he came and sat down by me, sending a boy for sherbet and dates, which he shared with me as a matter of course.

"Eh, Ibn Athir," he said, "this is a fortunate day."

"By the will of God!" I made response. "For in the cool of this evening I shall set out upon the road leading north."

"To what end?"

"To seek the court of the Mogul and behold his face."

"That is a long way, and I have heard that thieves beset the road. Verily, this is a land of thieves, both young and old."

He spoke bitterly as if remembrance stirred within him.

"By the beard of the true prophet, the nobles of each district demand a toll of strangers! The priests sit naked and hold forth their hands, and if thou givest not to them, they make outcry and a crowd comes with sticks. Moreover, Ibn Athir, the favorites of the Mogul go at will upon the roads, taking what best pleases them, of goods, weapons, or horses."

"O Hadji," I laughed, "it seems to me to be a rich land, and the lords thereof goodly in bearing and garments."

"Thou wilt see what thou wilt see," he made response, shaking his head. "Verily I say to thee, this is a land to be ruled by an armed conqueror, or by a woman, or by—the word of God."

"Such an empire, to be ruled by a woman?"

"Aye, by one—" he paused, musing—"but it will happen as it hath been written in the book that changeth not. Thou canst speak the Persian and that is good. Only remember, if thy road leads to the court, that the two favorites of the Mogul are Mahabat Khan and the Light of the Palace."

"What is that to me?"

Al-Mokhtar smiled and waved his hand. He was, as I have said, a man of discernment and guile. But now, at last, he came to that which was in his mind.

"The road is long, and thou wilt need a horse. I have a steed bred from—"

"I have seen the lot. Also, I have seen the horses of Kara Mustapha—"

"That son of a slave!"

"His prices are just."

"Just!" Al-Mokhtar spat. "That bladder of a swine! Now, bethink thee, O *hakim*,* I have—" he paused to run his glance over the horses, guarded by one of his swordsmen—"I have a roan that must be sold for a tithe of his true worth. Spirit he hath, and fire, and a tender mouth. Because he is lame I must be rid of him before setting forth. Yet the lameness, as thou canst see, Ibn Athir, is a slight matter, to be healed by a little warmth and rubbing."

"*W'allah*, am I to doctor a horse or ride him?"

"But the price! I will sell him for a dozen rupees."

This was less than I had expected his first price to be. Yet I gathered the folds of my mantle about me, and began the salaam of leave-taking.

"In truth, this is a land of thieves!"

"Nay, I am the loser, and my wish was to befriend thee."

"If so, make a fair price."

"Then I shall lose yet another two silver pieces, and make a price of ten."

In the end it was agreed between us that I should have the roan for eight rupees, also a bridle, lacking silver work, for two. As for the saddle, al-Mokhtar had one that he had promised to deliver to a certain man in Lahore, and, since he said Lahore lay upon my road, I pledged myself to take the saddle to its owner.

Nay, he trusted me because I passed my word, nor did he think a second time of it. The buying of a horse is a matter for bargaining, but a pledged word is otherwise.

There were indeed robbers upon the road that leads north and ever north through Ind, and I had wiped blood from my sword blade before I drew my reins into the *serai* of the blue mosque that lies by the garden of the emirs, in Lahore.

Here was a tank of stagnant water hemmed in by cactus and lime trees, where they who journeyed upon the great road halted to wash the dust from their eyes and ears and sleep under the safeguard of the mosque.

And here I was halted by two officers of the Hindu noble who ruled the district, demanding road toll, even as al-Mokhtar had said. The money, they said, was for driving the robbers away.

---

*Physician.

To them I made response that my sword had driven the thieves away, and besides, I had naught to give them. And this was truth.

But in this land all words are weighed in the scales of trickery, and the two officers went away looking angry. I thought then of what al-Mokhtar had forewarned and decided to watch for the next hours. I begged some rice seasoned with saffron from the keepers of the mosque and carried my portion to the edge of the tank where the roan had found a little dry grass to feed upon.

The tank was within a stone's throw of the road, and the light had not vanished when some twenty riders came galloping past, raising a great dust. They were excellently well mounted, the leader bestriding a black Tatar stallion with a glistening coat.

I stood up, the better to see the stallion, and an officer reined abreast this chieftain—the same officer who had failed to gather toll from me. It was then too late to withdraw and I stared at the rider of the stallion, fingering the hilt of my scimitar.

He was a slender man, wearing a small turban with a long loose end of white silk. His beard was black, and I saw his teeth flash as he laughed, without checking his pace.

"*Ohai hakim,*" he called out to me. "Ho, physician—may thy road be pleasant to thee!

The other officer said something, and the rider of the stallion shook his head impatiently, spurring on with his troop. The glow of sunset was still over the acacias, and jewels sparkled in his turban and girdle and saddlecloth.

Beyond doubt the officer I had angered had sought out this warrior lord and made complaint, but he had not wished to call me to account for the matter of the toll. Perhaps this was because of the nearness of the mosque, or a matter of mood.

"Art thou in truth a physician?"

So said one who squatted on the coping of the tank, by my feet—a barefoot and ragged Hindu, with a thin, knowing face and overbright eyes.

"In truth."

"From beyond the sea?"

"Aye, far."

The boy considered, trailing his fingers in the water. "Eh, I have seen the *hakim* from Iran and the fat one from Frankistan but not one who wore a sword as thou. What seekest thou, O wise physician?"

"Such and such a man," I made response, "to whom I must give this saddle. For this is the city of Lahore."

It seemed to astonish the boy that the saddle should have been given to me as it was, he knowing naught of the customs of the Arabs.

"Art thou friend to Mahabat Khan?" he asked then.

"Nay, I am a stranger in this place."

"But he greeted thee, even now."

The boy swore that the rider of the stallion had been Mahabat Khan, though at the time I cared little, one way or the other.

"I saw thee," the youth persisted, "stand erect and lay hand to sword when his eye fell upon thee. That was a sign!"

Now I had acted thus without forethought, and in any case it is better to rise and watch events than to bide. The Hindu did not understand. His people carry shield and sword and many daggers; still they like best to use their tongues and to intrigue. So I thought at that time, before I had met with the clans of the north and the riders of Mahabat Khan.

"Who is this khan?" I asked impatiently.

The brown eyes of the Hindu became knowing, as a dog's that has stumbled upon a marmot's hole.

"*Ai-ai!*" he laughed. "Shall I not know a sign when I see one? Nay, who art thou, Lord of Arabistan?" But when he looked into my face he became thoughtful. "He is a good man to have for a friend."

And he began to poke at the water with one finger. I think he suspected me of being a spy of this khan—this boy of twelve or fourteen years who begged his food by tricks of juggling. I had seen him, not an hour ago, performing with a single stout bamboo of the length of two men. He had set one end of the bamboo upon the earth and had climbed upon it unaided, shouting at those who were too intent on cooking food to spare a thought or a copper coin for this Jami, as he called himself.

For his pains, Jami had naught but the remnant of my rice that he had borne off on a leaf to eat in a corner. Since then he had come to sit and stare at me.

"I am thy friend," he said then. "Thy friend, Daril ibn Athir."

At this I smiled, for the youths of my land stand more in dread of the men.

"Nay," he said again, quickly. "I know thou hast not a copper in thy wallet. But tell me, O lord of *hakims*, is it true thou hast skill to cure the sick? The two others were great liars. Is it thy custom to cure with prayers written on paper, or a purge, or by letting blood, or spells?"

"Not by writing on paper or spells."

"If a man be dying, canst restore him to health?"

"The hour of a man's death is written."

Jami considered this and looked at the lanterns that were moving about the tank. One more question he asked—would I sleep in the *serai?*—and then darted off into the shadows. But he left his pole by my saddle and cloth, and when I had rubbed down the roan pony and had made the evening prayer, the pole was still there. I went to sleep with my head touching the saddle because, though the road might be clear of thieves, that *serai* was a nest of poverty-ridden men.

As with us during Ramazan, there was little quiet in the night. I smelled camels passing along the highroad and saw that armed riders bearing torches escorted the camel loads. Carts drawn by bullocks creaked past the tank, and men, women, and children too miserable to own a beast of burden filed by, bearing bundles on heads and shoulders. The air was foul with dust and gnats.

Whenever an emir, a nobleman, passed by, the beggars of the roadside would cry out in chorus. And perhaps the rider would reach into his girdle and fling them a coin. But the naked and dirty priests who sat by the highroad did not cry out.

Women passed like djinn wraiths among the tethered animals. And in the third and fourth hours of the night the air did not grow cool as in the desert, the *sahra.* Always I heard the low voices of men, speaking many tongues. Bare feet pattered near my head, and when I rose to an elbow, Jami squatted down, pulling at my sleeve.

"Awake, my lord! Come with me."

W'allah! The boy had returned to tell me of a sick man whose skin was purple and who was cursing all physicians. Jami had persuaded the family of the sick man to send for me. He swore that this stranger had especially cursed the Hindu priest who came to require money before offering up a prayer to various gods.

"Fool!" I chided him. "If the man gets well the others who have tended him will grasp the credit, and if he dies they will blame me."

"Thou are a bold man, Ibn Athir," he cried, "and, besides, the Rajput hath too strong a voice to be sinking toward the gates of Yama."

In the end I went with Jami, for—if the boy were to be believed—I had been summoned. I saddled the roan, not mindful to find horse and saddle gone from the *serai* when I returned. This seemed not to trouble Jami, who left his pole and ran, clinging to my stirrup.

He guided me from the highroad into an alley that led to wide gardens and an open gate filled with servants and horses and uproar.

"'Way for the benevolent Arab *hakim!*" Jami shouted above the tumult, thrusting at the Hindus. "At first he would not come. Send word! Stand back."

It was a small house, the lattices closed. Within, many people stared at me and crowded back to let me pass. In a room no larger than a single tent, twenty men were sitting, while two barefoot slaves stirred the heavy air with palm branches. On a matting lay a man of spare and muscular build, with a curling beard.

He was wrapped up in quilt upon quilt, and the skin of his head, as Jami had said, was nearly purple. I smelled opium and the fumes of burning hemp.

The skin of his corded arm, when I touched it, was hot and dry. Of Jami I asked the tale of his illness, and the boy stood forth, speaking importantly to one and another of the watchers.

"O *hakim*," quoth he, "since four days the Rao hath not mounted his horse. His head pained him, and on the second day he could not eat. By command of the other *hakim*, who is a piece of the liver of a dog, and a liar, being a Persian, he was wrapped up thus to bring forth the sweat. Look serious and shake thy head."

The sick man tossed impatiently under my touch, and it was clearly fever in him, perhaps from bad food. The quilts had only increased his trouble. Indeed, the matter was simple.

"Bring water," I bade the folk in the room, "heated in large jars."

"*Ohai!*" echoed Jami. "Bring water, or the Rao dies! Make haste, for this is the *hakim* known to our master, Mahabat Khan."

If the other physician had been a liar, Jami was no less! There was dispute when the steaming water appeared, but I bade them strip and bathe the man they called the Rao, and when they had done so, I gave him a draft to quiet him from the packets that still remained in my girdle.

"Far better to bleed him," the young juggler whispered. "Then the cure will be a greater cure. What was in the drink?"

A few herbs and rhubarb, no more. Still, I saw no need of telling Jami this, and no doubt he made a tale of the dose, for the watchers looked troubled and when I bade them rise and leave the sick man, they demanded that I stay in the house until the following day should reveal the efficacy of the draft.

Chapter II

Chieftains' Fees

Verily, if the Rao, whose name was Man Singh, had died, misfortune would have come upon my head. For, while I abode under his roof, during the next two days the Persian and the European physician came to attend him. When they learned of my presence, the European went away without saying anything; but the Persian swore by Ali and all the Companions that I had done ill to give the sick man the hot bath, and that the Rao assuredly would die.

But the Rao, who was nearly free of fever, gave command to his servants to beat the Persian on the buttocks and shoulders and send him forth without payment.

In fever or in health Man Singh had a short temper and a shorter purse. The food in his house was no more than fruit and boiled millet flour; yet the sword that hung by his matting was inlaid with gold upon the hilt, with sapphires and turquoise upon the handguard. Truly, like many of the nobles of Ind—and of my land—his wealth was all in his horseflesh and weapons. He did not lack for pride. When I came to bid him farewell upon the third day he praised me, and no word concerning payment was spoken.

I had returned to the *serai* with my roan, when Jami, who had been off on business of his own the last days, appeared with two servants of the Rao I had healed.

The servants brought silver from their lord, in an embroidered silk purse. When I poured the coins from the purse into one hand, I counted them and found them eight silver rupees—little enough for the service I had rendered.

And this insolent Jami could not contain himself at the sight, crying shame upon the two men for the niggardliness of their lord and whispering to me to toss them back the silver, since it was not sufficient.

For a moment I pondered. I had no dislike of Man Singh, yet I was in sore need of money, being alone in a land of thieves, priests, and exacting lords.

"Peace!" I reproved Jami. "It is sufficient." Then to the servants of the Rajput I added, "Indeed it is evident from this that thy master is not yet recovered. If the Rao were not feverish in his mind, he would have sent a greater reward. And I, who have attended greater lords, will accept no reward until the cure is complete."

So I dropped the coins into the purse and tossed it to them, while they stared, between anger and astonishment. Jami, for once, held his peace and squatted by me when they had gone.

"*Ai!*" he said. "There is wisdom in thee, Daril ibn Athir." After awhile he added shrewdly, "Still, I do not think the Rao will send anymore silver."

Jami had known that I would give him a coin, or perhaps two. He had been waiting for reward. Yet he had been wise enough to keep away from my side in the house of Man Singh, lest I lose honor by the association of a beggar, and he had been willing to sacrifice his little gain because he thought me underpaid. After awhile he could contain his impatience no longer, but must scamper away to learn what was happening at the Rajput's house.

Lo, it happened as I had foreseen. Before evening prayer, two other servants of the Rao entered the *serai* and brought me a good Tatar horse with a saddle horn ornamented with ivory, and also a robe of honor of brocade embroidered with silk.

I thanked them, and barely were they departed before Jami crept out from behind the cactus and stared at the fine robe with shining eyes.

"Well done, Daril ibn Athir!" he cried. "Oh, what an hour I have spent. Mahabat Khan himself was at the house of the Rao, and the khan laughed until his thighs cracked over the answer thou gavest the men of Man Singh. Eh, the Rao is a favorite officer of the khan, and this horse and robe are from the hand of Mahabat Khan himself, who wished to reward thee for healing his follower."

Now the servants had said naught of this, and I thought that they had not been willing to admit that their master was too poor to send such gifts.

"Now, imp of devildom," I asked sternly, "wilt tell me who this khan is?"

Jami had lost all suspicion of me. Indeed, he had attached himself to me as a stray dog follows a newcomer in the street.

"Mahabat Khan," he said at once, "is the finest sword from Malabar to the hills. He hath led the imperial standards to victory in all the provinces. Now he returns from whipping the Bengalis."

In the words of older men—for he was swift to pick up a phrase, and know the nature of the speaker—Jami explained that Mahabat Khan was of Pathan descent, and was well liked by the Rajput chieftains, who commanded the best of the Mogul's cavalry. And Jami dreamed of the day when he should possess a sword and ride in the following of his hero.

"Go thou," he urged me, "to the camp of the khan and greet him, and thank him for the horse. He will remember thee and may take thee into his service."

I smiled, because Jami, too, would then be in the camp of this warrior of Ind. But it seemed to me unwise to seek favor by making public the poverty of Man Singh. Besides, I wished to go to the court of the king.

When I told Jami this, he wriggled his fingers with excitement.

"To the *padishah*?"

"God willing."

Now this Jami was the most impertinent of mortals; even when he begged, he mocked men. But when I said this, he clutched his shoulders and shivered, looking around as if he meant to run away. For the time that milk takes to boil, he did not speak.

"Evil will surely come of that," he said at last. "Still, I will not leave thee, my *hakim*. We will go together to the Mogul."

And his sharp little eyes, lined and furtive, glowed in the dusk like the eyes of a cat. *W'allah!* At the time I thought he was angry at turning his back on the camp of Mahabat Khan. In the days that followed I learned otherwise. The wisdom of the bazaar children is not altogether good; but their friendship is a thing not to be despised.

Chapter III
Two Scimitars

Though a man choose his own path from the *serai* of a morning, how may he know what road the night will bring?

We were of good heart—Jami and I—that hot noon. We were near the end of that long highway leading north into the hills. It ran by a river, and the plumed grass and bamboo of the bank screened us from the sun.

Before leaving the dust of Lahore, I had given the roan's saddle to its owner—six days since—and now I rode the Tatar steed, having placed a light pack on the pony. Jami trudged at my bridle, his pole on his shoulder.

He was watching the kingfishers dart through the long leaves of the bamboo and out over the water, when he sighted a throng in the highway.

Cartmen and wandering soldiers, village women and dogs were gathered around a single rider.

"*Ohai,*" laughed Jami. "This is surely a punishment."

The rider was seated without a saddle, face to tail on a pony that was fit crows' meat. His wrists were tied behind his back and his ankles tied under the bony belly of the horse. Blood dripped from his feet into the dust, and flies swarmed about his bare head.

A woman held up a bowl of water, and he sucked it in through his lips without a word. The horse was plodding toward us, and we could not see the man's face, but Jami pointed out the *tamgha*, the brand on the animal's flank, saying that it was the mark of the Mogul, and this stranger must be an offender condemned to ride thus along the highway, it being forbidden to cut him loose until he died or met friends who dared the displeasure of the *padishah*.

Bidding Jami hold my horse, I dismounted, to see why the victim's feet were bleeding. I brushed away the flies and felt beneath one, and knew that it had been flayed upon the sole until the flesh was raw.

At once I drew my knife and cut the cords that held fast his wrists, paying no attention to the warning shouts of the onlookers.

"*Kabardar!*" cried Jami, pulling at my sleeve. "Take care, O my master! This is forbidden, and we are within a day of the Mogul's camp."

"Is it forbidden a physician to attend one who is suffering?" I asked.

"But it will be known, and thou wilt taste shame at the court."

I cut the cords around the man's ankles and lifted him down, being aided by a pair of soldiers—so I thought that all men were not content with the punishment. Placing the victim in the shade, I cleansed the flesh of his feet as well as I might, and put ointment on before binding up the wounds. Then I bathed the man's head. Jami had become voiceless. He had seen what I had known from the first glance, that this was the Rao called Man Singh.

By God's will there was no fever in him, though the veins stood out in his forehead and his seared eyes blazed like coals. The flesh had fallen in upon his bones, and it was no wonder Jami had not known him at first.

I had seen him last at Lahore, calling for his horse and his followers, to ride after the khan. Now he was alone, more dead than alive, and shunned by everyone on the highway.

"What now?" whispered Jami.

The voices around me had died away, but the soldiers still watched idly while they ate their rice in the shade.

"Hast thou strength to sit in the saddle?" I asked Man Singh, and his lips drew back from his white teeth in the snarl of a wounded leopard.

"As long and as far as need be," he growled, "so it be to Mahabat Khan."

Jami pricked up his ears and ran to ask the soldiers where the camp of the khan might be, then scampered back to plead for haste. What was I to do? To leave the Rao lying by the roadside were unkind, since I bestrode the horse that was his gift and had shared his salt. And I doubted whether he could sit in the saddle without help. Jami swore by his gods that the tent of the khan was no more than an hour's ride. I lifted Man Singh into the saddle of the Tatar horse, shifting the load of the pony to make room for myself. When his eye fell upon the animal with the king's brand, he shivered again and again.

Gripping the rein with numbed fingers, swaying from side to side, he followed us. And Jami, running by my stirrup, whispered the reason of this happening.

Where he had his knowledge only the beggars of the highway could say, but he said that Mahabat Khan in some way had displeased Nur-Mahal, the favorite wife of Jahangir, the king. The khan had been ordered back from Bengal. Reaching Lahore, he had sent his cousin, Man Singh, to plead for the favor of the king, that he had so long enjoyed.

Evidently Man Singh had risen from his sickbed to go to the court. And beyond any doubt he had been bastinadoed and bound to the back of a horse. Since the horse bore the Mogul's brand, this must have been done by command of the Mogul, but why and for what reason Jami knew not. And even Jami dared not ask Man Singh the reason of his disgrace.

It was three hours later and the sun was setting when we rode into an encampment in a broad meadow. Pavilions and round tents stood in orderly fashion between lines of picketed horses, and at the gate of each section of the camp standards fluttered.

Mounted warriors, coming in from hunting or games, beheld us with astonishment, and many reined after us—excellent riders, wearing small, knotted turbans with long ends and clad from thighs to wrists in silvered mail. They took the rein of Man Singh's mount and held him by the arms, but he said no word.

"They are Rajputs," Jami whispered to me, "of his command."

In the center of the camp we halted at the tent with the main standard before it, and here Mahabat Khan sat on a red cloth, eating fruit and talking with chieftains. Jami hid himself behind my horse when the khan looked up and saw the Rao.

He looked for a long moment, Man Singh speaking no word. Other chieftains who had hastened up gazed at the twain, waiting for what would follow.

Then Mahabat Khan sprang up, his lean face darkening with a rush of blood. He strode to his cousin, who was trying vainly to dismount. Taking him bodily in his arms, Mahabat Khan bore him to his own place and lowered him gently to the ground, kneeling to do so, and then stood with folded arms before the injured man.

"I cannot stand," said Man Singh, and touched the bloody bandages upon his feet.

"I do not ask it," responded Mahabat Khan quickly. "Only tell me which of Jahangir's emirs hath dealt with thee thus, and by the threefold oath I swear—"

Man Singh threw up his hand.

"Do not swear. It was done by command of Jahangir the Mogul—the bastinado, and—" he gripped his beard with writhing fingers—"the binding upon a horse's rump."

The officers about them fell silent, so intent on every word that no one thought of us. Mahabat Khan held his head higher and breathed deep through his nostrils.

"By command of Jahangir! If another had said that—"

"By now it is known between the rivers."

Mahabat Khan nodded grimly. By his lean cheeks and the corded muscles of his restless hands, by the way he met the glances of the other officers, swiftly and squarely, I judged him a man who loved deeds better than talk, who was prone to rashness rather than caution. Yet, after his first burst of anger at the shame inflicted upon his kinsman, he seemed bewildered as if a sure-footed horse had sunk beneath him.

"I should have gone!" he muttered. "The shame is not thine, but mine."

"If thou hadst gone when the summons came," cried Man Singh, heedless of anything but his agony of mind, "we would have lacked a leader ere now. There is one at Jahangir's side who seeks thy death."

"Who would dare?"

"Who persuaded him to shame thy messenger?"

The two exchanged a long glance, and one of the Rajputs, turning toward me cried out suddenly—

"He has heard!"

Grasping the hilt of his curved sword, he strode toward me, motioning back others who were crying eagerly:

"Strike! Strike!"

"Nay," quoth the slender swordsman, "this shall be my affair. I will clip his ears for him, and leave his tongue to slaves. Then may he prowl but he will not speak."

They were in a black mood, having beheld the shame of Man Singh, their blood brother. They thought me perhaps a spy, perhaps a seller of secrets, and for once Jami's tongue could not aid me. The khan and the Rao had observed nothing, nor was I inclined to raise the cry of mercy. I grasped my scimitar sheath and pulled the blade clear.

"My lord," I said to him in Persian—though I understood the Hindustani, I could not speak it readily—"look to thine own jewels."

In the lobes of his ears he wore two pearls. Some of his companions who had caught the jest laughed aloud and this angered him the more. He was a slender warrior, richly dressed, with the small mouth and full eyes of a woman, his skin as soft as a child's. Yet there were pale scars upon his cheekbone and chin, and he moved with the swiftness of a mettled horse.

Being angry, he smiled, advancing to within arm's reach of me.

"So," he cried, "the slaves must bury thee."

And suddenly he saluted with the sword and struck—once—twice at my side. I circled to the right, warding his blows and making test of his strength. He was light of bone, even more than I, an Arab of the *sahra*, but the edge of his blade bore down heavily upon mine.

In that first moment I knew that my danger lay in his quickness of wrist, and I knew also that his blade was like most of the weapons of Ind—thin iron, edged and tipped with steel. Good for parrying, and well shaped for a thrust, but inferior to mine, which could be gripped by hilt and point and bent double, being tempered steel of Damascus.

He too must have felt this difference. He stepped in closer and thrust again and again for the throat, while his companions shouted and the two blades moved in flashing light.

Eh, it is good to feel edge grind along edge, and to hear the whistle of the thin blades in the air. We of the *sahra* may carry spear and bow, yet our love is for the naked steel that leaps in the hand!

My blood was warming, and I yielded ground no longer. My adversary shouted and bent low, striving to force my weapon up and to thrust under the ribs. He was fearless—aye, he left unguarded his own head—and as swift as a striking snake.

"*Hai!*" the watchers cried out.

He had cut through a fold of my mantle, under the arm, but I knew that I was his master, having the longer arm and the better blade. This angered him the more. In the beginning, he had meant to wound me, or force my weapon from my hand; now he meant to kill if he could, pressing in upon me, and dealing blow after blow.

Then someone cried out near at hand, and the Rajput sprang back, breathing heavily, never taking his eyes from mine.

Between us stepped the speaker, Mahabat Khan, in his gold inlaid mail and damask mantle. In truth, he seemed angry.

"Sheath your swords," he said, and we obeyed. "Have I given permission, Partap Singh," he asked the Rajput, "to bare weapons in my presence?"

"Nay. This man heard what was not meant for his ears. I would have clipped them."

Mahabat Khan did not raise his voice or glance at me.

"This man is an Arab *hakim* who tended the Rao, my cousin, in his sickness and came hither, having met him upon the road, cutting loose his bonds and giving him a good horse to ride."

I thought then that Man Singh had looked up when the sword blades rang together, and had taken my part with Mahabat Khan. He could have done little less. And the noble who was called Partap Singh did a strange thing. He gripped his sheathed sword and held it forth to Mahabat Khan, the hilt forward.

"I did not know," he said. "If the offense is great, do thou, clear my honor with this blade."

He had asked the khan to slay him but Mahabat Khan smiled a little in his beard and spoke gravely.

"Nay, Partap Singh, thy sword hath served me too faithfully, to turn it against thee. I myself will deal with this guest."

And after the evening meal he sent for me, where I was eating with his Moslem followers and Jami. I was led to the tent of the standard again, and made the salaam of greeting upon entering.

Mahabat Khan sat alone on a rich carpet, leaning not against a cushion but a saddle. He motioned for me to sit before him, and this I did, while he kept silence. He seemed to be older than his years, for his brow was furrowed and his lips were harsh.

"O my guest," he said—and I took notice of the word—"I first saw thee near the blue mosque, and later I heard thy bold answer to my cousin, who is no man to trifle with. Lo, by chance thou hast met with him on the highway. And now thou hast crossed swords with that fire eater, Partap Singh of Malwa. Who art thou?"

He asked this question swiftly, biting off the words, nor did his eyes leave mine as I told him the story of my wanderings from the *sahra* to the great sea, and finally, to Ind.

"For a *hakim*, thou art rarely skilled at sword work."

"In my land there are foes to be met."

His face clouded, as if my words had called up a dark spirit within his mind.

"For the service rendered to my kinsman, I ask thee to accept a gift, Ibn Athir," he said, and called to one without the tent.

A Moslem soldier appeared and saluted him, bearing to me a small box or casket of sandal.

"It is not silver money," Mahabat Khan remarked, smiling, and I knew he was thinking of the purse I had given back to the servants of the Rao.

"*Yah khawand*," I said, "O lord of many clans, may thy pardon be granted me. How is it possible for me to accept a gift for aiding a man upon the road?"

"Open the box."

This I did, and astonishment came upon me. For, upon the satin lining lay four yellow pearls of size and luster, each the worth of a fine horse.

"A princely gift!"

I closed the lid of the casket, leaving it still in the hand of the soldier.

"Bethink thee."

Mahabat Khan looked at me intently.

"Thou hast bound up the hurts of my cousin and risked the displeasure of the *padishah*. Accept then the gift. Is it not sufficient?"

Now it was in my mind that Mahabat Khan was testing me, though how and to what end I knew not. So I spoke warily, yet openly. To tell the truth to talkative or inquisitive men is a waste of breath; but to some men it is not good to lie, and Mahabat Khan was such.

"Nay," I smiled, "the patient is not yet healed of his hurts. When he can walk again it will be time to think of payment."

"But thou seekest the camp of Jahangir."

I thought of Jami's idle tongue. After all, the boy was a Hindu.

"God willing, that was my purpose."

"And now?"

For a moment I did not speak. I had been sitting with the leader of the army of Ind for thrice the time water takes to boil, and he was certain that I had heard his cousin say that his death was desired at the court of Jahangir. Nay, I had seen his officers draw sword to slay me. I hoped for no more than that he would give command to bind me and keep me captive, so that I would not carry word of what I had seen in his camp to his enemies.

"I have heard what I have heard, O my khan," I said openly. "So, tell me thy purpose, that I may know what is in store for me. Verily, I am no spy; nor have I ever beheld the court of Ind."

At this he leaned back and combed his beard for a space. Once he parted his lips to speak and looked at me in silence.

"That Persian *hakim*, the one the Rao sahib had beaten, was a spy," he mused. "A creature who served Nur-Mahal. She, the favorite of the *padishah*, is Persian born. I do not think thou wilt see that *hakim* again, Ibn Athir."

His eyes gleamed and his long chin outthrust.

"Ho; go thou to the camp of the *padishah*! Bear a message from me. Is thy memory good?"

"At need."

"This is the message, not to be written down. Give it to no one but the person I describe to you. Thus: 'Mahabat Khan sends fealty. Are his deeds forgotten? Think, if the hawk that strikes down its quarry be not a better servant than the crow that feasts off others' game.'"

A strange message—an appeal fired with a warning. Its meaning was hidden from me, but it was a message that would go to one well known and of high rank. Moreover, it could profit little his enemies, if they heard it. They, I think, were the crows; and surely this warrior of Ind had the semblance of a hawk in his thin lips and down-curving beak of a nose and heavy brows. He made me repeat it thrice, until I had each word fixed in mind.

"To whom is the message?" I asked, wondering.

"To the *padishah*, Jahangir himself."

"*W'allah!* How am I to gain his ear, unknown to others?"

"In three ways. First, thou are a wanderer, and Jahangir loveth best the men of other lands. No man of mine would be suffered to live to speak to him. Second, thou art a physician, and may thereby approach and converse with my imperial master. Third, take the four pearls. Make a gift to Asaf Khan, the chief minister, and all doors will be open to thee."

So said Mahabat Khan, impatiently. And he advised me to give one pearl at first, promising the others upon fulfillment of the bargain.

"For Asaf Khan is a Persian, blood brother to Nur-Mahal, and a man with a price. Once his price is paid he may betray thee for a greater gain."

Another thing came into his mind. Indeed, he thought of all things.

"Some will cry out against thee, Ibn Athir, for freeing Man Singh from shame. Thy safeguard here is twofold. Others—my enemies—will know thou hast been within my lines, and will cherish thee, to question thee. And Jahangir likewise."

"To him, what shall I answer, if he question me?"

Mahabat Khan smiled bitterly.

"I lay no conditions upon that. Say what pleaseth thee."

Thereupon he summoned the follower who had in charge the casket of pearls, and these he put into a soft leather bag, bidding me wear it under my tunic.

"In the camp of my master," he said moodily, "thou wilt find, Ibn Athir, many to plunder thee and few to befriend thee. Let thine eyes be keen of nights, and fail not to deliver the message."

He made a sign of dismissal. A quiet man, not easily to be understood. A man oppressed by calamity, yet true to his salt, as I thought. One last glimpse of him I had, when we rode from the Rajput camp the next day.

Mahabat Khan, sitting a splendid charger, was inspecting his cavalry, riding down the ranks of five thousand, armed with sabers, each man wearing the garments and bestriding the horse of a chieftain. When he appeared on the *maidan*, a shout went up from the five thousand, a shout echoed by the servants and horse boys under the trees, such a shout as greets the leader of many clans and the victor of hard-fought fields.

Chapter IV
The Mogul's Door

As we rode north toward the river Bihat—for Jami had got himself some
stouter garments and had left his juggler's pole behind and had begged to
ride the roan pony—I pondered the meaning of the message I bore.

Why was the message sent? I knew not. How would the lord of all Ind
receive it? I knew not.

Perhaps Mahabat Khan had wished to be rid of me and had chosen
this way. Yet I did not think he was a man to let others do what his own
hand might do.

Two things were clear—that Mahabat Khan had lost the favor of Jahangir, since his emissary the Rao had been put to public scorn; and his
enemies at court were watching, that no man of his should reach the presence of the Mogul.

I noticed that Jami seemed joyful. His eyes were opened wide and he
had a quirk and jest for every veiled woman that passed under the hood
of a bullock cart. True, he liked to ride, and the lack of a saddle bothered
him not at all, kicking at the roan's lean ribs and pulling the pony's head.
But there was more in his soul than that, as I came to see in time.

And the women before our eyes became more and more—veiled and yet
shrill of tongue. They washed garments in streams and loitered under the
canopies of shops. For we were descending into the bed of a broad valley
where between steep clay banks a river ran, swift and turbid. Truly such
a river rises in hills where snow lingers. And this indeed was the Bihat
that races down from the northern mountains. I beheld the purple line of
them above the haze of the valley.

We drew rein then, to exclaim, each in his fashion. Beneath us lay the
lashgar, the great camp of the Mogul.

I have seen the camp of the true believers at the Stoning of the Devil,
within the Mecca hills, and I have seen the hunting camp of the sultan of
the Turks. But the *lashgar* of Jahangir was greater than either.

In the haze of the hot valley, scattered through the scrub, it covered the
earth as far as the eye could reach to the left and to the right. Near us were
the cotton shelters of the shameless women, booths of fruit and sweet-
meat sellers, and line upon line of horses; beyond them camels.

Far beyond, on the crest of a knoll, gleamed the gold and black iron of
artillery, and within the guns the tents were ranged in more orderly fashion, evidently housing warriors. Here again horses grazed and a hundred

standards fluttered through the dust billows. Near the river shone pavilions of red silk.

"That is the place of the king of kings!" cried Jami.

"He has not yet crossed the river," I made response.

We did not go at once to the red pavilions, because four Hindu horsemen came up the road and accosted us. The legs and bellies of their mounts were stained yellow with saffron, and they smelled, besides, of musk and ambergris. To me they gave courteous greeting, asking no questions, and turning back to escort me within the *lashgar*.

We had passed beyond the guns, which were placed in a kind of square, muzzles outward, and were among the elephants, when one of the horsemen said:

"Of all the pillars of empire, the thrice-worthy vizier Asaf Khan will be most fain to greet the *hakim*, Ibn Athir."

Now I had not said that I was a physician, nor had Jami opened his lips. I bore neither sign nor token that they should know me for a *hakim*. So was it clear that these four had been on the watch for my coming.

To them I said—

"Indeed, I seek the lord of lords, the earth-shaking Asaf Khan."

They led me around the elephants and through a cotton screen erected on bamboos that enclosed the space of a large village. Here dwelt the vizier, with his servants and slaves and watchdogs and his armed followers, of whom I saw several hundred loitering about. Once within the *khanate*, as the Hindus called the cotton screen, they showed me less respect. Others came to stare, and I did not dismount from my horse, though pressed to do so.

"Thy lord is not here," I assured them, "and before long I must seek quarters for the night."

"Thrice grieved will be Asaf Khan, if thou forsakest the shadow of his door before he has seen thy face."

This, I thought, might well be truth! But within the hour a shout arose, and a large elephant plodded through the gate of the enclosure—an elephant with gilt on its forehead and bearing a silver-inlaid chair on its back. Scurry and bustle filled the place when the elephant knelt, and two of my Hindus hurried forward to salaam to their master.

Now indeed I had to dismount, and someone led my horse away. But Asaf Khan spoke to me in Persian quite affably, bidding me take the evening meal with him. He carried himself well, a man broad in the face with a thick close-clipped beard. Diamonds of price gleamed in his turban aigrette and sword hilt.

Verily, that evening I felt ashamed of my plain mantle, for the least of his emirs wore velvet and fine linen. I had decided not to wear the robe of honor given me by Man Singh. I might as well have done so, since my packs were opened and ransacked and put together again, while I was with the vizier.

"Hast thou no better garment?" he asked when the others had withdrawn a little. "I will give thee one."

"Nay," I made response, "I have other garments, bought in Lahore; but it seemed to me fitting that I should go before the *padishah* in the dress of my country."

"Wilt thou seek audience of the king of justice?" As he said this, Asaf Khan leaned forward and touched the earth.

"God willing." I leaned toward him. "I have heard the men of Ind are excellent judges of pearls. No merchant am I; still I have some few precious stones. One pearl—I would like to know its value."

Before he could answer I took the leather purse from my girdle and placed it before him. He felt within it and drew out one yellow pearl.

"It is fair," he said, eyeing me sidewise.

"Honor me by keeping it as a journey gift, my lord."

He rolled it between his plump fingers, on which the rings of many-hued gems outshone my poor offering. At once—for I am not skilled at playing with words—I whispered that I was a physician, an adept at bleeding, and a well-wisher of Asaf Khan. That I sought the royal protection of Jahangir, and a chance to serve the lords of the court.

"And, though the pilgrimage hath left me bare of gear, I have three other stones the match of this one."

At this he became more friendly, calling me by name and bidding the servants bring wine, which I did not drink.

"Let me see the other stones, Ibn Athir," he cried playfully, "and I will judge if they be the equal of this."

Now I had the three pearls beneath my girdle, but I told him they were kept for me in Lahore against need, to be sent to me when I made demand. This he did not believe, nor did I think he would believe.

"What will be thy gift to Jahangir?" he asked.

I showed him a dagger set with a turquoise in the hilt, a long, curved blade of the kind the Hindus call *yama-dhara*, the death bringer, such a weapon as an assassin would choose, to slash open the heart beneath the ribs. It had not one tenth the value of the pearl, and Asaf Khan was satisfied.

In the end he swore that he would speak to Jahangir on my behalf and present me at audience, and I pledged him the three pearls.

Yet upon one pretext or another he put me off for one day and then two, saying that his master would think of naught but hunting. In this time his followers, as Jami told me, probed my saddle with their knives, and even lifted the ivory cap from the pommel.

"They are seeking a writing," the boy laughed, "and Asaf Khan is not easy in his mind as to thee. They know thou hast drawn thy reins hither from the *lashgar* of Mahabat Khan, who is the enemy of their master. They asked me many questions."

"And what answer didst thou make, O imp of the lower world?"

"I said thou didst seek reward from Man Singh, not knowing the peril of aiding one who had offended the *padishah*. And he turned thee away with empty hands."

"Good!" I praised the boy. "The roan horse is thine."

Jami grinned and cracked his fingers, saying truthfully that he could have stolen the pony, and I should give him now the *yama-dhara* in my girdle. His eyes brightened at sight of the weapon, that I had let him handle many times. But I told him he was over young to wear steel and, besides, it was to be a gift to the *padishah*.

For awhile after that he sulked, though he ceased not to pry about the encampment, eating with Moslem and Hindu alike, and often twice over.

"Eh, my master," he cried. "This is like a caravansary of all the world. Lo, this day have I eaten melons from Kabul and ginger fruits from Cathay, and rice and saffron of the plains." His cheeks were stuffed like a squirrel's that has combed the walnut trees. "And the women are fairer than in Lahore."

"How didst thou make certain of that, O lord of a hundred wits?"

"I walked behind the elephants, those with bells. Aye, when the *meharenis* hear the tinkle of the bells, they raise their veils to be seen by the rider of the elephant, if he be a famous emir. Besides, the tent walls are not like stone. Go, Ibn Athir, and cry thy skill to the *meharenis*, and from the women who thrust their hands forth to be bled or cured, thou wilt learn many secrets."

"Nay," I muttered, "only one thing I seek—to have speech with Jahangir."

"That is a simple thing," he responded idly.

Now I had watched the morning and evening audiences of the *padishah* from far off. And he sat in the opening of a pavilion by a fountain, surrounded by his emirs who stood within a teakwood rail, within guards. The lesser nobles thronged the garden of the fountain, to cry a greeting to the man in the tent, and a silken rope barred strangers from the garden. I might have cried out to Jahangir, as some Hindus did, but Asaf Khan stood ever at the ear of the *padishah*.

"And how?" I asked Jami.

"By the pavilion where the *padishah* sleeps hangs a gold chain, the end within reach from the ground. There are bells at the other end of the chain. This chain is for any man who has just cause, to give notice that he would speak with the *padishah*."

"Is it guarded?"

Jami nodded indifferently. I had not told him of the message I bore from Mahabat Khan.

"Aye, a spearman stands there to watch."

"No more than one?"

"Nay, my master—" Jami's eyes brightened—"only the one. Wilt thou go at night and sound the bells?"

"Perhaps."

Verily, what was not known to this youth? I thought that there were few men who would dare summon a king out of sleep, and that the chain of appeal was little used. Still, it seemed a way to what I sought. I had said to Mahabat Khan that I would deliver his message, and it was clear that Asaf Khan never meant to bring me to his master.

Chapter V
The Light of the Palace

When the cymbals clanged at the beginning of the fourth hour of the night I arose in the tent and clad myself in a loose black *kalifah*. To Jami, who had been sleeping curled up on a mat beside my quilt, I said that I was going forth alone.

"To return again," he asked, "O my master?"

On the threshold of the tent I thought upon this. Who can tell what the night may have in store for him?

"If I come not by the first light, when a white thread may be distinguished from black, do as thou wilt. Nay, take the black Tatar horse and ride him to the camp of Mahabat Khan. Say this: 'Ibn Athir, the Arab, delivered the message.'"

Jami, for some reason, began to grieve. He threw himself down and clutched at my ankles, bidding me take him with me. But this might not be. Within bowshot of the tent I waited to see if he would follow, and he did not. For awhile I heard him whimpering; then he fell silent, to watch, I think, for the appointed five hours.

It was a night of many stars. The earth underfoot was still warm, and a light wind rustled in the growth of thorn and flowering shrubs. Many men moved about the camp, carrying lanterns, and of noise there was no lack because that day the camel train and artillery had crossed over the river, escorted by most of the army, and on the morrow the rest of the *lash-gar* would follow in its journey toward Kabul, whither the Mogul went to pass the summer beyond the heat.

The lanterns made the darkness deeper, under the trees, and I passed from the lines of Asaf Khan without being seen. My black mantle merged with the night, and when I came to the place of the elephants, the lines of beasts chained among an army of keepers, I went forward slowly, beyond the fires where the men sat and gossiped.

Many times I had wandered through the camp, and the paths were clear in my mind. I turned aside into a place where few cared to go. In an open field by command of the Mogul some threescore thieves had been put to death.

Some had been trampled by elephants, some shot with arquebuses. But the leaders had been set on stakes, to die slowly. Two days had passed since then, and life had left the last of the thieves. In the starlight, they were visible, heads hanging on their shoulders. I came upon one suddenly and beheld his teeth gleaming between drawn lips. Eyes he had none, for the crows and vultures had visited this place of death.

W'allah! Jahangir delighted overmuch in torture. Even when hunting, he liked to have the carcasses stretched out at the end of the day for him to scan, and he kept at his side a servant whose duty it was to write down the total of each kind of game. For these unnamed miscreants, the thieves, the sword would have been punishment enough.

But they served me indeed that night, since I passed from the field into a trampled garden where a hundred soldiers sat about or snored by one fire. Beyond the fire was the *ata khanate*, the red cloth barrier around the imperial quarters. I went forward slowly, crawling in the dry grass, the sound of my passage unheard in the murmur of the wind.

The cloth screen that flapped and shivered over my head made a poor kind of barrier. I felt for the bamboo supports and thrust up the cloth between them, crawling beneath and standing erect all in a moment.

No fires glowed. Far off, lanterns swung gently on spears thrust into the ground, and the tops of the great pavilions swelled and sank. As I passed by the nearer tents I heard the tinkle of women's anklets, and laughter.

And straightaway I sank into the grass again. Torches came around the pavilion—torches borne by barefoot slaves before some young nobles who looked like Persians. One of them held in leash a pair of hunting leopards, and the eyes of the beasts glowed when they turned toward me, scenting a man.

I gripped the hilt of my sword and lay without moving, until one of the courtiers, noticing the restlessness of the leopards, held back his companions.

"Not that way," he cried. "Yonder lies the field of the dead."

Another laughed.

"Nay, Amir ul Amira, whoso kneels upon the carpet of Jahangir may win to immortality in this world, or the next."

Nevertheless, they went away to seek a more distant gate, and again I had reason to be grateful for the unfortunate thieves. I had marked by the torchlight a single spearman standing beside the largest of the pavilions, and toward him I made my way.

He was watching the departing nobles idly, and I waited until he had turned his back, walking away slowly. Then I rose to my feet and sped to him, drawing the curved dagger from its sheath.

The warrior stopped, listening. He faced me, peering into the gloom by the tent wall. Before he could speak, I gripped his tunic at his throat and pressed the tip of the knife under his beardless chin.

Eh, he had the long spear in one hand, a shield upon the other arm; the hilts of other weapons showed against his white garment. But for all his weapons, he trembled when he felt the steel prick his skin.

"Be silent and live!" I whispered. "Take me at once to the gold chain, the chain of justice that hangs by the pavilion of the *padishah*."

Doubtless he thought, if he thought at all, that I had come to carry off the gold. Before I let him move, I felt for all the knives at his waist and tossed them to the ground. In the darkness a long spear avails not at all, and a shield is of little worth; a sword may serve its turn, but the weapon that slays is a knife.

"This way," he muttered, drawing me with him. And, growing bolder in a moment, he asked what I desired.

"Speed," I laughed, and shifted the point of the *yama-dhara* from his throat to his back, beneath the left shoulder blade.

Indeed, he went swiftly around the pavilion, stumbling over ropes and his own spear shaft, until he ran full into another guard, who cursed him and warned him to be silent, in a whisper.

My man could not draw back and dared not speak. The other peered at him, recognizing him, and yet doubtful. My eyes were accustomed to the near darkness of the starlight, and I beheld within arm's reach something that hung down from the eaves of the pavilion. A post and a kind of bracket showed dimly against the tent wall, and from this bracket above my head stretched the thing that glimmered softly.

It came into my mind that this might be the chain of justice and the man he who stood guard over it. I reached forth and pulled upon it strongly.

W'allah! Above and within the pavilion bells without number tinkled and rang and chimed. The two soldiers cried out, and the one that had brought me hither, feeling my dagger withdrawn from his neck, turned and fled. The other grasped my arm.

"What madness is this?" He muttered. "O fool, there will come angry *mansabdars* to ask the meaning of this. If they find thee, they will drag thee before the king of justice and light of the law of Mohammed. And if they find thee not—"

He tightened his grasp on me. Truly, to free myself I would have needed to slay him.

"Has none come before me, to appeal to the Mogul?"

"Yea, desperate men, and—"

A lantern shone on the ground beside us, and came around the comer of the great tent—a lantern carried by a stout man in an embroidered robe who was followed by armed officers.

They held the lantern close to my face, exclaiming at my black garments. They spoke angrily to the guard by the chain, and the man in the robe of honor would have taken my weapons but I put hand upon hilt, saying:

"I am of the clan Nejd, a Sayyid, and the grandson of a chieftain. I have come to the light of the law of Mohammed in this fashion, at this hour, because evil men have kept me from his face."

The noble in command of the guard glanced upward fearfully. I had spoken in a clear voice, and doubtless many were listening, unseen.

"Come," said he. "The mercy of the Mogul is denied no one."

Indeed Jahangir, the Conqueror of the World,* sat awaiting us in the central chamber of the pavilion. His attendants led me through a curtain, out into the center of a wide carpet, holding fast to my arms, while others stood with drawn swords a spear's length at either side. The space was hung with tapestries woven into pictures, always of hunting, from elephant and horseback. And behind the Mogul stood a long screen of wooden fretwork, inlaid with mother of pearl. Above my head a canopy of cloth of gold swelled and shivered as the wind brushed into the pavilion.

Jahangir half sat, half reclined against a round cushion—a stout man without a beard. When he moved, his head turned from side to side, as a lion's. He had the broad chin and the full, slant eyes of the Mogul race. Only in a pearl armlet and upon the loose ends of his girdle did he wear precious stones; but his garments were the lightest linen, and he breathed at times with heavy panting, as if a hand had clutched his throat.

In the beginning I thought this shortness of breath might be due to the heat of the night. After another moment I beheld the gray tinge of his flesh, the coarse lips and bloated eyelids of one who has denied himself nothing of forbidden food, of opium and spirits.

Indeed, I beheld the living carcass of a man who would stand before the dark angels within the space of two years. I bent my head and shoulders thrice in the salaam of greeting.

"Thy hand caused the bells to sound?" His glance, that had been roving among the tapestries, passed over me fleetingly. "Speak!"

"O Lord of Ind," I said in Persian, which he readily understood, "dismiss thy followers and then hear me."

Again he looked at me and moved his shoulders in vexation.

"I was sleeping. Thou art armed. What is this?"

"A wrong to be redressed."

---

*The meaning of "Jahangir."

Suspicion, annoyance, and curiosity flickered across his broad, pale face. I asked the Hindus at my side to draw the *yama-dhara* from my girdle and to present it to the Mogul as a gift. He fingered it a moment, drew blade from sheath, and placed it beside him.

"Grant, O King," I cried, "that I may put my sword at thy feet and speak to no ear but thine." And I added, when his brow darkened, "The message is from one who would serve thee."

Eh, the ways of the court were strange to me; and I knew that already a messenger must have been sent to rout Asaf Khan from sleep, for his spies among the guard would have orders to report such happenings. So I took the boldest course unwitting. If only I had spoken otherwise . . .

But who may escape his fate? I did what I did. And a new look came into the eyes of the Mogul. He gave command that the chamber of the pavilion should be cleared. At once the officers objected, with many words, saying that I had come at night, without a friend. He bade them search me for other weapons, and, when they found none, he told them sharply to be gone.

In the end, they went. The chamber was great in size, and though they may have listened beyond the hangings, they could not hear a word. Before they departed I had drawn my sheathed scimitar and, holding it upon both hands, placed it upon the carpet within reach of the Mogul, stepping back three paces.

"Thy message?" he demanded, curling his bare feet under him and leaning forward, perhaps to understand the better, perhaps to have the sword under his arm.

"Thus was it." I reflected and said what Mahabat Khan had said: "Mahabat Khan sends fealty. Are his deeds forgotten? Think, if the hawk that strikes down its quarry be not a better servant than the crow that feeds from others' leavings?"

The Mogul's eyes widened and he frowned.

"Aye, a hawk indeed. He has drawn apart the heart of my army and follows upon my heels." For a moment he was silent. "Who art thou?"

It came into my mind that Mahabat Khan had told me to speak to this lord of men from an open heart. So did I, relating how I had journeyed to Ind to behold his face, and how I had fallen in with the Rajputs, and with the stricken Rao.

This seemed to trouble Jahangir. He started to clap his hands to summon a servant, then thought better of it and reached forth to pour with his own fingers a little amber fluid from a silver jar into a drinking cup.

Such a cup! Half a palm high it stood, glowing with all the fires of Iblis, for it had been cut from a single ruby. In gold inlay, there was upon it a single word—Nur-Mahal, the Light of the Palace.

Now as the Mogul lifted the cup and drank I heard the slightest of sounds, as if some one breathed deep nearby. But the hangings of the partition were five spear lengths away. Another sound came, the faint tinkling of a woman's anklet.

Eh, there was no woman within sight. Jahangir had not stirred, save to set down the cup, and he wore no bracelets or earrings. I looked covertly on all sides, and then at the wooden screen behind the Mogul's head, such a screen as bars the quarters of the women from the presence of men.

Jahangir choked and breathed heavily, feeling about with his fingers as if uncertain of what he touched.

"If I were sure," he chewed his lip, eying me. "Mahabat Khan was my sword arm until too much honor made him over-daring. He has been too long with the lords of Rajputana. If he had come into my presence, then I would know whether he be faithful or not."

"Verily he sent his comrade, Man Singh."

Jahangir moved impatiently.

"As to that I know nothing. If the Rajput came to the *lashgar*, he did not seek audience with me. I do not remember giving order for his punishment."

"Then others did so, in thy name."

"By the many-armed gods! Who would dare give out a *firman* in my name? Let Man Singh come before me and point out the one. Let him complain!"

So said the Mogul, yet his thought was otherwise. The eye of his mind contemplated Mahabat Khan and the five thousand riders bivouacked within a day's ride. Now in the *lashgar* were men without number, horse and foot and cannon men, slaves, huntsmen and their families. A multitude, perhaps a hundred thousand, perhaps more. Who knows? Yet the riders of Mahabat Khan worried him, because he questioned me—indeed I think it was for this purpose he had endured my words—as to the number of horses in the camp of the khan, and the names of the chieftains. "Do many come in from the countryside to talk with the khan?" he asked.

"More than a few," I responded. "And this, O King of Justice, is clear to me. Mahabat Khan is true to thee in his heart. When the chieftains cried out against thee, he would have none of it. Yet the wrong done to his cousin is his shame, and now he is like a man goaded into a path he did not mean to follow."

Jahangir threw himself back on the pillow, taking up and playing with the dagger.

"If a king's son, the firstborn, rebels against him, how is he to put trust in a Pathan?" Nevertheless, he seemed a little reassured. "What would Mahabat Khan have me do? He has lifted his standard apart from mine."

"He did not say. Why not send for him, pledging him safety, and then judge the wrong done his cousin?"

"Did he say that?"

"Nay, the thought is mine."

"Art thou a sorcerer, to read good and evil in a face? A *hakim*, thou! A curer of ills. This shall be a fortunate hour for thee if Mahabat Khan makes his peace with me. *Bism'allah!* I will give thee the healing of the women's quarrels and a robe of honor with a stipend of twelve silver crowns a month."

He smiled reflectively, and it was clear that he believed Mahabat Khan had charged me with this last message. His broad face shone with good humor, though he still breathed with difficulty.

"Ibn Athir, I find thee a discreet messenger, and I bid thee return to the khan and say—"

He paused, thrusting the point of the dagger against his palm, then casting it down, as if remembering it might be poisoned.

"Say to Mahabat Khan that if he comes to seek me with no more than two hundred followers, I, Jahangir, his king, swear that no harm will come to him. Much may be pardoned in a hawk that flies back to its master."

I bent my head and stepped forward to pick up my sword, when I saw the expression of the Mogul change. Turning, I beheld the hangings parted behind me, and a Hindu prostrate at the end of the carpet.

"Lord of the World," the fellow cried, not raising his head, "Nur-Mahal seeks thee, and even now approaches."

Alone, she advanced to the carpet. A triple salaam she made, her light body swaying with more than the grace of a dancing girl at each bending.

"It is the seventh hour of the night," she said, "and a nameless wanderer keeps the lord of my life from sleep."

Her voice was modulated as a singer's. An echo of it lingered in my ears, like the cry of a mocking djinnee. She looked down at my sword, picked it up and placed it under Jahangir's hand. Though she had said no word, she made it clear that she feared for his life.

"Nay," she smiled at him, "is it not the pleasure of my lord to cross the river at sunrise? And the hours of sleep are few."

"The *ata khanate* need not move until the cool of the evening," murmured Jahangir, "and I will sleep late. Have I not given command to hold no dawn audience?"

She had slipped to the carpet below him, and her arm rested across his fat knee that quivered a little when he breathed. Who can make clear with words what his eyes have seen? I saw that Nur-Mahal had draped herself in white, the folds of the linen hiding her shoulders and hips. Her eyes were of great size and almost as dark as the hair that was drawn back tight from her white forehead. One thing at a time I noticed, but always this. *She wore no veil.*

Eh, my pulse beat fast and strong. Unveiled, she had come into my presence, paying no heed to me. Though the Moguls made no great point of screening their women, still the favorite wife, the Light of the Palace, would not have revealed herself to one who would go from her presence and boast of it. Beyond doubt she did not mean for me to leave the pavilion.

"True, my conqueror," she said lightly. "So was the command wisely given. With the rebellious Rajputs drawing ever closer to our lines, one thing must be done swiftly. Surely we must put the river between us and their array."

"They advance?"

"With the last light Payanda Mirza beheld a band of two hundred horsed and in the brush trails."

Jahangir frowned, twisting his cup in his fingers. Nur-Mahal took it from him and laid it aside, as a trusted servant might remove some object in the way of his master. She spoke of the movements of Mahabat Khan with authority and clearness, without pleading or complaining.

Indeed I had heard that she herself directed the movements of the *mansabdars*, who were the officers of the Mogul. Until now I had not believed.

"When we are across the Bihat we can deal with the unfortunate ones who have raised their standard against us," she went on, watching the face of Jahangir from beneath heavy lashes. "Shah'lam hath brought thee a score of hunting leopards," she smiled, "and an elephant trained to fighting. They await thee, across the river."

No word she uttered concerning Mahabat Khan, but she had made the Mogul restless and uncertain. Until she entered the chamber he had spoken with authority, suspicious and hesitant, but open in mind. Now he waited upon her words, irritable and impatient, but confiding in her.

"Perhaps the Rajputs are merely making their way to some chieftain's hold, in the cool of the night," Nur-Mahal murmured, "or they may be coming to give their allegiance to us."

Jahangir grunted and breathed heavily.

"Asaf Khan," she laughed as if a little amused, "hath discovered a new *hakim* for thee, O lord of my heart. An Arab, who pretends to be well versed in bloodletting, who gave to my brother four pearls of size and good color. Three will Asaf Khan give over to thee. But this Arab *hakim* hath no mind to give thee more than a dagger such as that by thy hand."

Jahangir glanced at the *yama-dhara* and, angrily, at me. He rolled over on his haunches, like a badgered bear.

"A physician?" he muttered.

"Who tended one of the Rajput chieftains, the Rao of Malwa, Man Singh, during a fever and had a great reward from him."

Eh, Nur-Mahal chattered on, like a child with news to tell, and I wondered. I wondered how she had learned this, until I remembered the Persian *hakim* who had been a spy and had been beaten and cast off by the Rajput chieftain. No doubt he had sold his story well!

And now I knew that the coming of Nur-Mahal had not been by chance. There had been women who listened behind the screen, and had hastened to her as swiftly as limbs could take them.

She pressed against Jahangir's knee, to brush her fingers across his forehead, whispering softly. His eyes closed and opened without purpose. Verily of the twain, she was the one to command and he to question and scold—a woman's part. She had ordered the moving of the *lashgar* when she heard of the small party of Rajputs, or, more likely, she had used this as an excuse.

And now she beguiled and soothed the sick man into forgetfulness, until he reached out for his wine cup and his hand fell by chance on my scimitar.

In that instant a change came over him. His eyes cleared, and his lips tightened. He sat upright, like a man with a purpose.

"Go, Ibn Athir," he said clearly. "But tell Mahabat Khan he must come alone, and across the Bihat to me."

Nur-Mahal seemed to pay no attention, though Jahangir watched her. But when I advanced again to take my sword, she signed for one of the guards to bear it from the chamber.

Having permission to depart, I made the triple salaam of leavetaking and rose, from the last bending in the entrance.

At the instant I stood erect, the hangings were let fall before my eyes, shutting out sight of Jahangir and the Light of the Palace. And then all sight was reft from me. A heavy cloth was cast over my head from behind, and something closed around my throat, gripping tight through the cloth.

Who may escape his fate? I groped with my hands for the girdles of my assailants, seeking weapons, and feeling nothing. The noose about my throat put an end to breathing and by it I was dragged over carpets, until a red fire blazed up within my eyeballs and all strength left me.

Then the cloth and the noose were withdrawn, and in time I knew that I was bound at the wrists and knees, in darkness.

My head pained me and my throat ached. An hour might have passed before a torch appeared suddenly in the rift of a curtain and I rolled over, to stare up into the dark eyes of Nur-Mahal and the faces of a dozen armed men.

"Think, Ibn Athir," she cried, placing her slippered foot upon my throat under the chin and pressing down, so that pain anew shot through me, "think of this! It is unwise to meddle with strange affairs, and thy reward shall be to be carried upon the road in the carts of Asaf Khan, who will cover thee well with the fresh skin of an ox, sewn all about thee. Think—the sun is strong and great with heat, and an ox hide dries faster than any other."

Then, her foot still upon my throat, she bade her followers search me. They found nothing but the three pearls that were to have bribed Asaf Khan.

Chapter VI
The Fate of Ind

Until dawn I heard movement all around me. Horses trotted by in the distance, ox drivers muttered and swore, and carts creaked under heavy loads. Near my head the sounds were of bare feet moving about.

In all this time the eyes of Nur-Mahal were in my mind, the lustrous eyes of a proud and beautiful woman. She alone must have had me bound, keeping it secret from the sick and besotted man who lay upon pillows and

played with a jeweled cup. She had set me aside from her path as I might
have flicked a scorpion with my staff.

And Mahabat Khan—for what reason did she seek his ruin? Had he offended her, or had he grown too powerful? No doubt her spies had beheld
him on the road, and he had been taken and beaten by officers of the Mogul, who said the command had come from Jahangir.

So I reflected, and in time the light came. The stout *mansabdar* appeared at my side with two swordsmen.

"Pleasant by thy prayers," he grinned, bidding the men cut the bonds
from my ankles. "The cart waits and the hide is ready."

We went forth through the corridors of the great pavilion. At this hour
the sun did not yet shine full into the valley, and a light mist hung over
the river, casting its veil amid the clumps of cypresses and the high plain
trees. I had come forth on a carpet of red damask that stretched from the
pavilion entrance down to the mist.

The *khanate* had been removed, and I saw throngs of servants vanishing into the mists with their loads.

Overhead the blue of the sky became clearer, and the veil of mist thinned
slowly. The *mansabdar* stood waiting for his horse to be brought and watching the last of the elephants go down toward the bridge of boats.

I also was watching the outline of the bridge take shape, wondering
whether it were better to try to run from my guards and throw myself
into the river. Few men were about—the tail ends of followers. The *lashgar* with its guns and armed bands had all crossed over.

At last I could see the gray-blue bed of the river, over the steep clay
bank. And I saw a horseman trotting through the high grass toward us.
The sun shone full into our eyes and the rider was within a spear's length
before I knew him.

It was Mahabat Khan. Behind him rode a score, and after these still
other Rajputs galloped across the trampled fields.

The officer beside me shaded his eyes and peered up, his teeth striking together sharply.

"*Ohai!* This is indeed presumption! Mahabat Khan, wait and I will go
in and announce thee."

"Nay Salim Bai, I will go in before thee, this time."

The dark eyes of the khan met the startled gaze of the officer, and
Salim Bai drew back several paces. The twenty who escorted the Pathan

clattered up and some reined their steeds before the officer of the Mogul. Still others surrounded the great pavilion swiftly.

Servants came forth from the entrances and stared in wonder. The two men who had been watching me sheathed their weapons and went away. In all perhaps two hundred Rajputs had come to the *ata khanate* with drawn swords and dark faces.

And Mahabat Khan lost no least moment of opportunity. Eh, he was a leader, above all, a man fit to lead cavalry in a raid. Paying no attention to the bewildered servants or the irresolute Salim Bai, he summoned twoscore of his riders who carried bundles upon their cruppers. These he loosed like a flight of pigeons down the slope toward the river, galloping recklessly through the tail of miserable camp followers, until they dipped down the steep clay bank and smote the few guards who had been left at this end of the bridge of boats.

My blood warmed at the sight. The Mogul's men knew not what to expect, but they drew their weapons when the hard riding Rajputs were within a few paces of them. Some of the guards tried to mount their horses; some tried to form across the first planks of the bridge.

In a moment the Rajputs had broken them, knocking men and beasts into the swift current of the river and clearing the end of the bridge. Then they dismounted and fell to work with axes, cutting through the bottoms of the boats, cutting the lashings that held them together. From the bundles they had carried they took dried rushes and flax and kindled fire in this, starting a blaze in many of the boats that were swinging out into the current now. More than half of the bridge was destroyed in this way.

And, mounted proudly upon my black Tatar charger that scamp, Jami, reined up to me, tugging his own pony behind.

"*Ohai sahib*," he laughed, "they have trussed thee like a goat that is to be slain. I have ridden many leagues since the first light."

But he slid down by the stirrup that dangled far below his bare foot and cut the cords that held my wrists at my back. He used a half-moon dagger of a poor sort that he must have picked up in the disordered camp or begged from a servant. And he boasted without truth that the horses had carried him far, for the charger's coat was smooth, his limbs dry.

"The praise to the Compassionate!" I cried, stretching forth my arms.

Mahabat Khan glanced at me swiftly and nodded; then, seeing the boats burning out upon the river and all the armed forces of the *lashgar* save a retinue of young warriors waiting to escort the women of Jahangir on the far side of the river, he spoke to the chieftains near him and reined toward the imperial pavilion.

Nay, he did not dismount. Whipping out his light saber, he slashed down the entrance hanging and bent his head, urging his horse into the corridor between the tapestries. Several followed him in this manner and Jami quivered with excitement.

"Let us go in, my master," he whispered. "There will be a tumult, and—"

He meant there would be spoil for the taking. Without a weapon I followed, and the Rajputs made way for me with courteous greeting since they knew me for the man who had befriended the Rao. The horse of Mahabat Khan stood before the entrance of the audience chamber, pawing at the red damask underfoot.

Mahabat Khan himself paced forward slowly, and made a salaam, but without touching the carpet with his hand. Sitting among the disordered pillows, blinking in the sunlight, Jahangir the Mogul, without attendants and without armed men, faced him silently.

Mahabat Khan advanced to the feet of the Mogul and stretched forth his arms, holding high his head.

"I have come," he cried in a clear voice, "because the enmity of Asaf Khan hath sought my death."

In the court of the Mogul it was forbidden to pronounce this word, and Jahangir's dull eyes blazed with anger.

"If I am guilty of any wrong," went on the Pathan grimly, "I ask only to be put to death in thy presence; if I am blameless, it shall be known to thee."

At first Jahangir had trembled, his heavy hands moving across his weak knees. Verily, he had been roused from sleep a moment before, and he had seen me standing among the Rajputs at the chamber entrance. Perhaps he thought I had summoned Mahabat Khan out of the night, but surely he knew at once that he was a captive. The fleeing servants, the chieftains with bared swords, told him this.

So he sat upright, like a sick lion, barely showing his teeth, and striving to gather his wits together.

"Did I not send for thee?" he asked in his deep voice. "The sight of thee rejoices my heart, for with thee beside me I am safe from harm. Sit!"

Mahabat Khan hesitated for the space of a breath. The Rajput princes beside me murmured, fingering their sword hilts. They hated Jahangir, yet served him, as their fathers had served Akbar, his father. Their blood was up, and at that moment they would have rushed in upon the bloated and cruel Mogul, the alien who was master of Ind. By a stroke of the sword they would have made an end of him.

The Pathan, who was still faithful to the Mogul, seated himself at the edge of the carpet. Jahangir cried for his servants to bring wine, but no one came. Alone, with drug-dulled brain, he looked from one to the other, as if waking from a long sleep—he who had had men flayed alive and the skin torn from them for a whim.

"Nay, Mahabat Khan," he said, "is it fitting that I should sit, half clad, before these emirs? I will go to the women's tents and put on fresh garments."

"In time, O *Padishah*. But first there is need to go forth with me."

"Whither?"

"To the five thousand that await thee."

Blood rushed into the heavy face of the Mogul, and his fingers tightened on the ruby cup.

"I am thy captive," he said sulkily. "My fate is between thy hands."

Once it was asked of a certain wise man whence he had his wisdom, and he made answer—

"From the blind."

And his followers asked the reason of this. He said—

"Because the blind take no step without feeling the earth before them first."

Mahabat Khan had drawn near the *lashgar* that sunrise with his two hundred, intending no more than to look upon the camp. Seeing the armed forces withdrawn across the river and the imperial tents almost deserted, he had put spurs to horse and charged, intending to secure the person of Jahangir.

W'allah! He had succeeded. And if Jahangir had threatened him, or had tried to flee, a single stroke of a Rajput sword might have made Mahabat Khan a free man, free to deal with his foes and to stir into flame the embers of war.

"Now," cried Jami, at my side, "we shall see swords drawn."

This, at least, was true. The Rajputs were escorting Jahangir to another tent not so near the river bank. They had not allowed him to put on better garments, but had brought up an elephant from somewhere, an elephant without an umbrella and with only a plain chair in a wooden howdah. Jahangir mounted to his seat and the mahout made the beast go forward.

Then the imperial horsemen far off around the women's quarters realized what was happening. They ran about hastily, getting to horse and drawing sabers and taking the lances from the slings.

We followed—Jami and I—the elephant with its escort of a hundred Rajputs. It was no time to be without a weapon and I meant to find one and arm myself.

And it seemed as if there would be no lack of swords on the ground, for the *korchis*—the picked imperial guardsmen—charged at a gallop, shouting, and evidently determined to rescue their master. A hundred Rajputs put their horses to a trot and advanced through the dry grass to meet them.

In a moment the air was full of the clatter of steel and the war shouts. Saddles emptied all over the field. The Rajputs did not keep together, but fought each for himself, scorning the lance but wielding their light blades like *shaitans*.

The Mogul's followers soon lost their array, and in single combat the Rajputs beat them to earth and rode them down. Before long the *korchis* were flying from the field.

I went forward to pick up a sword when I encountered a woman coming from the nearest pavilion. She was veiled and wrapped in the colored mantle of a dancing girl and she walked with a swaying grace, without looking back at the fighting. Eh, it came into my mind that at such a moment a woman would keep to the tents—for the wives of the men of Ind are not like our women, who follow the clans to raid or battle.

When she came abreast me she turned away her eyes. And from her hair arose a scent that I knew, the perfume of dried rose leaves. I put forth my hand to stay her and she swerved aside to avoid being touched. Surely a dancing girl would not have acted thus.

"Thou art the Light of the Palace," I cried, certain indeed. "Is this the path to follow when thy lord is taken captive?"

She turned her head to look around, and Jami pressed close, alive with curiosity. In all the days of our wandering he had not seen me in talk with a woman.

Verily, this was Nur-Mahal. She lowered her veil with a swift motion and in the clear sunlight her beauty was no less than by night. But now her lips drooped and her eyes held appeal.

"I go where I must, Ibn Athir," she cried softly. "Calamity hath fallen upon us, and if I am taken by the Rajputs, they will take life from me."

Why did she withdraw her veil? Her skin was smooth and tinted by the blood beneath, like the rarest silks that come from Cathay. Startled, and dismayed, her pride hid all weakness as a cloak covers the rents of a garment. Only her eyes pleaded with me to keep her secret and suffer her to go, in her disguise.

"To go whither?" I asked.

"As God wills, perhaps to Lahore." Her eyes still dwelt upon my face, seeking my thoughts. "Will it profit thee, Ibn Athir, to deliver me to death?"

"Without honor, there is no profit."

At once she leaned toward me, half smiling.

"Thy sword! That is thy desire. Salim Bai took it, and thou wilt find it in his baggage."

Surely, she had read my thought! Even while I meditated, she fastened the veil in place and went on, moving without haste toward a clump of flowering shrubs. And I—I rubbed my fingers across my eyes, as a man will do who has been sleeping in strong sunlight. She was Nur-Mahal, and what was her fate to me?

Nay, if I had taken her then to Mahabat Khan the fate of Ind might have been otherwise. I thought: She is alone, flying from execution. Let God guide her steps.

And in the days thereafter I wondered whether she had not willed that I should think thus. But then I hastened to find Salim Bai and demand that my sword be given back. He was too afraid of the Rajputs to refuse.

Jami, meanwhile, had deserted me again.

After the dawn prayer on the second day I was summoned to the quarters of Mahabat Khan to attend Jahangir, who was worse than usual. I found the Pathan striding back and forth restlessly, while the Mogul lay prone on a white cloth with untasted dishes at his side.

"He thinks that I have poisoned him," cried Mahabat Khan angrily.

Jahangir glanced at me as a trussed criminal eyes the goaler who comes knife in hand. He was grunting and breathing with difficulty, and the blood throbbed in his pulse. Though the cool morning air blew through the tent, sweat hung upon his eyebrows and thick jowls. In spite of this, he pretended to be in excellent humor and called the khan his sword arm.

When I rose from his side I beckoned toward Mahabat Khan, and when we were beyond the hearing of the sick man gave my opinion.

"No man may outlive his allotted span, O my lord. The seal of *al-maut* is written on the forehead of the *padishah*. He will not live more than two years."

The Pathan started and clenched his sinewy hands.

"Nay, *hakim*," he responded grimly, "dose the *padishah* with physic, bleed him, purge him, and set him on his feet. Stripped of the parasites that have sucked his manhood, he may yet be king."

"No man may alter what is written. Though I were promised the emeralds of Golkunda, I might not lengthen his life. Others might promise more, and lie. I have spoken the truth."

For a moment his dark eyes bored into mine.

"I believe thee, Ibn Athir."

Then he turned back to the sick man, striding back and forth by the prostrate and panting form. The long, clean limbs of the warrior, and his clear eyes and firm step, gave him authority that the Mogul lacked. Suddenly he pulled at his beard and cried out in a loud voice:

"In my youth, I served Akbar the Blessed, thy father. And I will say to the son what no other hath dared to utter. Upon my head be it!"

He strode to the entrance of the tent, which was of heavy black velvet and, after looking out, let fall the flap.

"Thy great-grandsire Babar the Tiger conquered India, and he was a man in all things. Thy father, passionate in temper and too fond of intrigue, was yet a true ruler, who devoted every hour of wakefulness to the affairs of the myriads that worshipped him. Lo, calamity came upon his head in his children. Thy brothers died in drunkenness."

"Aye," nodded Jahangir, "they went out of the world in wine-soaked shrouds."

Mahabat Khan glared at his royal captive and pulled the wide sleeve back from his muscular right arm.

"These scars I had from the edge of steel in thy service. Because I was faithful to the salt, thy ministers sent me from the presence, giving me perilous tasks for nourishment, and stripping me of honor with their lies. Behold!"

He drew from his girdle a gold coin, of a sort I had never seen. It was a *mohur*, one side bearing the likeness of the beautiful Light of the Palace, the other that of Jahangir, smiling, a cup upheld in his hand. Mahabat Khan threw it down and spat upon it.

"Worthless! Asaf Khan the Persian hath taken the reins of authority from thee, and Nur-Mahal rules thee. Cease emptying cups and eating hemp and searching for new women! Give order to lead out thy horse and take command of the army, summoning the best of thine officers to thee. Then will we deal with Asaf Khan and his parasites."

The dark-faced Pathan checked in his stride and laughed.

"*Kya*! Asaf Khan is a jackal. Why did all but a few of thy *lashgar* cross the river, leaving thee defenseless when I was within a ride? Asaf Khan knew that I would strike, given the opportunity. He thought that the Rajputs would slay thee."

Jahangir rolled over on an elbow, his lips working.

"Nay, what gain to Asaf Khan?"

The Pathan's teeth gleamed through his beard.

"Think! Thy son hath drawn the sword against thee, and the daughter* of Asaf Khan is the wife of thy son. If they could put an end to thee, an end also there would be to the power of Light of the Palace, and Asaf Khan would rule from behind the throne of thy son."

Suspicion flared like a ray of sunlight across the heavy features of the sick man, and he felt at his girdle with a trembling hand as if feeling for the sword he no longer wore.

"Rouse thy courage!" stormed the Pathan. "Ride with me to the hills, and we will gather an army—a true army."

Jahangir sank back on his pillows, uneasily.

"Where is the Light of the Palace?"

"O my king, it is written, 'Unhappy the kingdom ruled by a woman.'"

Mahabat Khan gripped his beard, and I saw that his brow was damp.

"Nur-Mahal is a Persian, and a woman who sways thee as if holding thee in the meshes of her hair. They who know her—" he became silent, thinking. "O my *Padishah*, the Rajputs and the princes of the Dekkan, the Afghan emirs will not submit to have decrees signed by a woman in thy name."

---

*This daughter was Bibi-Khanum, called Mumtaz-Mahal, or Glory of the Palace, and the famous Taj Mahal is her sepulcher. She had as great an influence over her husband as Nur-Mahal had over Jahangir.

"She it was," muttered Jahangir, "who put thy cousin to public shame."

"Aye," nodded the Pathan grimly, "so that I would lift the standard of war against thee."

"I have always trusted thee, O *bahadur.*" Jahangir spoke too readily. "And in this moon I gave command to increase thy revenues to ten thousand *mohurs.*"

Mahabat Khan swerved as if he would have struck the sick man.

"*Bism'allah!* What care I for that? Nur-Mahal is a chain—a shackle upon thee. By scheming, by intrigue and by wiles, she rules India. And there is no help for it. She must be put to death."

These words had a curious effect upon Jahangir. He frowned, as if considering the torment to be dealt a criminal; then he shook his head helplessly, looking all around him. His hand stretched forth, fumbling for the cup that was not there.

"No help," he muttered. "But she is Nur-Mahal!"

Silent, with folded arms, Mahabat Khan waited.

"Where is she?"

The Pathan made a sign that he did not know, and Jahangir began to finger the pearls upon his armlet. Without Nur-Mahal at his side, he was no more than the husk of a man.

"Let it be so," he said at last, "Prepare a *firman* and I will sign it."

And he begged that some opium be sent him, his eyes glistening with real anxiety. Mahabat Khan gave an impatient exclamation and strode from the tent, gripping my arm. As he flung back the entrance flap, he breathed deeply, and I heard the words that came between his set teeth.

"May the Pitying, the Pitiful, have mercy upon me. This also was to come upon my head, after these years. Is there easement in all paradise for my spirit—I that have loved Nur-Mahal since she was a child upon the caravan road?"

Chapter VII
Battles

Within an hour we had tidings of Nur-Mahal. A messenger galloped up, raising dust among the tents, and crying that the imperial cavalry was mustering across the river south of us.

Eh, the bridge of boats had been destroyed, and a small party of warriors that had tried to surprise us in the night by swimming the Bihat had been drowned for the most part. But there was a ford within two leagues of

Mahabat Khan's standard, to the south, and here he had posted scouts to watch—a ford made treacherous by deep pools and by the swift current.

At these tidings Mahabat Khan was a man transformed. Now that he had to give battle to Asaf Khan and the other ministers, his eyes lighted and he called for his charger, riding out to where his Rajputs were already mustering.

Leaving a thousand to guard the camp and its royal prisoner, he hastened down the bank with his veteran cavalry.

And at the ford we found the fighting already begun.

At last the lords of Ind had stirred out of their stupor and were advancing to regain their monarch. Only the light cavalry was on their side of the river, but many thousand armored foot soldiers were massed on the far bank. From time to time white smoke billowed out toward us and a cannon roared.

But the range was too great and the khan and his Rajputs jested merrily at the balls that dropped here and there, or plunged into the steep clay bank. At the foot of this bank sandy spits ran out into the stream, making the current less; but the sand itself, so our scouts said, was evil footing.

The detachment left at the ford had gathered at the edge of the bank, firing from bows and matchlocks at a dozen elephants covered with leather armor. They were making their way slowly across the river, which rose to their bellies.

When Mahabat Khan had watched events for a moment, he gave command to draw back. The Rajput princes remonstrated, but he waved them away and they led their followers to a ridge more than a musket shot from the bank. Only a few were left to dispute the crossing.

And these fell back as the elephants began to top the rise from the river, their painted skulls showing first, then the howdah with its archers and finally their whole bulk of wet and glistening leather.

Once upon the bank, they waited for the footsoldiers—turbaned Mahrattas and shouting tribesmen. These were wet to the beards. Behind them came some Turks with matchlocks, and finally the first riders of the light cavalry.

The shouting and clashing of cymbals excited the Rajput chieftains, who grieved at beholding the van of the Mogul lords unharmed at the crossing.

"Let us strike!" They who stood nearest Mahabat Khan pleaded.

He made no answer, and the standards of the light horse came into view over the rise.

"By Siva," cried a raja, the lord of Jesselmir, striking his sword hilt, "it is not good to wait!"

But Mahabat Khan threw back his head and laughed soundlessly.

"Verily, it is good to wait when the foemen hath so foolish a leader as this."

"Yet they advance, more and more."

The khan nodded and, after awhile, to still the grumbling of the chieftains, he related a tale of a lion that lay in wait for a herd of horses. So long as the horses were not aware of their danger the lion kept himself hidden. Not until they scented him did the lion rush out and strike down his prey. For he was wise and knew that he could not slay all the herd, only the horse that came near his hiding place.

Some of the chieftains laughed, seeing the meaning within the tale. Verily, they could not strike the foemen across the river. Still more of the Mogul's bands appeared on the bank, spreading out to the flanks, the elephants advancing in the center. Perhaps four thousand were in sight when Mahabat Khan rose in his stirrups and cried out:

"Raise the banners!"

Eh, it was a goodly sight. The kettledrums rattled, and the lofty banners were lifted from the ground to the stirrup rests. The chieftains in advance of their men put their horses to the trot, down the ridge.

From a trot they spurred to a gallop. And, rushing upon the elephants, the lines of horsemen edged away to the right and left of the beasts. Some of the Turks began to fire from the matchlocks and there was noise and smoke. But some had wet their powder, and the Rajputs came on so swiftly, they had little time to settle their rests.

"Ho—nila ghora ki aswar!" Thus shouted the clans of Malwa and Jesselmir, remembering Man Singh.

They struck the hastily arrayed lines of the Mogul's officers as a torrent in the hills sweeps upon loose sand. Here and there the torrent was flung back—here and there it eddied—but the right of the foe was broken at once, and the Rajputs rode down into the center.

Who can tell all the events of a battle? I had kept behind Mahabat Khan, and I saw him strike two riders from the saddle, slashing one above the head of his own charger. I heard the deep trumpeting of the elephants, and the cries that rose on every hand—despairing shouts as the Mogul's men were pushed back to the edge of the steep clay bank.

They had crossed rashly, had formed without order and had been met by a well-timed charge of splendid cavalry. Hundreds lay upon the crest of the bank, hundreds more were slain by arrows as they struggled back to the ford. Meanwhile the Rajputs surrounded the elephants and slew the *mahouts* and archers from far off.

Mahabat Khan gave command to lead off the captured beasts, lest they run loose through our ranks, and he reined in his horse to gaze across the river.

"By the ninety and nine holy names, Ibn Athir," he cried, "would that Asaf Khan, the dog-born dog, had come over with those men."

But Asaf Khan, the wily, the covetous, did not show his person. We looked for a long time, trying to make out the leader of the foe. And in the end it was clear to us that somebody in the howdah of a fighting elephant gave commands. The elephant stood at the beginning of the ford, not moving from that place.

The howdah, of silver work, hid the riders, and at that distance we could only see officers coming up to the great beast and riding hence. Whoever it was—and we both, I remembering the three pearls, prayed that it be Asaf Khan—knew little about the maneuvering of men, yet lacked not determination.

Perhaps a hundred thousand of the Mogul's retainers had gathered on the far bank, and one after the other different chieftains led their followers down to the ford and essayed to storm our ground. But the four thousand Rajputs made good their ground.

Only for an hour was there doubt of the issue. Toward sunset the leader on the black elephant advanced into the ford with a multitude of footsoldiers. They plunged through the dark water in disorder, the current foaming about their shoulders. But they shouted with a mighty voice. Some of our clans had gone far to right and left to drive back scattered parties, and the Raja of Jesselmir held the crest of the bank with his veterans.

Above the turbaned heads of the oncoming warriors the black elephant loomed, feeling its way and flapping its ears restlessly. The level rays of the last sunlight struck full upon the glittering howdah, and Mahabat Khan and I cried out at once.

Under the tasseled hood we beheld the slender figure of the Light of the Palace. She, the empress, sat tranquil, a child on her knees. And it was said to me thereafter that this child was her youngest born.

We heard her voice, urging on the soldiery, and Mahabat Khan swore in his beard, looking this way and that like a man who knows not what path to take.

"May God shield her," he said under his breath.

But the lord of Jesselmir was weary of shooting arrows, and the Rajputs had no love for the matchlocks. He may have recognized Nur-Mahal; more likely, he could not hold back at such an opportunity.

Verily, he did well! He had been charged with the defense of the road and the bank; the assailants were too numerous to permit them to form on the top. So, before Mahabat Khan could send a galloper to him, he mustered his riders and charged down the winding road, slippery with blood and loose clay, and littered with the dead. He struck the head of the advance while the first hundred were crossing the sands.

Other Rajput clans rode up to take a hand, and the arrows began to fly about the elephants, some glancing from the silver work of the howdah.

The sun had left the surface of the river, though it still blazed in our eyes, and Mahabat Khan cried out to me—

"They will slay her, unknowing!"

Eh, this was what he himself had decided must be done, and surely it would put an end to the battle. But his eyes were dark with suspense and grief.

"If God wills it," I made response. "Nay, the issue will soon be decided."

Then Mahabat Khan remembered his leadership. Five hundred of his cavalry were fighting hand to hand down in the shadows, in the muddied and blood-stained water and the treacherous sands. He spurred off to lead up reinforcements. When a thousand had mounted and formed under his quick commands, he led them down the road, to rescue the chieftain of Jesselmir.

Wah! It was like the oft-told battle of the camel, when the woman Ayesha seated in the litter of a white camel cried on the avengers of Othman, and seventy of the clan Koreish died at the camel's bridle. Indeed, the spirit of a woman at such a time may put men to shame.

In the growing darkness there was heard only the screaming of the mortally stricken, the whir of steel, the shrilling of wounded horses and the trumpeting of the elephant.

I no longer saw Mahabat Khan. Swept away among the Rajputs, I was drawn out upon one of the sand spits. The elephant's *mahout* had been hurt by arrows and pulled from his seat. Masterless, the great beast swayed this way and that, and finally plunged out upon the sandbar.

With a loud shout the Rajputs around me made toward him, slashing down the spearmen and slaves who tried to hold us off. Once the elephant smote a rider with his trunk, and the man and horse went down. Others cut at the sinews of his legs which were protected by the leather armor.

"Bow and horse!" shouted a shieldless warrior behind me.

"Climb!" cried another, thrusting at me to get closer.

We splashed into water, and the horses reared. The great beast turned this way and that, infuriated with pain, and for an instant I beheld the face of Nur-Mahal.

The sky was still bright overhead, and her features were distinct, as she bent forward, no longer crying at the battle. The child on her knee seemed to be bleeding, and with cloth torn from her sleeve, the Light of the Palace was binding up its hurts.

By then the last of the Mogul's guards had been driven from the elephant by the Rajputs. But the black beast had had enough of pain.

Turning around, he made off through the welter and almost at once plunged into a deep pool.

The current tugged at him, and he struggled for footing, sinking and rising and drawing farther into the center of the river.

This was the omen of defeat for the Mogul's forces. Those in the ford, yet living, drew back, wet and dispirited. And fifty thousand eyes followed the laboring beast that carried Nur-Mahal.

We saw the silver howdah sway like a bush in a great wind. We saw the glistening head of the elephant move slowly toward the other shore.

Why make many words of our waiting? In the end the elephant reached shallow water and moved out to safety, far down the river. It had been written thus, and how was it to be otherwise?

Chapter VIII
Peace

After the battle, the sun of fortune shone upon us. Mahabat Khan had prevailed over the favorite, Nur-Mahal. And the chieftains who had held aloof until now hastened to ride into our *lashgar* with gifts and words of praise.

Venerable men blessed the Pathan when he passed by. And Jahangir, hearing of these things, announced that he had no friend so faithful as the khan. He proclaimed that the will of Mahabat Khan was his will. So the lords of the Panjab waited upon the khan with immense throngs of followers.

In those seven days I attended Jahangir daily, and it became clear to me that he was using drugs and spirits without cessation, buying them, I think, from the slaves.

"Nay," he said to me, "soon I will be able to mount my horse and review my followers."

Day followed day without his doing so. He did not like to have the emirs and *mansabdars* come to greet him; perhaps because he was a captive, and his nobles knew that the real power lay with Mahabat Khan.

Omar, the tentmaker, hath said, "Man is a magic lantern with a light within." And I thought that Jahangir was no more than a dull lantern, and Nur-Mahal the flame that had animated him and made him, at least, the figure of a king.

In those seven days I beheld a change in Mahabat Khan. He was victorious, bepraised, and besought. But he waxed moody; his eyes became dull, and the talk of government wearied him.

On the seventh night Jami appeared in my tent. At first I did not know him.

His tunic glittered with gold thread, and his trousers were bound at the ankles with strings of small pearls; his hair had been combed and oiled, and he smelled of mingled civet and musk!

"*Wai*, Jami!" I cried. "What is this?"

He grinned down at me where I sat, and thrust forward the hilt of a light saber—a hilt set with turquoise. Then he squatted and dipped into the bowl of rice that I was eating.

"I crossed the river, O my master," he laughed, "and I have had fowl and jellies and sugared fruits. I followed the Light of the Palace and hid in the fishing boat that took her over to the *lashgar*. She gave the boatmen five gold *mohurs*. I wanted to listen and learn what would happen and bring word of it to Mahabat Khan."

The graceless rogue glanced critically at the plain carpet and worn quilts of my tent.

"Has fortune not prospered thee, my master?"

"Only a thief prospers after a battle," I said severely, because conceit made Jami over-glib.

"I took no part in the battle," he remonstrated gravely. "Nay, I sat on a cart tail and watched. What a night!" He laughed and hugged his shoulders. "Ibn Athir, never was there such a running about. Baggage was cast from the carts and saddles tossed from horses. I slept in the tent pavilion of a Persian emir. By dawn the *lashgar* had dwindled to half—so many had fled the standards."

He reflected a moment, fingering his newly acquired sword.

"I wanted to hurry back with the tidings, but not until tonight could I find a boat and men who would cross."

"Is Asaf Khan planning to advance again?"

Jami shook his head idly.

"Nay, when he is not watching the men who guard the imperial treasure, he is quarreling with the nobles who still adhere to him. He has no stomach for more fighting. It was the Light of the Palace who went to the emirs and made them ashamed that they had not attempted to cross the river. She gave commands."

"And now?"

"Eh, my master, we will see what we will do."

Jami cocked his head and looked at me curiously. Near at hand we both heard the strumming of a rebec and the clink-clink of women's anklets. Someone was singing a song.

"What?" asked the boy, licking his fingers.

"Do not go near that place. It is Jahangir's, and the guards are wakeful."

It was an old custom of the Mogul court every week for the dancing girls, or a troupe of them, to come into the presence and bow down, to receive some gift. Jahangir had formed the habit of keeping some three or four to divert him.

"I will sleep." Jami picked out the quilt that lay nearest the entrance. "Hast thou aught of sugar, Ibn Athir?"

"Nor thou, of caste!"

Jami chuckled and lay down, making much ado of taking off his sword and girdle.

"*Ohai*, my master, dost remember the evening when we first met by the blue mosque on the Lahore road? Thou wert then a wanderer without friends, and I a boy." His bright eyes considered me and he nodded.

"Hearken, Ibn Athir, bear thou my message to the khan, and accept of the reward."

Indeed, he knew very well that he would not be admitted to speak with Mahabat Khan, if he were not bound and held to be questioned.

"As to the reward," he added, "it is time and more than time thou hadst a servant and a few horses. Mahabat Khan is verily thy friend."

"Peace!" I assured him. "What profit is to be taken from friendship?"

Yet it seemed good to me to go to the Pathan with the boy's story, and I left Jami curled up asleep. It was no more than a bowshot to the tent of the khan, and I went slowly, deep in thought. Even at that hour the sun's heat lingered in the dry grass. Against the stars rose the thin-leafed stalks of bamboo. A dim gleam from the sickle of the new moon showed me the guards by the wall of the garden in which the Pathan's tent had been pitched.

They knew me and suffered me to pass through a clump of cypresses to the edge of the trampled jasmine bed. The Pathan's tent was no richer than mine and he sat motionless on a carpet in front of it. Two soldiers standing beside him peered at me, but he knew me and cried out—

"O *hakim*, pleasant be thy coming!"

Yet his voice lacked the hearty ring of a month ago, and he seemed weary. He ordered me to sit and sent a man for a tray of sherbet and fruit, listening while I told him Jami's story.

"Aye," he said at last, "many of the emirs have come from Asaf Khan's following to mine. They were at the *durbar* this evening."

He folded his arms, twisting his strong fingers in his beard, frowning. I saw then that he wore the long signet ring of the Mogul, and even in the faint glow of the night sky the diamonds and sapphires gleamed against his dark hair.

"They urged that an army be mounted and sent to seize the treasure before Asaf Khan might carry it into Persia. At the same time came Hindus of the Multan plain to render fealty and ask that the collection of the revenues from the Panjab be allotted them. By God, the spittle of wrangling fouled the carpet of our council! And lo, even at this hour another comes!"

A palanquin with four bearers had passed the outer guard post, and our two swordsmen went forward to learn what it might be. I rose to ask leave to depart, but the warrior-lord bade me stay.

"Happiest of men art thou, O *hakim*, who wanderest at will, guiding with thy hand the reins of one horse. For those who hold the reins of government, there is neither rest nor ease of spirit."

Drawing in his breath suddenly, he sprang to his feet. Out of the palanquin stepped a *pateran*, moving gracefully toward us, veiled, her mantle cast about her shoulders.

"Protector of the poor," said the soldier who had accompanied her to us, "this one swears she is here at thy will."

"Get thee gone!" cried the khan harshly. "And thy fellow, and suffer no other to come in to us."

Verily, in the starlight and veiled as she was, he had recognized the Light of the Palace, as I had known her by the proud carriage of her head and shoulders. Hours without number his eyes had dwelt upon her in the past, from afar.

"What madness is this!" he whispered fiercely the instant the guards had passed obediently beyond hearing, taking with them the litter and its bearers.

Perhaps we both doubted that this was really Nur-Mahal, or perhaps our hopes made us doubt, because the *firman* of her death had been signed these seven days.

"At thy summons, O Well-Beloved Lord,* am I here!"

When she spoke, we no longer doubted, for the voice of the Light of the Palace was like the chime of golden bells.

"The order for thy—" he blundered upon the word.

"For my execution hath been signed. That is known to me, Mahabat Khan."

Even defeated and forsaken by half of the nobles, she had had the tidings from spies in bazaar and household. Nay, she quoted to us the next of the decree: "Because she hath displeased us by her ambition, causing coins to be minted with her likeness, and *firmans* signed with her name, and the conduct of the empire discussed and decided in her presence, she, the daughter of a Persian singing woman, a child abandoned on the caravan track, hath presumed too greatly, and is to be given to the sword of judgment."

"And is not this true?" demanded Mahabat Khan.

---

*The meaning of "Mahabat Khan."

"True. And so am I here at thy summons." She had seen the signet ring and she laughed a little under her breath, turning toward me. "Wert in the right, Ibn Athir; my place is with my lord husband."

The tall Pathan, hands thrust into his girdle, made answer without mercy.

"Hearken."

Beyond the brush of the garden stood the pavilion of the Mogul, and little bursts of laughter could be clearly heard, and the voice of a singing girl.

"Others are in thy place, beside thy lord husband," he said.

Nur-Mahal fingered the dancing girl's scarf that had helped to disguise her within the palanquin.

"Not so, Mahabat Khan! Many days hath Jahangir spent with his idlers and slaves, but I alone know his weakness, his failing health. For years I have ministered to him, and none can stand in that place."

"Thou art clever," he growled.

"As I have need to be."

"And faithless."

"But not to him."

The Pathan bent, to look full into her dark eyes, and she did not flinch.

"God alone knows whether that be true. Jahangir hath set his feet in the wrong path. He tortures his nobles, or buys them. He lacks heart and is not fit to command an army in the field. In the last days I have seen this."

"And not before now?"

"Nay, how was I to know?"

"Nor did the other emirs know." The Light of the Palace flung back her head, pressing both hands to her forehead. "I—I have kept them from knowing. How often have I sat at Jahangir's side at *durbars* when his wits were muddied? Aye, thy *firman* spoke the truth; I have tried to rule his subjects, so that his weakness should not be known."

Mahabat Khan uttered an exclamation and turned, to stride back and forth between us. And I thought of the morning and evening audiences in which Jahangir had barely shown himself to his court—a glittering and remote form, to be greeted and gifted. I thought of the chain of mercy, the gold bells that announced a supplicant, bells that the Light of the Palace could hear.

"What matter now?" he cried under his breath. "Between us the sword has been drawn."

"Aye, now." The Light of the Palace bent her head, rousing to look about the garden. "Rememberest thou, O my khan, a garden like to this and three children, thou and Jahangir and I, when he was prince and thou his playmate, and I a foundling of the caravan paths? We had two doves, and Jahangir gave them to me to hold and one escaped; the other I tossed into the air. Jahangir was angered, because he had been tormenting the doves, and that was why I freed them."

The Pathan checked his stride at a sudden thought.

"And by whom was Man Singh put to shame?"

"Tell me this, O my khan, is thy mind firm? Am I to die?"

He caught his breath at that, devouring her with his eyes, his hand closing and unclosing upon the hilt of his sword. Then he nodded.

"If so," responded Nur-Mahal after a moment, "I can say that I had no part in thy cousin's torment. It was a whim of my husband's when he was in his cups. For he feared thee, as I did."

"With good reason. For now is our strife ended."

"And the decree written."

Defeated in the field of battle, she had come alone and without defenders, to play another part. I wondered whether she meant to throw herself at the feet of the Pathan, or whether she was in reality resigned to death.

"By the Resurrection and by the hour when our deeds shall be weighed against our naked souls," cried Mahabat Khan, "I swear that Jahangir has not been threatened. Of his own will he signed the *firman*!"

Just for an instant she caught her breath and swayed upon her feet. Then she closed her eyes and responded quietly—

"Wilt thou suffer me to speak with Jahangir alone—now?"

I looked at Mahabat Khan. If he allowed her to talk with Jahangir, nothing was more certain than that the idle and capricious Mogul would change his mind and cling to Nur-Mahal as in the past. And if Jahangir publicly countermanded the *firman* and shielded her, Mahabat Khan might not put her to death without blame.

"Why come to me?" he said, musing.

"Nay, art ruler of India!"

"I? God knows I seek no throne!"

"Who puts foot in the stirrup must mount to the saddle." She looked at him gravely and stretched forth her hands. "Suffer me to go to my husband."

The Pathan began again to pace to and fro between us, with bent head. And this I took for a sign that he would not grant her request. But then the silence of the garden was broken by the twanging of a dulcimer, yonder where lay the Mogul and his companions. A voice shrilled out a snatch of song, without sweetness or melody:

> My heart is like a rosebud spotted with wine—
> Lo, when my petals have fallen, I am thine!

Again the lute twanged, and laughter resounded. Mahabat Khan ceased his pacing and stood, grimly silent. A dozen voices of young girls seized on the refrain—

> My heart is like a rosebud—ai-ai-ai!

Mahabat Khan raised his head, as if goaded into speech.

"It is time to make an end. Our strife has come to this point; it is thy death or mine. I will summon my men."

He raised his hands to strike them together, when Nur-Mahal seized his wrists, and cried softly:

"Nay, I will not have their hands upon me. Let it be by thy sword— here—now."

Indeed she knew that if he gave her to the keeping of his guards, he did not mean her to see another sun. At her touch he shivered, looking down upon her dark head, and now she spoke without hope or cunning, but with the fierce eagerness of one who casts off old bonds.

"That *firman* lied! O blind that thou art! Have I struggled during these years for myself? Thou hast no child, Mahabat Khan, but I have a daughter, who—" she ceased and raised her head proudly, lest we think she begged for mercy.

But in that moment of silence I thought of Nur-Mahal in the howdah of the wounded elephant, shielding the young girl with her body from the flying arrows, intent on binding up the scratch that had pained the child. Surely Nur-Mahal was fearless and surely she loved her daughter. These few words of hers were naught but truth.

Then she sighed and smiled up at the tall Pathan.

"Does my face trouble thee? I will veil it—thus may thy stroke be swift and sure!"

Drawing a fold of the light mantle from her left shoulder, she held it over her head, her slender arm gleaming in the starlight. Motionless she stood, that faint scent of dried rose leaves clinging to the air about her.

Mahabat Khan laid his hand upon his sword hilt and half drew the blade. The muscles of his face twitched and his eyes glowed like embers beneath black brows.

And lo, my eyes beheld a strange thing. The woman, standing erect and tranquil, seemed at peace and joyous, while the man, his hand clenched upon the steel, his face tormented, was in an agony of spirit.

Only for an instant. Then his arm thrust down—the sword was rammed back into its scabbard, and he folded his arms.

"Go to the Mogul. I give thee life, Nur-Mahal."

We sat together, the Pathan and I, until the seventh hour of the night. The men at the garden entrance changed post with other guards, but the two at the tent had been sent to escort the Light of the Palace. It was quiet among the jasmine beds, and a slight breeze stirred the cypresses. The revelry in the imperial pavilion had ceased.

Mahabat Khan was sunk in reverie, and by degrees his brow cleared. When the cymbals struck for the seventh hour he reached out his hand and ate some of the dates that had remained untasted upon the tray.

"Eh, Ibn Athir," he said. "Mount thy horse and go."

The glitter of the precious stones in the signet ring caught his eye, and he drew it from his finger, weighing it in the palm of his strong hand.

"Come," I said then, "with me."

"Whither?" he smiled.

"To a ship. A little voyage and we can reach the land of Athir that is my land. There the horses are excellent, and the folk of the desert are hospitable. Thou canst draw thy reins at will, to north or south."

Verily in that moment something came into my spirit—a longing to see my people again and wander with the sheep and the herds.

"Why?" he asked again.

I made bold to voice my thought. Mahabat Khan was an upright man, a daring man, and a companion to be desired.

"It will happen in this place that Jahangir will forgive Nur-Mahal and she will regain her influence over him and his nobles. She will contrive to set him free from thy restraint, and the influence will be lost. What then of thee?"

He swept his arm toward the silent camp.

"I cannot leave my followers." And after a moment he smiled. "Thou art a true prophet, Ibn Athir, and—having made enemies in this court—'tis best for thee to depart while the way is open." He thrust the ring into his girdle and rose. "I serve the salt. And they have need of me. They may send me to the frontier with my cavalry."

And this thought pleased him, for he stretched forth his arms and breathed deep, as if casting a burden from his shoulders. To the guard post he walked with me, and lifted his hand in farewell. I watched his tall figure moving with its long, noiseless stride toward his tent in the deserted garden, among the shadows.

The warriors, newly arrived at this post, were looking at the palanquin that stood where it had been left by its bearers.

"Eh, *hakim*," said one, "what was the woman who went in to the lord *bahadur* in the last hour?"

"Some say," whispered another, "that she was the empress, but this is the litter of a dancing girl, a shameless one."

I considered this in my mind, wondering what would be best to say.

"She was the mother of a child," I made response, "come to beg of the lord *bahadur*."

The Way of the Girl

Nadra left the trail and curled up in the thin shadow of some date palms. She was not tired, but for appearance's sake she drew the sandal from a slim, dusty foot and looked at it earnestly. Out of the corners of her dark eyes she watched the tribe go by.

They went swiftly, the camels pacing under their loads, the donkeys urged on by children with sticks. Her father rode by with the older men, carrying shields and bamboo lances, because the tribe, the Banu's Safa, was passing near the land of an enemy.

They were not rich, the Banu's Safa. Drought in the lowlands had forced them to seek new pastures for their animals at risk of their own lives. The camel packs and the donkey loads carried all their possessions—sacks of precious grain and wool, scraped hides, brass bowls and water jars, the chests of the women, and weapons captured in battle by the men.

Dust hung over the trail like a mist, dust in which flashed the horns of the cattle. Beside the trail the horse herd roamed, searching out the dry grass, and Nadra stared at it until she recognized the color of Yarouk's cloak. Yarouk, as usual, was taking more care of his gray mare than of her!

While the dust still hung about her like a veil, Nadra slipped down into a wadi and began to run back, beside the trail. Avoiding thornbush and devil rocks, she sped away, the silk head-veil caught by a silver pin, flapping in the wind gusts. Nadra was proud of that silk, and of the embroidery she had worked laboriously upon the breast of her gown. Other girls might embroider more skillfully but they had not her beauty.

She was going back for the two kids—those playful little goats without a mother; goats with brown, silky hair. Nadra had taken them for her own, tying a collar of scarlet thread about the neck of each one. They used to follow her and sleep in the shade of her father's black tent. Now they were missing, and Nadra felt certain they had been left behind at the last halting place.

None of the men, of course, would turn back for a girl's goats. Yarouk especially would mock her if she begged him. Nor would they let her take a horse. It was the duty of the nomad girls to care for the animals, not to use them—nor to speak boldly to the men, who could ride to hunt or to war as the whim struck them. They would not even let her go back while the tribe was within a day's ride of Sultan Ibrahim's castle. But no one in the tribe had seen her go.

When she was tired of running, the Arab girl walked swiftly until she came to the last halting place, a patch of gray, trodden grass. For a moment she searched the spot with her eyes. If enemies had been following the Banu's Safa, they would be nosing about this place now. But nothing moved except the tips of the brush on a rocky knoll. Nadra thought she saw a glint of brown, and she hastened forward.

In a gully behind the rocks she found the two bleating kids.

"Foolish ones!" she scolded in delight as they bounded up unsteadily and rubbed their heads against her hands. When she stooped to pick them up, she paused, listening. There was a rushing sound, not made by the wind in the brush.

"Ai!" The girl crouched, clutching her pets.

A black shape bounded into the gully, turned with a scattering of gravel, and vanished between swaying bushes with a rending snarl. It was a black panther, and Nadra breathed a prayer of relief, until she heard a thudding of hoofs and a crashing of brush.

She had not time to hide before the horse burst into the open space. Reined in, it went back on its haunches and its rider flung himself from the saddle. Nadra prepared to run desperately, when she discovered that the man was paying no attention to her. His eyes questing along the ground, he went after the panther among the overgrown rocks. And Nadra stared, amazed.

Even Yarouk, she thought, would not go after a fleeing black panther on foot. And this man was not like an Arab. For one thing he carried an iron shield as if it were straw; and on his head he had no more than a light steel cap, from which hair the hue of gold fell to his broad shoulders. True, his face was darkened by the sun-glare, but the eyes that flickered over Nadra were the blue of deep water. He carried thrust before him a light lance, and from his hip hung a long, straight sword. Nadra had never seen anything quite like him before.

When the stranger had vanished among the rocks, she inspected his horse, a powerful bay stallion. It was a fine horse, and the girl moved toward it eagerly. It would be a prize to delight her father—but, more than that, it would be safety for Nadra, who had no illusions about the fate of young women found in the desert without armed men to protect them.

The stallion, however, was on edge, with the scent of the panther and the sight of a robed woman carrying two goats. It wheeled away, snorting, when Nadra reached for the rein. And then a second man galloped up on a laboring pony, an armed servant of the first, apparently. Nadra dropped her goats and turned to flee, only to find the warrior of the tawny hair striding back toward her.

Nadra darted to one side and fell heavily. The stranger had thrown his light lance, butt end first, in front of her. And before she could gain her feet he had lifted her bodily. Feeling the clasp of steel-like fingers under her knee, the girl lay passive, panting.

"Look, Hassan," he laughed. "I have lost a panther and caught a girl."

"Eh, master—" the attendant shook his head—"the panther would be less dangerous."

They both spoke Arabic, but the one, noble-born, who held her, did not speak it as her own people.

"O man," she besought him softly, "do not dishonor me."

Alan, Sieur de Kerak and baron of the marches, had little mercy in him. He rode with a loose rein to hunt or to war. They who followed him had more wounds to lick than gold to count. It was said of him that never had he turned his back upon quest or quarrel.

He had grown up on the border, where were the outposts of the crusaders who held Jerusalem. It was the land of Outremer—Beyond the Sea. Sir Alan had never set foot within hall or hamlet of Christendom in Europe—all his days he had lived here, in Beyond the Sea. Many a night had he watched for the gleam of moonlight upon helmets. And so in time he had been sent to hold Kerak, the easternmost castle of the crusaders, the farthest watch post beyond the Jordan—a tower and a walled courtyard on a rocky height that the Arabs called the Stone of the Desert. It was his duty now to watch the caravan track to Mecca, to send word of any rising of the foe, and to hold Kerak safe if he could. If an attack came, he need expect no aid. Meanwhile, he amused himself with hawk and hound and riding after antelope.

In spite of the protest of Hassan ibn Mokhtar, his sword-bearer, an Arab of the Hauran who had eaten his salt, Sir Alan had gone out that morning without other guard, along the southern trail.

Now he looked down at the frightened girl in his arms, scrutinizing the smooth forehead under its tangle of dark hair, and the quivering lashes of the closed eyes.

"And why not?" he laughed.

"Because," she whispered, straining her head away from him, "I am daughter of a *rais* of the Banu's Safa. If harm comes to me, my father will hold blood feud against thee until the shame be finally ended with thy life."

"O girl, have I no enemies? Yea, Sultan Ibrahim and others have sworn to take my life, yet I live."

"Then, by Allah, take ransom for me."

"What talk is this?" Sir Alan smiled. A strange girl who, found wandering in the desert afoot, spoke of ransom like a baron taken in battle.

"True talk." Nadra made up a tale without any hesitation. "Wait, and in an hour or so will come a *kaid* of the tribe who will bring a gray mare. A swift mare, worth more than that charger of thine. The mare he will give thee for me."

"And what name will he have, this noble squire?"

"Yarouk, son of Yahiya."

"And what robe will he wear?"

"A white robe, with a blue cloak."

"Now I see well that I have caught a true houri of fairyland, who knoweth the secret of what is to be!" Laughing he unclasped the silk veil and drew it from her face.

Among her own people, Nadra was not particular to keep her face covered. The tribe had never visited a strange city, and in the desert the better-looking girls liked to be admired. But never had a man snatched the veil from her. Swiftly her hand dropped, closed upon the hilt of the hunting knife in Sir Alan's girdle.

Before either of the men could move to prevent, she struck with the knife, beneath her captor's arm. And she cried out angrily. The knife blade jarred against chain mail under the knight's surcoat. The next moment he gripped her wrist and took the weapon from her.

"O she-panther! O witch, destroyer of men!" Hassan exclaimed furiously. "Set her loose, lord, or give permission that I slay her. If you keep her captive, we shall eat nothing but trouble."

"Nay," replied Sir Alan, "first we will drink."

They led the horses down the gully to a second clearing. Here, hemmed in by rock nests and brush, were a well and the shade of a few poplars. When the horses had drunk, Hassan loosed their girths and tethered them among the trees. But he tied Nadra firmly about the knees with a long rope.

It was past the middle of the day—the shadows told her that—and the hot air quivered above the baked ground. By now, Nadra thought, the caravan of her people would be hours away. And Yarouk would be searching out grazing for the swift gray mare that was like the very blood of his heart to him. Once on a moonlit night Yarouk, the *kaid*, the young warrior, had sung outside her tent—"O heart of my heart"—Nadra knew every word of that song. But she had waited for his wooing, so that every man of the tribe should see the warrior sitting at her feet, beseeching her. She had waited . . .

And now this infidel lord with the lion's mane sat by her, eating barley cake and drinking thirstily. She had turned aside from the goblet they offered her . . . this Lord A-lan was a man of steel—steel-like the clasp of his fingers, and steel-bound his body. He was like the sword he bore, unyielding.

The brown kids leaped over her feet and thrust their heads against her. Nadra caressed them absently and refastened the veil about her head.

Then down the gully came Yarouk, leading the gray mare with a saddled pony.

"*Salaam aleikum*," he said, lifting his right hand to forehead and breast, so that even Nadra could see, when the blue cloak fell back about his shoulders, that he carried no other weapon than the ivory hilted dagger in his girdle. "I am Yarouk, son of Yahiya."

"Upon thee also be peace," responded Sir Alan courteously, taking note of the white headcloth and the graceful horse that followed the Arab. "Sit, eat."

"May Allah lengthen thy days." Yarouk seated himself carelessly a lance length from the knight. "Nay, I have no hunger. O lord, thou art far from thy tower."

"As thou art from thy *kafila*."

"By Allah, that is true. Yet this is not safe ground." Apparently he seemed not at all surprised to find Nadra lying under the trees; certainly he paid no attention to her. "I came back to look for some stray goats and a girl."

Toward the end of the morning he had noticed that Nadra had left the caravan. Hearing that she had been seen under the date palms, he took out a saddled pony and, riding the mare he had picked up her tracks in the wadi and followed them into the gully. Seeing the three at the well, he had pondered for a moment . . . the caravan hours away, and Sir Alan clearly making only a brief halt at the well . . . Nadra bound and impossible to reach without alarming the infidels . . . Sir Alan he knew as the devil of the Stone of the Desert; no other crusader would be within three days' ride of this place.

So he waited, his dark eyes impassive, while Nadra's blood hummed in her ears.

"Here are the goats," said the knight. "Take them. But the girl is mine."

For an instant the Arab's lips twitched and the breath caught in his nostrils. "I say she is mine!"

Hassan, who had satisfied himself that no other tribesmen were coming after the lone rider down the gully, moved forward and put his hand on his sword hilt, waiting expectantly for new trouble to come. Sir Alan's blue eyes gleamed. "*Inshallah*, if God please. But now she is mine, and how will you alter that? Will you give that mare for the girl?"

For a moment the Arab warrior glanced at the mare's lifted head, with the long mane combed clean of thorns. "Yes," he said suddenly.

Sir Alan seemed not to hear. He thought of his bare room in the tower top, of the hours spent gazing into the fire while his men-at-arms rested over their cups and the hunting dogs crunched bones . . . Nothing more than that to go back to, and at the end of it all in any case the slash of an arrow in his throat, or torture under the knives of his foes . . . He had held her in his arms for a moment—in time she would forget her people. "And I also," he said, "prize the girl more than the horse."

The veins stood out upon Yarouk's bare arms. "Then let the sword be between us. Give me this one's sword, and we will try the judgment of Allah!"

Sir Alan smiled. "Nay, that would be no judgment between us! For if we cross swords I shall slay thee. Now go!"

He had no wish to kill the younger man. And he knew the frenzy of excitement that seized upon those nomads when swords were drawn. With Yarouk he had no quarrel; on the other hand he had no intention of giving up the girl.

"O man," cried Hassan, "thou hast heard the command—"

"Be silent, thou!"

Yarouk leaned his elbows on his knees. His eyes were closed but the veins throbbed in his temples, and Hassan waited for a moment when he could spring at Sir Alan with his knife. There was silence about the well, except for the slow breathing of the three men and the rustling of Nadra's garments as she moved uneasily. The gray mare lifted her head and paced forward daintily to nudge Yarouk's shoulder with her nose.

As she did so, the Arab's expression changed. "Have you enemies who would seek you here, Lord A-lan?"

"That have I. This is the land of Sultan Ibrahim, who would like well to roast me over a fire—" the blue eyes gleamed—"as he did one of my men."

Yarouk edged closer to him. "*Wallahi*, speak softly or he may hear thee. There are men hidden in the rocks behind thee."

But Hassan drew his bow from its shoulder quiver and strung it. "Fool!" he muttered, "Think ye to throw dust in our eyes with such talk?"

"Look!" Yarouk whispered urgently. "By Allah—look at the mare, if ye will not turn." Sir Alan did look at the mare, as she flung up her head with ears twitching. If there were foemen among the boulders, screened by the brush, drawing closer while he sat in talk by the well, they would have bows and they would loose their arrows without warning. If he ran to the horses with Hassan, their backs would be turned to Yarouk . . .

Suddenly Nadra screamed, "*Aida!*"

And Hassan dropped to his knees, whining. An arrow in his back, another in his neck. With the snap of the bows a yell burst from the rocks: "*Yah kafir!*" Sir Alan threw himself back on the ground, reached for his shield as two more arrows flicked over him. Thrusting his arms through the straps, he sprang up, drawing his sword.

The boulders behind the poplars seemed to be alive with men scrambling forward. Five—six—seven. Instinctively the knight made up his mind.

Instead of standing his ground, he lowered his head, raised his shield and ran toward his foe. An arrow crashed against the iron shield and he leaped high. The first man, running swiftly, was taken by surprise and had no time to swerve. The edge of the shield struck the Moslem's throat and the pommel of Sir Alan's sword smashed down upon his forehead. He was thrown to the ground, unconscious.

"Kerak!" Sir Alan shouted. "Come ye and taste the sword!"

Two of them came—two who wore chain mail and bore leather shields and scimitars. They drew apart and darted in from the sides, the long, curved blades shining in the sun. One slash Sir Alan took upon his shield, the other grated upon the chain mail that sheathed his ribs. And he struck once, with full sweep of arm and sword . . .

"Bows!" screamed a voice. "Slay the devil with arrows."

Sir Alan kept his head bent, his shield high and close to him, so that only his eyes could be seen between metal and metal. An arrow whipped between his legs, and he ran forward again so that they would not make a mark of him.

But they had seen him strike once, and they dodged like hunting dogs at the sweep of a bear's paw. A thrown javelin thudded into the iron chains over his chest, the point of it grating against bone. He could not spare a hand to pull it out. A sword-tip raked his thigh and warm blood ran down into his shoe. With his sword he met the slash of a long scimitar and broke it, the steel tip, whirring off.

"*Yah Muslimin!*" the same voice shouted. "Oh, Moslems!"

It was the one who had thrown the javelin, and he came on now, with a swordsman at either hand. Sir Alan planted his feet, flung up his shield, and struck to the side. His blade caught an uplifted arm and swept on, while the severed forearm, clutching a scimitar, fell to the ground.

But the third man—he of the javelin—was untouched, a stabbing spear gripped in both hands over his head. Fleetingly, Sir Alan glimpsed a jutting gray beard and slavering lips. And then the man stopped, rigid as if turned to stone in the act of slaying. From the gray beard protruded the feathers of an arrow, and Sir Alan saw that these red feathers were Hassan's—the shaft had come from the quiver of his dying sword-bearer. He dared not look behind him.

Another arrow flashed over his shoulder and ripped into the shield of the third Moslem. The man shouted and turned to flee. He was not quick enough. Sir Alan leaped and struck . . .

"*Div—div!*" voices screamed in fear. "A demon—a demon!"

And they fled.

Then Sir Alan went back. Straight to Yarouk, where the young Arab, chanting with excitement, was stripping shield and armor and sword from the body of the graybeard.

"Friend or foe?" Sir Alan asked, sword in hand.

"Look!" cried Yarouk. "Look, it is the king of the vultures, the scavenger of the caravans. He is slain—Ibrahim the sultan, the accursed, who followed after my people this day with his swordsmen. By Allah, this is his sword and now it is mine!"

"Didst thou slay this Ibrahim with an arrow?"

"Nay—" the Arab, in his fever of exultation, hardly heard—"I watched, knife in hand. It was a stray shaft. It was his fate. Ha—there are rubies in this clasp."

"It was an arrow from Hassan's bow."

"Do the dead bend a bow? What foolish words. Look!"

By the well Hassan's body lay outstretched, a cloak thrown over its head. Beside it sat Nadra, tying up her goats with the rope that had bound her legs. Near at hand a bow lay on the ground. Uneasily she lifted her head as the two men approached.

"O girl," said the knight curiously, "did thy hand speed the shaft with red feathers that struck the chieftain?"

Her eyes luminous with excitement, she nodded.

"But why? It gave me life."

"Truly, I feared for thee. If they had cut thee down, harm would have come to us."

Leaning on his sword, Sir Alan looked down at her.

"And how," asked the knight softly, "could you come hither and shoot arrows from a bow when you were tied upon the ground beneath yonder trees?"

Nadra shifted uneasily. "Eh, I untied the rope while I played with these little kids, when Yarouk came—"

"What is this?" The Arab gave heed at last. "Thou wert loose and free when we talked? And thou didst not flee? We could have escaped, thou and I."

"I know—but, O Yarouk, I longed to hear what thou wouldst say. If thou hadst not valued me more than the gray mare I—I—"

Her voice faltered. Here she stood, the young veiled girl, the voiceless servant of the men of the Banu's Safa, who had sat for hours at the threshold of her father's tent, longing for a single glance from Yarouk. And she had dared speak boldly to Yarouk before a strange infidel lord who was certainly a hero. "I would have gone with this unbeliever," she whispered. "He wanted me."

Yarouk's breath hissed in his teeth. "Thou, Nadra!"

But that day Nadra had been carried off by a man of steel. Yea, more, she had struck him with a dagger, and then had slain her father's foe, the sultan Ibrahim. By reason of her, Yarouk's arms had been loaded with spoil. If she did not speak now, when would she have the courage again? She stamped her foot and tossed back the black mane of her hair. "Yea, I, Nadra!" she cried all in a breath. "By Allah, this one is more of a man than thou—herder of mares. While thou didst stand shouting like a horse boy, he ran against seven. While thou didst sing about that bold heart of thine, he took me in his arms—"

She stopped, panting. And Yarouk stared at the girl he had never seen before—at this new Nadra with a will and a voice and a defiant beauty. Then he stepped forward, his arm went out, and he struck her with his open hand across the face.

His brow dark as if with fever, his eyes burning, Yarouk picked her up and carried her to the gray mare. He flung Nadra over the back of the mare behind the saddle.

"O girl," he said between set teeth, "be still. Tonight thou shalt be a woman and the wife of Yarouk."

Fleetingly Nadra glanced down at him, and laughed a little from sheer joy. She had seen his eyes. When he turned back for the bundle of armor, she slipped down and retrieved her goats that were tumbling about the cord she had put upon them. With them under her arm she climbed back into her seat.

Sir Alan watched, motionless, leaning upon his sword.

A few moments later Yarouk turned in the saddle to look back at the well where the kites were dropping from the sky toward the bodies, and the solitary crusader, limping about his task, was piling rocks upon the dead Hassan.

"*Wallahi*—he is a man," Yarouk said.

But Nadra had looked back more than once. Now she tightened her arms about Yarouk's waist and laid her head upon his shoulder.

"But a man of steel unfeeling," she said contentedly. "And thou, O warrior, art lord of my heart."

The Eighth Wife

Sakhri was loyal to her lord and, moreover, obedient. She was also lovely, as many Circassian girls are—tall, with a tawny mane of hair and long, drowsy eyes that slant up in the corners, strong-bodied and a little indolent—like healthy animals and still capable of unchanging devotion to the men who buy them.

Not slaves exactly. They used to be that, in the days when the sultans sat behind the Sublime Porte and few wealthy Turks lacked a Circassian girl in their harems. Not wives, as we understand the term. Just the veiled women of the household, the mothers of sons, the most alluring of them being the favorites. They could not read, and they were told that after death they could not share the Paradise of their lords, the men. Still, they knew a lot and the future never seemed to worry them. What was written would come to pass.

For centuries the Circassian families in the mountains sold their girls. When a child was thirteen, fourteen or so, she would be sent off with a merchant—disappearing without trace. That happened to Sakhri, after she had tended the cows for five years and worn the veil for three. The lads of the village used to follow her about, and she would throw stones at them, being a fastidious child. She also carried a curved knife, which she could use very effectively, having been called upon to slaughter lambs frequently when the men were off at war. The night before she went with the merchant she prayed in the stone *masjid* by the tombs and bathed herself all over. Then she put on her silver armlets and inlaid headband, not forgetting the knife that had an ivory handle. She was sold to one Uzbek Khan, who was fifty-six and already had seven other wives—Sakhri the Circassian being the youngest and the eighth.

Uzbek Khan was a man of note, since he held Al Arak, an almost impregnable tower by the caravan road—impregnable so long as he could pay the two or three hundred unbridled tribesmen who served for a mounted army. An experienced fighter, generous to his women, who had separate rooms and slave girls of their own. With Sakhri he was patient and gentle, smiling at her jealousy of the other women. She paid little attention to the ox-eyed Greek, or to the older ones who had borne children; but she waged a war of her own against Lali, the dancing girl from Isfaban who melodiously sang mocking songs about her. Sakhri, who was not unusually clever, could not think of a retort. But one day, with her knife she cut off half of Lali's dark hair, and when Uzbek Khan was told about this he laughed.

"Eh," he said, "she is a little dove with strong wings."

He loved her passionately because she was no more than a child. Her jealousy of the others and devotion to him pleased the khan, who preferred her fierce love-making to the more languid arts of Lali, who, besides, now lacked half her hair.

And Sakhri thrived under his adoration. She had armlets—silver set with opals, cat's-eyes, turquoise, and moonstones—all the way from slender wrist to shoulder, and she used attar of rose—plundered from Lali—to scent her straw-red mass of hair instead of the musk that had satisfied her until now. She learned to chew mastic and to eat sugared ginger by the handful. When Uzbek Khan and his riders went out to raid, she stood on the arched gate and screamed encouragement after them.

On such occasions the khan always rode a white horse with unclipped mane and tail. He carried a round wooden shield studded with silver bosses, and he wore two knives beside the long yataghan thrust into his waistband. But his pride was the Enfield rifle slung behind his shoulder, the stock ornamented with gold tracery. When he left his women on such occasions for a month or so, he placed no guards over them. Neither eunuchs nor armed slaves. His wives, he believed, would cast their eyes on no other men. Once a young dancing girl had done so, and Uzbek Khan had cut away her nose and ears and had sent her, unveiled and screaming, mounted on a donkey's back, to the other man—a visiting merchant who, upon this apparition of his amorata, had made haste to flee on the first horse ready at hand, taking no thought of his camel string or of the mutilated girl. Uzbek Khan let the man go—knowing the dancing girl, he did not consider the merchant guilty—but he kept the camels in trade.

During his absence with the army, he sent news to his family from time to time. At Al Arak they had a dovecote with trained messenger pigeons. The old Tatar who watched over the khan's falcons took care of the house of the pigeons, as he called it, and put a half dozen of the swift birds into wicker cages to accompany the khan upon a journey. If the khan wished to send word to Al Arak, he would repeat it to his writer, who would copy it down upon a slip of rice paper and put the paper in a tiny silver cylinder, which in turn would be fastened to the wing or claw of the carrier pigeon. When the bird alighted at the dovecote on the roof of Al Arak, the Tatar falconer would remove the cylinder and take it to someone who could read the message—to the old hadji or the mullah. So, those in the palace could hear the message of Uzbek Khan.

It was the only post in this waste of mountains between the snowcap of Ararat—where the people say the remains of the ark of Noah are to be seen, if any human being can scale the mountain—and the salt-encrusted shore of the Caspian. Civilization, with its telegraph wire, its siege gun and cinema, has not yet penetrated this limbo of pine forests that soar upward to bare rock and the eternal snows.

Sakhri found life honey-sweet, until another woman took her place as favorite of the khan.

It was Sultan Hussayn's doing. He was lord of Irivan, and a few thousand square miles of mountains, including the tiled fort of Al Arak. Generations ago the khans of Arak had paid tribute to the sultans of Irivan—the white-walled city by the lake. But Uzbek, and his father before him, discovering that their stronghold was impregnable, had defied the sultans, who, after a fruitless attempt or two to storm Al Arak, perched like a bird's nest atop the cliff, had contented themselves with threats.

A little while before, Sultan Hussayn, a young man and a spendthrift, had sent Uzbek Khan an invitation to visit him in Irivan. The khan, aware that such a visit would end in a cell, declined politely, protesting that he was incapacitated by a wound, and sending Hussayn a swift-paced black horse and a brown peregrine falcon as gifts.

Now Hussayn returned the present—in princely fashion. Protesting that in his turn he had nothing but love in his heart for the Eagle of the Snows, he dispatched to Al Arak two camels loaded with bales of silk garments and carpets and one eunuch and one girl. This girl was Zuleika.

At the first sight of her Uzbek khan muttered under his breath praise of Allah the Compassionate. Her skin, he thought, was soft and clear as silk; her hair darker than the storm cloud; her shape slender as a young willow; the scent of her sweeter than musk, aloes, or burning ambergris. Moreover she could play melodiously on the lute and sing love songs he had never heard before. He wondered why Hussayn had been moved to such generosity until he questioned the enunch who brought her, and learned that the sultan of Irivan had fared badly in war. Hussayn, it seemed, had need of the Eagle of the Snows and his twelvescore horsemen.

But he soon ceased to wonder, in Zuleika's arms. He even neglected Sakhri. No more armlets or sugared ginger came to the flame-haired Circassian girl, who shut herself up in her room, enraged. When Uzbek Khan failed to beg her to show the moon of her countenance to the night of his misery, she wept. Then the new eunuch, Vali, came to bid her move from her quarters, in the summit of the tower.

Incredulous, she saw Zuleika installed in the room—upon the finest of carpets and embroidered silk cushions, while Vali fetched and carried for her like a porter. Sakhri complained, in a tempest of tears and beseeching, to Uzbek Khan, who stroked her head gently and listened unmoved.

"Thou hast called me," she cried recklessly, "the illumination of thy soul and the solace of thy liver. *Wallahi*, thou knowest no other man owned me while that lute tinkler—"

"Still thy tongue!"

"I will cut off her nose."

It seemed to him very probable that she would do that. "Nay," he grumbled, "but I will have thee beaten now, Sakhri."

"Not by her creature, Vali."

Sakhri was beaten with a stick, but by Arslan the Tatar falconer, not by Vali. After the beating she grew quieter and made no more outcry. Lali mocked her a little and then grieved with her—much preferring to have the youthful Sakhri favorite instead of the more sophisticated Zuleika with her watchdog Vali.

"It was written, perhaps," she consoled the girl. "Besides, Zuleika is a beauty."

"She is an old woman, without shame. She does not love our lord."

This, in Sakhri's eyes, was the greatest of crimes. To make matters worse, Uzbek Khan—who had perhaps grown weary of the feuds among his women—announced that he would ride off with most of his men to raid a caravan moving up from Tabriz. When he mounted and passed under the gate, it was Zuleika who melodiously cried encouragement to him

from the arch of the gate. Sakhri had to content herself with stealing up
to the deserted tower summit to watch the men ride off.

The tower top, being part of Zuleika's domain, was forbidden to her,
and she peered around with lively curiosity at the new canopy to keep
off the sun, at a silver samovar, and at a wicker cage in a far corner. The
cage held, she discovered, six pigeons. For an instant she wondered if they
were trained tumblers in the air, or only fattening for pies—until her eyes
blazed, and she loosened the small door of the cage.

No plump doves were these, but stout-breasted blue flyers. Hastily she
grasped one and drew it out. Running to the edge of the parapet she cast it
into the air and watched intently, The blue pigeon circled the tower several times and then headed swiftly to the south.

These blue pigeons, Sakhri reflected, were carriers—and Irivan lay to
the south. She shut the wicker gate of the cage and chewed a strand of
hair while she meditated.

She meditated too long. Footsteps ascended the stairs, and Vali's round
turban and bulging face appeared above the flagstones.

"Eh," he shrilled, "what doing is this?"

Waddling toward the girl, he tried to seize her in his hands. Sakhri
smiled and drew her curved knife, while she kept out of his reach.

"Thou art no keeper of mine," she exclaimed. "If you touch me, your
heart will be on the carpet."

Vali was no heroic spirit. He spat as close to her as he dared, and when
she slipped down the stair he raised a cry of "Thief!" after her. And that
noon in the bathhouse, Zuleika came over to Sakhri and accused her of
stealing a girdle clasp of silver-gilt and turquoise.

"That is a lie," said Sakhri calmly. "I took nothing from the tower."

But the Circassian knew that if Zuleika wished, such a girdle clasp
would be discovered at the proper moment among her own belongings.
Zuleika had described it before witnesses in the bath, and the khan, being under her spell, would believe her tale. Still, they had not noticed that
one of the pigeons was missing.

Late that afternoon Sakhri veiled herself heavily and went to sit in the
women's garden, summoning Arslan the falconer to her.

"Hast thou," she asked, "in the pigeon house six gray-blue messengers,
dark in the head and long in the wing?"

"Aye so, little Head of Flame."

"Are they pigeons of Al Arak?"

The Tatar nodded. What else would they be?

"At the hour of sunset prayer, when the family of thy lord, the khan, are in the mosque, take thou those six in a carrying basket to the tower top where dwells the beautiful Zuleika. Canst thou tell one bird from another?"

"Doth a she-lion know her cubs?"

"Well, then, remove the five blue pigeons from the wicker cage there, and put in their place the six thou hast brought. And if and when one of thy birds of Al Arak—one of the six thou hast put in the tower—returns to the pigeon house with a message upon it, bring thou that message to me. I will take it to the hadji to be read."

Arslan shook his head, scenting a trick. "What fool would write such a message?"

"I know not. Yet I loosed one of the birds from the tower cage and it flew off, to the south. Bethink thee, if the khan returns and finds that one among his women has been sending messages unknown to him, with what punishment would he reward thee, O Keeper of the Birds?"

Arslan became thoughtful and finally went away, remarking that what was written would come to pass, but only God knew what was written. After three days he waited for her in the garden, and showed her a tiny silver tube, saying that one of his six pigeons had returned to the pigeon house bearing this tube. He had brought the old hadji with him.

Under the watchful eyes of the two men Sakhri drew a roll of rice paper from the tube and spread it out between her fingers, which trembled a little. It bore several lines of delicate writing, and the scent of it was sweeter than attar of rose. Sakhri recognized Zuleika's handwriting and perfume. She handed it to the hadji, who murmured in surprise: "It is in Persian."

"What says it?"

"'To the Lord of my Life, the Delight of My Eyes, greetings from a heart consumed by the flame of passion.' Tck-Tck. That is clear enough. Now follows—'Come swiftly. Come in the hour before sunrise, I will meet thee, and lead thee to a fitting place. But delay not, for the old eagle flies far and returns not during this moon. Written by the hand of one who is trusted—'"

And the old hadji peered down at the Circassian, his eyes pensive under his white turban. "It is signed with thy name, Sakhri."

"My name!" The girl stared. "But—but I know naught of it."

"Still," the hadji pointed out, "it is here." And he folded the letter within his girdle cloth, while Sakhri chewed her lips with rage.

Surely Zuleika and Vali would not know one gray-blue pigeon from another! Surely this missive had been meant for Irivan! And yet—it was apparently a summons to a lover, and bore her own name.

"Did any see thee place thy pigeons in the tower?" she demanded of Arslan.

"Nay. Yet in one thing wast thou mistaken. Instead of five pigeons I found only four within the tower cage."

"Four! And how many didst thou put in, after taking out the four?"

"Six, as thou bade me."

"Fool! Father of fools! Go away and do not speak to me."

Sakhri ran back to her room and threw herself down, to weep in comfort. It was quite clear what had happened. Zuleika had caught Sakhri in her own trap. Now Sakhri was accused of theft, and the old hadji held the love message signed with her name—and even Zuleika's fateful pigeons had been removed from the tower.

She was certain Zuleika meant mischief. Had not she and Vali sent one of the original pigeons from the tower toward Irivan before Arslan substituted his birds for the others? Had it not carried a message?

Sakhri felt as if she were battling against cobwebs—the more she tried to brush them away the more they entangled her. She became moody and began to dread the hour of Uzbek Khan's return.

At the end of the week Arslan brought another missive from the pigeon house. The khan had sent word to his castle. He was going farther west, for antelope hunting, and he warned Arslan and the hadji to look well to his house.

Encouraged by this, Zuleika and Vali began anew tormenting of Sakhri, who had grown too listless to resent their abuse.

Then Sultan Hussayn appeared before the gate of Al Arak.

The lord of Irivan came prepared for war, climbing the hill trails with fivescore mounted riflemen, a small mortar on a camel, and a throng of grooms, body servants, well-wishers, and spectators. He came with five large banners snapping in the chill wind and a bareskulled dervish prancing in front of him, mouthing curses upon the rebellious heads of Al Arak and praise of the magnanimous, the wealthy, the all-wise and loving Muhammad ibn Mokhtar Hussayn al Aziz Kutb ud Din, Sultan of Irivan, Lion of the Hills and Protector of the Poor. And he summoned Arak to surrender unconditionally.

In answer Arslan closed and barred the gate. He had with him some fifty men and boys capable of using weapons. But they found in the arsenal of the castle only a dozen damaged rifles, and any amount of cartridges for those Uzbek Khan and his men had taken away with them.

Sakhri, delirious with excitement, demanded that he send gallopers after the khan.

"Whither?" the Tatar demanded plaintively. "The eagles of the air might find him now, but we could not."

For the first day the sultan contented himself with making camp in the level summit of the ridge before the gate. He watched his servants erect his commodious tent and rope it down against the buffeting of the wind. Then, in a striped silk *khalat*, he rode forward to see the mortar, set up by his engineers, batter down the gate. The two round shells they had fetched on camelback dropped harmlessly within the castle, and when the engineers tried to fit a stone into the mortar's mouth for a third shot the thing exploded, nearly blowing Hussayn off his horse. Sakhri was certain that Zuleika, ensconced on her tower summit, had waved a veil, encouraging the invaders.

"What will happen now?" she asked Arslan after the sunset prayer.

"Perhaps tomorrow perhaps the next day they will attack the wall with ladders." The Tatar had seen more than one siege in his day and knew what was to be expected. "They may get in, if Allah wills it. Otherwise, they will wait until we have no more food. In two weeks they will take the castle."

"That she-devil sent for the sultan as soon as our lord rode from the gate. She is a spy, and it would be better to throw her over the wall."

"Women always cause trouble," Arslan admitted philosophically. "But I am not such a fool as to throw my lord's favorite wife over the cliff."

"What wilt thou do?" Sakhri demanded of him.

"Eh what is there to do? Wait, and learn thy destiny."

Another day passed, and the ladders were nearly finished. Sakhri could see them lying on the ground by the Sultan's tents.

"Then give scimitars to us women," she demanded of the Tatar. "We will take our places on the wall and die in the fighting rather than be led like sheep to the slave market of Irivan. Thus, the honor of Uzbek Khan will be preserved."

"Wilt thou go to thy room?" Arslan retorted. "By Allah, thou hast caused more trouble than all the men of Sultan Hussayn!"

Bitterly offended, the Circassian went off to shut herself in the tower room looking out upon the gorge, when the assault upon the castle began with a volley of rifle shots. She heard the loud roar of muskets on the wall and much shouting and running about. The crack-crack of distant rifles punctuated the din, and Sakhri listened for the chorus of triumphant shouting that would mean the wall had yielded to the attack.

The crack-crack of rifles dwindled, while horses galloped about furiously and the mountain echoes flung back the screams and the shouts of men. She heard the war shout of Al Arak—"Aluh—aluh—aluh!" The Eagle, the Eagle so they called Uzbek Khan, but now, reft of his eyrie, what would become of the gentle and tender khan, who had been tricked by the art of Zuleika?

At last she heard a knock on her door and a summons to come out. The noise of fighting had ceased. It was the old hadji, his fingers trembling and his eyes watery from excitement.

He led her up to the tower top, and she looked in vain for a sign of Zuleika. Then she cried out.

There were bodies lying under the wall—there was a reek of smoke in the air, and the gate stood open. But the banners of Irivan had been flung down. Beside them among his men sat Sultan Hussayn, weaponless as they were. And sitting his white horse by the tent of his enemy was Uzbek Khan. Sakhri screamed with exultation.

"An hour ago," the old hadji said, "our lord came down from his hiding place by the snow-fed lake. Like a panther he leaped upon the back of Sultan Hussayn. Aye, when he mounted to ride away, half a moon ago, he said to the Tatar Arslan that he smelled treachery—when Hussayn sent such gifts as a slave girl who could write, and had messenger pigeons for pets—and he would watch, unseen, from the height. He said he would wait to see if Hussayn paid him a visit."

"And ye said naught to me!" Sakhri cried.

The old hadji spread out his hands, and a smile wrinkled his beard. "A secret is no longer a secret if it reaches a woman's ear. As it is, thou didst discover the carrier pigeons."

But Sakhri had left him to hasten down to the window over the gate. For Uzbek Khan was riding back into the castle with loot piled on the saddles of his men, and the mighty Hussayn, Lion of the Hills, walking captive at his horse's-tail. No eagle's mate ever screamed a shriller greeting than the Circassian girl, while the war drum roared and the echoes clamored back.

That evening when the shadow of the height fell over Al Arak and the dust settled down in the courtyard—after the old hadji had wailed the summons to prayer—Sakhri sat happily in the summit of the women's tower. Her arms rested over the knee of Uzbek Khan, and her flaming head, pressed against his side, felt the beating of his heart. With adoration she looked up into the cold gray eyes. Like an eagle's they seemed to gaze far off, without expression.

Since the old khan said nothing, Sakhri contemplated Zuleika's possessions contentedly—they were hers now. Zuleika and Vali had been sent to the cell wherein Sultan Hussayn would wait until his ransom should arrive from Irivan.

"Wilt thou give orders to cut off her nose, O my lord?" she ventured at last.

"For what reason?" Uzbek Khan passed a sinewy hand through the tangle of the girl's hair. "By Allah, she was faithful to her lord, even as thou hast been to me. Besides," he sighed reminiscently, "she is beautiful as a young white horse."

Sakhri wriggled jealously. "If I had not been, if I had betrayed thee, what then?"

Removing his hand from her head, he swept it out over the gorge where the crimson of the afterglow was fading to gray on the far rock wall. "I would have cast thee into that."

Down into the blue shadow of the depths Sakhri looked, and glowed with satisfaction. Uzbek Khan loved her, then. He would not even harm that unspeakable woman, that one full of guile. But he would have slain her, if she had looked away from him. She pressed closer to him, stroking his hand. A last doubt troubled her.

"God knows," she whispered, "I am not beautiful, as she is."

A gleam crept into the gray eyes of the khan. After all, the gentle devotion of the girl pleased him.

"Thou art," he responded guilefully, "the illumination of my soul."

"And what else?"

"And the solace of my liver."

Sakhri sighed with utter content. The cup of her joy was full.

Appendix

Adventure magazine, where many of the tales in this volume first appeared, maintained a letter column titled "The Camp-Fire." As a descriptor, "letter column" does not quite do this regular feature justice. *Adventure* was published two and sometimes three times a month, and as a result of this frequency and the interchange of ideas it fostered, "The Camp-Fire" was really more like an Internet bulletin board than a letter column found in today's quarterly or even monthly magazines. It featured letters from readers, editorial notes, and essays from writers. If a reader had a question or even a quibble with a story, he could write in and the odds were that the letter would not only be printed but that the story's author would draft a response.

Harold Lamb and other contributors frequently wrote lengthy letters that further explained some of the historical details that appeared in their stories. The relevant letters for this volume follow. Also enclosed are a number of essays concerning the Crusades. *Adventure* editor Arthur Sullivant Hoffman published excerpts from Lamb's books about the Crusades as Lamb was drafting them and sometimes printed explanatory letters about these excerpts in "The Camp-Fire." While the text of these book excerpts was similar, if not completely identical, to the text in Lamb's Crusades volumes, the text of Lamb's related "Camp-Fire" letters is not, and they are reprinted here for the first time. They provide insight into how Lamb perceived the time and people he was writing about in both his histories and his fiction.

All of editor Arthur Sullivant Hoffman's introductory editorial comments and segues are included in the letters that follow.

The appendix concludes with two anecdotes about Lamb from the pages of the *Saturday Evening Post*, making brief reference to Lamb's contemporary stories, not contained in this series.

August 8, 1926: "The Shield"

Something from Harold Lamb in connection with his complete novelette in this issue. I don't read enough history these days for my opinion on histories to be worth anything, but I have a strong hunch, not coming altogether from thin air, that Mr. Lamb is right in what he says about modern historians in the bulk.

Berkeley, California.

It is the story of an Arab, in Constantinople, in 1204 when the crusaders took the city from the Greek emperor.

It introduces a new character, Khalil, the Beduin. That is, an Arab of the Ibna or elder chieftains, of al-Yamen, or the desert country. I've become quite interested in these chaps. Every place we follow a Venetian or Genoese or French or English pathfinder, an Arab seems to have been there before with his horses or his ship. They were in China four centuries or so before Marco Polo—the first authentic account of the Chinese is that of Abu Zeid al Hassan, about 900 AD. They rambled through Central Asia with their caravans, and their ships penetrated to India before Spain and Portugal emerged from the dark ages. They were born fighters, of course, and lovers of horses. Also they were chivalrous fighters. A crusader's code of ethics was much less formidable than that of a clean-strain Arab, and there were no indulgences issued in Yamen. Two different codes of course, and there were rogues as well as splendid men on both sides—crusader and paynim.

But the Arab, and the saracin-*folk, were more intelligent than our Croises, more courteous, and usually more daring. They had a sense of humor. Remember that the Baghdad of Haroun al-Raschid, the Alexandria of the Ptolemies, the observatories, academies and the gardens of all Near-Asia were their heritage. Read side by side, the Moslem chronicles of Ibn Athir, Raschid, or Ibn Battuta are much more human, expressive, and likable than the monkish annals of the crusaders—Matthew of Edessa, Matthew Paris, Archbishop William of Tyre. And, strangely enough, these Arab and Persian historians bring out values that have been unknown to us, at least in our histories of the Crusades. They are very fair—more so than our chroniclers—in giving an enemy credit for gallantry. Figures like Alexander the Great (Iskander) and Richard of England (Ricard Malik) were talked about in Asia for centuries, and became heroes of the first magnitude.*

Our existing stock of histories of the Crusades is unfortunate. The early stock was taken from the main Church chronicles, and consisted of a lot of silence and a great deal of fanfare, exaggerating the deeds of the Croises. Then appeared the cynical history, making much hay of the fact that the crusaders usually fought a losing fight, and were sometimes the very opposite of saints. Lastly the ultramodern history has cropped up, making much of the superstition and ignorance of the crusaders, and tracing out with great pains the "advantages" of the Crusades in establishing contact between the East and West, introducing Asia's inventions into Europe, etc.

In decrying the exaltation of the crusaders, and in hunting out the mercantile gains from their efforts and deaths, we have somehow rather lost sight of the intimate personal story of the crusaders—which a reading of the Arabic chronicles serves to bring back to us.

So MUCH of our history and biography and fiction, too, has been written out of prejudice, or a preconceived bias. "Catherine the Great was one of the most gifted women of all time" vs. "Catherine the Great was one of the greatest —— of all time." "Alexander of Macedonia was a superman" vs. "Alexander was mad." You know how those things shape up.

Nowadays one cannot enter a book shop without seeing on all sides "The Truth About This" or "Outlines of That." The desire of readers to learn is real enough. The fault is with the writers, who lack both scholarship and inclination to devote months or years to finding out the truth as nearly as possible. The result is that the very modern histories are usually "outlines" right enough.

Scholarship seems to have died in the last century. Anyway, I'll wager you can't name a better story of the Crusades than Scott's "Talisman." Sir Walter admitted that he wrote from meager information—there was little to be had in his day—but he was a scholar and a conscientious student of his epoch.

History, our dictionaries say, is "a narrative devoted to the exposition of the unfolding of events."

Discarding this husk of Latin phrasing, the dictionary says that history is the story of what actually happened. By the way, it's interesting to notice that the dictionary ranks fiction equally with chronicle. And "unfolding" is just the word. What is history but the uncovering or the unfolding of the past? The story of what certain men did—their adventures, because it's more interesting to read about what they did than what they were. And easier to get at the truth, that way.

It's so absurd to sit down and start in to whitewash some individual or people and call it history. And equally absurd to assemble a few facts and draw personal conclusions from them, without taking the trouble to get at all the facts.

This is beginning to wander. But it's so tiresome to look for history in many modern publications and find only personal opinions, deductions, vilification, or deification, and references to faulty authorities. And so many modern "historical" novels, written by hasty Americans, are enough to make Sienkiewicz or Tolstoy walk the earth again.

Getting back to our Arab—it's been awfully refreshing to read about the crusaders from Arabic sources. But "The Shield" is not a story of the Crusades—the Croises figure only in the taking of Constantinople. I've tried to reconstruct the city as it was then, with its afterglow of Greek and Roman splendor.

The garden of the Patriarch was there, and the Place of Horses, as in the story. I've told the story as Khalil might have told it—many of the incidents befell Ibn Battuta in real life. The storming of the city follows the actual event, except that the siege actually lasted longer. Regarding the disparity in numbers between the crusaders and the Greeks, Mills relates that the crusaders numbered twenty thousand while there were four hundred thousand men capable of bearing arms within the city. Villehardin confirms this, and DuCange. And it is borne out by others.

Khalil rather appeals to me. Also an Arab story to the effect that the sword of Roland—Durandal—taken by the Saracens, after the death of the hero, and hidden away in Asia Minor.

So I'm thinking of a second tale, dealing with the search for the sword by a crusader.

August 15, 1927: "The Guest of Karadak"

Harold Lamb tells about tradition among the Arabs, in connection with his long novelette in this issue.

A word about Arab tradition. It is like no other tradition because the spoken word was handed down from generation to generation rather than the written. Until the ninth or tenth centuries very few Arabs could write, and it was customary when two riders met on the trail to stop and exchange anecdotes. "So-and-so says, on the authority of Such-a-one—"

Naturally when the first annals came to be written they were merely a collection of hadith*—tradition. So we find the early Arab histories to be brief and matter-of-fact, almost invariably truthful. They deal with men and deeds, weapons, and the amount of spoil taken in the* razzias*—with covenants and herds and the position of wells. And especially with the manner in which the great warriors of the books met their deaths.*

These fragmentary histories were jotted down on "date leaves, bits of leather, shoulder blades, stony tablets, or the hearts of men." But, put into words by men born and bred to war who spent most of their lives in the saddle, the written hadith *have a real ring to them. Here we find no lengthy memoirs, no monastery-compiled chronicles, or histories written long after events. We have the word-of-mouth narrative of men who were on the scene.*

That is, perhaps, why the medieval histories of Al Tabari and Ibn Khaldun are better reading than anything that came out of Europe in those days. The Arab then had a fine sense of chivalry, a keen wit, any amount of pride in himself and his deeds, and a full appre-

ciation of what was due him, and others—in the way of money, but more particularly, of honor.

As an example, take an incident in a famous battle—Cadesiya, when the small host of invading Arabs was confronted by the great mass of Persians under Rustam, in the year 635—as related by Baladhuri and Mas'udi.

(To explain the situation, Sa'd, the Lion, leader of the Arabs, was sick that day and was watching events from a cot placed on the rampart of a tower. So his horse, a white mare, was without a rider. Every able-bodied man was in the lines, and the women had been put in charge of the wounded and the prisoners. Among those confined was Abu Mihjan, a hotheaded but redoubtable warrior who had not long since charged single-handed against an elephant—the first to be encountered by the Arabs.)

Abu Mihjan was sent away to Badi by Omar (the caliph), because he drank wine. Somehow, he managed to escape and rode after Sa'd. In the army of Sa'd, Abu Mihjan again drank wine, and Sa'd flogged and imprisoned him in the tower. Then he was heard to sing:

> Bury me by the roots of the vine,
> The moisture will wet my bones;
> Bury me not in the open plain,
> Lacking the fragrant grape.

When he heard the shouting of the battle he asked Zabra, a concubine of Sa'd, to set him free to take part in the fight, after which he would return to his fetters. She made him swear by Allah he would do so. Mounted on Sa'd's mare he rode against the Persians, piercing through their line several times, and once cutting with his sword into the trunk of an elephant. Many did not know who he was, and others thought him to be Al Khizr (one of the angels).

But Sa'd said, "If Abu Mihjan were not safe in chains I could swear it were he and the mare my own." Abu Mihjan afterward rode back to his gaol, and Sa'd exclaimed, "The mare is indeed mine, but the charge is that of Abu Mihjan!"

When the issue with Rustam (the battle with the Persians) was ended, Sa'd said to Abu Mihjan, "By Allah, I shall never punish thee for wine drinking after seeing what I saw of thee."

"As for me," Abu Mihjan answered, "by Allah, I shall never drink it again."

I have tried to tell the story of the Guest of Karadak as Daril would have told it, relating it in his own way as hadith—tradition.

The hospitality and the fighting qualities of the Rajputs are too well known to need comment. They would, as one chronicler put it, "find cause for quarrel in the blowing of the wind against their *faces." The feud between Kurran's clan and the clan of the cousins Awa Khan and Sidri Singh was only one of fifty—or a hundred—going on at the time. Perhaps its first cause had been no more than an unintended word, or a fancied grievance. Nothing would appeal more to a Rajput chieftain than an opportunity to defend the honor—against a stranger—of another Rajput with whom he was at feud.*

In one case a raja, flying for his life from the pursuit of his enemies, stopped for a night at the dwelling of a third chieftain who was not involved in their quarrel. This Rajput considered that the fugitive was now his guest and he was obligated to protect him, so he defended his house against the pursuers and lost his life in doing so.

December 1, 1930

A few words from Harold Lamb relative to his historical piece "Saladin's Holy War," in this issue. It ought to be repeated here that this, like the others of the series to follow, is an extract from the manuscript of the author's second volume on the Crusades, to be published in book form sometime in the spring.

Mr. Lamb has condensed and arranged these articles for *Adventure*, writing a special foreword in several cases to serve both to orient the reader and to make each piece as complete in itself as possible. This will enable those of you who should happen to miss one (and you shouldn't!) to go right on with the next without losing the swing of the Crusades movement as a whole.

Probably as rich in color and drama as any in recorded history, the period covered includes roughly the years between the fall of Jerusalem and the coming of the Mongols. Mighty figures play the leading roles—Saladin, Richard the Lionheart, Pope Innocent III, Baibars the Panther, St. Louis—and turbulent and stirring is the story of their exploits. None of his previous books, all splendidly received by the reading public, has offered Harold Lamb such an opportunity to display his mastery of the historical narrative. Nowhere has he succeeded so brilliantly in catching the spirit and movement of one of the world's great epics.

New York, N.Y.

The battle of Hattin was one of the turning points of the Crusades. In fact it was pretty much the turning point. Until then the Moslems had looked on the crusaders as invincible in ranged battle. Even upon the eve of Hattin, Saladin's emirs had urged him to withdraw and content himself with the old policy of raiding here and there, and retreating when the Christian army of Jerusalem took the field. Sala-

din, however, saw his opportunity to break the power of the armored knights, and the event proved that he was right.

Various stories are told to explain the disaster to the army of Jerusalem. Some chroniclers of the time accuse Raymond, Prince of Galilee, of treachery. But it is clear that Raymond kept the field until the issue of the battle was decided. He had urged the other leaders not to advance, and had gone forward with them against his better judgment.

And later-day writers have assumed that the crusaders of Hattin were incapable and weak compared to the men of Godfrey of Bouillon and the first Baldwins, who conquered Palestine. That is not so. Individually the men who fought their way to the Horns of Hattin were as courageous, and certainly as able soldiers, as the first crusaders. Only a decade before Hattin, the Templars had routed Saladin on the southern coast, forcing the sultan to flee at the full speed of his horse for a day and a night to escape capture. After that, Reginald, or Renault, of Kerak had transported ships across the desert to the Red Sea and sailed down the coast to raid the Moslem holy cities—a bit of sheer daring that astonished the Moslems. The adventurers from Kerak were killed or taken prisoner almost to a man, and the Arab chroniclers said, after questioning the prisoners, "the stories they told us of their hardships and exploits almost burst our hearts with astonishment."

The exploit of the Wolf of Kerak aroused Saladin and his emirs to settle the issue once and for all—to risk a decisive battle after generations of border warfare.

The crusaders lost this battle, but not because they were weaklings. They had no leader able to cope with Saladin. The lord of Kerak and the master of the Templars were responsible for the fatal advance toward Hattin, and Saladin, seeing clearly their mistake, hemmed in the wings of the Christian host and penned it on the barren plateau where it could not get at water.

A day and a night without water finished the crusaders' horses, and in a few hours more the men themselves were done.

A little over a year ago I visited the battlefield of Hattin, and understood a bit of what the crusaders faced. The plateau from Nazareth to the edge of the Galilee depressions is without shelter or water of any kind except occasional deep wells in the villages. The lake of Galilee lies some six hundred feet below sea level, and down by the shore of the lake—in the sunken valley—the air is bearable enough, cooled by the breeze over the water.

But on the height of Hattin over the lake the heat is stifling. The hot air from the depression seems to hang on the edge of the slope. I visited the place on a cloudy day in October. What the heat would do to a man under a clear sun, in early July—after a day's march in armor and under arms—can be imagined.

And after a day's fighting without water, and after the brush was set on fire!

A word as to Saladin's character. Recently the great sultan has been painted as a man merciful in all things. A kind of chivalrous saint. Saladin was more than that—a just man, and very wise. Moreover he held inviolate his given word.

There was nothing emotional in the mercy he displayed. He ordered the men of Kerak to be executed after the Mecca raid as retribution, and the Templars after Hattin. With his own hand he struck down the lord of Kerak, as he had sworn to do.

He granted the best of terms to the Christian garrisons which surrendered after Hattin, because it was essential to him to take possession of the crusaders' citadels before a new army could arrive from Europe to take the field against him. No, Saladin was not a sentimentalist. He was merciful beyond his age to women and children who appealed to him, while he dealt sternly with men under arms.

One of the wisest generals who ever lived, Sun Tzu, who won battles in China long before our era, said "Never attack desperate men, and never attack men who have no way of retreat open." Saladin's policy of mercy made it easier to surrender than to resist, and we are beginning to understand how his sagacity gained more for Islam than his armies.

December 15, 1930
A note from Harold Lamb in connection with his Crusades narrative, "The Walls of Acre," in this issue:

New York, N. Y.

We are all beginning to understand after the last show in France that wars are not decided by grand strategy alone, in spite of what the brass hats say. We have been realizing it more and more after each war. The strategists and disciplinarians point to Austerlitz as the perfect battle; but Austerlitz was fought on terrain like a parade ground—and strategy and tactics alike went by the board when Napoleon's grande armeé *was confronted by the bare plains of Russia in early winter a little later.*

Weapons and ground, and the thing called morale—the character and feelings of the men themselves—are apt to settle things once the actual fighting has begun. Genghis Khan rather than Napoleon gives us our best example of a strategist who was supremely successful. Napoleon's plans usually went astray when his armies maneuvered outside the familiar and easy terrain of middle Europe—failed, for instance, in Syria, Russia, and Spain. While the plans of the Mongol conqueror stood the real test—they worked.

Genghis Khan won his campaigns upon every kind of ground, under all conditions. But we are apt to forget that his Mongol horsemen, believing him invincible after the first years, had what might be called a trouble-proof morale, and their bows out-ranged and out-hit any opposing weapons. Fra Carpini, one of the first Europeans to journey to the court of the Mongol khans, said emphatically that the Mongol mounted archers were so destructive that they would cut the enemy forces to pieces before the "battle" began.

Take the late war, the Gallipoli campaign. The Allies had all the odds but one in their favor, and a strong fleet to back their landing. They had numbers, morale on their side, and the element of surprise. Military critics say the strategy of the landing was perfect. For nearly two days the detachments landed had only a few battalions of Turks, badly bewildered, and still fewer machine guns concealed in higher ground, to oppose them.

What happened is familiar enough. The detachments lost touch, and proved again what the Allied higher command proved so often—that riflemen in the open cannot advance against concealed machine guns.

Leaving Constantinople the last time, I passed over the Gallipoli peninsula in a seaplane, and saw only sheep moving on the shore where the Australians and the others had landed. There was also a gray stone monument of some kind on the tip of the land. A Greek captain of aviation was with me, and writing in French on some unused vomit bags in the plane, he pointed out to me the gray tracery of trenches still visible, and a cemetery enclosure. Those trenches and the cemetery were the real monument to the men who carried rifles against machine guns. And there are plenty of similar monuments around northern France.

Weapons, ground, and morale have all been used to the last, ultimate advantage by the great captains of history. It may be heresy to say it, but it does not look now as if the Germans were beaten in the last war until the advantage in weapons and morale passed over to us, and they were driven out of their prepared strong points. Even at the last, in Palestine, Allenby's fine sweep up to Damascus—strategy that really worked—only took place when the British and Arabs had enormous superiority in weapons and transport—in such things as motors and planes—and when the Turko-German morale was about broken.

This is rambling off the subject. What I'm getting at is the odds faced by the crusaders. We are accustomed to think of them as men physically stronger than the Arabs and Turks, and wearing heavy armor, equipped with much heavier weapons. That is mostly wrong.

The crusaders had heavier shields and lances—those who had lances. The Moslem shield of the time was usually leather strengthened by metal, small and round—shaped to the forearm of the riders. Not at all lance-proof. The Arabs and Turks relied on their agility and the speed of their horses to avoid the long, massive lances.

And it seems that the crusaders did most of their fighting with their swords and short axes. Lighter Moslem lances, with six- to eight-foot bamboo shafts, were handier than the long ash weapons of the crusaders.

Crusaders' swords were shorter and heavier than the Moslem curved sabers, and had more iron in them. But the long blades of the Moslems met the crusaders' weapons on even terms, by and large. The Moslem horsemen also used javelins and the short, curved khanjar and yataghans with considerable effect, while the crusaders did not. Nobles and knights who came out of Europe had more complete body armor (link or chain mail) than the average Moslem horseman. But the Christian archers and miscellaneous soldiery did not.

This was before the day of plate armor, long bows, and closed helms with visors. By 1220, in the later stages of the Crusades, the closed helm came into use, gradually, among the Christians. The Moslems never did take to it kindly, favoring light helmets with chain mail drops, and nasal and sometimes cheek pieces. The English longbow with the cloth-yard arrow only reached its great power a century later.

About the time of the siege of Acre the crusaders were beginning to bring in crossbows, which did a lot of execution in close siege fighting and little elsewhere. Coeur de Lion was the first king to use the crossbow—the French chivalry always looked on it as unsportsmanlike, and the Popes banned it until about 1210.

This was about the only weapon the Moslems adapted from the crusaders, and they never liked it very much because it was clumsy to handle on a horse. The same applied to the long two-handed sword that some crusaders, mostly Germans, carried in the thirteenth century and later.

It is clear that in arms and armor, the Moslems were on even terms with the crusaders. In other matters, they usually held the advantage. They had better horses, bred in the country, and greater strength in mounted men. The Christian archers were usually on foot. The Moslems had more serviceable kits for carrying water and rations; they were adept at scouting and maneuvering. Saladin had a portable siege train and a pigeon post as well as a pony express to carry messages.

Zangi, Saladin, and Baibars were much better strategists than the leaders of the crusaders, and were of course more familiar with the terrain.

One advantage that Moslems always held: flame weapons. The Arabs were as skilled as the Greeks of Constantinople in the use of the mysterious flame that the crusaders called "Greek fire" or "wild fire," and sometimes "sea fire" because it burned on the water. It was made variously out of naphtha or the ingredients of gunpow-

der. The crusaders never learned the secret of it, and were besides unwilling to use it, looking upon it as black magic. The church forbade its use.

The Moslems employed it in siege warfare, beginning with Acre, and also in hand grenades and "fire-maces." In time they learned to cast barrages of it, and smoke screens, before or into an attack. It gave them a decisive advantage for generations—until serviceable firearms were in use.

This fact has escaped the notice of most historians. But it is clear enough when we read the amounts of men on both sides who were present at such events as the siege of Acre.

It is also clear that the crusaders in their long conflict with the armies of Asia had only one real advantage—command of the sea at their backs. And in their morale. All the other advantages were on the side of the Moslems.

January 1, 1931

A note from Harold Lamb, relative to his narrative, "Richard the Lion Heart," in this issue:

New York City

Richard of England, Coeur de Lion, must have a word said about him. Long before Scott wrote "The Talisman" the errant king of England had been a hero in legend. But of later years the debunkers have been busy, and they have not forgotten Coeur de Lion. They have plastered mud over the great warrior of legends, saying that Richard was "a bad son, a bad husband, a worse king." A kind of all 'round black sheep, a waster, good for nothing except carousing and treacherous fighting at the head of his boon companions, the mercenary men-at-arms. We are not concerned with Richard as a king. It is true that he was one of the bravest men and the worst monarchs ever to rule England. But then we must remember that Richard was practically an exile in his youth, and when he came to the throne he was already pledged to the Crusade. Unlike his rival, Philip-Augustus of France, he devoted himself to the Crusade instead of the government of his realm. And when he journeyed back from the East, he was seized and made captive by the European princes unlawfully—for it was against all written and unwritten laws to seize the person of a crusader returning from the war in the East. When Richard was at last ransomed—at a further cost to England—he not unnaturally devoted himself to vengeance.

So much for Richard's motives as a king.

The real interest of his life lies in his crusade, the brief years between 1190–1194. And here we are faced with a puzzle. Was Richard an invincible fighter—the real Lion Heart of the crusade—or a *dismal failure?* Scott pictures him as a hero incarnate, and modern historians, especially of the French school, picture him as a trouble-maker and an inefficient leader.*

Consider his actions: His march toward Jaffa delays and delays again; he keeps his army on the defensive, even in the open fighting at Arsuf; he fortifies Jaffa and tries to rebuild Ascalon; constantly he importunes Saladin for terms of peace; twice, when the army crawls† toward Jerusalem, he is the first to urge a retreat. No doubt about it, the debonair Coeur de Lion has become a timid general. Why?

It is not that Richard was wholly unfit as a commander. A worth-less leader usually sacrifices his men to try to gain an advantage. St. Louis of France did so two generations later, without being blamed. Richard safeguarded his men and fought the veteran Moslem army led by the ever-dangerous Saladin on slightly better than even terms during his year of command in Palestine.

I think the answer is this: The moment he set out from Acre, at the head of a great army of all nationalities, Richard found himself con-fronted by what the French call the **grande guerre**—the war of large armies maneuvering over open country. The country was strange to him, and the fate of the crusade itself hung upon a decisive battle. Until then the Lionheart had only experienced the foray-and-siege warfare of Europe, where his own prowess in arms could wrest suc-cess out of a struggle in which at most three or four thousand men were engaged on each side.

And it seemed as if Richard realized at once his inability to com-mand in such a war as this. He could not relinquish the command. For one thing, the other leaders of princely rank—even Conrad, the ablest of them—had deserted him. The rank and file of the army was deter-mined to press on to Jerusalem, and Richard had to lead them.

So he became afraid, not of personal peril, but of disgrace and di-saster. Unable to turn back, he must go on, realizing his own inabil-

---

*Scott, who was a conscientious historian even in writing fiction, represents Richard as harassed and abandoned by the princes, who plotted against him. Mod-ern writers explain that Richard's arrogance estranged the other princes, who withdrew from him on that account. The truth, here, lies between the two views. Richard was overbearing in seizing the leadership, and he lost prestige by taking sides in the Montserrat-Lusignan feud—the two parties claiming the kingship of Jerusalem. But by then some of the best of the leaders—Barbarossa, and the count of Flanders, and William of Sicily—had died, and it is clear to this writer at least that Philip-Augustus and the Austrians were only half-hearted in the Crusade. They seized upon Richard's conduct as an excuse for getting out.

†It must be remembered that the crusaders lacked horses, having perhaps only one man mounted to five or ten Moslem horsemen. This brought about the curi-ous situation in which Saladin, on the defensive, was able to attack at will, while Richard on the offensive could only crawl about.

ity to cope with the Moslem armies. The blind devotion of the common men only made his situation more intolerable. The bad tidings from England, where his brother, John Lackland, and Philip-Augustus were overrunning his lands, in spite of their oaths to him, added to his mental torment.

We do not know what Richard thought about it, but what he did in his dilemma is pathetically clear. While he shielded his army in camp and town, he went out himself, with a small picked following, to engage the Moslems at every chance. Instead of sacrificing his men, he risked his own life. Tried to win a war as he had won tournaments so often. He stormed hill towers, captured the Egyptian caravan, drove the Moslem warriors before him in a dozen hand-to-hand encounters. Possibly he sought death in these ventures. It was a hopeless task, to gain victory by such minor feats. It was not war but it was magnificent, and Richard's final stand at Jaffa when he waded ashore in the face of a victorious army is about the finest thing of its kind in the records of history.

Grant that Richard of England was a poor king, a troublemaker, and a failure as a general in his greatest test. But remember that he hazarded his own life, not his men's, and stuck to his cause. He was one of the most courageous men who ever breathed. Saladin himself said that he would rather lose the Holy Land to Richard than to any other. And the name of Malik Ric (King Richard) has been preserved among the Moslems as the greatest of all the crusaders.

I have tried to set down Richard's actions during those years, 1191–1192, without prejudice for or against the English king. Those actions tell their own story of his character. And I think that Richard will keep his surname of the Lion Heart in spite of the debunkers.

February 15, 1931

A few words from Harold Lamb, in connection with his narrative, "Beausant Goes Forward," in this issue:

Piedmont, Cal.

The Battle of Gaza in 1244 is one of those little-known affairs that shaped destinies. The pages of history have little to say about it because we have almost no authentic reports as to what happened and why. Nearly all the crusaders were killed. Like the Custer fight, it has come down to us as a name and a date and a casualty list. We will probably never know just what happened there.

The Moslem chroniclers, however, have shed some light on the campaign, and we have learned some details from them. Such details are given in this article. The battle itself changed the whole course of the Crusades. It marked the final loss of Jerusalem—until Allenby walked into the city with his army in one of the last cam-

*paigns of 1918. It marked also a new force on the Moslem side, the
arrival of contingents from Central Asia, driven west by the hard-
fighting Mongols, who had first appeared under the horned standard
of Genghis Khan.*

*Before Gaza the crusaders on the coast and the cultured Arab sul-
tans, the descendants of Saladin, managed to live and let live, and
probably Jerusalem would have been recovered in time by the Christians. But the incoming of the new fighters from mid-Asia, who increased in numbers as the years went by, brought the conflict to a
head again, and gradually turned the scales against the crusaders.*

*From that time the tolerant Arabs were pushed out of power by
the masses of Turks and Tartars, who gathered together in Cairo,
and presently founded the Mamluk dynasty that endured until Napoleon entered Egypt.*

*For another thing, Gaza saw the rise to fame of that redoubtable
fighter, the Panther, who was destined to do what Saladin had not
been able to do. And the battle brought about the great Crusade of
Saint Louis, the last general crusade to reach the East.*

March 15, 1931

A note about the strongholds of the crusaders, by Harold Lamb, in connection with "The Panther," in this issue:

Piedmont, Cal.

*Few of us know that the frontier line of the crusaders' castles still
exists in the hills of Syria and Palestine. There is a good reason why
this line of citadels remains almost unknown. Outside of a magazine article or two, the only description in print that I know of is
by a French archeologist, Rey, published in 1871 in the* Documents
inedtes sur l'historie de France. *And the country remained, until Allenby's campaign late in the World War—the one Lawrence had a
hand in—under the Turk. Few visitors did more than look in along
the coast. For two good reasons the crusaders' citadels along the coast
are pretty much demolished: first, Baibars, Kalawun, and Khamil
made a point of destroying them, so that crusaders thereafter could
not use them as landing points; second, during the last seven-odd
centuries, the people of the country have taken the building stone
out of the crusaders' ruins for their houses.*

*So on the coast, only the castle at Triploi, the little cathedral at
Tortosa, and the ruined citadel of Chateau Pelerin are well preserved.
The Turks used the Triploi as a garrison post and prison, and Chateau Pelerin (the Arabs call it Ahlit now) was too far from any village to serve as a source of building stone. The church at Tarous—as
Tortosa is called now—was turned into a mosque, with a minaret
tower like a sentry box stuck up on one corner. It's a beautiful thing,
deserted now.*

Of course you can find ruins of other points along the coast—part of St. Louis' castle at Saida (Sidon), and then the buildings of the Hospitallers are well preserved at Acre. They were digging out a fine little chapel that had served as a Turkish stable when I was there. But the walls and most of Acre, as they stand now, date from the Napoleonic era.

But the great castles back in the hills take your breath away. There are a dozen big fellows stretching south from Antioch, down to Kerak east of the Dead Sea—a line of about 540 kilometers or, if my reckoning is right, 280 miles. And a half dozen strong towers interconnecting.

These are not the miniature medieval castles of feudal Europe. Most of them are twice the size of Coucy, the largest of the feudal castles of France. Moreover, the European structures have been built over for the most part, and restored until little of the twelfth-century construction remains as it was. The cité of Carcassonne, in southern France, for instance, was restored by Vollet-le-Duc in the last century. By way of comparison, Carcassone (which was really a fortified town, not a castle) is said to be 1,600 yards in the circuit of its outer walls. While Kerak, across the Dead Sea, in Palestine is, I think, 2,700 yards in its outer circuit.

You see, the crusaders had to fortify whole summits of mountains. The war out there was a real war, and the fortified points had to accommodate several hundred to five thousand or more human beings, with chargers, cattle, and sheep—granaries and reservoirs. They had to plan out the water supply in a dry country.

Most of the castles have interior wells. The Arab villagers under the hill where Belfort stands still go up to the castle to get their water. The well at the Kerak is deep. I dropped a stone in it and had to listen five or six seconds for the splash. Also, because a single well would not serve the big places, they had reservoirs for rainwater. At Marghab the reservoir was some thirty yards outside the great tower, within arrow range of the walls. It has a healthy forest growing in it now.

I don't suppose that any other war has left monuments like this line of deserted citadels in the hills of Syria and Palestine. No government had done anything to restore or repair them—for five hundred years, anyway. The French shelled brigands out of two of them recently, but the artillery did little more than scar the great stones.

Tourists don't visit them, and they will probably remain as they are, deserted and slowly crumbling under sun and rain for some centuries yet. I've seen a good many things, but nothing quite as impressive as those strongholds of the crusaders.

April 1, 1931

A note from Harold Lamb, in connection with "The Trial of the Templars," in this issue. This piece, as you know, concludes his series of true stories of the Crusades. His next efforts for our pages will be, he expects, some more of his colorful tales of the Don Cossacks, which many of you have been asking for.

Piedmont, California

One last word about the crusaders. In my books, and in the Adventure *narrative, I've tried to show the men and the happenings of that time as they actually were. To do this, I used the chronicles of that time—leaving out present-day opinion.*

Recently, however, the crusaders have come in for debunking, along with other characters of the past. In the last generations we've been fed up a bit too much with heroics, and the present tendency to kick down pedestals is a healthy one, so long as it is honest and intelligent kicking.

The debunkers say something like this: "The Crusades were a vain undertaking, a mistake, resulting only in waste of lives and treasure. The crusaders themselves, instead of being saints in arms turned out to be human sinners, who massacred and pillaged, while they made of the idealistic Kingdom of God around Jerusalem a kind of robbers' roost. They were really adventurers, who became degenerate and lost everything."

Some cynics say one thing, some another. But their point of view is pretty much the same. And in this case it is wrong. Because you can't lift men out of the twelfth century and set them down beside men of today, for comparison. Not that the world today is any Utopia. But the comparison is meaningless.

As to the question of the gain and loss in the Crusades, the wisest of the historians admit that they cannot answer it. We have no scales vast enough to weigh the inventions and the knowledge that came out of the great venture, against the destruction of goods and life.

Nor is modern civilization, which has seen itself torn asunder by a world war, without apparent cause, entitled to cast a stone at the crusaders, who fought for what was to them the greatest of earthly causes.

Remember, to the men of that time, the Crusades triumphed for more than a century. Whole people were torn loose from their isolation and merged with their fellows. Men who had been to the East returned with new knowledge—the rudiments of the knowledge that gave birth to the Renaissance thereafter, to the era of voyages of discovery. Four centuries before the first voyages, the crusaders set out over the sea to Outremer. And long before the first modern European entente the Crusades brought about the first international alliance.

As to the crusaders themselves, they were a cross-section of the humanity of the time; if anything, they were the best with the worst. And the debunker errs when he assumes they looked upon the venture as a kind of shortcut to salvation. The Church granted them absolution from their sins during the time of the crusade—usually fixed at three years—because the danger of the venture was so great.

Many of them, of course, hoped to carve a fortune for themselves in the East. Beside a Godfrey of Bouillon you will find a Bohemund; and with a Coeur de Lion, a Conrad of Montserrat. That happens in any great movement. And far outnumbering the fortune-seekers were the multitude who sold or pawned their possessions at home to pay their way on crusade, and brought back nothing but memories with them.

There were adventurers, no doubt of that. Probably—except for the Vikings and Varangians who formed clan units—they were the first massed adventurers. Certainly the first recruited from all nations to take part in a single enterprise. They paid their own way and put their lives at hazard for a cause. Of course they pillaged and took land where they found it—women too, at times. How else were they to live in that age when commissaries and paydays were things undreamed of?

But the kingdom they founded and held—Antioch was held for two centuries—knew more peace than the countries of Europe. There were quarrels in Jerusalem, but worse in Rome or Paris or Venice. And their code of laws, the Assizes, is now looked upon as the model of the early Medieval Age.

The crusaders have been accused of callous massacres. When they first penetrated the East they killed without discrimination, but they stopped this as soon as they found out that the Moslems were human beings very much like themselves, and not servants of Anti-Christ as they had been taught. Moslem chroniclers do not accuse them of any massacre except the slaughter at the capture of Jerusalem.

The crusaders who settled beyond the sea became colonists in earnest, and adapted themselves to their surroundings and the peoples of the East. They were exploited by the Italian merchant-republics, upon whose fleets they were dependent, and by the Church of Rome, which turned the Crusades into armed movements against enemies and heretics at home, leaving the exiles in Outremer to fare as best they could.

That they should lose their conquests was inevitable, when the new masses of Moslems, trained in the Mongol method of fighting, came against them from the East. At the end they were dozens against hundreds—garrison posts against armies. Degenerate they were not.

Their devotion and their chivalry cast a light upon an age otherwise dark and grim and treacherous. No words of ours can alter what these men did. They reached the summit of daring. They drained the cup to the very dregs of suffering and shame. They followed the light of their star, until they died. And in spite of all that modern cynics can say, the Crusades will always remain a cherished memory.

May 25, 1946: "The Lowdown on Jonah"

In Harold Lamb's entertaining story of an American in Persia—"Oracle by Hafiz," page 16—some of the most spirited action takes place at a pass. The pass Lamb had in mind—he knows the Middle East as well as most Americans know their own country—is one called Young Woman Old Woman Pass. It is exceedingly high, and gets its name from the idea that a young girl starting up would be an old woman by the time she got down.

Lamb wrote "Oracle by Hafiz" in his home in Beverly Hills, California, out of knowledge gained in some 59,000 miles of travel in the Middle East. He spent more than two years there in wartime, sometimes in palaces, sometimes in tents. He came back with an unbroken record of defeats at various sports. The Middle East is the homeland of chess, and Lamb was not surprised to lose to Emir Abdullah of Transjordan at that game. He was a little surprised, however, to find that the Shah of Iran, Mohammed Reza, could beat him at tennis, and that his bridge wasn't good enough for official circles in Tehran.

"It's a fine country to visit," he said. "Anywhere in the desert, you can still drive up to a village, pick out the best house and tell the owner you are going to be his guest for the night. In one Zoroastrian home we stayed three days, telling the servants what we wanted done, before seeing our host. You don't pay for things like that.

"I wanted to meet the people and live with them, and it is very easy to do, whether they are Arabs, Turks, Iranians, Kurds, Armenians, or Asiatic Jews. My only real grief was an excess of hospitality. Most of the folks out there look on an American as a visitor from the Promised Land. The United States seems to them to be a composite of the biggest, toughest, and wealthiest nation, expounder of the Atlantic Charter, President Wilson's idealism, typhus control, and Snow White and the Seven Dwarfs. It's a reputation very hard to live up to."

Like the hero of his story, Mr. Lamb got along very well with the mountain tribes, in spite of some differences in viewpoint. He found the tribesmen living quite well, getting such luxury items as tea, sugar, and gasoline by raiding highway convoys. One British military attaché arrived at Shiraz, during Lamb's stay, wearing nothing but gray woolen underwear. He had come through the mountains at a moment when the tribesmen needed clothes.

One of the many Middle Easterners Lamb visited was Fattah Agha, a tribal head in the mountains south of Lake Urmia. Fattah Agha's tribe, the Hirkli, was getting along fine, finding good grazing as it moved around and carrying a little contraband salt across the frontier as a sideline. Fattah Agha asked with interest how Lamb's tribe found the grazing and such in the United States. "Do Americans migrate with their animals," he asked, "or do they build homes in settlements?"

Lamb told him the Americans had a tendency to build homes and stay in them, although they did migrate around a good deal with their women. Fattah Agha said he supposed it was all right if you liked that kind of life, but added frankly that he couldn't see how Americans would ever make any money staying in one place all the time.

Mr. Lamb also picked up a new version of what happened to Jonah. The real story, he was assured, is not the one he had been taught in Sunday school. It seems that Jonah prophesied that the wicked city of Nineveh was due to feel the wrath of the Lord, who would demolish it in forty days. And for forty days a wind shook the strongest of the city's walls and torrential rains flooded the city's streets. But when the storm ended, the city was still there. So the inhabitants went looking for Jonah, who lived up the Tigris River, and told him that while they were glad his prophecy had not come to pass, with an inevitable lowering of real-estate values, he must realize that they couldn't put up with a prophet whose predictions didn't come true, and they would like to have a word with him down by the river. So they tossed him into the Tigris, where the biggest fish—big, but by no means a whale—swallowed the prophet at a gulp. "They assured me," said the traveler, "that this is official."

February 24, 1951: Those Delightful Turks

Girl meets Lieut. Comdr. Terry McGowan in Istanbul's Great Bazaar on page 31, and in that same famous market—where one buys strictly at his own risk—author Harold Lamb once met an extraordinary bargain. One day he bought a fine Armenian manuscript book, which had a yellowed parchment page stuck inside it. While Lamb was examining something else, he noticed the dealer slip out the parchment. When the dealer went to get wrapping paper, Lamb slipped the parchment back in. The dealer obviously saw this, but said nothing, and the sale was gravely consummated, the whole business being considered fair and aboveboard by Bezistan standards. The parchment turned out to be a fragment of a rare early Gospel and is now in the University of Chicago collection labeled "The Harold Lamb Gospel of Mark."

But outside of the bazaar's free-for-all Turks are apt to be so honest that they get Americans all mixed up. One day a boy walked eight miles with three of Lamb's shirts to get them washed. The clean shirts returned with some rents tastefully embroidered. Price: twenty cents. So the grateful Lamb added eight cents for the needlework. The boy seemed upset, but presently returned in better humor after another eight-mile constitutional, reporting that the wash woman said the charge was twenty cents, and twenty it would be. Lamb took back the eight cents, dazedly apologized for his mistake, and everybody was happy.

Lamb, who worked the ancient Turkish Sultan Suleiman into an earlier *Post* story and now is being acclaimed for his new book *Suleiman the Magnificent*, loves the way the Turks use few words to say much. Example: once he got a Turkish ambassador to inscribe a helpful visa in his passport, expecting many flowery sentences. His excellency wrote seven words. Lamb got worried and had them translated. They said, "Do what you can for this man, lawfully." Another example: several years ago the Kremlin employed a vast number of paragraphs explaining to Turkey that for mutual security she should cede various territories and let Russia police the Dardanelles. Turkey's economically worded official reply boiled down to five English words, "Then come and take them."

About the Author

Harold Lamb (1892–1962) was born in Alpine, New Jersey, the son of Eliza Rollinson and Frederick Lamb, a renowned stained-glass designer, painter, and writer. Lamb later described himself as having been born with damaged eyes, ears, and speech, adding that by adulthood these problems had mostly righted themselves. He was never very comfortable in crowds or cities and found school "a torment." He had two main refuges when growing up—his grandfather's library and the outdoors. Lamb loved tennis and played the game well into his later years.

Lamb attended Columbia, where he first dug into the histories of Eastern civilizations, ever after his lifelong fascination. He served briefly in World War I as an infantryman but saw no action. In 1917 he married Ruth Barbour, and by all accounts their marriage was a long and happy one. They had two children, Frederick and Cary. Arthur Sullivant Hoffman, the chief editor of *Adventure* magazine, recognized Lamb's storytelling skills and encouraged him to write about the subjects he most loved. For the next twenty years or so, historical fiction set in the remote East flowed from Lamb's pen, and he quickly became one of *Adventure*'s most popular writers. Lamb did not stop with fiction, however, and soon began to draft biographies and screenplays. By the time the pulp magazine market dried up, Lamb was an established and recognized historian, and for the rest of his life he produced respected biographies and histories, earning numerous awards, including one from the Persian government for his two-volume history of the Crusades.

Lamb knew many languages: by his own account, French, Latin, ancient Persian, some Arabic, a smattering of Turkish, a bit of Manchu-Tatar, and medieval Ukrainian. He traveled throughout Asia, visiting most of the places he wrote about, and during World War II he was on covert assignment overseas for the U.S. government. He is remembered today both for his scholarly histories and for his swashbuckling tales of daring Cossacks and crusaders. "Life is good, after all," Lamb once wrote, "when a man can go where he wants to, and write about what he likes best."

Source Acknowledgments

The following stories and novellas were originally published in *Adventure* magazine: "The Shield," August 8, 1926; "The Guest of Karadak," August 15, 1927; "The Road to Kandahar," November 15, 1927; "The Light of the Palace," August 8, 1928.

The following stories were originally published in *Collier's* magazine: "The Way of the Girl," November 11, 1931; "The Rogue's Girl," October 29, 1932; "The Eighth Wife," December 31, 1932.

www.ingramcontent.com/pod-product-compliance
Ingram Content Group UK Ltd.
Pitfield, Milton Keynes, MK11 3LW, UK
UKHW022049060225
454777UK00012B/1030